AF887325

Brigitte B. Fischer

My European Heritage

Life Among Great Men of Letters

Translated from the German by
Harry Zohn

© Copyright 1986
by Branden Publishing Company

Library of Congress Cataloging-in-Publication Data

Fischer, Brigitte B., 1905-
My European heritage,

Translation of: Sie schrieben mir.
Includes index.
1. Fischer, Brigitte B., 1905-
2. S. Fischer Verlag. 3. Publishers and publishing—Berlin (Germany)—Biography. 4. Publishers and publishing—Europe—Biography. 5. Authors and publishers. 6. Europe—Intellectual life—20th century. I. Title.
Z315.F4913 1986 070.5'092'4 [B] 85-31433
ISBN 0-8283-1897-2

Branden Publishing Company
17 Station Street Box 843
Brookline Village
Boston MA 02174

I am one of those old-fashioned people who regard a letter as a means of communication, one of the most beautiful and productive ones. Rainer Maria Rilke

The happiest person is one who can establish a connection between the end of his life and its beginning. Goethe

Contents

Part Two
What Life Brought Me

Preface

For my ninth birthday— it was in 1914— my parents gave me an album. These *Stammbuecher,* as they were called, are a bit out of fashion now. But in those days every child got one so his or her schoolmates might inscribe their verses "in perpetual remembrance." *My* album, however, was inscribed by writers and poets.

To the little girl these people were strange figures, at best "uncles" and "aunts"; for the growing daughter of the house, who was already beginning to be familiar with their creative work, they were admired and idolized geniuses; and in the later years of my life they were close friends tied to me by a common fate. In that album they would write a greeting, a souvenir of hours shared, or verses of their own. With the passing of the years, however, my little album no longer sufficed for what we had to say to one another. We began to exchange letters, and this gradually led to a constant exchange of ideas and in some cases developed into a dialogue about life in our world of radical change. But my album became a volume in my library like many another, half-forgotten one.

It came to hand again when I was rereading those letters from friends that had survived the vicissitudes of the Nazi years. At that time I noticed that what had been started in my little album had been continued over a period of sixty years in those letters.

Part One Awakening to Life

To my daughters
and grandchildren

1
How I Experienced My Childhood in My Parental Home, 8 Erdener Street, Berlin-Grunewald

One day, when I was five, something quite unusual happened: I was dislodged from my bedroom and had to spend the night in a guest room in the attic, where there was a faint smell of mothballs and bygone times and where it was possible to crawl into the primeval beds of my grandparents.

I did not learn until years later that this had come about because my parents had invited guests to celebrate the first night of *Der Rosenkavalier,* the opera that had had its first performance amidst great jubilation in Dresden a week earlier.

"It was in the winter of 1911," wrote my mother in her memoirs, "that we attended the premiere of the opera in Dresden under the direction of Max Reinhardt— an event for which the entire artistic and musical world had assembled. Hugo von Hofmannsthal's libretto and Richard Strauss' music evoked the same delight as the wonderful performance, and when the waltz in the second act had died away, vigorous applause roared through the hall. Everyone was enraptured. What the poet and the composer had envisioned, that mixture of seriousness, gaiety, and poetry, had here found its full expression. From Dresden the Hofmannsthals went to Berlin, and in their honor we gave a party in our house at which people danced to the strains of the *Rosenkavalier* waltz for the first time."

I sat hidden behind an old chest up in the gallery. From there I had a view of our vestibule, which extended over two floors and had an old Dutch chandelier with festively burning candles hanging from the ceiling. I marveled at the elegant people who had gathered down below. The long, flowing evening gowns and the gleaming jewels of the ladies and the tailcoats of the gentlemen kept me from recognizing most of the accustomed friends of my parents. The fragrance of the perfumes, the gaiety of the festive mood, and the golden glow of the candles rose up to me, however, and surrounded me like an enchantment. Later, when I was buried in my old-fashioned high bed up there, I could still hear in the distance the *Rosenkavalier* waltz, soon to become famous, for my mother had taken the arm of her friend Julius Meier-Graefe and was leading her guests through the whole house in a polonaise based on its strains.

For a long time to come, the *Rosenkavalier* party in our house on Erdenerstrasse remained a milestone of memory in the artistic circles of Berlin.

A lot of "people" frequented my parental home, a beautiful, bright, and roomy villa in the Grunewald section. The outside wall of our house was decorated with the S. Fischer logo, a fisherman with his net, as a relief. I knew every nook and cranny from the cellar to the attic, having absorbed them with all my senses. In the basement there was a large, open kitchen with a stove in the middle. Next to it was a good-smelling pantry which I often visited. Down there it smelled of ironing, but also of apples from the fruit cellar, whose wooden bins were always full. From the kitchen a small staircase led to the serving table, which was supplied by a dumbwaiter from the kitchen. From there the food was carried into the long dining room, which my father had provided with an arched coffered ceiling. The dining room had five large windows that extended to the floor; along the walls stood old Dutch baroque buffets with silver candelabra; and in the middle was a spacious dining table of the same walnut, surrounded by highback leather chairs on which the fisherman with his net was embossed. The glass doors to the small, dainty tearoom always stood open. It had light cherry paneling, a round Biedermeier table, sofa, and chairs, covered with silk bearing green and white stripes, as well as Biedermeier glass cabinets along the walls. From there one could go to the covered terrace and into the garden. These rooms had a Sunday atmosphere, and it was always a pleasant surprise to step from the main entrance, in whose walls were embedded casts of the two side reliefs of the Greek altar "Birth of Venus", through the coat room into the large, open vestibule. It was a festal house, designed to receive and entertain the growing family of authors and the large group of Berlin artists.

Felix Salten, one of my parents' closest friends and at that time the cultural editor of the Viennese newspaper *Die Zeit,* gave the following description of our house in his 1910 essay "Strolling in Berlin":

The railing is white, the house is white, and the doors are painted white. Gleaming white gravel paths run through the greensward of the garden as bright stripes. When I come to Berlin, I like to visit this house—at night, when the lights are burning, in the afternoon, when tea is served on the terrace, or in the morning for tennis. There is a matchless charm in staying in the city as a dawdling or bustling stranger, to run around in the city, letting the seething tumult of this life clang and roar around you, but then rush out to the house in Grunewald in an automobile with the speed of lightning and sit still there. It is like swimming under water till there is a buzzing in your ears and a throbbing in your temples, till there is a steely pressure on your chest. But then you emerge, you feel a reassuring breeze on your cheeks, and you have the heavenly bliss of drawing deep breaths.

In the vestibule hangs an old chandelier of Dutch brass. A white staircase gracefully rises to the upper level where an open gallery goes along the row of bedrooms. This vestibule is like a little festival. Adjoining it there are a few other little festivals: That library with its dark cupboards and the low bay window, tastefully decorated with white tulle curtains. Then the salon with the old Dutch secretary, the dainty Nymphenburg china dolls, and the double door that opens on the garden terrace. A gentle festiveness pervades all these rooms, something clean and shiny, something Sunday-like. That is why all the objects here are so congenial to me, so familiar and pleasant, almost like living friends. When I arrive, I greet them all: the chande-

lier and the Nymphenburg figurines, Holbein's "Erasmus" in the library, Liebermann's "Riders by the Sea," Cézanne's "Still Life," Van Gogh's "The Chestnuts," and Pissaro's "Quai d'Orsay" . . . Here everything is shiny down to the most hidden nooks. Here everything is young and inwardly clean. Here nothing is dusty, nothing is permeated with, or confined by, the debris and the junk of many past times. Here everything has grown like the resplendent rhododendron in the Botanical Gardens: wrested from the arid soil. That is why I overflow with so much confidence and enjoyment of creativity and a Sunday kind of joy here. That is the house in Grunewald.

When I bounded up the winding staircase, I often paused on the landing in the middle where there stood two bronze figures, Adam and Eve. On the opposite wall, above the open fireplace of the vestibule, there was a frieze in the form of a pictorial broadsheet which always posed new puzzles for me. They were dark-green ovals depicting, in changing surroundings, children and adults in antiquated attire, some strolling under trees in a garden, others by a lake in which a swan was stretching its long neck, in a traveling coach or in a shabby hovel with an iron stove and a long, winding stovepipe. An itinerant journeyman played his lute; a girl in a wide hoop skirt waved to a young man; and on a green hill, beneath drooping willows, a fire burned on a high altar toward which a muffled figure was walking hand in hand with a slender woman. What was all that supposed to mean? Time and again I stood up there and stared at those figures. They seemed to be moving, though their gestures seemed so unnatural to me that there was something mysterious about the whole thing. At a later date I was able to decipher the captions under each picture: The Swan, Friendship, The Traveling Minstrel, The First Trip, The Encounter, Unrequited Love, The Poem, In Distress, Immortality. The series was called "A Poet's Life"; it was a Biedermeier fresco by Karl Walser, who had thus decorated the vestibule of the publisher's house.

I used to stand up there by the railing of the gallery from where I was able to see, observe, and hear everything without being heard or seen myself. When Mama sang, when guests came, or when my brother was giving a musicale— always the vestibule was the center, and I crouched hidden away behind the gallery and participated in the activity down below in my own way. There on the upper floor were my parents' bedrooms as well as my own, which was connected with the playroom I loved so much.

The top floor was reached from the gallery via a narrow back staircase. There the smell was quite different from the rest of the house. This was the location of the guest rooms— small, low garrets with slanting walls— and of a bathroom dating from grandfather's days with a bathtub of snowy white porcelain that rested on curved feet of iron and had presumably been built for giants. And there also was an attic, a huge attic in which one could get lost, as well as an upper attic to which one climbed on a ladder and from whose skylights one had a magnificent view of the entire Grunewald section. This upper attic was full of mysteries; it contained boxes with old letters, and there one could find old household items of all kinds as well as strange furniture of our ancestors. The attic was a forbidden no man's land; actually, it was always locked, and it was a lucky break for me when I was able to sneak in. For me it remained the part of the house that was shrouded in mystery. After World War II the rumor circulated among our neighbors that my father's death mask, which had been hidden there during the Hitler period, had shielded the house from the air raids, whereas almost all the surrounding houses had been heavily damaged or completely destroyed by bombs.

In the garden, where the massive plane trees stood, it was so good to bicycle around the circular flower bed. An arbor led to the tennis court, which later became an important meeting place and combat zone for me and my friends. On the other side of the house was a playground with many pieces of gymnastic equipment and a gazebo where I always took my supper in summertime. This is where my friends came every day, and there we played our games of croquet which occasionally ended with quite a ruckus, so that my friend Peter had to climb over the fence to escape my attacks with a croquet mallet. Together with my two friends and neighbors Esther and Peter I took my first steps into life, proceeding from play with dolls to long discussions about religion and politics.

Although I had received two quite normal names from my parents, Brigitte and Eva, everybody called me Tutti. I have never been able to find out how I got that name, which has stuck to me since early childhood. Thus I had to content myself with being called Tutti, which means "all" in Italian. At a later date Alfred Kerr teased me by asking how it would be if "Tutti" sang a solo.

My playroom with the round marble table in the middle and the big pendant lamp above it was the center of my childhood. I loved its warmth and security. There I gradually outgrew my first playthings, such as my "hurdy-gurdy" on which one had to put records with holes in them and then turn a crank to hear the music. I could never get enough of the chorale "Praise the Lord"; I had to listen to it over and over again and learned to recognize the record by the position of the holes. Another of my companions was the doll Butzi in a white sailor's suit; it went with me everywhere together with the faithful dachshund Pitt, which had already watched over me in my baby carriage.

For years the dollhouse, which occupied a part of the playroom, was the center of my play. It was so big that one could enter it through a door. It had real window panes and window sills, and inside it was furnished with a table and chairs, so that I was able to treat my friends to dishes I cooked myself on the dollhouse stove.

Only at a much later date did I realize that the "people," the grown-ups who came to see my parents, were mostly artists, poets, writers, and musicians. I gradually learned to distinguish among them and to love them— or, in some cases, merely to be polite to them. It was years before I was allowed to sit at the table in the evening when such "people" had been invited. I was glad if they did not send for me, for I much preferred staying in the isolation of my playroom and eating my supper at the round table under the pendant lamp. The semolina pudding certainly tasted wonderful, especially when grated chocolate was on it and "Lau" read to me while I was eating it.

Oh, Lau! Her real name was Bertha Seele [Soul], but no poet could have invented a better nickname for her. She had been there ever since I could remember. Her outward appearance was so unremarkable that I am unable to remember details of her face, but I do remember her loving kindness. She was part of that warm shelteredness of my childhood, and she protected me from anything that could cause fear. At night, when I heard her busying herself with the carpet sweeper, I felt that I could safely fall asleep. She was harmony personified, always kind in the same way; when she was around, there was no getting excited or nervous. My brother Gerhart, eleven years my senior, loved her too, and although he often had a temper and could be difficult, she got along well with him. In the evening he would sometimes tutor her, for he thought it scandalous that not all people had equal educational opportunities. She submitted to this with infinite patience, for she was patience personified. Later she took care of my own children, and she remained close to us till her death.

We also had a puppet theater. It was a big box carved out of wood with a real stage on which the sets could be changed. There was a room from a castle with elegant murals as well as a wild mountain gorge. But the main thing was the colorfully painted curtain which we raised upon the ringing of a bell. The figures were also carved of wood and wore sumptuous Biedermeier costumes. We could move them by means of long wires. My brother used the puppet theater for his own sketches of operas, and together with me and my older friend Benvenuto, Gerhart Hauptmann's youngest son, he performed scenes which often ended very dramatically, with artificial storms and rain, in the darkened room. Most of the time I was in charge of the sound effects. If things got too wild, Lau broke in and put a stop to the drama.

On my birthday there usually was a children's party. On such occasions we were allowed to sit at the long table in the dining room. There was a lot of cake, hot chocolate, and above all cracker bonbons and little presents that had to be won in all sorts of games. The finale was a parade through the whole house to my mother's piano accompaniment. My little friends always asked anxiously, "Is Butzi Hauptmann going to be invited to the party?" His ability to create terrifying disturbances was limitless. One of his favorite acts was to switch off electric fuses and to plunge the entire house into darkness, and this caused fear and terror among us.

I moved out of my childhood playroom when I was eleven, for in that year, 1916, my sister was born, and this filled the children's rooms of our house with new life.

Her birth was, of course, a great and joyous event for the whole house and changed every member of the family in his or her own way. Since the death of my brother Gerhart, whom I had lost three years earlier, I had been the only child in the house, excessively cared for by my parents. But now I felt freer, more grown up, more independent, and I joyfully assumed increasing responsibility for my little sister. With the arrival of the new child my parents seemed to have become rejuvenated and more cheerful, and every day the baby gave them fresh joy.

In the tiny workroom that I now moved into I assembled everything that was important to me. There I could read, study, and reflect without being disturbed. There I had a library of my own which I had slowly accumulated, containing the literary and philosophical classics that especially interested me: Lao-tzu, Confucius, and the Upanishads were important stages for me at that time. My own piano also stood there. In my piano lessons I preferred playing Bach and studied "The Well-Tempered Clavichord" and the suites. I also began to accompany my mother; with her beautiful contralto voice she would sing the songs of Schubert, Schumann, Brahms, and Hugo Wolf, and she particularly loved Mahler's "Songs of a Wayfarer" and "The Song of the Earth." She was a born musician and had a unique memory for music. She filled our house with her love of music, and she passed this love on to me.

Very soon I discovered chamber music, and this kind of music has enriched my whole life to this day. I found young musician friends who got together to play trios, quartets, and quintets, and at times we also formed a small chamber orchestra with which I played Bach's piano concertos.

Occasionally I even made music with Albert Einstein, who is known to have been no great musician. He was a great music lover and an impassioned violinist, but could not take any criticism of his playing and was apt to fly into a rage when he botched something. One day he was playing Bach's Double Concerto with an excellent professional violinist, Gerhart Hauptmann's daughter-in-law, and me at the piano. Suddenly he lit into his partner, whose big tone was drowning him out: "Don't play so loud!" I believe he got more excited then than he ever would have in a scientific dispute.

Only gradually did I get accustomed to participating in my parents' "loftier" conversations with their friends and to listening to them. Today I realize that in those days many important things were being stored up in me.

2
School in My Parental Home and First Friendships

My schooling took place in the attic of our house next to those mysterious guest rooms. Our class usually consisted of four or six children from the neighborhood. We loved our teacher, a very dynamic elderly woman with a French name, Leviseur. She was intelligent and had a sense of humor as well as a peculiar style of rapid-fire teaching. Her first questions were asked when she was still on the topmost step of the staircase, even before she had pulled the long pin out of her hat and set foot in the classroom. The whole lesson continued at this breathless pace, and in this way we learned quickly and a great deal without ever getting bored. At a later point, when we were older and Miss Leviseur could no longer handle the ever-increasing curriculum by herself, we had five different teachers. In this setting it was appreciated if we wrote essays that did not necessarily conform to the teacher's opinion and contained original ideas that could be discussed in class. This was not possible in the state schools, which were still in line with the ideology of the Prussian imperial state. Anyone whose thinking deviated in the least from the premises of this ideology and who tried to expose his or her own ideas was ridiculed or, even worse, impeded in his or her scholastic progress.

It was the latter kind of institution that I attended during my last two years in school. At length I could no longer stand the musty atmosphere and the regimentation, and I prevailed upon my parents to let me enter Professor Auerbach's private school to prepare for my *Abitur,* the school-leaving examination. There I found a female teacher who inspired me. With her enthusiasm for literature— particularly Goethe, whose works she virtually knew by heart— she opened my ears and my mind to poetry. To read Goethe's *West-Eastern Divan* with her was quite an experience. For the first time I read with my ears, as it were, and understood that language can be music. This gave me access to a new world. At the same time I took an introductory course in philosophy and began to study Nietzsche and Kant; but time and again I was more fascinated by the philosophy of China and India than by anything else. Today I have the same experience with my grandchildren, for whom the Far East has become the world of their dreams, since the world surrounding them is currently in a state of confused self-destruction.

Unfortunately I was not vouchsafed a few years of quiet study far from home. Even though I had grown up in my parental home in independence and freedom, my parents later insisted "egotistically" on refusing to let me leave home to continue my higher education. Thus I had to curb my curiosity about life "out there"; for the time being I was obliged to quench my thirst for knowledge by reading books and to content myself with six months of practical work at a school of home economics. This school was located on the old estate of a banker, Eduard Arnold, in the Brandenburg March. I liked the sparse, flat, sandy landscape with its magnificent forests, and I loved country living.

At that time, in 1923, postwar Germany's diet consisted mainly of turnips and potatoes, and hence the culinary arts that I was supposed to acquire there could not have been on a very high level. Actually, my duties did not matter to me; what I considered important were those adventurous bicycle rides through fields, meadows, and woods as well as our discovery of country life in the nearby old villages where we spent the night in haylofts. One day I found out that Moritz Heimann, a close friend of my parents who had also become a fatherly friend to me, lived in the vicinity. His native village, Kagel, was tucked away in the sandy oases of the March woods. The small, cheerful farm house, the parental home in which he had grown up, was very attractive to me with its well-scrubbed wooden floors and its beautiful, simple, old furniture. Heimann received me there like his daughter, and he always had time for conversations about all the things that mattered to a young person. There was no need to be shy, for one could ask him about anything and get his advice— on one's relationship with one's parents, on questions of religion, on how to cope with life. My hours with this kindly and wise man became more important to me than anything else around me. He had known me since my birth, but now he took me *into* his heart, as it were, and guided me. His thinking was clear and unsentimental, and thousands of years of Jewish knowledge of human nature were stored up in him. He was a man who suffered—not just physically, but I felt how an unmerciful world made him suffer. That is why he was so open to the problems of his fellow men and why he was able to help so many young people— artists, poets, and writers— who came to see him by speaking to them in a way that dispelled their doubts. He was a great listener; with his uncommonly large ears he listened with a devotion that enveloped the other person and at the same time encouraged him or her to confide in him completely. On such occasions one had the impression that at that particular moment one was the only person in the world as far as Heimann was concerned.

For my fifth birthday, which I spent in Rome, he had sent me an Easter card with the following little poem:

Leg' das Ohr an, horch genau:
Die Osterkätzchen schrein miau,
Sie ringeln ihre Schwänzchen.
Und wenn die Sonne lustig scheint,
Und wenn der Wind es auch so meint,
Dann machen sie ein Tänzchen.
Es kommen alle Blumen vor,
Die ganze Erde steht im Flor
Und lacht im neuen Frühlingslicht
Und ist so dumm wie dies Gedicht.
Und dumm und lustig muß man sein,
Denn so sind auch die Engelein.
Nun hör' ich auf, der Platz ist aus,
Ich grüße Dich, komm bald nach Haus!

(Apply your ears and listen closely: The little Easter cats are crying meow and curling their little tails. And if the sun shines merrily and the wind blows the same way, they are going to do a little dance. All the flowers are coming out, the whole earth is in bloom, smiles in the new light of spring, and is as silly as this poem. But one has to be silly and jolly, for that's how the little angels are. Now I shall stop, for there's no more space. Greetings to you, come home soon!)

What nice children's poems Uncle Heimann was able to write! I liked them very much and was able to recite them from memory, including another, a bit more serious spring poem that he wrote in my album for my ninth birthday in March of 1914:

Murmeln trägt ein Jung in seinem Hut,
Alle Eisenbahnen riechen gut,
Alle Kindermädchen haben Zeit
Und die Kutscher tun mir nicht mehr leid.

Bald, ach bald
Machen sieben Bäume einen Wald,
Aus der grünen Wolke wird es dringen,
Wird auch durch die blauen Lüfte springen:
Eingeschlungen in die Himmelskette,
Sing' ich schon mit Lerchen um die Wette.

(A boy carries marbles in his hat, all trains smell good, all nursemaids have time, and I no longer feel sorry for the coachmen. Soon, oh soon seven trees will make a forest, something will come out of the green cloud and jump through the blue air. Entwined in the heavenly chain I am already engaging in a singing contest with larks.)

A letter he wrote me on June 12, 1915 shows that he already treated me as an adult when I was ten:

My dear friend Tutti! Your photo gave me much pleasure. May you always have flowers in your basket. If I did not already represent a somewhat autumnal scenery, I would give you a photo of myself in return. When my son Fritz comes, I shall ask him to try to make me "say cheese"; then you will get me, because you already have me, as your friend with my best regards, Moritz Heimann.

3
My Brother Gerhart. His Short Life and Early Death

I had a big brother. His name was Gerhart and he was eleven years my senior. To me he was an idol; we loved each other, I loved and adored him. He seemed to me like the consummation of the future. Though he was so close and so akin to me, the world that surrounded him was an alien and undreamt-of one. He teased me a lot and was capable of playing with me quite exuberantly, usually laughing uproariously as he did so. I liked his boisterousness and enjoyed romping and fooling around with him, for unfortunately I was still much too little to be a partner for him. When he and his friends came home from time to time on vacation from the Freie Schulgemeinde Wickersdorf, the boarding school of which my father was one of the founders, this was my first contact with the mysterious world of men. Gerhart and his friends, who were so high-spirited and so full of *joie de vivre,* appeared as something unattainable to me.

For my first birthday he wrote this lullaby for me:

Schlaflied für meine Schwester Brigitte Eva
von ihrem Bruder Gerhart
Grunewald, den 5. März 1906

Schläfst Du, Evchen, mein Kind?
Hörst Du, wie draußen tobet der Wind?
Wie er fährt über die Häuser und Dächer dahin?
Ja, er hat keinen freundlichen Sinn.
Jauchzet nicht und lallt nicht freudig wie Du. –
Schlafe Evchen, in süßer Ruh!

Schläfst Du, träumst Du von besseren Tagen,
Frei von allen Sorgen und Plagen?
Wo Du in schöner Frühlingsluft
Atmest der Blumen würzigen Duft?

Schlafe und träume in süßer Ruh
Schließe Deine Äuglein zu
Und öffne Dir des Traumes Pracht,
Daß er mit seiner Liebe Macht
Gesegnete Strahlen auf Dich sende
Und Dich tröste – bis an Dein Ende!

(Lullaby for my sister Brigitte Eva from her brother Gerhart, Grunewald, March 5, 1906

Are you asleep, Evie, my child? Do you hear the wind roaring outside, moving over the houses and roofs? Oh, it is not kindly disposed, it does not shout and babble joyfully like you. Sleep, Evie, in sweet peace! Are you asleep, are you dreaming of better days free from all care and toil, when you will breathe in the beautiful spring air and the spicy fragrance of flowers? Sleep and dream in sweet peace. Close your little eyes and open up the splendor of your dream so that it may send beams of blessing upon you with the power of its love and console you—to the end of your life!)

These were mature and wistful verses for a boy of twelve.

When I was eight and he had just turned nineteen, I lost him. He had contracted typhoid fever while staying at the Adriatic Sea, and when he joined my parents and me, who were spending our summer vacation on the Lido near Venice, he was already in very bad shape. I remember those radiant August weeks, the wide, sandy beach of the Hotel des Bains, so comfortable with its bathing cabins and deck chairs, and the many friends (the Beer-Hofmanns, the

Schnitzlers, and Peter Altenberg) who had joined us. My parents' horror at their son's illness destroyed this summer idyll; they decided to leave the Lido immediately and to return to Berlin. The nocturnal voyage to Venice in the rocking gondola with the mortally ill boy seemed to take forever. The flashing lights in the darkness of the nocturnal sea; the splashing of the long oar and the uncanny, long-drawn-out calls of the gondoliers; the fear in my parents' faces— all that has been engraved on my memory since that eerie night.

My brother was taken home, but despite all medical efforts and the tireless care of my mother, who kept an around-the-clock vigil by his bedside, he died after ten days of terrible suffering.

This blow of fate burst into my children's world, hitherto so sheltered and protected, like a disastrous stroke of lightning and transformed my childlike dream world. Gerhart's death, which I witnessed in the house, though it seemed to be happening far away, was to me a sinister and cruel presence and an alien force to which I felt helplessly exposed. The doctors were powerless, because in those days there was no remedy for that disease. Through my brother's death I experienced for the first time the ineluctable force of destiny and a feeling of profound sadness. I tried to hide my feelings from my parents, however, and usually acted cheerful and frolicsome in front of them. As a result they probably wondered whether I had "understood" that bitter death at all. I understood it in my own way, meaning that I had been left all alone, and I tried to get accustomed to the loneliness that surrounded me.

For three years, until the birth of my sister, I remained the only child in the house.

My brother had begun to write music and poetry when he was still a child. He played the piano and later studied at the Musikhochschule (Academy of Music) in Berlin. He wrote Lieder as well as pieces for piano and for orchestra, and he began to work on several operas for which he wrote his own libretti. Together with his friends at school he had formed a small chamber orchestra which he conducted and with which he also performed his own compositions. Among his best friends in this musical circle were the Humperdincks, the children of the great composer. Wolfram frequently conducted the chamber orchestra and Senta sang Gerhart's Lieder. There were festive evening concerts to which my parents invited friends and sometimes even music critics of their acquaintance. There was very serious music-making with long rehearsals; in addition to first performances of Gerhart's compositions, the programs included Bach's Brandenburg Concertos and other concertos by him. When he was not busy with the orchestra, my brother usually sat at the piano and composed, or he played Brahms, whom he loved very much.

Gerhart had a distinctive personality even as a boy. After his death I read the diaries which he had started keeping at the age of ten, and I marveled at his maturity. His self-analyses and his impressions of works of art and music assumed increasing importance and grew into finished essays like "The Salzburg Mozart Festival," "Some Thoughts on Brahms," "Impressions of *Tristan*," "Verdi's *Otello,*" and "Gustav Mahler's *Lied von der Erde.*" It is astonishing how modern his views on this work sound. The following diary entry by the eighteen-year-old is from the year 1912: "Mahler fashioned the poems into a very appropriate foundation for the expression of his own nature, and thus he was able to draw from his fullest sources. Above all, one's ears revel in lush, minutely crafted orchestral hues which suffuse this atmospheric poetry with an abundant flow of color and shape it with a truly visionary insight. What emerges from all this harmony is a noble, warmly perceptive soul with a frequently disconsolate, frequently smiling melancholy as well as a pure sensuality based on a love of nature."

To express himself and communicate in music was Gerhart's innate talent, and soon outer experiences also had a share in his musical development. Thus a trip to Italy in 1910 inspired him to compose a three-part Rhapsody—the first part being an elegy on Monte Pincio, the second a Good Friday procession in Sorrento, and the third a Scherzo depicting the bustle at the Rialto of Venice.

But what touched me particularly about him was his kindness toward others and his feeling of social responsibility. This was so strongly developed in him that he felt ashamed in front of those who were on a lower educational level. His diaries reveal his great concern with social differences. In 1913 he wrote under the heading "The Social Obligations of Man": "In my opinion, this is the main point: The advantage that every person who has grown up in comfortable circumstances and with a good education has over other people is only a credit voucher, an obligation to let others benefit by it, and it is utterly worthless if the person does not use it for the benefit of others and does not attempt to give them in kindly fashion what they lack. This obligation would be a reassurance for everyone who asks himself in astonishment whether he is a better person by virtue of birth or a kindly fate and deserves a better life than any child from less fortunate circumstances. I certainly know how many apprehensions and obstacles within us militate against such a course of action and how hard it is to overcome deep-rooted prejudices, but I do believe that we have to work on it anew every day. Jakob Wassermann has chosen the beautiful words *Die Trägheit des Herzens* (The Indolence of the Heart) as the subtitle of his novel *Kaspar Hauser.* It is this indolence within us that we foster deliberately, provided that we are conscious of it at all . . . I am far from believing that all class differences could be eliminated without incurring complete chaos, but I think that our interpersonal relationships ought to be expanded. I believe that more light could be conveyed from one person to another and that both parties could give each other and help each other more than they are doing now. A contribution in this spirit could be made by every individual who continually makes a clean sweep of his acquired and engrained prejudices and recognizes only human differences between himself and other persons . . . "

When Gerhart died, their entire circle of friends and authors shared in the terrible loss which my deeply shaken parents had suffered. The voices of the poetic friends consoled them. On the occasion of my brother's death Richard Dehmel wrote a text for one of his melodies and dedicated it to my mother.

Fremdlinge sind wir, laßt uns nicht weinen
Seht wie die Sterne über uns scheinen
Aus ihrem Schimmer stammt unser Blut
Mitten in Finsternissen
Träumt sich's gut.

Mutterhaus, Glück, Geburtstagsstunden,
Fern liegt ihr, fern,
Seitdem ich heimgefunden.
Oh, wieviel Lichter sind hoch um mich her!
Mutter, Geschwisterchen klagt nicht mehr!

(Strangers are we; let us not weep. Look how the stars shine above us. From their shimmer comes our blood. It's good to dream in times of darkness. Maternal home, happiness, birthday hours—you have been so distant since I have come home. Oh, how many lights shine high above me! Mother, little sister, lament no more!)

Moritz Heimann spoke the following words at Gerhart's grave:

He felt the responsibility of life—not the small one from which no one is exempt in his pursuits, but the big, mournful one which is imposed upon nobler spirits over and above civic duty. He did not want to live from day to day, and so he went into the too early night—too early by our standards and knowledge. But if we ever are capable of higher knowledge, it is when we are taught by a dead person. I looked this young human being in the face when he was dead, in his peaceful and austere face, and I felt that he had completed his life and was complete . . .

For Gerhart's tombstone Heimann wrote these verses:

Er wollte singen und wurde Gesang,
Wir hören ihn unser Leben lang.

(He wished to sing and himself became song/ We shall hear him our whole life long).

A year later Heimann wrote to my mother for her birthday, which was also the day of Gerhart's death:

It is, of course, your little girl who is on my mind, and if I send you my best wishes now, I know that I can do so joyfully, for you have to accept these wishes joyfully. And so I congratulate you and your husband and Tutti so that the three of you in your loving and exemplary community may use the new young light in your house to enjoy the imperishable light in your own souls. I know full well that the shadow which has been cast on your life cannot go away, but like all shadows, it will only make the colors, those evidences of light, deeper and more distinctive. May everything that is part of you thrive.

The writer Max Dauthendey, a friend of my parents, visited them a few months after my brother's death. The rooms in our house in Grunewald were still suffused with the aura of his death, and Dauthendey captured this atmosphere in his novella "Zwei Reiter am Meer" (Two Horsemen by the Sea) which appeared in a volume of his short fiction entitled *Geschichten aus den vier Winden* (Stories from the Four Winds):

The wide open doors to the illuminated adjoining rooms, the music room, the dining room, and the salon, all of them suffused with soft lights and an infinite calm, had made my thoughts wander ever farther afield, and it seemed to me as though my chair did not stand in the library of an elegant country home on the outskirts of a cosmopolis. Instead, I seemed to be standing at the edge of a continent and looking out on a grey ocean whose waterline turned into wispy clouds on the distant horizon. Only at great intervals did an extensive wave raise a cloud of foamy spray over the beach . . . The picture which I saw so vividly and which depicted two riders by the sea hung in the adjoining music room in a golden frame over the grand piano. It was by Max Liebermann.

A wide-ranging, muted, festive atmosphere surrounded me; I could not escape it and yet I was not able to feel part of it, because this festivity did not belong to me. It was the festivity of the hour of death that harmonized sorrow and joy, a festivity that had not left the rooms of this house as yet and that had been able to impart a higher transfiguration to the everyday rooms than any noisy festivities had managed to do.

The dead person had been a young musician. Mother and son had frequently spent hours over there by the grand piano. The mother sang what the young man had devised, and he played for her what the voice of his youthful feelings, his youthful seriousness, and his youthful solitude had made him give sound to.

At such times the hearts of the mother and the son had been like the two riders by the sea whose horses walked in the same rhythm and who moved along melodiously in front of the infinity of the sky and the sea, in front of the future and of the past . . .

Months had passed. The mother had never been able to bring herself to open the grand piano in the music room. She had had to bury her dead son over and over again; she had not yet found the strength to let the son arise before her transfigured. But every leavetaking must be succeeded by a return; the separation brought about by death is followed by the return, the hour of resurrection. Life, including dead life, does not allow itself to be buried unto infinity. Death, too, contains a tide, and past life also has its departure and its return.

On that evening I had unconsciously realized that the dead man had returned to his mother and his father in transfigured form. He had arisen again in the rooms of the house . . . His death wave, more inspatial than the spatial waves felt by us, the living, was trying to assume shape before us.

Under the spell of this mood I ventured to ask the mourning mother whether she would like to sing a song by her deceased son or play one of his compositions . . .

When the mourner sat down at the gleaming black grand piano between the two screened bright lamps, with her narrow shoulders, swathed in black, standing out against the snowy white tulle curtains that hung vertically from the windows behind her, I was not yet certain that life would be awakened by the piano . . .

But she was ready to receive her returning son. With wonderful courage, as though she herself were joyously crossing the threshold to death, she coaxed the old pleasant sounds from the piano . . .

And when she was singing one of his last songs, something wonderful happened before my eyes: As the mature, beautiful woman sang the youthful melodies of her son, she sang her way back to her own earliest youth, and her woman's face became girl-like, free from all disappointments . . . And I saw mother and son ride along the sea of infinity on two super-lifesized young horses, each of which seemed to be the embodiment of a destiny.

To this day I see these two as riders by the vast sea at the edge of the world, and I shall see them thus forever.

4
My Mother and My Father

My parents married in 1893 in Berlin. At that time my mother was twenty-two years old, the daughter of a prosperous businessman's family who had spent her youth in Stettin. The world of my father, whose newly founded publishing house placed him in the midst of social, political, and artistic upheavals, was totally alien to her. She had no idea what to expect and what was in store for her, but she appears to have adapted to the new life in short order and she wholeheartedly became an integral part of it.

My grandmother was a singer—not a professional one, for that was frowned upon in her circles in those days, but a well-trained soprano. As my mother frequently told me, her beautiful voice, her graceful figure, and her great charm made her an ideal interpreter of Mozart. Grandma must have been a beauty. As early as age twenty-five her hair was snow-white and framed her lovely, intelligent face. All sorts of delightful stories circulated about her that demonstrate her childlike naiveté despite all her motherly femininity. On one of her birthdays my father described her as follows in a letter to my mother: "This was quite a festive morning . . . .Mother's wishes really were touching: a pot for making bouillon, a baking dish, a sugarloaf, a scouring cloth, and other items of kitchen poetry . . . "

It was grandma who brought music to the family. In the great oratorios conducted by Siegfried Ochs at the Berlin Singakademie she sang the soprano solos; this much was approved of as being "standesgemäss" (in keeping with one's social standing). She took her children—my mother and her brother and sister—to the rehearsals for those concerts, and thus the children received their first musical education at an early age.

This love of music and enthusiasm for it dominated my mother's life as well. Even as a young girl she attended numerous concerts; thus she heard the great Russian pianist Anton Rubinstein play under the baton of Hans von Buelow and experienced the memorable evening on which Buelow conducted Beethoven's Ninth Symphony twice in succession. But her greatest musical experience, one that she talked about again and again, must have been the first performance of Gustav Mahler's Eighth Symphony in 1910 under the composer's direction. On that occasion she experienced the birth of a new world to which the audience reacted with profound emotion and tremendous ovations for Mahler.

My mother was a unique mixture of childlike naiveté and mature intelligence. She had good instincts about people and encountered them with trusting openness. There was something disarming about the way she dealt with people.

"Zitternd unterm Schicksalsjoch/ Ganz in Gott geborgen doch" (Trembling under fate's yoke, yet wholly sheltered in God), wrote her friend and admirer Jakob Wassermann, and her friend Felix Salten called her "the most innocent woman I know." Our friend Hans Reisiger, however, displayed an even more profound knowledge of her when he described her as follows:

It is not as though she were unkind, but precisely out of love of mankind she had, thank God, strong dislikes. One cannot be a wife and mother presiding over a house and an important area of life without being able to wrinkle one's brow when this is necessary. She was a very emotional, passionate, and intellectually sensitive person—and here I equate intellect with beauty, the highest form of intellect. . . . For a woman like her in whom femininity and artistry, hospitality and intellectuality harmonized in such natural fashion, a place by the side of a great publisher of predominantly literary works was certainly the appropriate one . . . . The publishing house was a home for its authors, a warm, homey world which made everyone who entered it feel good, but that would not have been the case without the dear and noble femininity of 'Mommy'; it would not have been so without the stimulation that emanated from her—less from her intellect than from her personality.

The Baltic writer Eduard Graf Keyserling, published by my father from 1900 on and whose books my mother loved very much, said about mama's share in the shape of the publishing house that a manuscript was not really and truly accepted by Fischer until a tear from Frau Hedwig's eyes had fallen on it.

Once she had become convinced of the sincerity and the worth of a person, she befriended him or her. Friendship was her element—something unconditional and fixed for all times. She was always there for her friends, with complete caring and devotion, such as she was there for her husband and children. She always maintained contact with her friends, and I have heard it said that she wrote about 50,000 letters in her lifetime.

Every year our Christmas celebration with the big, decorated tree by the window of the dining room with the beautifully arched ceiling was a radiant festival. The big table, extended to its full length, was covered with presents for all members of our household. The cook, the chambermaid, the chauffeur and his family, "Lau" and we family members had our regular places at this table, side by side, and in front of each of us was the fragrant "mixed" plate with all sorts of gingerbread and marzipan. Before the presents were distributed, Mama sang Christmas carols with us—those by Peter Cornelius being her favorites— and then everyone found something specially selected for him or her, for mother was a genius at giving. All her friends were gifted with colorfully wrapped packages, and it was hard to understand how she could manage all that, for her acts of friendship never ceased.

For many years she was at the center of Berlin's intellectual and artistic life as the heart of the great publishing house. Her activities and her personal aura may have resembled those of the famous women of German Romanticism, who were living models to her. Thus our house on Erdenerstrasse became the home of our family of authors.

It is strange, though: Now that I reflect about it, something that I didn't do at the time, she devoted less time to her own children. Their growing up was something self-evident that one need not waste any thought on. That is what her relationship to me was like.

To be sure, she did worry when something was wrong with me and lovingly took care of me; but in daily life she never asked what I was doing, working on, or thinking. She was pleased that my musical education was progressing well, and she was proud when I was able to accompany her singing, but she never tried to steer me in any direction. When I was preparing to work in the production department of our publishing house, she did not take this very seriously.

My mother was an optimist by nature, and this made her an ideal companion for my father, who was frequently subject to depressions. She simply believed that everything would turn out for the best. When, at a much later date, her world collapsed and the Nazis threatened her very life, she was speechless in the face of the absolute evil that surrounded her. Her naive faith in man's goodness kept her from seeing that she was clearly endangered. Her innocence scared friends like Joachim Maass, who was still in Germany in 1938 and faithfully visited her. Some lucky star must have protected her, for danger lurked about her daily until finally, in response to our constant urging, she decided to leave her house, Berlin, and Germany, abandoning all her possessions, including her diaries, the guest book, and the entire archives of our publishing house, and to join us in our Stockholm exile.

My mother's grandparents had still been pious Jews, but her parents had already assimilated to German culture intellectually and emotionally. In the memoirs of her youth which she wrote as an emigrant she described this as follows:

In those days there were multifarious social, cultural, and artistic struggles, but we knew nothing of racial hatred and hardly anything of anti-Semitism. In our sphere at least I encountered only seldom traces of it. We experienced little or nothing of even 'moderate' anti-Semitism in our house and at the office. In our family and among our friends, mixed marriages were nothing out of the ordinary, and most of them worked out rather well . . .

When Nazism overtook Germany, she was not able to comprehend that people wanted to deprive her of her old home, her country, and her citizenship, that they cast her out and robbed her of her property because she was Jewish, and that they were trying to kill her and her kind. The conviction of her entire life— that there are no Jews and Christians but only human beings— was being destroyed. All this was such a profound shock to her that in her years of emigration in America she lived only like a shadow of her former self. She became mistrustful toward everyone and could no longer find her bearings. Only her grandchildren were able to give her joy.

Life had taught my father to make extreme demands upon himself. Only in this way, striving for the highest things from the humblest origins, did he manage to build up his publishing house. Yet he was reserved by nature, constantly questioning himself and examining himself critically.

"Everything that happens, that I hear and see only serves me as a standard for my own self— gives me clarity about dormant powers within me, my ability and desires, about the worth and unworth of my being." This is an excerpt from one of the few sketches which he began in the form of a diary in 1907 but unfortunately did not continue. "I do not estimate my worth too highly because I measure it against the best of my contemporaries, and to have met them constitutes the value of my life. I have never found the time and the composure to draw up a balance-sheet of my energies, to calculate where I can expend and where I must save so that I may strengthen my weak points and within my capabilities make a harmonious person out of myself. At an early stage my environment and situation compelled me to view a rise to a higher social existence as the goal of all labor. With this goal in mind, I was a person totally bent on acquisition. Gradually my horizon brightened and broadened."

Papa was a Sunday child and the youngest of four siblings. He was named Samuel, but as a child everyone called him Sami; in later life only Mama called him that. He always signed his name as S. Fischer.

He hardly talked about his youth in the ancient town of Liptó Szent Miklós, located in Transylvania at the foot of the Tatra Mountains and at that time part of Austria-Hungary. In that Hungarian-speaking region he attended the German-language school of the Jewish community and then, for a few additional years, a Jewish private secondary school. Even as a boy he displayed a great passion for books. The Jewish community of Liptó had established a reading circle with its own library, and his first acquaintance with the German classics stems from that. Full of curiosity he looked at the books in the windows of the town's only bookstore, located on Market Square.

At the age of fourteen he left his parental home and a hometown that had become too narrow for him. One day he found himself in front of a bookstore in the capital city of Vienna. There he was accepted as an apprentice and thus took his first step toward his life's profession. He really must have received a "call" from the calling which he felt in himself, a call that he obeyed blindly. After a few years he felt impelled to move to Berlin, where he became an assistant in the Steinitz Bookstore on Friedrichstrasse and soon rose to be a partner.

Around the turn of the century Berlin had become a new literary center almost unparalleled in the rest of Europe. As in its earlier history, Berlin's soil now proved to be fruitful for the "new age." As a fellow fighter for intellectual renewal my father had founded his own publishing house as early as 1886, and in the very first decade of its existence it gathered round itself nearly all the great writers and dramatists of the period.

In a letter to Julius Bab dated 1923, my father wrote:

All that I thought I knew, everything that helped me to form my own thought and feeling I owe to the arts, especially literature, and in large measure to living contact with their creators. By the growth of my own spiritual and intellectual powers I can gauge the effectiveness of art changing into experience. I have personally witnessed, and at extremely close range, the development of a cultural epoch. Fate has favored me by putting into my hands the most important documents in all their immediacy. In the course of a lifetime these constitute the continuity of human growth and suffering, the connection between life and development. At any rate, between my youth and my maturity these manifestations have become a source of knowledge and life for me. I have been privileged to derive reality from an imaginary world. G. C. Lichtenberg once said: 'Books do not make a person good or bad, but they do make him better or worse.' They have made me better.

The road to his first successes was not an easy one. When he married, he had been on his own for seven years, and his publishing house, though still small, was known beyond Germany's boundaries. One of his first authors was Henrik Ibsen, at that time known as a starry-eyed idealist. Every other year my father published a new drama by Ibsen whose revolutionary dynamite horrified the imperial Prussian authorities. The works of Ibsen were soon joined by the first German translations of Dostoievski, Tolstoi, Zola, and the Goncourt brothers. These writers brought fresh air to Germany and gained for my father the reputation of a progressive and modern publisher. In 1890 he and Otto Brahm founded a weekly that bore the same name as the theatrical association Freie Bühne (Free Stage). The first issue of this weekly with a programmatic declaration, a document that breathed the spirit of the new times: "Where the new is greeted with joyful shouts, the gauntlet must be flung down to the old, and it must be fought with all the weapons of the spirit . . . "

At the end of 1889 the theatrical association Freie Bühne, a thorn in the flesh of the imperial authorities, already had 360 members, and later there were 900. The membership list included such outstanding names as those of Theodor Fontane and his wife, the theater directors Barnay and L'Arronge, and the critics and actors Kainz, Agnes Sorma, and Paula Conrad. Ibsen had joined from Munich and Anzengruber from Vienna. The "anonymous" members came in large part from the Jewish circles in Berlin, and Fontane declared that "here in Berlin all freedom and refined culture is conveyed to us chiefly by wealthy Jews." The Freie Bühne inaugurated its theatrical program in 1889 with Ibsen's play *Ghosts*. "A well-constructed truth lasts thirty years," this great dramatist had said. I believe that his truths have lasted longer and changed many things, and thus they have been effective to this day.

Ibsen hated the state as such and called it "the curse of the individual."

The state must go! In that revolution I shall participate. Undermine the idea of the state, establish free choice and intellectual affinity as the only decisive criteria for an alliance— that is the beginning of a freedom which is worth something. The state has its roots in the temporal, and it will have its apex in the temporal. Greater things than it will fall; all religions will fall! Neither moral concepts nor art forms are eternal. How many things are we really duty-bound to preserve?

At a later time, all our intimate friends congregated in my paternal home in Grunewald: Gerhart and Carl Hauptmann, Thomas Mann, Rainer Maria Rilke, Moritz Heimann, Richard Dehmel, Otto Brahm, Julius Meier-Graefe, Annette Kolb, Otto Flake, Hans Reisiger, Walther Rathenau, Franz and Alma Werfel, and Alfred Döblin— to name only a few.

The "northern" writers came, friends like Hermann Bang, Peter Nansen, Björnstjerne Björnson, Johannes V. Jensen, Aage Madelung, Ellen Key, and Eduard von Keyserling. In the meantime a circle of writers had formed in Vienna that joined my father and his publishing house. Some of them became intimate friends, and on their trips north they visited our house in Grunewald whose hospitable white gate was always open to our friends. Among those who came whenever they had occasion to go to Berlin were Hermann Bahr, Peter Altenberg, Arthur Schnitzler, Hugo von Hofmannsthal, Richard Beer-Hofmann, Jakob Wassermann, and Felix Salten. On Erdenerstrasse there was no dearth of occasions for minor and major celebrations—for example, when my parents invited people to attend concerts of chamber music by the violinists Wolfsthal and Max Rostal, the violist Emil Bohnke, and the cellist Alexander Schuster. Frequently we were joined by Gerhart Hauptmann's wife Margarete, who was a pupil of Joseph Joachim and owned a beautiful Stradivarius, or by the young pianist Ansorge, who played Beethoven's Sonata opus 90, a favorite composition of my father's which he could not hear often enough.

In those days the theater was the great focus of intellectual life in Berlin. Almost every year a new, incendiary play by Ibsen or Hauptmann was performed on the stage and issued in book form by my father's publishing house. Otto Brahm, the co-founder and first director of the Freie Bühne, was succeeded by Max Reinhardt, who lifted the Deutsches Theater to an artistic level that had hitherto been attained only by the Russian Stanislavski ensemble. Many of the actors were personal friends of my parents— among them Joseph Schildkraut, Joseph Kainz, and Rudolf Rittner. As a young girl I had a crush on Alexander Moissi, who often visited us, and at a ball on Erdenerstrasse Tilla Durieux fell in love with the publisher Paul Cassirer. My parents' parties often led to marriages or divorces. At a later date Max Pallenberg and his wife Fritzi Massary, Elisabeth Bergner, Else Eckersberg, and Leopold Jessner, the director of the Schauspielhaus, were frequent guests in our house.

To this day the passionate performances of the great Beethoven sonatas by the brilliant pianist Eugen d'Albert ring in my ears. I particularly remember a concert that he gave in honor of his friend Gerhart Hauptmann in the big auditorium of the University of Berlin. In a state of enthusiasm and rapture he transported not only his friend Hauptmann but the entire audience, which was profoundly moved when it rose after his performance of the Appassionata and the Waldstein sonatas. D'Albert and his almost annually changing wives were frequent guests in Erdenerstrasse. When he introduced his "latest" wife to the Berlin painter Max Liebermann, the latter responded as follows: "Think I'll skip this one." Arthur Schnabel and his wife Therese, a great singing teacher who had also taught my mother, frequently called on us, as did the pianist Bruno Eisner and his wife, Olga, a fine mezzo soprano.

Bronislav Hubermann's violin playing, his tone and his phrasing, has remained just as unforgotten as the person— a passionate and enthusiastic champion of a United Europe. Bruno Walter, who conducted at the opera house in Charlottenburg and whose performances of Mozart operas are particularly memorable, was a steady visitor of my parents. Their shared love of Gustav Mahler bound my mother and him especially together.

My parental home was no less hospitable to graphic artists. My father had a great love for innovations in all forms of art, and he had as keen a perception for graphic artists as he had for poets and other writers. He was among the first people in Germany to acquire in Paris, toward the end of the nineties, paintings by Van Gogh, Cézanne, Gauguin, and Pissaro— to the great dismay of his friend Gerhart Hauptmann, who shuddered at such "modernists."

I still clearly remember how I became aware of this new world of the Impressionists. Suddenly I saw that they had transformed the atmosphere of our house, that they had brought in a new language. The "Still Life" of Cézanne, today one of the best-known paintings from the epoch, exuded a warm life-like atmosphere: on a wooden kitchen table a green earthenware jar, light-blue majolica pots, a bowl with yellow-red apples, behind it a boldly folded linen cloth in front of an old wooden cupboard— how this picture filled our salon with its rather stiff Empire furniture with new, young life! The Van Gogh painting that hung next to it shocked me at first. There were wild, shaggy, giant chestnut trees with white, candle-shaped blossoms that jutted upward, and beneath them a broad avenue on which only one solitary, strangely indefinable figure, sketched with a few green strokes, was walking. I had never seen anything like that before. It struck me as uncanny, and it was some time before I became aware of the great power behind this wildness.

My father's art collection also contained some sculptures by Maillol, Renée Sintenis, and August Gaul. Max Liebermann painted his portrait. My father, ever eager to meet new talents, belonged to the Sezession, an association that organized exhibits of modern artists, and befriended many artists, such as Emil Orlik, Lovis

Corinth, Max Slevogt, Max Pechstein and Alfred Kubin (both of whom he commissioned to illustrate books for him) as well as E.R. Weiss and his wife Renée Sintenis, Karl Walser, and Emil Preetorius.

Berlin became an international center of music. Every Sunday morning Richard Strauss conducted the great symphonies and in the evening operas in what was then still the Royal Opera House. There I surrendered for the first time to the enchantment of a musical play, the opera *Hansel and Gretel* by Engelbert Humperdinck. Papa Humperdinck, who seemed like a good-natured old "uncle" to me, asked everyone who entered his house to admire the electrically illuminated starry sky in his entrance hall.

The Charlottenburg Opera House was directed by Bruno Walter, and Otto Klemperer was chief conductor of the Kroll Opera. These three opera houses with their outstanding orchestras and important conductors were a unique magnet for singers from all over the world.

I still heard the concerts of the Berlin Philharmonic under Arthur Nikisch, whose personality radiated some secret power. How he was able to produce music, as if by magic, with great economy of gesture! What a contrast to the music-making of Wilhelm Furtwängler, his great successor, who conducted by swinging his long arms.

At the Singakademie Siegfried Ochs performed with his chorus the oratorios of Bach, Handel, and Haydn, and there I was also introduced to chamber music by the Rosé, Busch, and Klingler quartets as well as the duos Arthur Schnabel/Carl Flesch and, later, Rudolf Serkin/Adolf Busch.

My father was always attracted to what was "in the air" and what he perceived so strongly, and he was not satisfied until he had made it his own. That might be an idea, a book, a plan for a play—or the first timid attempt of a young, unknown writer whom he strove to encourage. On such occasions he would cautiously try to find the garb appropriate to the new work. When a book was printed, bound, and provided with an attractive dust jacket, he took it in his hand, weighed it, and looked at it from all sides as lovingly as if it were a living being. Yes, a book *was* a living creature for him, and he lived with these his "children." He had a very critical eye for the outer garment of a book and for the proper proportions of the typeface. A well-set page was capable of delighting his eyes. One after another he attracted the graphic artists whom he needed to do covers and dust jackets, and he did not forget to give the total graphic promotion of his publishing house an original note. More than anyone else, it was Professor E.R. Weiss who designed the most important new books of the S. Fischer Verlag and who created a new typeface that was used for many of its books. In line with my father's requirements, Weiss brought a new style to the form of the modern book.

For my father, who was given to procrastinating and carefully weighing his judgment, it was not easy to make decisions—and decisions had to be made every day. But usually his temperament carried the day; renunciation was not for him.

My father was completely immersed in his work, and the constant expansion of his publishing house claimed all his energies; consequently he had little time left for his private life. He usually did not get home from the office until the early afternoon, and so we were starving by the time we were able to have our noonday meal. My mother had a hard time prying him loose from his work and also calming the cook, whose food was burning. A publisher's work does not cease when he leaves the office, but actually bears fruit only in the atmosphere of his private life. Thus there hardly was a day on which my father did not bring an author home with him. Sunday dinner in Erdenerstrasse was famous, and "turkey at Fischer's" became a byword. To please my father, dessert usually was one of the sweet dishes from his Austrian homeland—a strudel made with homemade dough or a Kaiserschmarren (a cut-up and sugared pancake with raisins).

My father was a solicitous father, but the world of a child was alien to him. Everywhere he sensed dangers for which he felt he was not a match. He applied rather high standards to his children. Although he kept away from any so-called "education" and had no interest in our daily progress at school, he still was capable of suddenly springing some questions on us in order to test us and make sure that he was not dealing with a substandard intellect. One afternoon, on one of our walks through the Grunewald woods, he once again asked me one of his intricate questions, and when I answered correctly, he said in astonishment that I was not as stupid as he had thought after all. He seldom praised us, but he did not like to censure us and was never strict; instead, he preferred to correct us with a smile or a roguish remark. I sometimes had the impression that he did not think very highly of girls in general. But even in those days I realized that I owed him the measure of all things, in the visual as well as the literary spheres, and above all in every realm of the humane. His fatherly kindness and modesty as well as his firm critical judgment in his association with his authors and their works have always remained an example for me.

On the last page of my album he wrote these fine, clear verses:

Was dir die bunte Welt
nicht hält,
mag dich nicht arg verdrießen.
Du hast dein Feld
sehr gut bestellt,
stehst du auf eigenen Füßen.
Dein Vater, Glücksburg, den 16. 8. 1919

(The promises the colorful world does not keep should not vex you. You have cultivated your field very well if you stand on your own two feet.—Your father, Glücksburg, Aug. 16, 1919)

In the summer of 1916 Moritz Heimann had written to Papa:

I was very pleased to receive your card with Tutti's address. I remain convinced that Tutti will never disappoint you if you expect her to be a physically and mentally sound person. Kiss her for me; I frequently read Goethe's conversations, and the kisses harvested there by young girls and women gives people like us the right to be envious.

At Christmastime of that year my father gave me the S. Fischer Almanac celebrating the thirtieth anniversary of the firm with this inscription: "Dear Tutti, your 'industrious' father places his report card for this year in your hands. He already feels rewarded by the confidence that some day you will be satisfied with it. Your father, on Christmas Day 1916."

How greatly his "industriousness" became a model for my life!

Ten years later, in the Almanac for the fortieth year, his old friend Julius Elias, who had translated Ibsen for him together with Paul Schlenther, also wrote about my father's "industriousness":

You always were the man whose eyes were on everything in his profession, in his workshop—from the writing of books to their covers, from the estimate to the collection, a man who did not let even the smallest detail go unexamined, who worked as much as a dozen men at a tremendous pace, a man who as a vessel filled to bursting. Sometimes your omnipresence became a bit scary . . . And it was your skill and your secret to maintain this pace and yet often seem like a procrastinator, an irresoluteness, and the melancholy were something like a mask behind which you wanted to catch your breath so as not to dissipate your energy . . .

My father was in the habit of understating things, in particular his own achievements. Doubt was among his first reactions to his environment, and his friends knew this. Hans Reisiger described it as follows: "An undefined fearfulness, something like listening for something threatening from afar, and a tendency to brood that increased with the years probably overwhelmed him at certain times." And his friend Wassermann wrote: "He has been steadfast of spirit, faithful, righteous, and friendly . . . Strangely enough, he inspires a love about which one does not reflect but of which one is constantly aware. He is so timid about this that one has to tell him about it."

The fullness of his love for me gave me the wordless encouragement that a young, growing person needs, and I felt his love at all times; it enveloped me in our daily togetherness. Thus I was bound to be all the more shocked by his last conscious glance which reached me before his death.

At the celebration of the fortieth anniversary of his publishing house my father made a speech in which he discussed his firm's working methods:

It is in the nature of our firm that no rigid work scheme can develop. Every book is different, every day brings new tasks. A living, functioning publishing operation must be able to rely on the living interest of all fellow workers. That is why over a period of years a good tradition and a good spirit of comradeship have developed among us. In our work we have found our life's task. True, a publishing house is an economic organism like many others, and it is the duty of its management not to lose the economic balance—something that really is not easy nowadays. Beyond that, however, such a firm has obligations that far transcend purely economic considerations. We do not produce merchandise that can be sold daily because it retains its material value; rather, we are mediators for intellectual products that are either bought or stay on the shelf. Success and failure alternate with each other and are not in balance, for a success is something that, in Ibsen's parlance, can be called "wonder." Our work aims at giving every book its due . . .

As early as 1911, when the house was celebrating its twenty-fifth anniversary, a word of thanks for my father's literary mediatorship came from the north. Hermann Bang wrote: "If the situation for us Scandinavians has changed, it is due to our having found a bridgebuilder who built a bridge across the stream. In the broad expanse of water that separated Germany from the north S. Fischer saw a rock jutting out from the middle of the sea. This granite rock bore the name Henrik Ibsen, and Fischer recognized that this rock could become a pier from which an entire bridge could be built. Fischer fashioned such a bridge— the bridge that led from the north to the world. And we owe him more than access to Germany, for his bridge took us farther. The works published by his firm bear a name that attracts international attention. The road to Russia and France went through the door that he had opened for us. He built for us a bridge to the world."

Papa's 70th birthday in 1929 gave his friends an opportunity to express themselves about him and his work. Thomas Mann wrote:

I know the profound spiritual intelligence of this man, his unerring instinct for values, his awareness of what is needful. I also know his drivenness, the productive unrest which will surely not leave him till his last moment. And I believe I also appreciate the delicacy and vulnerability of his humanity, the fact that he had to learn how to stand his ground in the forms of dry and cold commercial life, and above all, that he made his way in the world and proved his mettle by means of great achievements. During a lifetime's collaboration loyalty toward this man has become deeply rooted to me; I consider myself fortunate that I am associated with a publisher whom I truly respect and trust. To use a phrase of his forefathers, he is 'blessed of the Lord,' and I cannot deny that the poetic-human attraction which the phenomenon of a "blessed one" exerts upon me is in some measure responsible for the admiration and the liking which I have for his life.

On the same occasion Jakob Wassermann wrote:

With a brilliant flair and an instinct that seldom deceived him he cast his fisher's net after all sorts of colorful, wild, predator-like, hard-to-catch and hard-to-retain amphibians and branchiate animals in order to transport them carefully to his aquarium and there to take care of them . . . There undoubtedly is a specific kind of greatness in the ability to gather round oneself prolific and creative people and to bind them together through a community of interests . . . For many years he had an incomparable helper and adviser in Moritz Heimann . . . To find such an aide is in itself a gift and a merit, not merely a matter of luck. Only he who knows how to serve can be served. He has always been a servant of his servants; therein resides his humanity.

When my father's energies waned and he was no longer up to making decisions, when he was increasingly beset by anxiety in the face of threatening danger, I promised him that I would devote the rest of my life to the preservation of his work.

5
My Fatherly Friend Moritz Heimann

"One winter evening in 1895," reminisced my mother, "we were visited by a young writer, who sat with us by our fire-side. His name was Moritz Heimann. His simplicity and goodness as well as his forthright judgment appealed to us, and that very same evening my husband invited him to become the editor of our publishing house. Heimann gladly accepted. He remained our editor until his death thirty years later; he became our friend and the friend and confidant of our authors."

My father's daily collaboration with Heimann became of decisive importance to him. In addition to his infinite patience and his inexhaustible energy, Heimann brought to his work extensive knowledge in all fields of intellectual endeavors. Literature was his element, however. As a creative writer and critic he was a staunch champion of his opinions and offered determined resistance when it was a matter of defending his point of view. The discussions between him and my father, in which the formal *Sie* was used as a form of address for many years and the informal *Du* only in the last ones, almost never ended in the office but were continued on the shared trip home or in our house. In addition to the daily personal exchange of ideas, Heimann often put his advice and his criticisms into letters to my father:

We must not let the hard times force us onto the defensive. The best defense is an offensive. One has to think, and if people starve they will read as they do so; they cannot do without books. This pride, this inner conviction are the all-important things! . . . A publisher thrives when some books do not sell, for if all books sold well, publishers would be unnecessary and could simply be replaced by special departments of printing houses. "Verleger" was originally a term for the financial backer of a printer. The professional standing of a publisher gradually rose far above that, and publishing became a very honorable profession, one that works in the intellectual realm and has responsibilities to it. You have fulfilled these requirements in large measure . . . Enough is not enough— this is true of life generally and also of the life of a publisher. Even the most successful books would suffer if they were not nourished by the great, tempestuous circulation of the humors, for it is this very circulation that constitutes the reputation and the respect of a publisher.

Heimann addressed my father with the kind of openness that can exist only between close friends, and in his every word one can sense that the future of the firm was close to his heart. Heimann admired my father's generosity of spirit, as witness the following letter: "Fate has placed us in the same boat for the brief crossing from one shore to the next (this is my permanent image of our existence); in his own way everyone must help his fellow man and serve him; everyone needs forbearance so as not to disturb and impede the voyage or to turn the narrow space between the banks into a prison or hell. I know how much forbearance I need and how much I receive from you. That so paradoxical a relationship as that between you and me has not only endured for so long but has perhaps become absolutely unique and exemplary is to your credit more than it is to mine. You have made it possible for me, your salaried employee, not only to become your closest friend and that of your family but also to remain a completely free man. I am profoundly conscious of the amount of indulgence, patience, deference, solicitude, foresight, and self-control that this has taken. I thank you for this, my dear Herr Fischer, and in equal measure your wife, who has over the years become like a guardian angel to me . . .

In Dec. 1922, when gravely ill, he wrote to my father:

Dear Fischer, after such a great number of gifts you have given me the most beautiful one and one that honors me the most: the form of address that you have used for the first time and now permit me to use in addressing you. I was as touched by this as I was pleased, for I was allowed— That is as far as I got before I had to go to bed, and I am still laid up. But my letter to you torments me, the one that constantly writes itself inside me, because I cannot finish it today. But I will not let the day go by without thanking you for everything and especially for the informal du. Forgive me for confessing that I have often affectionately stood beside you and your house. Most cordially, Moritz Heimann.

In 1924 Heimann became concerned over a certain stagnation of the periodical *Die Neue Rundschau* and looked around for new and vital centers of world problems. He wrote to my father:

. . . You will laugh at me or get angry if I again undertake to draw your attention to American affairs. It is becoming ever more glaringly evident that a writer, a journalist, or a publisher cannot have a direct effect on our conditions. What we need is a long period of reflection and instruction. This cannot be accomplished in parliaments but is the task of the great periodicals and the intellectual leaders. I believe that in no European country, and certainly not in the history of our own people, do we have such enlightening material about a possible constitution as in America. Sooner or later we shall have a second national assembly in Germany for the purpose of discussing a constitution, and it would be disastrous if it set to work with no more preparation than the first one had . . . The question whether Germany's future should be federalistic or unitary is of vital importance. I do not expect anything of a direct investigation of this question, but much more if it is viewed as in a mirror. The history of America, from the Revolution to the Civil War, is this desired mirror. It would therefore be desirable to get a noted historian to write for us a treatise entitled "The Contest Between Federalism and the Concept of the Single State in America" . . .

You will remember that I once talked to you about an American Library. I regard such a series as intrinsically useful and promising, and I also believe that it would pave the way for our books in America. An exchange between nations is even more natural in the intellectual sphere than in the economic one. And in this connection the importance of the Rundschau cannot be overestimated; it must always be a factor in such deliberations.

What farsighted, prophetic remarks! In the early 1920's there were only few people in Europe who had a clear view of the great internal and external development of the "New World." Europe was still regarded as the center of all culture, and America was viewed as the "Wild West." My father, however, took Heimann's advice. He sent authors like Arthur Holitscher on a "trip around the world" (the phrase became a book title) and had them write reports for the *Neue Rundschau.* Samuel Sänger wrote regular political chronicles. Coudenhove-Kalergi reported in many issues of the periodical about his plan of a united Europe, Emil Ludwig wrote about Wilson and Heinrich Mann about European problems. A new international atmosphere found its way into the journal. The translation rights to great American authors were acquired. John Dos Passos' *Manhattan Transfer* was published. Hans Reisiger made an exemplary free translation of Walt Whitman's *Leaves of Grass,* and the house of S. Fischer introduced the dramatic works of Eugene O'Neill on German stages and published book editions for German readers. Personal contacts with American publishers like Ben Huebsch of the Viking Press and Alfred A. Knopf were established, and translation contracts for works of Thomas Mann, Jakob Wassermann, Alfred Döblin, and others were signed. The gates to the "New World" were open.

In early September of 1925 Heimann became mortally ill and was taken to the Charité Hospital. There was little hope that he would live. I still remember the small antechamber of his room in which we all sat, worried and trying to say farewell to him. I was losing a second father. I hoped in vain for an auspicious moment for introducing my future husband to him, but it was not to be; Heimann was already too weak.

Mama wrote in her diary: "When his great heart stopped beating, it was like the expiring of a saint."

Oskar Loerke spoke the following words at his grave:

For the last time, before the earth covers him up completely, we stand beside Moritz Heimann— at his feet, which knew so well the blessings and hardships of human paths; near his head, which was a pure shelter for the image of this world, just as the world offered his head and his heart a beloved and enduring shelter . . . He had luminous words of wisdom for many of his fellow men when they were beset by petty problems and dark urges. An indefatigable bringer of freedom, a master of patience and forbearance, he always thought first of the needy and last of himself . . . He used to say: 'There is no difference between happiness and suffering. There is enough quiet in me for noise to find room in this quiet. There is enough darkness in me for all the brightness of the world to find a place within it.'

6

Three Friends of the Family: Peter Nansen, Hans Reisiger, Otto Flake

After my brother's death there were, first and foremost, three friends who attempted to stand by my completely shattered parents. They spent the winter months after the very distressing time with us in St. Moritz, and each managed in his own way to spread some cheer with little jests.

Peter Nansen was already a writer widely read in Denmark when, in 1897, he came to Berlin from Copenhagen. My parents immediately fell in love with the charm of his person and his books. He was close to my father not only as an author but also as a professional colleague, for Nansen was a director of the Danish publishing house Gyldendal. "Fischer, let's calculate" was his standard saying, and then the two would withdraw into a corner to talk shop. Nansen could also tell amusing stories about old Ibsen, whom he knew well and whose vanity was so great that he used to carry a mirror in his top hat and have his publisher set the medals bestowed upon him in diamonds.

"Uncle Peter" was delicate and ailing; with his aristocratic face he must have been very handsome as a young man. In 1914, when we were all staying at the Hotel Calonder in St. Moritz, we teased and apostrophized him a lot, for he used to sleep late and did not participate in our outdoor activities, such as skating and sledding. He usually appeared in a fur coat and patent-leather shoes, stuck his nose out of his fur for a moment, and then disappeared into the hotel again.

"Ach lieber Onkel Peter
Du kommst ja immer später.
Was bist du für ein Mensch?
Du kommst nicht mal zum Lunch!"

(O dear Uncle Peter, you keep coming later and later. What kind of a person are you? You don't even show up for lunch!)

When he finally did appear for breakfast at a time when lunch was already being prepared in the kitchen, he would say in his delightful German:

Frau Calonder kann sich seine Eier selber essen.

(Let Mrs. Calonder eat his eggs herself).

In my album he wrote the following poem that was still under the shadow of my brother's death:

Meiner Freundin Tuddi gewidmet

Die Welt kann noch so traurig sein,
trüb und grau
für Pappi und für Mutti:
Es wird doch plötzlich Sonnenschein,
der Himmel blau,
wenn Du es willst, Klein-Tuddi.
Denn:
Wo die Kinder wand'ren, ist der Himmel immer rein
und uns're Thränen regnen in mildem Sonnenschein.

Peter Nansen, 2. Januar 1914, St. Moritz

(Dedicated to my friend Tuddi. No matter how sad, gloomy, and gray the world may be for Daddy and Mommy, suddenly the sun will shine and the sky will be blue if you wish it, Little Tuddi, for where children walk the sky is always clear and our tears rain in the mild sunshine).

Hans Reisiger was an author of our firm from 1911 on. About his first encounter with S. Fischer, he wrote:

Those who have not experienced it can hardly imagine today with what love the young intellectuals of Germany looked to the S. Fischer Verlag around the turn of the century. It hardly occurred to us that a man named S. Fischer existed at all. What stirred us so was the whole atmosphere of literary creativity gathered around a name. Utterly unpretentious cordiality enveloped me, twenty-five years his junior, when I met him face to face for the first time. The little work [Reisiger's first novel, Maria Marleen, published in 1911] that I, trusting to luck, had sent to this publishing house, which we regarded as the foremost gathering place for everything we loved about the present, had been accepted— and thus I was part of it now.

"We spontaneously became friends with Reisi," wrote Mama, "and he accompanied us on many trips, always lively and able to shake my husband out of severe depressions and to cheer him up."

He bewitched Mama with rhymes about fine shirts, and when they went for a walk through the city he would very skillfully and seemingly by accident steer her to the shopwindow in which the desired object was displayed, whereupon she simply could not resist making him a present of it. When he appeared at the table afterwards, happy and grateful and adorned with the new shirt, his verses produced the irresistible laughter that was part of Mama's nature and that the whole family found infectious. The most amusing games, however, Reisiger had devised for my father. For hours on end they would harangue each other as if they were old captains of commerce, dashing officers of the Prussian army, or two old and quite senile aristocrats reminiscing about their youth around the turn of the century. My father was often convulsed with laughter during these games, and they could make him forget all his sadness and pain for hours.

Reisiger became something like a new son in our house, and he and I were like brother and sister. When I became older, it was natural for me to have a crush for a while on the handsome young man who was always surrounded by so many adoring women. At that time he wrote in my album:

Besuch in München, April 1914

Mir ist, meine liebste Tutti,
Ein herrlicher Weg bekannt,
Hoch über ihm steht ein Tempel,
Monopteros genannt!

Die jungen Birken lachen
Neben den Pappeln groß,
Darunter sitzt das Frolli
Und hält das Buch im Schoß.

So nahe strahlt der Himmel,
Mir scheint, sein Blau färbt ab:
Wirft man den roten Ball hinauf,
So kommt er blau herab.

Dann wieder kann man sitzen
Und ruhn vom wilden Lauf,
Man gibt sich in dem Schatten
Die herrlichsten Rätsel auf.

Miss Fisch weiß zu erzählen
So manchen heitern Scherz!
Wie lachet da dem Pimpo
Das edle Männerherz!

Man denkt der weißen Höhen
Des Engadiner Schnees,
Man spricht von den blauen Tiefen
Des schönen Gardasees.

Die schöne Mittagswärme
Füllt rings die ganze Welt. –
Komm wieder, liebste Tutti,
Eh Schnee und Regen fällt!

(Visit to Munich, April 1914. Dearest Tutti, I know a magnificent path, and high above it stands a temple called Monopteros. The young birches gleam next to the tall poplars; underneath sits Missy with a book in her lap. The radiant sky is so close that its blue color seems to be coming off. If you throw a red ball up, it comes down blue. Then you can sit again and rest up from the mad dash; in the shade people ask one another the most marvelous riddles. Miss Fish has many funny jokes to tell; how Pimpo's noble manly heart leaps with joy! One thinks of the white heights of the Engadine snow, one talks about the blue depths of Lake Garda. The fine noonday heat fills the entire world. Come back, dearest Tutti, before the snow and the rain fall!)

Otto Flake was spending the month of July 1914 with us at the Hotel Waldhaus in Sils Maria when the outbreak of the world war surprised us there on August 2. The sudden flight of the vacationers caused such a stampede on the trains that children were in danger of being crushed by the mad crowd. My savior was Otto Flake, a giant towering over the crowd, who carried me on his shoulders and handed me to my parents through the train window.

Soon thereafter, in September 1914, he wrote in my album his thoughts on the outbreak of the war, still quite shaken by "this powerful moment." He envied my later knowledge of how everything had come out. However, he lived to see the end of that war with all its terrible consequences— Germany's defeat and the ensuing inflation and unemployment— as well as Hitler's assumption of power, World War II, and the destruction of Germany. Flake died in 1963, resigned and sad though he had lived to witness Germany's rise.

September 1914.

Does it always have to be verses, dear Tutti? Surely not—so let me give prose its due. And since I want to be straightforward, I shall proceed from the events that are agitating all of us at the moment. And that is truly a great moment, such a powerful one that in your entire life— and this is what I wish for you— you will not experience a more anxious one.

Actually, it is too bad that you are only a little girl. And yet, when I see you in your garden on my evening visits, engaging in military maneuvers with your friends from the neighborhood and the little fugitives whom your parents have taken in, waving a flag and singing the same songs that our warriors sing when they march through the streets to the railway station and then, when they get off the train, move into battle through the open field— when I see all that, I think that you will retain memories and impressions of the war of 1914.

And, you see, a sensible person derives profit from anything—without schoolmarmishness, of course. Today, on September 17, we are waiting with fear and anxiety for news from the East and the West and four times a day buy newspapers that tell us nothing. A fearsome battle is raging outside Paris— we don't know what the outcome will be. Behind Lemberg the Austrians, who recently were before it, await the Russians; we don't know whether they will stand their ground. We don't know anything— whether we shall dictate the course the world will take or whether we shall lie on the ground destroyed. But when you dig this book out at a later date and read these lines, all will be over— the fears and the hopes, the dead and the tears shed for them will be forgotten, the torments of the wounded will be a thing of the past, as will the blather of those who even now cannot be anything but phrasemongers, and the devastation of Belgium and East Prussia will be complete.

Thus you will be much smarter than we are today, and I envy you that. And yet at bottom it will all be the same. It will make no difference if the one great upheaval has long since been replaced by the sum total of the many small, entirely personal ones. You will be a young woman subject to the law of life which you will call your fate—but remember that everything passes. That can lead you to resolve to do two things: never to become so closely attached to something that you break down if you lose it, and to feel the good, or rather the strong and eternal, aspects of a given moment— be it sorrow or grief, surely the whole meaning of life is the ability to feel.

This is not a new philosophy, you will say; but there is no new philosophy. Everything human is age-old, and you really do not need writers, poets, or artists to proclaim that. But being too wise is not good either. The best proof of that is this sermon by

Your friend Otto Flake.

For me the most important thing about this "sermon" remained his advice to feel the strong and eternal aspects of the moment and his insight that this ability to feel gives life its meaning. That made sense to me then and has given me strength and confidence throughout my life. I shall always be grateful to Flake for that. Evidently people do need writers, poets, and artists to proclaim such a simple truth.

My parents met Otto Flake in 1912, and the "blond Alsatian beanpole" became their friend. He brought my father the manuscript of his first novel, *Das Freitagskind* (Friday's Child), and after my father published it Flake remained an author of the S. Fischer Verlag. He was a wise and dependable friend and a loyal companion in hard times. During a shared winter vacation at Partenkirchen we children teased the long-legged man about being so clumsy on the ice. A young rascal from Munich shouted at him, "Hey, poet, gimme a pome!" Flake greatly resented that, for he did not have much of a sense of humor. But in other ways Flix, as we called him, was a good children's companion, for he took us all very seriously.

He had a loving manner toward me. He would take my little hand in his giant one and wander with me through the forest and fields, always talking about and explaining the many things an adolescent would like to know about. Yet he was not didactic as a schoolmaster would be, but like an older companion and brother.

Since Flake lived in Berlin for years, he was a frequent guest at our Erdenerstrasse home. My mother was his trusted advisor in his personal problems, particularly the difficult ones relating to his marriages. For my father, however, he was an important partner in conversations about political and literary questions which he evaluated with his keen intellect and in his unsentimental, objective way. He became a regular contributor to *Die Neue Rundschau* and made a name for himself as one of Germany's most brilliant essayists. In 1934, when we brought my mortally ill father down from Freudenstadt to Baden-Baden, the deeply concerned Flake stood by us.

7

Uncle Gerhart Hauptmann. With "Gift" and "Galle" through the Silesian Countryside

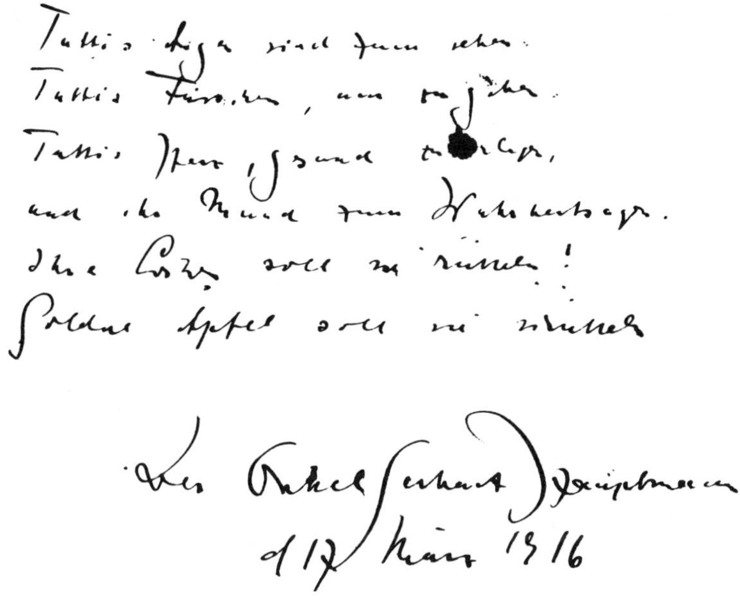

Tuttis Augen sind zum sehen
Tuttis Füßchen, um zu gehen.
Tuttis Herz, gesund zu schlagen,
und ihr Mund zum Wahrheitsagen.
Ihre Locken soll sie rütteln!
Goldne Äpfel soll sie schütteln.

(Tutti's eyes are for seeing; Tutti's feet are for walking; Tutti's heart is for beating soundly and her mouth for telling the truth. Let her shake her locks! Let her shake golden apples. Uncle Gerhart Hauptmann, March 17, 1916).

Ever since I could think, he was was "Uncle Hauptmann" to me; to the world, however, and in particular to Germany, he was the famous prince of poets who was admired by all and cheered by the crowd wherever he appeared. When he walked through the streets of Berlin, both adults and children recognized him by his impressive figure with the mighty head on which he usually wore an enormous slouch hat. When he drove through the villages of the Silesian homeland in his open carriage and pair, drawn by the two wild ponies Gift (venom) and Galle (gall), peasants and burghers stopped and greeted him respectfully. And when he came to Rapallo every winter, everyone said *"Il poeta tedesco è arrivato"* (The German poet has arrived.)

When I was a child, "Uncle Hauptmann" was to me a supernatural figure that exuded magic. When he came to our home— and he frequently stayed in our guest rooms— he filled the entire house with his personality, and it seemed to me as though a secret power emanated from him. He loved children and was close to them in a natural way, since he was himself still close to the primal state of mankind. His large, expressive hands accompanied and underlined his speech. In those days I believed that he could look inside me with his small, very bright eyes, and I shuddered a bit at the thought. He associated with me familiarly, almost as if I were the daughter he had wished for in vain.

When I was an adolescent, my parents took me along on one of their trips to Agnetendorf, to the Wiesenstein, Hauptmann's castle-like house that he had built in 1901 at the foot of the Riesengebirge. My father had visited him there as early as 1902 and reported about it to Mama: "In the vestibule of the castle— it is an exceedingly tasteful house— Grete received us by bright candlelight and an open fire in a very stylish Empire dress of black satin with a white lace collar." Shortly before that, Hauptmann had written to my parents: "The house is already rather animated— not only by hobgoblins and poltergeists but also by the spirit of music . . . All good spirits praise the master of this house, and so I praise all the good spirits in it . . . " The Wiesenstein, which overlooked the Riesengebirge, was situated in a wild garden with old trees wholly embedded in meadows. It was a veritable castle with a large open entrance hall that extended over two floors and from which a wide staircase led upstairs. Hauptmann had built a round watch-tower for himself; it contained his study which reminded one of Faust's study with its giant globes and astronomical charts. Only those specially favored were allowed to enter it. It was the holy of holies, the center of the house, his realm, and there the spirits he invoked whispered their secrets to him. It seemed to me as if his spirits came from the earth in which he was so deeply rooted.

On a trip in his two-horse carriage to which he had invited me we sat side by side. It was a glorious summer day, and Gift and Galle pulled us through fields and forests at a wild trot. Then we sat by the edge of the forest and he held my hand in his big, strong hand that was such a vibrant part of his being. He whispered sweet nothings to me, a bit in love with the young thing next to him that he would probably have liked to seduce. But he had too much respect for Herr Papa and for the penetrating glance of his wife Bocchi. Thus we returned home from this splendid trip as two people who shared a beautiful secret, and it seemed to me as though I had taken a long trip through a fairyland hand in hand with a great magician.

"A handful of light was put into a handsome man," said the poet Franz Werfel about him.

On a number of occasions my parents took me along to rehearsals of Hauptmann plays. I watched him play a dramatic scene on the stage for the benefit of the actors, thus transferring his poetic conception to the boards. In this way, I became acquainted with many of his plays— the fairy-tale drama *Die versunkene Glocke* (The Sunken Bell), *Die Weber* (The Weavers), *Florian Geyer,* and the comedy *Der Biberpelz* (The Beaver Coat). I became especially fond of *Und Pippa tanzt* (And Pippa Dances), a delicate fabric composed entirely of musical elements and full of longing for another world. But the greatest theatrical experience of my youth was Max Reinhardt's performance of *Hanneles Himmelfahrt* (The Assumption of Hannele) at the Deutsches Theater, with Helene Thimig as Hannele and Alexander Moissi as the teacher Gottwald. Both actors seemed to me like such incarnations of their roles that for me they remained these two characters in real life as well. The fate of this poor Hannele moved me to tears, and for a long time I remained wholly under the spell of this half-awake "dream play." When, still quite stunned, I had to accompany my parents to a post-performance dinner that Hauptmann gave for the actors and his friends, it seemed to me like a profanation of what I had just experienced. I did not want to encounter the actors, now completely stripped of their aura, as ordinary people.

But *Hannele* played a special role in the life of my parents, too. My mother met Hauptmann for the first time in 1893, when she was a bride and the poet gave a reading of *Hannele* in my father's bachelor apartment. In her diary she reported about this as follows:

. . . Here I saw for the first time the wonderful person and poet with the magnificent head, which then still looked somewhat ascetic. Those present in addition to me included old Frau Marschalk with her son Max, who had composed the incidental music for Hannele, and her three beautiful daughters, including the youngest, Margarete, who later became Hauptmann's second wife . . . A few months later, in October 1893, we celebrated our wedding. It must have been strange: ultramodern writers and poets mingling with Jewish solid citizens . . . Hauptmann had his first full-dress suit made for that occasion.

My parents' honeymoon— and this was quite typical of my father— began with a trip to the Leipzig printing firm that was supposed to complete the book edition of *Hannele* in time for the premiere at the Königliches Schauspielhaus in Berlin, which was scheduled for November 15, 1893.

From then on my parents' relationship with Hauptmann grew into an affectionate and even devoted friendship. Nothing could destroy their absolute admiration and allegiance, not even the well-nigh unfulfillable financial demands that Gerhart Hauptmann later made of my father. My father did everything for his friends, even if this involved the greatest sacrifices. But Hauptmann also knew what a friend and publisher he had. Forty years later he wrote: "I was vouchsafed the great good fortune of finding you, dear Fischer, when I was taking my first youthful step into the limelight."

8

Summer at the Berghof on Attersee. The Austrian Friends Felix Salten, Hugo von Hofmannsthal, Arthur Schnitzler, Peter Altenberg, Jakob Wassermann

The Berghof was an old Austrian estate situated on a plateau overlooking the Attersee. It belonged to the family of the composer Ignaz Brüll, a friend of Johannes Brahms. My parents were taken there by their Viennese friend Felix Salten with whose family we shared one of the beautiful, spacious country houses in the summer months of 1910, 1911, and 1912. Our house was covered with Virginia creepers. The branches of the apricot trees climbed up the green trellises. From the wooden balcony that encircled the first floor there was a magnificent view of the Attersee and the mountains surrounding it. Next to the entrance door there was a long wooden bench, and when one entered the house one could walk across scrubbed floors and up a worn wooden staircase into a fine old rustic room with cozy, old-fashioned furniture and a massive tiled stove. In the courtyard between the houses the clear mountain water spurted from a well with a gurgling and splashing that lulled me to sleep every night.

Behind the houses there was a playground where we children cavorted, and then there was an expanse of broad meadows up to the Hausberg, where the forest began and there was an odor of fir trees and cyclamen which bloomed in great profusion in the forest soil.

Frau Marie Brüll, the composer's widow, lived in one of the houses with her family, and her house was always filled with music. On his way from Ischl, Brahms had stayed with her on a number of occasions. Photos of his hung everywhere, and manuscripts lay on the grand piano on which he himself had played frequently. Madame Brüll told us about Brahms's visits and how much everyone had loved him despite his difficult and self-willed habits. The aged composer Karl Goldmark still came for a few months' visit every summer and sat in his ground-floor room that faced the playground. When we children were romping around there, he would stick his venerable white head, covered with a round black skullcap, out the window in order to put a stop to those frightening children.

"In the summer of 1910 Hofmannsthal came over from Aussee to visit us at the Berghof," reminisced my mother. "He stayed with us for a few days and in the evening read to us the first two acts of *Der Rosenkavalier.* We were greatly impressed with his work full of poetry, esprit, and humor. I have always remembered these words of the Marschallin: 'Time is a strange thing. While one is living one's life, it is absolutely nothing. But then, suddenly, one is aware of nothing else. Sometimes I hear it flowing, inexorably. Sometimes I get up in the middle of the night and stop all the clocks. However, one must not be afraid of time. It, too, is a creature of Our Father who created all of us.' That same summer we went over to Aussee and heard there the third act with its magnificent closing duet: '"Tis a dream, it cannot really be true that we two are together."'

On the occasion of the opera's premiere at the Dresden Opera House, my father issued Hofmannsthal's play in book form. It continues to live as a work of art quite independent of Strauss's music, though Hofmannsthal says in his "Unwritten Afterword" of 1911:

. . . Anyone who sunders will do the wrong thing. He who lifts out one thing forgets that always the whole dies away unnoticed. The music should not be torn from the text nor the word from the animated picture. This was made for the stage, not for a book or for an individual at his piano.

I was the only "German" child at the Berghof, though it took my Austrian friends to make me realize this. As Austrians they looked down upon me with some pity, and often they sang in a proud chorus their national anthem with the words "Gott erhalte Franz, den Kaiser" (May God preserve Emperor Franz), while my *Deutschland, Deutschland über alles,* sung to the same Haydn melody, only made my situation worse.

The most beautiful part of the summer was the annual Kirtag, the great fair. The marketplace, in fact the whole village of Unterach, was full of booths in which one could buy anything one's heart desired. The farmers brought fine old things that they wanted to sell: old silk cloths, colorfully embroidered silk dirndl dresses, embroidered vests with silver buttons and cords, and above all their old peasant jewelry— wide necklaces consisting of many graduated chains and intended to conceal a goiter, earrings, belt buckles, and bracelets. My mother received as a gift many fine pieces, some of which I still own today. The fair usually lasted several days, and I have hardly ever experienced more festive hours than those in which I was allowed to pass through the rows of booths with my friends in the hot sun and enjoy the hurdy-gurdy music and the carrousel rides. We would make excursions to the mountains, with rucksacks, hobnailed boots, and alpenstocks, up to the colorfully blossoming mountain pastures where we picknicked near the dairy farms among herds of cows, or we would go to Ischl for a *Jause* (afternoon tea) at the celebrated Cafè Zauner, whose Sacher and Linzer tortes had already been famous for generations.

"Uncle and Aunt Salten" were like my second parents in those days. When we went to Vienna, which happened almost every year, I usually stayed at the Saltens' house in the Cottage district and was really spoiled there. Uncle Salten was always cheerful and friendly; I greatly admired him and found him nice to look at, especially when he was in the country and wore his Lederhosen, green loden jacket, and colorful neckerchief. He would tell us children to behave, but without any strictness, and I never saw him angry. He wrote in my poetry album:

Alles kommt noch! Liebes Kind,
Unsres Lebens Tage sind
Manchmal von Erfüllung schwer.
Hochbeladen, Glückgefeiert;
Manchmal wieder kahl und leer.
Oft von Thränen ganz verschleiert –
Aber sieh, – es sind nur Boten,
Boten sind es, ernst und heiter.
Ob sie lachten oder drohten,
Merkst Du nicht? Sie gehn ja weiter.
Steh und warte! Das gibt Mut.
Warten, Tutti, ist so gut!
Was die Tage Dir auch bringen,
Immer hör' die Zukunft singen.
Was die Tage auch genommen,
Glaube: Alles muß noch kommen!
Alles kommt noch! Denn das Leben
Hat sein Letztes nie gegeben.
Nie! Man darf sich nur nicht weigern,
Und es wird sich immer steigern.
Dieses Warten Dir bewahre,
Reichtum ist's aus Kindertagen
Über viele, viele Jahre
Wird's Dich sanft hinüber tragen.
Wie viel Tage auch vergangen –
Denk': es hat erst angefangen!

Dein Freund Felix Salten, Berlin, 12. V. 14

(Everything is yet to come! Dear child, the days of our life are sometimes heavy with fulfillment, piled high, festive with good fortune, at other times bare and empty, often quite veiled with tears. But look— they are only messengers, grave and cheerful messengers, whether they are laughing or threatening. Don't you notice it? They do pass on. Stand and wait! That gives courage. Waiting, Tutti, is so good! Whatever the days may have taken from you, have faith that everything must still come! Everything is yet to come! For life has never given its final things. Never! One simply must not refuse and it will always intensify. Preserve this waiting for yourself. It is a wealth from childhood days; over many, many years it will gently carry you across. No matter how many days have passed, remember: It has only just begun!

Your friend Felix Salten, Berlin, May 12, 1914)

Felix Salten's friendship with my parents extended over many decades, with many joint trips and shared experiences. My mother loved "his radiantly cheerful nature" that could catch fire on everything beautiful, be it music, the graphic arts, or literature. They had this receptiveness to the multiplicity of the world in common. Rainer Maria Rilke envied her such a good traveling companion and wrote her about him:

I like to associate with this man in whom all Austrian qualities are united, well-kept and shiny as in a soft case. And there is so much amiability in the way he looks at things, though he makes no compromises. His disposition works soundlessly like a scale, indicates everything, and resumes a natural equilibrium with a graceful swing. Such qualities, I imagine, make him a very suitable traveling companion, and they probably accrue to those who are privileged to have him as a friend in quite precious and beneficial fashion.

Felix Salten was an enthusiastic Viennese and guided my parents with loving expertise through old Vienna and the Beethoven houses of Heiligenstadt. He took them to the early baroque church Maria am Gestade, in which one seems to hear Mozart's music, and to the old cemetery with the graves of Schubert and Beethoven.

Vienna marked a new phase in my father's development. Through his contact with the "Vienna Circle" in 1895 his publishing house, which had hitherto been oriented toward northern Europe and its literature, also received an Austrian note, one that it was to retain.

In the Cafè Griensteidl in Vienna the new circle of Austrian writers, "Young Vienna," had been born, and that is where the young friends met regularly: Arthur Schnitzler, Richard Beer-Hofmann, Felix Salten, Hermann Bahr, and the seventeen-year old *Gymnasium* student Loris. Hermann Bahr, who in prophetic presentiment as early as 1891 sensed something of a "new Idealism, a new Romanticism" which to him were "precursors, warnings" that literature was approaching a turning point and removing itself from "obsolescent Naturalism," wrote: "An artist's nature should no longer be a tool of reality . . . but, conversely, reality should again become the material for an artist to proclaim his nature in clear, effective symbols . . . Thus I believe that Naturalism will be overcome . . . There will be something laughing, scurrying, fleetfooted . . . a rustling as of green sprouts . . . a winged, earth-unbound climbing and floating . . . " Were these thoughts of Bahr's not like a presentiment of Hofmannsthal's genius?

This young *Gymnasium* student Loris, whose name was Hugo von Hofmannsthal, read to the astonished and skeptical circle of poets his first plays, *Der Tod des Tizian* (The Death of Titian) and *Der Tor und der Tod* (Death and the Fool), and his listeners were deeply shaken by the youth's intuitive knowledge and linguistic perfection. Schnitzler said he had "felt that I had encountered a born genius for the first time in my life."

In 1899 Hofmannsthal became an author of the S. Fischer Verlag, and very soon his relationship to his "dear publisher" became one of trust and friendship. Hofmannsthal had married in 1901 and settled in Rodaun near Vienna. His little house, which had been built in Maria Theresia's time and was situated in a garden full of old fruit trees, had a salon and baroque furniture that made it seem like a little castle well suited to its "chatelain." That is where I met his daughter Christiane, who was my age. My parents frequently met with Hofmannsthal—either in the Salzkammergut, for he usually lived in Alt-Aussee during the summer, or in our house in Grunewald. I often encountered him there. He was of medium height, his figure was frail, and he had dark, expressive eyes. He spoke much and fast, as if he were trying not to miss a moment of life, and his entire being seemed to quiver nervously. Perhaps he felt even then that he would not have much more time in this world and that his life was threatened. There was always something mysterious about him, and one sensed an inner tension, a flame that was bound to consume him.

My mother had called him a "favorite of the gods." I often listened in on the conversations between him and my father. They mostly concerned attempts to make his work known beyond the small number of his admirers. Hofmannsthal evinced a distinct impatience, almost a fear that he would not be known or receive recognition.

On March 12, 1922, he wrote my father from Alt-Aussee:

I have received your good, detailed letter of March 8 and thank you very much for it. It is extremely gratifying to me to have a human being and not a businessman as a publisher, and every turn in our relationship that reminds me of this gratifies me all over again. As a person with a multiplicity of blood strains and as an Austrian I am completely attuned to a connecting line, to the conciliation of contrasts. A pensive nature from childhood on and the terrible teachings of the epoch have intensified this characteristic in me, and anyone who meets me on other terms pulls the rug from under my feet and makes me rigid with fright and repugnance . . . My destiny is special in every sense: there is my Austrian orientation— in a certain sense I am perhaps the only Austrian; I would call Schnitzler a Viennese, but not an Austrian— and then there is a certain loose attachment to the epoch, though half of me stands somewhere else, too— not out of capriciousness but because of destiny . . . Your faithful Hofmannsthal.

In 1929 a great misfortune befell the house of Hofmannstahl. The poet's 26-year-old son Franz took his own life. When Hofmannsthal was getting ready to attend the funeral, he suffered a stroke and died that same evening at the age of 55. Thus father and son were buried in the same grave. Horror and profound sorrow seized all who had known and loved him.

On July 9 Mama wrote to Schnitzler from Pontresina:

Our thoughts are now so often in Vienna, ceaselessly occupied with the tragedy in the Hofmannsthal house which also shocked you, one of his oldest friends, as much as it did all of us . . . You, who lived in such close proximity to the man who died so young, have lost so much more than we more remote people, and yet we, too, have shared so many happy, festive, and cheerful hours that are connected with the name Hofmannsthal, and we owe him so much that this farewell is accompanied by profound sadness and sorrow . . .

Here is Schnitzler's answer:

Vienna, July 23, 1929

I thank both of you for your kind words. It was only a few weeks ago— a few days before I went to the Semmering for two weeks— that Hofmannsthal came to see me and we talked for a few hours. As you know, talks with him were experiences, and this last one was no less so than our first ones of almost forty years ago. That last time we talked quite a bit about his health; he seemed much less sick to me than some feared, and who knows whether he would not have lived many more years if that misfortune had not happened. It is a hard blow to me that he is no longer on earth— let us not shrink back from big words at such a moment. I loved him very much— not only because of many poets I admire he was (to me) perhaps the most real one, but also because he was a companion of my youth, though he was twelve years my junior; then, too, because, despite the problematical nature of his personality, he was a most humane being in a very comprehensive sense.

As you see, I am still here and my traveling plans are still uncertain. Olga is in Berlin and has undergone a not entirely minor operation. She is at the Franziscus Sanatorium, and as telephone conversations with her indicate, she is out of danger; Frau Dora Michaels is taking care of her like an angel.

After a few somewhat disturbed weeks in May, my physical condition is not bad at all. I am even working and shall probably send a play [Im Spiel der Sommerlüfte] to your publishing house within the next few weeks. Only six characters (who no longer need to go in search of an author) and only one Dekoration [set] (quite a Freudian slip— I started to write Diskretion), so perhaps a theater might even muster the "courage" to perform it (curtain time 8 o'clock, end at 10:15— provided it starts in the first place).

Of course I know about the April child [our daughter Gisela]; I have congratulated the dear parents and already received their thanks. I am glad that everything is fine with you; I am desirous of learning about your future plans and hoping for a good reunion under favorable circumstances.

It was very nice of you to think of me. Most cordial regards to all of you.

Yours, Arthur Schnitzler.

On July 11, 1929, four days before his death, Hofmannsthal had written my father from Rodaun:

Dear Mr. Fischer, as I date this letter I realize that it has been thirty years since my first book was published by your firm, which has since become so big and famous, and reflecting on the length of time during which we have been so attached to each other, I give you an amicable handshake in thought.

With cordial regards and loyally as ever,

Your Hofmannsthal.

Arthur Schnitzler visited my parents, in company with his friend Richard Beer-Hofmann, for the first time on the Rudolfshöhe near

Ischl, a favorite summer meeting-place of the Viennese writers at the turn of the century. Schnitzler came from a Viennese medical family and became a physician himself, but he soon devoted himself completely to his writing. Mama reminisced:

His melancholy and laughter will remain unforgettable to me. By virtue of this he seemed to be coping with a life that was marked by frequent afflictions. He was one of the few sages of our time . . . Even as a writer he remained a doctor and a healer. In his time there may have been no more profound and more sensitive interpreter of women, or anyone who more vigilantly observed death for the sake of life and who was therefore able to bestow on life that mellow melancholic serenity that informs every one of his works . . .

A warm friendship was formed at this very first meeting. Mama sang a Brahms song for him that he later asked her to sing over and over again, *Nicht mehr zu Dir zu gehen:* "Never again to go to you, I resolved and swore it, and I go every evening, for I have lost all my strength and stability."

"Later," Mama wrote, "we often visited Schnitzler in his nice house in the Cottage district and spent good evenings with him. On some of these I heard him play Mahler symphonies with his mother on the piano, four hands, and he frequently accompanied my singing."

The Berlin premiere of Schnitzler's play *Liebelei* (Light o' Love) took place at the Deutsches Theater in 1896; directed by Otto Brahm and featuring such great actors as Agnes Sorma, Rudolf Rittner, Josef Jarno, and Emanuel Reicher, it was a great success. In 1910 my parents attended the premiere of *Der junge Medardus* in Vienna. On that occasion they stayed at the famous old Hotel Sacher, and Mama remembered the pillows on the window sills on which people leaned while watching the people in the street below. The legendary Frau Sacher, the mistress of those venerable rooms, who had the strange habit of smoking fat cigars, swept through the hotel and restaurant every day wearing a black silk dress as well as numerous ringlets in her hair and surrounded by a pack of fine young dogs. Even in those days the Sacher served the best beef as well as the famous Sachertorte, and all the waiters were like refined patriarchs.

We frequently met Schnitzler on our summer and winter trips, especially in the Engadine, which he loved and where I can still picture him wearing knickerbockers and a sports jacket on the walks we took together. He was an ebullient and extremely amusing raconteur. When he walked through the Engadine meadows with my father, both of them engrossed in an intensive conversation and gesticulating animatedly, I sometimes followed the two and noted with amusement that their adult problems kept them from seeing the magnificent nature all around them. Schnitzler wrote about this to my father:

In these all too short hours of your stay in the Engadine I felt the warmth and permanence of our relationship with particular gratification, and the kindness of your dear wife as well as the unaffected vigor of your charming daughter also contributed toward giving the atmosphere of this get-together the clarity and serenity which heaven has not fully favored me with. May our relationship remain as it has basically always been. With the most cordial regards to all of you, yours faithfully, Arthur Schnitzler.

In spite of some severe blows of fate—the separation from his wife and the suicide of his greatly beloved daughter— and despite all his suffering and sadness one sensed in Schnitzler a positive attitude toward life that transfigured his entire being. I felt admiration and awe for him. There was something well-rounded, mellow, and awe-inspiring about his personality. His eyes, which always seemed to be blinking a bit, smiled into the world. His kindly glance rested on the people he was speaking with, and he looked at them penetratingly, as though he had to help them bear all their sorrows. Yet he was capable of unexpectedly bursting into a guffaw. Thomas Mann referred to this as follows: " . . . this cheerfulness and childlike to laugh inclination that so becomes a man of mind . . . " Alfred Kerr wrote about Schnitzler's poetic quality: "As if by gentle magic there appears a painfully sweet world full of sad, roguish grace, ironic melancholia, and gently laughing tenderness . . . Pain and games, smiling and dying . . . What no one can acquire he was given in his sleep . . . He forgoes completeness . . . and replaces it with intimations."

Schnitzler wrote a verse in my poetry album:

Tiefsinn hat nie ein Ding erhellt:
Klarsinn schaut tiefer in die Welt.
Arthur Schnitzler, Lugano, 29. 8. 1924

(Profundity has never illuminated anything; clarity affords a deeper view of the world).

These lines later served as the motto of *Buch der Sprüche und Bedenken* (Book of Sayings and Thoughts), a volume of Schnitzler aphorisms that the Phaidon Verlag of Vienna published in 1927.

In 1895 my mother, who frequently served as an editor during the first decade of my father's publishing firm, received a big cardboard box filled with loose sheets covered with a large, childlike writing. It almost looked like a woman's handwriting, and the manuscript contained nothing but short prose sketches. They bespoke a very singular personality that championed the natural, childlike, and healthy elements in life and rebelled against human mendacity, malice, and unnaturalness. The author loved children, and young girls were his heroines. He saw how children were made to suffer by the unreasonablesness and obtuseness of adults. And he loved women, sang their praises, and was so touched by their suffering as oppressed and misunderstood wives that his writings declared war against the narrow-mindedness of members of a certain stratum who had, "for the sake of decorum," forgotten how to treat their fellow men humanely. When my mother read all those written sheets, she burst out in tears, and that sufficed my father. He became the publisher of these sheets, these writings of a great human soul, the fellow sufferer with human misery: Peter Altenberg.

The following year the first volume of his prose sketches appeared under the title *Wie ich es sehe* (As I see It) and instantly gained its author a public that loved him and remained loyal to him.

In the publisher's catalogue announcing his work, Altenberg wrote:

I have tramped around forests, have been a law student without studying law, a medical student without studying medicine, a bookdealer without selling books, a lover without ever marrying, and finally a poet without producing poetry. For, are my little things poetry? By no means. They are extracts. Extracts of life. The life of the soul and the random day boiled down to 2-3 pages, stripped of superfluities . . .

S. Fischer Verlag introduced him a bit differently: Altenberg is a writer for whom triviality does not exist. He seeks the lost paradises, and he finds them in the souls of children and young women.

While others write with long windedness works that people forget the next day, he can with his short-windedness say things that are simply unforgettable.

Altenberg's work has remained both "unforgettable" and alive, particularly by virtue of the childlike naiveté that enabled him to recognize human problems. In Vienna he became a popular figure. Every coachman knew "Herr von Altenberg," the bald-headed, moustached writer with the flowing cape that made him feel he could fly. In the Central, his favorite Viennese café, he was always surrounded by a bevy of female admirers. He never had a coin in his pocket and in general was not able to cope with life. My mother started a collection that was presented to him as a "Testimonial Gift of German Women" and for which he thanked her by addressing her as "noblest of women." In 1913 we met him at the Lido near Venice. I was eight years old at the time, which made me the ideal object of his adoration, and he presented me with "the most beautiful shells" of the beach in a little bag together with a poem that has unfortunately not been preserved.

In *Märchen des Lebens* (Fairy-tales of Life), he writes:

A poet actually has only the hypertrophied soul of an ordinary person, and the overly energetic activity of this soul keeps him from remaining an ordinary person! Under the microscope of the soul these ordinary things become extraordinary and many uninteresting things become interesting! The "romance of everyday life" is the noblest educational device. We are surrounded by precious treasures which the days and the hours give us of their own accord; why, then, flee to the poets if we ourselves could experience this poetry called "life"?!?

I once observed a young, beautiful woman putting the worse part of a roast on the plate of her husband, who loved her most tenderly, and taking the better part for herself. To me that was a profound, tragic poem. For I immediately sensed all the sad things that this unfortunate man would still have to suffer at the hands of this great beauty, and at the same time I had a presentiment of her own tragic conflicts, for fate, after all, leaves nothing unavenged— in the end! Actually, with that piece of roast meat that woman had already cheated on her husband, who was taking such loving care of her, offering him despicable egotism in return for his noble friendship . . .

All that I am really asking people to do in this little book called Märchen des Lebens is to get a bit more out of this moment 'life' than they have up to now. Let everyone discover the poet in himself!

"Uncle Wassermann is stuffing himself." That is what my brother once wrote in his diary, and my own first memories of the dark-haired, dark-skinned young man with the pitch-black eyes are of shared meals in our Grunewald house at which he used to eat and talk much and fast. It was the writer Jakob Wassermann. I liked his natural, boyish ways. We could fool around and play with him and then listen to him tell stories. There was much kindness and yet also a great deal of roguishness in his personality, and I grew quite close to him. He had known me since I was little, and for my ninth birthday he wrote in my album a poem which showed in a loving way that he was well acquainted with my parents' nature:

Liebe Brigitte Eva, Du denkst wohl gar,
ein Gedichtlein für Dich sei leicht erfunden?
Ein paar Reime schnell zum Strauß gebunden?
Ach, es ist ja nicht wahr,
momentan sind die Dichter rar.
Frag nur Deinen Vater darum,
vielleicht gibt er mir Recht, vielleicht bleibt er stumm,
aus Artigkeit, um mich nicht zu verwunden.

Doch was ich kann, ist mühlos erzählt.
Ich kann Dir gut sein, kann Freundschaft bewahren,
darin trotz ich Gefahren und Jahren.
Mir ist die Welt
ein Bau, den das Herzblut zusammenhält.
Frag nur Deine Mutter danach,
die kennt sich aus in diesem Fach,
hat viel Freundschaft gegeben und erfahren.

Leb wohl, bleib mir treu gesinnt,
das ist mein Wunsch
und Geburtstagsangebind.

Dein Jakob Wassermann, Wien, März 1914

(Dear Brigitte Eva, do you really think it is easy to invent a little poem for you and quickly bind a few verses into a bouquet? Alas, it is not true; at present poets are scarce. Just ask your father; perhaps he will agree with me, perhaps he will say nothing— out of politeness, so as not to hurt me. But it takes no great effort to tell you what I can do. I can be fond of you, can preserve our friendship; in this I defy dangers and years. To me the world is an edifice kept together by heart's blood. Just ask your mother about that; she is an expert in that department, having given and experienced a great deal of friendship. Farewell, stay true to me; that is my wish and my birthday present.

—Your Jakob Wassermann, Vienna, March 1914).

My mother told me that Arthur Schnitzler brought Wassermann along to their summer place in 1899. "The dark-haired youth who looked like a Savoyard boy was a Franconian from Zirndorf near Fürth. His mother, who died young, must have been especially beautiful; in her home region she had been known as "Jette the beauty," and surely Wassermann had inherited his sparkling dark eyes and his gypsy-like nature from her . . . We liked his book— it was his first novel, *Die Geschichte der jungen Renate Fuchs* (The Story of Young Renate Fuchs)— as much as we did its author. My husband accepted the work, and with him that always meant the publication of all the author's writings. Jacob Wassermann became one of our most successful authors . . . "

From that first meeting our friendship with him was firmly founded. Wassermann often came to Berlin, for that city fascinated him more than his new adopted city, Vienna. He called Berlin "an impressive city that astonishes one with the power and speed with which everything meshes." He became a regular guest in Grunewald, and my parents, each in his or her own way, tried to civilize the "somewhat gypsy-like" writer a bit.

Soon he not only admired my mother, but also carried a bit of a torch for her, and he wrote for her an acrostic on her name, Hedwig:

Helles Herz, erwachte Seele,
Ernst in innigem Verstehen,
Dunkelheit im Wege – Gehen
Wissend aber um ein Ziel.
Immer zuckend unterm Schicksalsjoch
Ganz in Gott geborgen doch.
Spital, Febr. 1908, Jakob Wassermann

(Bright heart, awakened soul, earnest in heartfelt understanding, obscure in walking along paths, but knowing a goal. Always quivering under fate's yoke, but wholly sheltered in God).

Wassermann was a "rouser," and in his books he appealed to the conscience of men. His book *Caspar Hauser oder die Trägheit des Herzens* (Caspar Hauser or The Indolence of the Heart) deeply impressed not only my brother but also me, an adolescent at the time, and it always accompanied me as an exhortation. In the book he managed to tell about a tragic human fate in his customary suspenseful way and in so lively a fashion that even a child could follow the story. I read the book like a fairy-tale and let his indictment of human apathy and indolence shake me up. I recognized my own responsibility toward my fellow men and the commandment to take helpful action wherever it was necessary. In the great, wide-ranging narrative works that I did not get to know and admire until later Wassermann repeatedly took up similar themes that appealed to men to act morally.

Wassermann sincerely sympathized when my parents mourned their only son, and a short time after the misfortune he wrote them a deeply felt letter in which he said, among other things:

Everything is swallowed up by the day, everything is killed by the moment, and only a great destiny makes us look to the heights; suddenly we have a presentiment of the divine, of what created us, destroys us, and renews us again. I have an unshakeable belief in this renewal and transformation, and just as in the physical world no energy is lost, no feeling, no image, no figure is lost in the psychic realm . . .

9
Rainer Maria Rilke and his 'Buona Pasqua'

When I think back on my earliest impression of Rainer Maria Rilke, I see him as a delicate young man of medium height with a delicate head with blond hair, a thin face, and very expressive eyes. There was something ephebic and ethereal about him— as though he were really not quite of this world. He always had a smile that expressed melancholy rather than joy.

He was extremely kind to me when I was a child and spoiled me. When I was in Rome at the age of five, he sent me a giant Easter egg with a card saying *Buona Pasqua a tutta la famiglia!* (Happy Easter to the whole family). "Here is an egg for Tutti to hunt, but please regard its contents as inedible." In almost every letter to my parents he included kind words of greeting for me.

Later, when I was older, he spoke to me as to an adult. When he tried to explain the essence of a work of art to me or picked up one of the little bronze horses by the sculptress Renée Sintenis from my father's collection, stroked it, and lovingly traced its lines with his expressive hands, it hardly took words for me to understand what he meant. And for the first time I comprehended that art is an emanation of the spirit and can manifest itself through any medium.

To what extent the various art forms coalesced for Rilke I discovered from a letter he wrote on July 15, 1924 to the princesses Mary and Antoinette Windischgraetz:

In the great cathedrals, in Notre Dame in Paris, St. Mark's, or on Mont St Michel, I often brought myself to believe that over the centuries the ever-swelling waves of organ music have had some influence on the curves of the arches, the intertwining of the ornaments, or the more customary smoothness of the pillar flutting and of the columns . . . Perhaps at some time in the future it will turn out not to have been so daring and adventurous to claim such a side effect for sound, for do not iron filings form figures when a string is bowed near them? The great interaction and interplay of the world as well as the discovery that the stimuli of our various senses touch one another somewhere, in some as yet undiscovered periphery—these facts, which lie within the realm of possibility, will hardly be surprising to our descendants; experiments and surprises will combine and increasingly bring these facts to the fore . . . Imagine music having not merely the ability to move a mind or a soul but also the power to transform a body or change a face . . . perhaps heal a wound! . . . What is to prevent us from believing in this?

At a much later time I read Rilke's poems with mounting excitement, and I would have given a great deal to have been able to discuss his sonnets and elegies with him. But by that time he was no longer on this earth.

Rilke was not one of my father's authors, but he did belong among the closest circle of artist friends. My father had no special feeling for poetry, but he still very clearly sensed the great evolving artist in the young Rilke and gave him financial support at a time when Rilke had to struggle greatly. Rilke thanked him in a letter from Capri dated March 19, 1908:

My dear Mr. Fischer . . . I will put your letter aside for today and wait to see whether it is still there tomorrow and the day after—just as it is now, just as natural in its friendship, as though it were the most natural thing in the world to be a letter, to arrive, and to read thus. The proposal you make me opens up to me the most fortuitous opportunity, one that seemed impossible just a short while ago: I would be able to go to Paris, lock myself in, and work impulsively as never before. You know what this means to me: Everything . . .

To my mother Rilke was tied by very personal and warm bonds of affection, and they corresponded regularly. In her memoirs she writes:

On a winter day in 1897 a reading took place in our apartment at Burggrafenstrasse 3, Berlin, as was frequently the case in the literary circle that had formed around my husband's publishing house. Carl Hauptmann, Gerhart's elder brother, wished to read his play Ephraims Breite (Ephraim's Breadth) before a rather large group of friends. In the audience was Frau Lou Andreas-Salomé, a Russian writer as beautiful as she was distinguished and a woman known to have been Nietzsche's friend at one time. Frau Salomé had brought along her young friend Rainer Maria Rilke, and this is what made that evening meaningful to me. I had never heard of him or read anything by him, but this delicate, quiet, good-looking man (about twenty-two years old at the time) made a big impression on me. He was slim, blond, and blue-eyed, and he wore a high-necked waistcoat of black silk with a cross suspended from a chain. Having just gotten over an illness, I was still somewhat weak, and with an empathy that he had especially for women he immediately sensed this. Thus he helped me after the reading, in an extremely nice way, with my household chores at the teatable and the samovar. We immediately became friends, for we soon noticed that we liked the same people. We both loved the Viennese writer Peter Altenberg whom I had discovered in 1895, when I was an editor of the publishing house, and we both admired Gerhart Hauptmann and loved his works. Our friendship, which of course included my husband as well, became firmer, and we enjoyed it for many years till his early death in the old tower of Sierre in the canton of Valais.

There was hardly a Christmas at which he was not present, be it through a letter or one of his new books. He sent them all to us, year after year, all of them inscribed, and he wrote that he knew his books "felt at home" among us.

When he was living in Paris as a secretary to Rodin, a man he greatly admired, he met his future wife, Clara Westhoff, a pupil of the sculptor. But he was not made to be a husband; he was and remained a loner, and thus they lived apart. Clara Rilke often stayed with us in Grunewald for weeks, and she always remained our loyal friend. In those days she sculpted our little daughter Tutti, and I sent photos of the bronze sculpture to Rilke in Paris.

Rilke wrote my mother:

So Tutti's bust really grew and matured in a good atmosphere, and I think it actually shows. From the little photograph one can see how calmly and distinctly the little, resolute personality has been captured and reproduced. This may well be Clara's best work to date.

And in a second letter from Paris, dated November 6, 1969, he wrote to my mother:

Dear Mrs. Fischer, I must write you right away that Rodin has just seen the photos of Tutti's bust. He looked at them all repeatedly with great concentration, most of all the one made by artificial light. He found this work very beautiful, 'très vivant, plein de force et d'éloquence' (very beautiful, full of power and expressiveness)—and told me I should immediately congratulate my wife on it. His joy, which is just as concentrated as his observation, is absolutely wonderful in such a case and carries one along with a heartwarming effect . . .

In one of his earlier letters from Paris Rilke told my mother about Rodin's portrait bust of George Bernard Shaw:

A few days ago Rodin started the portrait of one of your most noteworthy authors, and it promises to be something very special . . . Not only does he stand very well (energetically holding still and surrendering absolutely to the sculptor's hands), but he also knows how to collect and concentrate himself in that part of his body which, so to speak, will have to represent all of Shaw within the confines of the bust in such a way that his essence is transferred to the bust, feature by feature, with incredibly heightened tension.

Mama noted the following:

We had our most beautiful encounter with Rilke in the spring of 1910 in Rome where we lived together for seven weeks in the Hotel de Russie on the Piazza del Popolo, directly below the Pincio. Rilke accompanied us on our art trips, and with him I saw the El Grecos in the Corsini gallery for the first time. After lunch we often sat together in the sun on the topmost terrace of the gardens, enjoying the magnificent view of St. Peter's and the city. Rilke never took his meals in the hotel, but only drank a glass of milk and ate some fruit in his room. After the meal he would come to our blue salon, always announcing himself with his card; he was always welcome, of course.

After our departure, he wrote:

. . . Not just Rome mourns you so expressively and distinctly; the hotel itself did not want to lag behind and expressed its dismay in

its own way. The electric light failed and could not be restored for an hour. The others, of course, did not know what that meant, but I comprehended the grandeur of this manifestation of mourning and silently participated in it. The dinner downstairs had to take place with candelabra, and it was strange to stand by the window and see single candles moving along in the long corridors. Suddenly it was quite exciting and extraordinary, as in a hotel in Hofmannsthal's time. The garden door of the blue salon always keeps its shutters closed . . . Give my regards to your beautiful house, which will surely do you good. Cordially as ever, R.M.R.

In his first letter, dated October 25, 1911, from Duino Castle, which was to become such an important milestone in his life, Rilke wrote to my mother:

. . . *Now I shall tell you right away where I am: with my friends, in this castle which towers so immensely over the sea and with many of its windows (including mine) overlooks the open sea (one is tempted to say, directly overlooks the cosmos and its generous, all-transcending spectacles like a promontory of human existence. The inside windows of a different level afford a view of quietly contained, ancient baileys in which later times have twined around old Roman walls the attenuations of baroque balustrades and figures playing with themselves. Behind them, however, when one steps out of all those secure gates, there towers the bare karst, no less impassable than the sea, and the eye thus cleared of all smaller things develops a particular fondness for the little castle garden . . . At the next promontory on the shore stands an even older castle that antedates the other one, which goes back to time immemorial; tradition has it that Dante stayed at that ancient castle.*

April 26, 1922 is the date of Rilke's report to my mother from his last abode, Château de Muzot in Valais:

. . . *The little castle is from the thirteenth century and is a typical medieval Valaisan nobleman's residence. When I moved into it last summer, it seemed to be a heavy and hard fit, like a suit of armor, but as I lived there, the old walls seemed to become increasingly soft and supple, as it were. In any case, it has afforded me the most wonderful protection. In this uniform stillness, I was finally permitted to finish the work I had begun in 1912— and only this has made me a contemporary of myself. Owing to the unfortunate interruption of this work I had felt throughout all those bad years that I had lagged far behind myself; now I breathe like a person who has found himself. Because of this recovery good old Muzot will always remain unforgettable in my gratitude . . .*

On January 29, 1924, he wrote:

You are too good and old friends to surmise that I have forgotten you this time as I sent out my two new books! The (Sonnets to Orpheus) came out around Eastertime 1923, but I wanted to send these poems out together with the ten great elegies that had been completed simultaneously with the very rapid composition of the sonnets, in February 1922 . . . In the elegies (which are particularly dear to me) you will recognize the poems, collected at Duino in 1912, which the war had interrupted for me so profoundly that I already thought I would have to forego their continuation and completion forever. My present quiet abode, with its great— often almost too great—solitude has rescued these endangered poems for me, and saved them with such purity that not a fragment of earlier days had to be abandoned as lost! A blessing for which I cannot be grateful enough. I thought I ought to keep this completion attached to the name Duino, especially since the old castle was destroyed in the war, so that it has permanence only in these lines . . . From me . . . Oh, let the books speak!

In old friendship, Yours sincerely, Rilke.

Rilke's last letter to my mother, dated Muzot, December 12, 1925, sounds like a farewell:

Dear Mrs. Fischer, to have a birthday is hard, a matter of enervating passivity, and I notice that it is easier if one may exchange good wishes. I hastened to send mine to you and Mr. Fischer and Tutti, who is mainly involved. You can imagine that these are my most cordial wishes, based on so many memories . . . What a pleasant experience it is for me to read Erdenerstrasse 8; despite the fact that Tutti is a bride this line looks so unchanged, and behind it there are all kinds of unchangeable good things among you and between us. These are constants, believe me, that slow us down a bit and keep us from being only old at one stroke.

In old, grateful friendship and devotion, Your Rilke.

Rilke's poems accompanied me through all the stages of my life, and time and time again they revealed to me a new, different, hitherto unrecognized world. Through his poems he spoke to generations, but his words were also addressed to individuals. For many years I carried with me a few lines from his letter to a friend:*

. . . I am not fond of the Christian conception of a beyond; I am moving farther and farther away from it, without of course thinking of attacking it . . . To me, first of all, it involves the risk of making the departed less distinct and for the time being less accessible to us, but it also makes us less definite, less earthly as it draws us over there and away from here in our longing— and yet for the time being, while we are still here and akin to trees, flowers, and the earth, we should remain distinct and earthly in the purest sense of those terms—in fact, we must always evolve in that direction . . . I reproach all our religions with giving their believers consolations and palliations of death without implanting in their hearts means of accommodating themselves to it and coming to an understanding with it.

Ever since I met him, the figure of Rilke has remained alive in me— not just the figure of the poet but above all that of the truth-seeker, the truth-perceiver, the visionary invoker, and his words as well as his music have resounded in my ears to this day.

**Countess Margot Sizzo, Château Muzot, on Epiphany.*

10
Thomas Mann's Epistle in my Album. A Memorable Boat Ride

In 1945, toward the end of World War II and shortly after his seventieth birthday, Thomas Mann inscribed for me a copy of his book *Das Gesetz* (The Tables of the Law) in America, the country that had become a new home for him and for us: "To Tutti whom I used to dandle on my knees, most cordially, Thomas Mann."

Thus he had known me much longer than I had known him, for I was twelve years old when I first consciously met him. It was not an altogether cheerful encounter for me. The Manns had invited my parents and me to dinner at their home on Poschingerstrasse in Munich; it was a big dinner party and the Mann children were included. The atmosphere seemed a bit tense to me; there was something imperious and severe about the father, whom his children called the *Zauberer* (magician), and his ironic remarks were apt to frighten children. The master of the house did make some jokes, though they sometimes appeared like barbs aimed at his children, who were making him nervous, but I was relieved when we were allowed to get up from the table after a dessert that had been praised by the Zauberer.

The *Zauberer* cut a strange figure in the midst of his children, and I very distinctly felt the secret and ambivalent currents within his family. Between the "big ones" and him there was a special, humorous dialogue composed of a mixture of somewhat bantering irony and love, and toward the younger children there was a stance of strictness that could lead to the command "Go stand in the corner" as well as a great, emotional affection of the kind that he himself so beautifully described in his story "Disorder and Early Sorrow." All in all, there was a certain tension in the house that affected me, the child, and frightened me when I was a guest there.

The next encounter with Thomas Mann took place two years later and in an entirely different atmosphere. It was summer, and a vacation trip had taken us to the Flensburg Fiord, to Glücksburg, a town a bit north of Thomas Mann's birthplace Lübeck but with a similar climate and situated in a similar landscape, on his native sea, the Baltic.

It was 1919, one year after the end of World War I. Even though people were not exactly starving, it was difficult to feed a large family. I am sure Frau Katia knew a thing or two about that. Every day she had to ride her bicycle all over Munich and environs in order to produce the absolute essentials for her family.

Thus it was a pleasant relaxation for Thomas Mann to be spending a few summer weeks with his friend and publisher S. Fischer and his family in the fertile countryside of Holstein—by comparison with the big cities a "land of milk and honey." Those were harmonious weeks of daily proximity. The northern Baltic countryside brought his childhood and youth back to Thomas Mann; the soft light, the air and the hues of the north put him in a gentle and nostalgic mood after the many years he had spent in the "harsh" southern city of Munich. Every day he took me for a walk through the radiantly green fields that extended to the sea and told me many things about his life and his work. He talked about *The Magic Mountain* and told me how such a work "imperceptibly" and unintentionally grows from a story to an extensive novel, and he spoke about Hans Castorp, the novel's unheroic hero, who was a reflection of its author.

These walks concluded with an hour's bathing at the beach on which he felt so at home. One day we also went boating together. It was an old fisherman's sailboat that took us out to the fiord, and the calm sea and the blue all around us reminded him of his boyhood, the vacations he had spent in Travemünde. Those vacations on his beloved Baltic Sea had been the happiest and most carefree periods of his youth, for the constricted atmosphere of the old city of Lübeck and the dreary, provincial atmosphere of his school had caused him quite a bit of suffering. For this reason the short annual seaside vacations with his siblings and friends really opened his eyes and his heart.

All this came back to him in those hours at the Glücksburg fiord, and we were so enveloped by a magic from an entirely different sphere that we completely forgot about the homeward trip. But since the wind had now died down completely, we were "stuck" in the middle of the sea and of necessity had to start rowing hard to bring the heavy boat back to the shore, where my parents were already keeping an anxious watch for the two of us.

Thomas Mann described these shared weeks in my Album:

«Brigitte-Eva Fischer!
Der Onkel wird träumerischer.
Es hebt ihn zum Gedichte, –
Was sagt er seiner Nichte?
Er sagt ihr – – –

(Brigitte-Eva Fischer: The Uncle is getting dreamier; he is lifted to poetic heights. What does he tell his niece? He tells her . . .)

No, dear Tutti, not this way, let us forget about the verses. It is most unlikely that I could sustain such a high poetic level for more than two or three lines, and the result might be a fiasco that would be particularly shameful in nature in such illustrious company. I will permit myself to sink back into the native element of prose to write in this pretty souvenir book of yours a word of remembrance of our weeks in Glücksburg . . . A native element? Remembrance? But here we already have the theme and the key words of these lines— two sentimental key words, veiled in sentiment and a colorful haze like paintings of the coasts of my northern homeland, and they taste salty like tears and the water of native northern high tides in which one bathes once again after many years spent in the harsh atmosphere of the south. Yes, the south is harsh, but the northern homeland is soft. Art is hard, but our heart is soft, isn't it, dear Tutti? This is an old melody that has been ringing in my ears since I have been here— the melody of the old song and the prose piece about Tonio

Kröger, and it is a pity that it has already been written, for otherwise I would write it down today. You will read it shortly— if only out of filial piety, for Papa has published it, or 'brought it to light' as people used to say. Then you will think of our weeks in Glücksburg. And just as your good grey eyes were always present, and will be present in my memory, at all the dear and beautiful things that these weeks told me and gave me, please remember, when you recall brisk, salty sailboat and steamboat rides and the park of Augustenburg and good meals and many strolls through the fruitful Holstein countryside— please remember kindly, I say, your affectionate Uncle Thomas Mann. Glücksburg, July 31, 1919.

Thomas Mann's visits with us on our summer trips and during vacation weeks recurred a number of times. Thus we met with him on the Feldberg in 1923 and stayed together at the Hotel Feldberger Hof. Those were still lean years and the room prices went up every day. In order to help indigent artists in that difficult inflationary period, Thomas Mann and my mother decided to put on a joint "evening" in the hotel. The writer read the "Snow" chapter from his then still unfinished novel *The Magic Mountain,* and my mother sang Gustav Mahler's four "Songs of a Wayfarer." The evening was very successful and netted the artists' fund a pretty sum that both of them were very proud of.

There, too, I was allowed to accompany Thomas Mann on his daily morning walks. Since I was very interested in music in those days and had already made some progress on the piano, we had a topic in common: music. His knowledge in this field was not only extensive but vivid and passionate as well, and he was open to every new impression, as now to the Mahler songs that he had just heard my mother sing. "Actually," he said with deep admiration for his friend Bruno Walter, "I would have preferred to become a conductor."

11
Annette Kolb, Who Outlived Generations

Annette Kolb once told me that her most vivid memories were of her childhood and that she remembered herself best as a seven-year-old. At that time she told herself: "I shall love people, but I shall never be able to be like them. After seven years workaday life has begun. Up to now everything has been festive, new, and fresh, but actually I have never liked grown-ups. And when I had to say hello to them, I smeared my face with soap in advance."

Even as a child, Annette Kolb always seemed ageless to me. Her slim, frail figure was enveloped in shapeless garments that had neither beginning nor end, and yet it always appeared elegant. There was something distinguished and aristocratic about her face with its big, narrow nose, broad cheekbones, long chin, and intelligent, alert eyes. Her hands were narrow and her fingers long and bony; she had remarkably big and masculine ears. She radiated a charm that embellished and transfigured an ugliness that was full of character. There was no escaping the impression of a great personality.

When she visited us— during our summer or winter trips— my father bade me dog her footsteps. I had to follow her and be sure to pick up all the things she lost or left lying somewhere. Once it was her gold watch, another time her purse with the royalties that the publishing house had just paid her. Her eyeglasses and her penholder— everything disappeared mysteriously and was only rarely found again. But she took these losses in good part, just as her whole being seemed to consist of a mixture of feminine cleverness and masculine humor.

Thomas Mann has immortalized her in his *Doctor Faustus,* where he calls her Jeannette Scheurl, "a writer of novels . . . grown up between two languages . . . she wrote ladylike and original studies of society that did not lack psychological and musical charm and were definitely part of higher literature . . . Of stylish ugliness, with an elegant sheep face in which peasant elements were mixed with aristocratic ones, just as in her speech the Bavarian dialect mingled with French, she was extraordinarily intelligent and at the same time enveloped in the naively inquiring innocence of an aging spinster." Despite all her friendship with Thomas Mann and Frau Katia, she never forgave him the "sheep face."

But she remains indescribable and her age indeterminable. Nobody knew the year of her birth. She is said to have told a passport official who inquired about her age: "This is *my* age, right? It ain't yours, and it's none of your business." She was probably a hundred when she died. To the anniversary almanac of the S. Fischer Verlag in 1911 she contributed reflections entitled "Balloon Perspective": "I do fear that there will be another war; there will have to be one, though the diplomats deny it . . . I can't say how I feel about our planning to pull another war out of the junk-room of mankind." How right she was to be! She had to live to see *two* world wars. In 1912 she wrote a little "Vignette" about a party in the Fischer house, "where the publisher gave his receptions with tremendous dignity . . . All rooms on the ground floor were open for this purpose. Among them was the salon that was adorned with what was perhaps Max Liebermann's most beautiful portrait and that could easily be converted into a ballroom, and I remember dancing with Walther Rathenau— but our host did not show up there; his mind was only on literature, and when he had company, he would stay in a book-filled nook of the big room . . . I shall never forget with what brilliance, interest, assurance, and concern this little self-made man could express himself about his authors. They were his hobby . . . "

Annette's first novel— whose title, *Das Exemplar,* had been invented by my mother— was published by S. Fischer in 1913 and immediately made her name known. Mama wrote: "Annette's first work was a travel book . . . Her feeling at home in the big world, interwoven with charm and deep feeling with a simple and yet exciting plot, gave the book its truly unique tone. I found only the title, *Mariclees Erlebnis* (Mariclee's Experience) bad, and I insisted that the book be rechristened; it had to be called *Das Exemplar.* That is the title it was given, and it made its way."

In one of her later books, *Kleine Fanfare* (Little Fanfare), she describes a visit made together with Richard Beer-Hofmann to my parents in Unterach on the Attersee in 1912:

I had just made my debut as a novelist. We were sitting in the car of our common publisher and driving like the wind zigzag along the sprawling shores of a mountain lake; the weather was like a godsend . . . When we reached the villa in which our publisher was holding court, it gleamed snow-white in the moonlight, its mighty terrace overhanging the lake. I walked up and down lightheartedly, as if the little silk coat I was wearing could easily waft me to the other shore or up to the transfigured mountain tops.

Annette Kolb participated in the life of our family; she became part of us, of the publishing firm as well as the house. For me she had an understanding ear, and with her wise instinct she observed my development from childhood to adulthood. Her little entry in my poetry album is from that period: "August 22, 1923. Dear Tutti, these times are horrible, and thus an excellent girl like you is doubly valuable. I wish you luck, and make your way. Most cordially yours, Annette Kolb."

In 1928 Papa published Annette's new novel, *Daphne Herbst,* in which she described her girlhood and her family history. Her father, a royal Bavarian court gardener, married a Frenchwoman who said about herself: "J'avais quatre enfants et un piano" (I had four children and a piano). Annette inherited her musicality from her mother, who is said to have been a very gifted pianist, and she herself lived in the world of music with true enthusiasm and played the piano well. Visitors to her apartment in a Paris hotel always found her baby grand opened, for she played a lot for herself, improvised, and loved to participate in chamber music. Her heart belonged to Mozart in particular, and her books about him and about Schubert found many readers. Annette was at least as attached to France as she was to Germany. For years she had a little house in Badenweiler, next to that of the writer René Schickele, a close friend, and like him she felt most at home near the French border. She belonged to both cultures, and her sense of responsibility was torn between them. As a true and convinced humanist she became a passionate Hitler hater. She was capable of being hard as nails in her absolute and principled stance, her rejection and contempt. When her novel *Die Schaukel* (The Swing) was published by S. Fischer in 1934, during the Hitler regime, she insisted on the following footnote being included on page 176 of the book: "From the time when the Jews achieved influence in intellectual life, certain chances became perceptible in the endangered life of the artist— that he would no longer have to make his way with a drudgery that, viewed subjectively, only too often was tantamount to falling by the wayside. In other words, and viewed retrospectively: a Hölderlin might have been preserved from playing the impecunious tutor, and Franz Schubert might not have died so young and so penniless. However that may be, in today's Germany there are a small number of us Christians who remain aware of their debt of gratitude to the Jews." To publish these lines in a prominent place in her book was at that time a provocation that could have had dangerous consequences for her and her publisher. Only as upright and intrepid a character as Annette Kolb could have dared to do such a thing.

She went into exile, to America. One of the last planes that she caught in the nick of time in Spain before the outbreak of the war in 1939 took her to New York; she was wrapped in a huge cape and her face was hidden behind black glasses, and so she was taken for an Arab sheik. "Desperately unhappy in body and soul" in New York, she yearned for Europe and was almost crushed under the wheel of the big buses in the skyscraper city that was so alien to her. She was not made for the "New World." Immediately after the end of the war she returned to Europe, living alternately in Paris and Munich, where she felt "at home" overlooking the English Garden. To a ripe old age she remained full of ideas and delicious humor, and to the delight of the public she liked to give public readings from her last, mostly autobiographical books.

A few years before her death we received these greetings from her from Munich:

May 7, 1964. Dear Tutti, Many thanks for your very kind words. Of course, I too care most about the last pages of this new and last book "Zeitbilder" (Pictures of the Time) . . . I hope you will come soon. I plan to be here till the middle of June and then to Paris for a little while, as usual, because I cannot give it up. My eyes are giving me a lot of trouble; I hope you can read my writing. Oh, that beautiful, happy evening on which Gerhart Hauptmann's son [Ivo] told such charming stories and we laughed such a lot is so far away! Where does he live? Shall we not send him my book with my regards? With best wishes— we would have so much to talk about if we saw each other— your Annette.*

On April 5, 1965 she wrote:

Dear Publishers, since my return the day before yesterday, I have been the owner of a beautiful blue dressing-gown that makes me forget the cold. My very best thanks for it. What a pity that I missed you here! I did forget; I am a foe of money, which is there only to be spent. It is the greed for the Golden Calf that I am fighting— this is the reason that I am not selling my house, though this may place me in a difficult position. That is why I am still working, but I can do so only with the aid of a secretary because of the sad condition of my eyes, which unfortunately cannot be operated on and which I can keep open only with a great effort. I cannot read and can play only from memory, nor can I travel. Nevertheless, I will not lose courage. I hope you will come to visit me. Again, my cordial thanks. The beautiful robe gives me pleasure.

Annette.

The dressing-gown is a dream.

That was her last message for us.

**S. Fischer Verlag, 1964.*

12

At Age Seventeen. Walther Rathenau. Storm Clouds Foreshadow an Evil Force

On my 17th birthday my "fatherly friend" Moritz Heimann wrote:

Kagel, March 4, 1922.

Dear Tutti,

Things are coming full circle for us— and now all that Fräulein stuff makes it hard for me to recognize the little child and girl in you. It really is quite mindless praise when one says "Oh, you still look as you did before; doesn't she look as she did when she was a child?" If I were now to say to you, "Tutti, you look as you did seventeen years ago," would you like it? No. And as you did a year ago? Truth to tell, you wouldn't really like that either. And so it probably is best to stick to the present at its presentest and to tell the seventeen-year-old young lady who polishes off last night's ball as easily as she does two or three chocolate creams: Tutti, congratulations! Everything else is up to you: You are so touched that you fling your arms around your uncle's neck, and he smiles . . . Give my regards to your dear parents and to Miss Seele, who so faithfully and soulfully counts and seals your years. I almost forgot: cordial greetings, and at least seventeen of them, to you from your Moritz Heimann.

Otto Flake also sent me congratulations on my seventeenth birthday, writing from Partenkirchen on March 10, 1922:

. . . I am surprised that you are already having such a high birthday, and I shall check my calendar again: It quite clearly says the seventeenth birthday. When I was seventeen, I was an obstreperous boy, but a girl that age is already a young lady—so let me congratulate the young lady. When you become engaged, I shall use the formal form of address. Perhaps I shall say Sie soon; how about that? But I assume you'll wait until I can shake your hand in person. Until then a cordial auf Wiedersehen. Your friend Flake, who hardly dares to call himself Flix any more.

If people addressed me so solemnly, I must have crossed a "threshold" with my seventeen years! I had already entered a more aware phase of my life a few years previously: that sort of thing does not happen on a definite date. I recall experiencing occasionally that people suddenly listened to me when I tried to say something and formulate a thought. At such moments I knew that I was no longer a child; perhaps I was no longer an "adolescent" but one of the grown-ups.

While I had until then lived instinctively, without reservations about the outside world and within the sheltered confines of my parental home in the Grunewald, I now began to observe the world around me with more critical and more open eyes and to explore the history of my origin and that of my parents in certain directions.

My maternal ancestors still lived in the Jewish tradition. Provided with civil rights by the German Kaiser, they had become good, successful businessmen, and my mother had grown up in the peaceful period following the Franco-Prussian war of 1870-1871, a time that was so propitious for the German middle class. Her parents had emancipated themselves from the Jewish rituals, and so she felt as a free citizen of the world, a feeling that she tried to instill in me.

My father's ancestors lived in a German-Jewish enclave in Austria-Hungary. Evidently my father was never hurt by anti-Semitism; he never spoke to me about that. Thus the two ancestral streams that converged in me had made me a person that was striving for self-knowledge.

My parents' cosmopolitanism thus made it easy for me to be a "Jewish" child. Only once— I must have been eight at the time— did a fellow pupil tell me that I bore part of the blame for the crucifixion of Jesus Christ. This accusation was utterly incomprehensible to me at the time, and after my parents tried to explain it to me, this experience left me with astonishment rather than injury or trauma.

Later I became more aware of my Jewish origin. To my friend Suse and me it frequently seemed as though we both reacted to our surroundings more skeptically and sensitively than our schoolmates. Our parents, too, seemed to us to be more "heavy-hearted" and more care-worn, and we often wondered how they had got that way. Did we Jews perhaps bear the invisible burden of our everlasting fate? At that time this being different seemed an advantage in our eyes. Learning came easily to us, and we had open eyes and ears for literature, philosophy, art, and music— a world that was not as open to most other girls.

I met Suse at the Grunewald Lyzeum where I spent my last two years of school. As the only Jewish girls in a class of thirty-five we immediately found common ground. Although we had friendly and usually intelligent schoolmates, albeit often with a nationalistic upbringing, we two felt as though we had been akin and close since time immemorial, and soon we knew that this mutual confidence would bind us together for life. We shared every care— the little worries about the solution of difficult problems in school and the big worries about problems of development as well as the sorrows of friendship and love.

Soon I had an opportunity to become better acquainted with the changes in my environment after the lost war. So there no longer was a "Kaiser" and Germany had become a republic, but between the nationalistic right and the Social Democrats and their leftist friends there was hatred and contempt; political unrest was the order of the day.

One dramatic afternoon in March of 1920 we heard that there was street fighting in the city. In front of our house there stopped a truck with soldiers who presumably were supposed to watch the surrounding houses. What was the meaning of that? Had a revolution broken out? We inhabitants of Grunewald were completely cut off from the city of Berlin by a general strike of all workers. There was no public transportation, no telephone, and no electric light. We had to walk to Halensee in order to look for food. In the evening we sat by candlelight with Gerhart Hauptmann and his wife, who were staying overnight with us. They had come to our house from their nearby home to share the uncertainty with their friends. We got as comfortable as we could and made music by the light of the flickening candles . . . We were disquieted, but we did not take things very seriously. Faith in the security of government authority and in the absoluteness of the law was so strong in my parents' generation that they did not give any thought to serious danger. Not until two days later did we learn what had transpired in Berlin. Wolfgang Kapp, an extreme nationalist, had wanted to overthrow the government with the help of his henchmen, the later Free Corps men and a Prussian general. The general strike of the workers and the resistance of the civil servants had frustrated this attempted putsch.

Life went on— but a new age seemed to have dawned. I witnessed this only as a spectator and was still too young to feel any responsibility, but I did sense that something new was in preparation. It became increasingly clear that things would no longer be as they had been.

I received my first great shock by the irruption of brutality and force, the murder of Walther Rathenau. He was a friend of my parents and lived near us in the Grunewald. As a child I had been impressed with his characterful and imposing figure. Even though he was admired and respected by the world around him, his life was surrounded by loneliness. His villa, which he had painted and furnished with exquisite taste and modeled somewhat after Goethe's Weimar house, could be entered only through a narrow door. Just wide enough for one person, it was a symbol of his life! With his works on political economy he became an author of my father, and as a neighbor and a friend he would often come to our house after his duties as president of A.E.G., the Allgemeine Elektrizitäts-Gesellschaft founded by his father.

Presiding over such a great industrial enterprise meant that he had a great deal of power in his hands, and he was well aware of that. Despite his position as a "big capitalist" he was a person with a marked social conscience; the world around him, however, had no understanding for his views. It was his plan to revolutionize the entire economic system; he foresaw the great social revolution in the western world. In his book, *Von kommenden Dingen* (Of

Things to Come), issued in 1917, he wrote: "Mechanization is the destiny of mankind and thus a work of nature. It is not the willfulness and error of an individual or a group; no one can escape it . . . The goal toward which we are striving is called human freedom."

On March 24, 1917 he wrote my father:

My dear Herr Fischer, I am very grateful to you for your intention of bringing my book to the public . . . As regards my collected works, I thought that I might use the summer weeks in Freienwalde to put together and rework all my pertinent writings. There would perhaps be two or three volumes in addition to my books "Kritik der Zeit" (Critique of the Times), "Mechanik des Geistes" (Mechanics of the Spirit), and "Von kommenden Dingen"; I think these should constitute the first three volumes . . . You know with what high regard I have followed your work for decades as well as my delight in a great and successful endeavor to lift what is truly good out of the mass of the indifferent. It may be an idealism that is hard to realize, but I cannot bring myself to abandon my assumption that an intelligent people may finally be induced to prefer good production to bad, even in mass consumption. Very sincerely yours, Rathenau.

On August 31, 1917 he wrote: "My dear Herr Fischer . . . About half of my new work is ready. I estimate that it will amount to 60 to 80 pages. Its title (confidentially) is *Die Neue Wirtschaft* (The New Economy), and I believe it will be the revolutionary and fundamental document of the future reconstruction. Unfortunately it will cause even more excitement and opposition among my fellow industrialists than my last book did. But our future is more important than my profession, and *pour faire une omelette, il faut casser des oeufs* (you can't make an omelette without breaking eggs).

In addition to his book publications he thought that he could have a great influence on the world around him with a new periodical as well. He wrote to my father on June 18, 1917: " . . . One of my customers, not all of whose ideas are altogether far-fetched, proposes that your publishing house start issuing a journal with the title *Der Volksstaat. Monatsschrift für sittliche Wiedergeburt* (The Republic. Monthly for Moral Rebirth). Since one should take good things where one finds them, I believe that this title might really be considered . . . Yours in friendship, Rathenau."

Rathenau was a person devoted to the arts. He was musical, knew the musical repertory, and often insisted that my mother sing his favorite Schubert and Brahms songs for him. When chamber music was played at our home, he would show up even if he had to cut short important negotiations.

I thought I could sense behind his cosmopolitan, assured manner something mysteriously concealed, a profound sadness. Within a few years the "yoke of fate" under which he had been placed was to take hold. I remember evenings on which he carried on passionate debates with friends of my parents and not only foresaw that the war would end badly for Germany but also foretold the "things to come," the world revolution. I listened to the expressions of his keen intellect which for the first time revealed the great political connections to me. In those days he surely was one of the most progressive German politicians. His planned economy became the first step toward a reorganization of Germany after the lost war. In 1921 he became Minister of Reconstruction, and the following year he was named Foreign Minister. Regarding the latter appointment, Moritz Heimann wrote to my father on June 1, 1921:

Dear Mr. Fischer, man certainly is a being quite jealous of what little discernment he has! I cannot help giving you my opinion on a matter that is none of my business. You see, Walter Rathenau will do a very good job, better than anybody else, provided that he is permitted to get to work. The hasty declaration by the Hanseatic League is a despicable act of the worst caliber. He will provide for the country an altogether inestimable economic drainage, but this will get him neither gratitude nor affection. All this is a grand sensation, and yet he would have been better off to decline . . .

Rathenau was the great liberal "patriot"— one of those German politicians who spoke the language of Europe and had the ability to build a bridge to a common future. But this very fact, coupled with his Jewishness, added fuel to the hatred of the German nationalists. He had to be brought down. The assassins' bullets hit him from an ambush; his murderers were Free Corps men, anti-Semites, and precursors of Hitler. I can still see myself on my way home from school facing frightened people at our streetcorner who gave me horrified reports about the monstrous murder that had just taken place there. On the previous day we had waved to our friend, at the very same corner, on his daily drive from his home to his office. His death was like a harbinger of the disaster that was to befall Germany.

Socialist and liberal Germany mourned him, but the rest of Germany cheered. The democratic, internationally recognized Jew had been a thorn in the flesh of the nationalistic upper middle class. His murder was the prelude to Hitler's seizure of power.

Only now, at a more advanced age, was I able to gauge the extent to which my parents had influenced my development. The air that I had breathed as a girl in my parental home, that lively center of intellectual give-and-take, had educated and formed me. Only now did I realize to what extent I had become an integral part of it, and this gave me a great inner support and the determination to make something of myself, to explore and develop my abilities, and to capture a place of my own within the publishing world.

In this, Moritz Heimann played a decisive role. It was he in particular who confirmed my decisions and encouraged me, especially when my father denied me permission to attend the book-trade school in Leipzig. Instead I had to look for the teachers and the place for such training in Berlin. I found both— two excellent teachers of script in E. R. Weiss and his pupil, Frau Marks, and in Otto von Holten's printshop I learned block printing and hand-setting. It gave me great pleasure to become absorbed in the world of scripts, to familiarize myself with them, trace their historical development, and learn to write them. Immersing myself in writing with a quill I had cut myself afforded me a peace and a concentration similar to those with which medieval monks used to cover parchments with artistic writing and adorn them with such marvelous ornamentation. I wrote the old uncial, Gothic letters, and the classical antiqua, and my eyes were trained by the ancient models. To produce next to the written and drawn letters a well-set book page was a welcome task to me. This work gave me an eye for my later assignment, the creation of the graphic aspect of the publishing house.

In addition to my studies, those years meant being in love with being in love. I believe there hardly was a day without inner excitements, expectations, and tensions. It was not so much that I was in love with a specific person but rather the state of being in love *per se* that filled me with high spirits and charged me with energy. It was like a game, a test, a preparation for my future life.

The friends of the house, everyone of the "people" who had in those years given the little girl's hair a friendly stroke and written such beautiful verses in her poetry album— by and by, they turned into new personalities toward whom I had to take a stand, whose works I became acquainted with, and whose greatness and importance I became aware of.

Part Two
What Life Has Brought Me

13
A Family and Home of My Own. My Three Daughters. Death of My Father

The times of my poetry album were past. I had awakened to life. Everything around me seemed full of wonder and promise. The fullness of phenomena knew no bounds and the world was open to me; I only needed to reach for it.

At that point happened the encounter with the human being with whom I was to share my future life. "He" came from a different environment, being a surgeon at a large hospital in east Berlin. He already was in charge of his own hospital ward and bore a great deal of responsibility. In his free time he played the violin and the viola, and after his gruelling occupation and an hour's bus ride he did not shrink from playing chamber music with me and my friends. His calm and manly resoluteness, his goodness and his love enveloped me and captivated me completely. Both of us knew very soon that life had destined us for each other.

Now it was a matter of making our decision clear to my parents, but that was no easy task. Both of them, especially my father, still believed that they had a claim of ownership to their children, and the idea of losing me to "someone" was hard to bear for my father.

Hence we had to meet secretly at the country estate of mutual friends who had introduced us to each other in order to have heart-to-heart talks and make our decisions. However, soon enough the secret was revealed to my parents. They immediately removed me from Berlin and took me along on a trip to Bad Gastein, strictly forbidding me to be in contact with "him." It was an anxious waiting period for both of us, and we lived only from letter to letter which we smuggled to each other in roundabout fashion.

After our return to Berlin my father had the decisive conversation with "him," asking him whether he would consider exchanging his profession of surgeon for that of a publisher. "He" was profoundly taken aback and also deeply touched by this unexpected proposal, and so he asked for time to consider. He had been so wedded to his medical profession that he could not imagine any other life. But the realization that a life's task was waiting for him and for "us"— namely, to safeguard the continued existence of the publishing house— won out, and he accepted the idea of becoming my father's successor. What a benign providence had been at work there! But for him the S. Fischer family and publishing house would have fallen into the hands of the Nazis eight years later!

My father personally initiated Gottfried into the secrets of a publishing house and into the profession of a publisher. He sat opposite my father in his office and experienced the daily routine, the conversations, planning sessions, discussions, and decisions. Soon he had a clear picture of what was expected of him. His unprejudiced, modest and knowing way of dealing with people, even if they were such famous and difficult authors as Gerhart Hauptmann and Thomas Mann, removed all prejudices against the neophyte.

I had a big step to take: I was to exchange my freedom, the life that had hitherto belonged only to me, for the constraints of a marriage. There was something awe-inspiring about the finality of this step— but my joy at the good fortune that was now coming my way was greater and stronger than everything else. Gottfried exuded a great confidence that captivated me, and so we took this step together into a new life that very soon took its normal course after the tremendous wedding given us by my parents.

Thus began our first years of marriage in which each of us attempted to get to know the other and our three children were born. Getting to know each other and at the same time becoming parents was not a simple matter, and added to this were the difficult first years for Gottfried in his new profession of publisher. It was not easy for him and it took infinite patience to grow into this complex structure of the publishing house step by step and to have to start all over again after the independence he had already gained as a medical doctor. It soon turned out, however, that all would go well and that he was quickly growing into a world that was new to him. His medical and human experience soon made him an adviser to the authors whom he was able to help in their often difficult situations. After a short time Gottfried moved to the top of the firm next to my father, whose burden he sought to ease more and more.

Our apartment, which was located around the corner from my parental home, soon became a second center of the publishing family, and a circle of younger writers and artists gathered around us: Carl Zuckmayer, Kurt Heuser, Alexander Lernet-Holenia, Manfred Hausmann, Joachim Maass, Joseph Roth, Klaus Mann, Ernst Toller, Walter Mehring, and Erwin Piscator, who created a modern theater for the young dramatists in the Berliner Volksbühne. The painter George Grosz was a particular friend of ours. Writers from all over the world, especially France, came to see us: Jean Giraudoux, Jean Richard Bloch, René Crevel, Pierre Bertaux, Pierre Viénot, Raymond Aron. One day we were visited by a son of Leon Trotzki, who was then living in exile and writing his memoirs for the S. Fischer Verlag at the suggestion of my father.

Naturally, music was part of our new life as well. I had formed a small chamber orchestra with my friends, and Gottfried joined it with his viola, which had become a "sacred" instrument to us, for it had brought us together.

Our three daughters were growing up. What joy they gave us, and what discoveries and experiences there were every day! How different they were from one another— like contrapuntal variations on a theme.

Gaby, our oldest daughter, was a pensive and dreamy creature. We often observed her sitting in a corner of her room, listening; this attentive listening and thinking was to remain peculiar to her even later, when she became grown-up. She displayed a liking for the arts; she painted, studied music, and developed an exceedingly fine ear and understanding for the music world of Mozart.

Gisi, our second daughter, had a diametrically opposed temperament. From childhood on she was an extremely alert personality, saw and noticed everything around her, and took an active interest in everything. She breezed through school; I rarely saw her do any homework, though she was always among the best pupils. She loved games and sports, had many friends and beaux, and was a connoisseur of human nature. Even as an adolescent she was something like a counseling center for the problems of her fellow pupils. She observed people minutely and was able to amuse an audience with her very witty initiation of their manner of speech. Her humor and her imagination, both of which were already developed when she was a little child, caused Thomas Mann to call her, at age three, "little Herr Fischer."

Annette, our youngest daughter, was from the moment of birth harmony personified. Born a Libra, she was a contented and always smiling baby that never cried, and so our neighbors did not become aware of her existence until months after her birth. She remained a cheerful child that was in tune with the world around her and was surprised when there were squabbles among her older sisters. She always appeared to us like a gift from heaven, and she won the heart of every person that crossed her path.

We were vouchsafed a few more years of peaceful family life in our young marriage in the midst of the turbulent and vitality-charged atmosphere of Berlin. Work at the publishing house carried over into domestic life, and not a day or evening passed on which there were no joint consultations and planning sessions with my parents. We had gradually become the young publishing couple, and my relationship with our authors, particularly the "grand old man" Thomas Mann, also assumed a different aspect.

The year 1929 brought him and us the greatest success. Two important events occurred: He was awarded the Nobel Prize for his novel *Buddenbrooks* and the S. Fischer Verlag had previously published a clothbound popular edition of this great, voluminous novel that became a runaway bestseller at only 2.85 marks. Sales figures mounted from day to day; after two months the book had sold 600,000 copies, and soon thereafter more than a million copies were in print.

This external good fortune was not to last long, however. The signals of the impending storm increased, and the stratagems of the Nazis, who had hitherto worked underground, became ever stronger, more distinct, and more official. While Thomas Mann was delivering a lecture, "Appeal to Reason," in the Beethovensaal in Berlin on October 17, 1930, he was interrupted by furious abuse from the Nazis scattered through the audience. We had to help him leave the hall by a rear exit to keep him from being physically attacked. This was the beginning of the end of the carefree years that my husband and I were able to spend at the side of my father.

Until our emigration in late 1935 we had to live with daily and nightly threats from the Nazis, who had come to power in 1933, and this was hard to bear in our last years in Berlin. Often the fear that Hitler's murderous brown gangs would break into our house would wake us up in the middle of the night, for this is what had happened to many people we knew. Then we would take our bedding under our arms and spend the night with friends. We had, of course, tried every day to find out how we could leave this witches' cauldron as soon as possible. As long as my father was alive, it was impossible to think of emigrating. He would not even hear of transferring part of his property to a foreign country— while that was still possible, that is— and to turn his back on his publishing house and on Germany was inconceivable to him. Thus we had to stick it out for the time being.

In the evening we would read to each other Thomas Mann's *Die Geschichten Jaakobs* (The Tales of Jacob) from the proofsheets. What comforting strength emanated from this great work! At that time I wrote the author:

. . . Today, at a time of great inner anguish, and in the daily struggle for existence, your work has blended with the unshakable and exemplary elements of your figure and has become a support to me . . . I believe that if someone carries and nurtures such treasures within him, the world cannot harm him. For this I must thank you. (Berlin, June 1935).

After the death of my father in October 1934 Gottfried took over the direction of the S. Fischer Verlag. Thomas Mann left Germany and lived in exile. It was a stroke of fortune and a blessing that my father had been spared the conscious experience of the irruption of barbarism into the country that he had loved and for which he had worked. Thomas Mann's last two letters to S. Fischer testify to their close relationship:

Küsnacht, November 18, 1933

Dear Mr. Fischer, Your letter deeply touched me and filled me again with the most respectful and most amicable feelings for you. We admire you for the sovereign wisdom with which you look at things and for your perdurable activity. Your life has been long, full, and basically blessed. This will remain so till the end, for even the most insane and most adverse circumstances cannot substantially change the basic character of a life. We two really have nothing to complain about, even though we are now being hit with some unavoidable things. Life has been kind to us, and even though, as Goethe says, "man must be ruined again," I am confident that even there we shall get off lightly. I now find myself in exile— oh well, I never dreamt of this and I certainly was not born for it, but it was meant to be. Where do we go from here?

"I did not think it was right," writes Elisa Wille in her memoirs, "when I read and heard here or there that Wagner knew visible sorrows of exile in Zurich. The banished man was respected by all; he lived in the safety of his own hearth and had friends who stood up for him." . . . Well, then, Zurich is not so bad, and for you, too, the real thing will shine through to the end— which is, I hope, far away. In the safety of my "own hearth" I am working on my "Götterdämmerung," the Egyptian volume of Joseph und seine Brüder (Joseph and His Brothers). People will have to chew for a while longer on the prehistory of "Das Rheingold," and so there is no hurry for "Young Siegfried" to appear. Cordial regards from your Thomas Mann.

And here are his last lines to my father:

Küsnacht, August 23, 1934.

Dear Mr. Fischer, I was very touched by the friendly letter which you recently dictated in the forest; I have read it repeatedly. Above all, I am pleased that Freudenstadt is doing you good and that this peaceful place is letting you face the Fall hopefully. I have always loved the Black Forest, though I am not acquainted with the part in which you are staying now. But since that time we were together on the Feldberg (remember, it was the inflationary period), I have on a number of occasions driven to the Titisee area, and the enchanted forest of black fir trees with the fine undergrowth of fern is among my dearest memories . . . You say that you are one of the old ones, but all of us are, you no more than I, and experiences are old and keep recurring. In 1811 Goethe said to Boisserée: "You would not believe how maddening it is for us old people to have to watch the world around us decay and return to its elements, so that, God knows when, something new may come from it." Does this not sound quite familiar to us? Most cordial regards and wishes for you and yours, your Thomas Mann.

A scant two months after Thomas Mann's last letter to him my father was released from his sufferings. His death seemed to us like a release from the "primal fears" that had beset him during his last years. He died on October 16, 1934 in our Grunewald house. The "blessing" had remained upon him and had preserved him from all the brutalities that the near future was to bring to his family and his publishing house.

14
Emigration to Vienna. Founding of the Bermann-Fischer Verlag. New Friends. Escape from the Gestapo

After extremely difficult negotiations with the Ministry of Propaganda we succeeded in 1935 in transferring a large part of our publishing house, along with the rights and the inventory of the authors prohibited or "undesired" by the Nazis, to Vienna and in leaving Germany. It was a powerful and liberating feeling to have escaped all that!

The newly opened Bermann-Fischer Verlag was immediately at the center of Viennese literary life. We had found a small old house in the Viennese district of Hietzing near the Schönbrunn Castle. The house at Wattmanngasse No. 11 was painted a Maria Theresia yellow and had a cast-iron balcony with baroque ornaments facing the street as well as an old, stone-paved courtyard adjoining a wild garden. The children called it *Klebehaus* (glue house), since it was one of a row of similar small yellow houses. The rooms were nicely proportioned. The ground-floor library was filled from floor to ceiling with the books we had brought from Germany— with first editions, manuscripts, and collections of letters, the biggest among them the correspondence between Thomas Mann and my husband. Our furniture, and especially the paintings from my parents' collection that we had been able to save when we emigrated, made this house a beautiful and livable home for us. It soon became a gathering place for old and new Viennese friends, and many a friend from "the outside" came to visit us.

My domain in this house was on the second floor. There I had turned two small rooms into a large music room with two grand pianos. On the wall hung El Greco's "Sudarium of Saint Veronica," a picture that cast its spell on me whenever I looked at it. I regularly played music with our friend Victor Zuckerkandl, the musicologist, literary historian, and pianist, and I received much musical knowledge from him. He became an editor and literary advisor in our publishing house.

The family of the composer Prohaska lived next door to our garden. The three brothers were all musicians who played many instruments, and they lived in the house in which Johann Strauss had composed his operetta *Die Fledermaus.* The one that played the cello frequently came over the fence with his viola da gamba, and I played with him on my 1790 clavichord that I had been able to bring along from Berlin and that I had to tune daily with its old key.

On July 6, 1936, Thomas Mann reported to my mother about his first visit to our new home:

Dear Mrs. Fischer, . . . Your letter was forwarded to me in Budapest where we spent a number of colorful and amusing days. After that came Vienna, which was also rich in impressions . . . I enjoy the thought that you will soon be able to see with your own eyes how nicely your children have fixed up their home in Vienna. We again spent charming hours in their nest, and the city charmed us all over again despite stink bombs at a performance of Tristan . . .

Yes, we shared a bad experience in Vienna. After Thomas Mann had read from his *Joseph in Ägypten* in the smaller hall of the Konzerthaus, we walked together to the State Opera where Bruno Walter was conducting Thomas Mann's favorite opera, *Tristan und Isolde.* He himself described our experience in a letter to his brother Heinrich dated July 2, 1936:

. . . After my reading we caught the third act of Tristan under Walter in an opera house that smelled terrible. The Nazis had thrown some stink bombs, but the performance continued— finally only

with the orchestral portion, for the singer portraying Isolde, who had vomited during the intermission, only made a fine gesture of incapacity and no longer rose from Tristan's corpse . . .

We found a half-empty opera house almost abandoned by the audience, and in Walter's box his weeping wife. In this weird atmosphere we listened to the conclusion of the opera, conducted by Walter with the last of his strength, but with all the greater devotion.

In January of 1937 Thomas Mann again gave a reading in Vienna and visited us in our house in Hietzing. He said that he wanted to read to us something he had just written. Thus we were the first to have the privilege of hearing from his mouth the document that later became famous. I can still see him before me, taking a seat at the little baroque desk and putting on his glasses slowly and carefully before he began to read. It was his answer to the "Dean of the Philosophical Faculty of the University of Bonn" who had recently stripped him of his honorary doctorate— a powerful indictment of the Hitler regime: " . . . To what a pass, in less than four years, have they brought Germany! Ruined, sucked dry body and soul by armaments with which they threaten the whole world, holding up the whole world and hindering it in its real tasks of peace . . . "

Our Viennese circle of friends had increased considerably. Old friends like Gerty von Hofmannsthal, the Beer-Hofmanns, Lernet-Holenia, Heini Schnitzler, and the Zuckmayers (who were living at Henndorf near Salzburg) were joined by new ones. Our circle was expanded by the publisher Paul Zsolnay and his wife Anna (the daughter of Gustav Mahler), Robert Musil, Egon Friedell, Ödön von Horváth, Fritz Stiedry, and Bruno Walter (who had also left Germany). A wine party in the little, ivy-encircled yard of our Hietzing house, where we had put up wooden tables and benches and served our guests by candlelight, still reflected lighthearted Viennese gaiety and was crowned by the appearance of Franz and Alma Werfel. Alma and "Franzl" were a unique pair— each an artist who really understood and inspired the other. Both lived in the world of music and the world of literature. One simply had to love Franzl; he was a man of love— love of life, love of people, and love of the whole world surrounding him. He had a big heart and believed in the overcoming of evil and the victory of good. In his work he fought for his belief.

Alma was a lady of great stature. Even her outward appearance was impressive, and the aura of her personality was to become fateful for many artists. She spun her multifarious webs not only in Viennese society but in the intrigue-ridden circles of the church and politics as well. She had access to all dignitaries and exerted her influence as though she were living at the time of the courts and their power. With her great craving for recognition and her almost masculine resoluteness she could have been a Medici in Renaissance Florence. Through her passion for art she dominated the artists whom she knew how to bind to herself. Hosts of great musicians, painters, and poets had close ties to her. The painter Gustav Klimt was in love with her when she was still almost a child, and the musician Zemlinsky, who discovered her great musical talent and taught her, wanted to marry her when she was an adolescent. He brought her together with Gustav Mahler, whose wife she became at age 23. When Mahler died, she was 32 years old— a young, beautiful woman. Later she told us about her passion for the young painter Oskar Kokoschka, who had wrested her from her unhappy second marriage to Walter Gropius, until she met Franz Werfel six years later. For both of them it was a great love at first sight. Their first encounter was under the sign of the music that bound them together. He loved Mahler's music and sang, and she accompanied him. "We exulted music," she wrote later. My mother remembered an evening at Grunewald on which Wassermann brought the two along for the first time: "Werfel was smitten like a page boy; he always blushed when Alma spoke to him." It was in 1917, when Alma had met Franz Werfel in Vienna; at the time Werfel was 27 and Alma 38. "Werfel is a stocky man with sensual lips, beautiful big blue eyes, and a Goethean forehead"— that is how she described him.

He had two different voices— a musical speaking voice and a passionate vibrant reciting voice with which he presented his poems, almost singing as he declaimed them.

Possessed by an uncompromising love of truth, he worked on himself with unsparing self-criticism. His union with Alma became his destiny. Her dominant personality was a great weight for so tender and sensitive a poet's soul as his, but she took in hand his outer life, which he was apt to fritter away between temptations and distractions. He found it hard, however, to do creative work when she was around, and thus he usually fled to some hotel room in order to complete his great novels in perfect solitude— "inspired by Alma's genius from afar."

Our life in our Hietzing house in Vienna still went on undisturbed, though the signs of approaching disaster were multiplying. For as long as it was possible, the Viennese remained true to their tradition of "live and let live"—filling the theaters and concert halls and celebrating feasts together. The Werfels' house on the Hohe Warte was at that time an artistic center of Vienna, and Alma's parties in her villa, whose walls were decorated with Mahler's musical manuscripts, were a favorite meeting place of great conductors, poets, writers, and artists from all over the world. The last of those sumptuous feasts in which we participated was also to be the last before the "end" and a farewell to the "old" world.

One day Hitler's troops stood at the border. At noon on March 13, 1938 our telephone rang; a friend who was close to Chancellor Schuschnigg informed us of his resignation. The German army had started its invasion. We immediately packed the essentials. To this day I can see our three children—seven, nine, and eleven at the time— dressed for traveling and waiting in surprise for what the future might bring. Several strokes of luck helped us out of the terrible danger—particularly our still valid German passports that enabled us to pass the already existing checkpoints at the Vienna railroad station and later the Austro-Italian border. Thus all five of us reached Italy safely. Two days later the Gestapo already occupied our house in Hietzing. Once again we had escaped by the skin of our teeth.

This time everything was really lost. All that our house contained was confiscated and later sold off at the Dorotheum, the state-owned auction house. Our publishing firm was placed in the hands of a Nazi engineer who specialized in bridge-building, and some time later it was closed. The entire inventory was in the hands of the Nazis. We had to start all over again. Once more a kindly fate guided our steps and led us to Sweden, where the large Bonnier publishing house took us under its wings. The Bermann-Fischer Verlag— which, thank goodness, had retained its authors' rights— resumed its work there. All of Europe, parts of which were occupied by Hitler's troops, anxiously awaited the things to come.

15

New Beginning in Stockholm. The Congress that Never Took Place. War Breaks Out

Sweden, the land of social justice and general prosperity, the homeland of Alfred Nobel, who endowed those prizes, opened its doors to us. In May 1938 we received permission from the Swedish government to settle in Stockholm and continue our publishing house there. The Swedish press welcomed the new enterprise. We opened our offices in the center of the city and immediately resumed our work with some of our collaborators who had been rescued from Vienna, among them our loyal friend and advisor Victor Zuckerkandl. In short order new books were completed, including such important ones as a new edition of a biography of Madame Curie, Carl Zuckmayer's *Herr über Leben und Tod* (Master over Life and Death), Stefan Zweig's only completed novel *Ungeduld des Herzens* (Beware of Pity), and a volume of Thomas Mann's essays (Listen, Europe).

Here, in extreme northern Europe, far away from the murderous Nazi hordes, we thought we were permanently safe. In this peaceful country, where everything still went on in quiet and orderly fashion and the taciturn and reserved people had received us with kindness and helpfulness, we started a new life that was filled with the rebuilding of our destroyed publishing house and the raising of our daughters. In the meantime our family had been augmented by a new member: we had taken in the twelve-year old son of Gottfried's sister, whose parents had been transported to a concentration camp. Sweden became his new home; he had professional success and is now leading a happy life there with his wife and children.

We found an apartment in a settlement located on the outskirts of Stockholm. Its big windows overlooked green lawns in the middle of the wide road that led to an extensive field. For the children, who soon spoke Swedish fluently, it was an ideal playground during the short daylight hours of fall and winter. In the summer months, however, we all moved to Dalarö, a beautiful, quiet place in the Skärgarden, where the Bonniers had made their summer home available to us. Every day Gottfried would drive our little car to his office on Stureplan in Stockholm. I took long hikes with the children or climbed down the steep cliffs with them to the sea. The Skärgarden is one of the glories of this world. Thousands of small rocky islands, some of them with thick woods, line the Swedish coast. We would spend whole days with the children on those Robinson Crusoe islands, enjoying the profound peace of a fortunate country. The children attended a French school and during the long winter months developed into excellent skaters.

Our friendship with Fritz Busch brought music to our home again:

In his book *Bedroht-Bewahrt* (Threatened— Preserved), Gottfried wrote:

Fritz Busch had come to Stockholm from Argentina, the first stage of his emigration, and became active as regular guest conductor of the Philharmonic Orchestra and at the opera. In 1933 he had left Dresden, where he had been general music director of the opera, as a protest against the encroachments of the Nazi party, just like his brother Adolf, the famous violinist, who had also turned his back on Hitler's Germany. Fritz Busch was one of the few now directly threatened German artists who left voluntarily, motivated by profound hatred of the destroyers of German culture and aban-

doning their possessions and their careers, and who then represented its best in foreign countries.

Busch's concerts and performances with the extraordinary ensemble of the Stockholm Opera are among our most beautiful memories of those years. I shall never forget his Stockholm Così fan tutte, an opera he had performed a short time previously in Glyndebourne, with his friend Carl Ebert as director. All that can be lovable in a human being was combined in him. He was open and straightforward, free from the intrigues that exist among conductors no less than in many other professions. His warm cordiality and his humor, coupled with a healthy skepticism toward uncritical thinking and irrational speculation, led to an amicable relationship between us, Busch, and his wife, who had a great knowledge of artistic matters but also managed to regulate the practical sides of her family's life.

Fritz Busch was wholly committed to music, and it seemed to me as though he were made of music. Those were happy hours when he sat down at the grand piano to play four-hands with me. How he enjoyed everything we played! He could never get his fill of Schubert's *Fantasie,* and we always had to repeat his *Grand Rondeau* and his marches. He took Mozart's Sonata in D-major at breakneck speed, and Mozart's *Tema con Variazioni* was his favorite piece. Busch often visited us, usually in the evening after strenuous rehearsals. When we did not make music, he had us tell him about our publishing activities, for he also had a burning interest in literature.

In the meantime we had resumed contact with our authors, who were scattered all over the world. Thomas Mann and Zuckmayer were in America, Stefan Zweig in England, the Werfels in France, Joachim Maass en route to the United States. With the two exile publishers active in Holland, Albert de Lange under the direction of Walter Landauer and Querido under Fritz Landshoff, we agreed on a certain collaboration. Our shared production and distribution found visible expression in the Forum-Bücherei, a paperback series.

We were vouchsafed two happy and peaceful years in Sweden. At that time we had no idea that these would only be part of our long odyssey.

In late August 1939 the festive opening of the International PEN Congress took place in the Stockholm City Hall, a building of unique architectural beauty. Thomas Mann was among the great authors who had come from all over the world. In his honor we arranged a small reception in the house at Dalarö together with our partner Bonnier, Mann's Swedish publisher. Gottfried welcomed him with these words:

We are delighted to be able to welcome Dr. Mann and his dear wife as well as all of you here in our buon retiro, in the circle of our magnanimous helpers in a country that received us so hospitably. When after the loss of our second homeland the active helpfulness of the house of Bonnier enabled us to settle here, we were deeply touched by this confidence in our cause. Our cause— that is the cause of the spirit, that is the cause of gathering and preserving the values that are threatening to fall prey to the oblivion and evanescence of exile, and of rebuilding what has been destroyed. Above all else it is your great work, my dear Mr. Mann, that is the object of our entire care. In accordance with your words we will confidently believe that the cause of freedom and right will be victorious, confidently believe that we shall succeed in preserving the values for which we are fighting for better times.

The aforementioned congress, however, never took place. Hitler had already invaded Poland, whereupon England and France had declared war on Germany. The Manns took the next plane to England to try to find a boat back to the United States from Southampton. We were happy to receive word from Katia of their arrival in England, because the previous day the same plane had been shot at by the Nazis while flying over Germany. After their landing in the U. S., Mann wired us: "Escaped safely; grateful wishes, Thomas Mann."

In a letter from Princeton dated September 22, 1939 he wrote:

It is now almost like a dream to be here again and to follow the unpredictable European events from such a distance. Even so it remains oppressive enough, and at my age I must wonder whether I shall be able to set foot on the other shore in this life . . . We hope with all our heart that you will be able to carry out your business plans, albeit in modified form. After all, it seems entirely possible that Sweden might even benefit from the increasingly apparent rivalry between the horrendous giants Fasolt and Fafner by remaining unmolested by the two . . . Give my cordial regards to your family and the Bonniers. That last evening seems so long ago and is as though enveloped in a dreamlike veil. I hope the contact between us will never be broken . . . In any event, it is fine and useful that we have seen one another and had a heart-to-heart talk before this prolonged affliction. Your Thomas Mann.

Shortly thereafter Thomas Mann's new novel *Lotte in Weimar* (The Beloved Returns), appeared in the Bermann-Fischer Verlag in Stockholm. On the occasion of its publication I chose an excerpt from it and wrote it for him on parchment. He thanked me in a letter:

65 Stockton St., Princeton, N.J., January 14, 1940.

Dear Tutti, with your fine artistic manuscript from and about Lotte in Weimar you have given me extraordinary pleasure, and I must immediately give you my heartfelt thanks for it. The parchment which you made with monastic care will be the showpiece of the little collection of documents that I have started on this subject. It cannot, of course, be very substantial, for the response has not been multivoiced . . . But there are a few letters from readers who have been moved, and all in all I do have the impression that some joy has been bound into the book that is released when it comes in contact with readers still receptive to such things. Goethe himself once said that the all-important thing about a work of art is the conception. And right from the start there was something attractive about the conception that endured and seems to have prevailed even in the face of boring aspects of the execution. We recently wrote to old Mr. Bonnier to tell him with what concern, suspense, and anxiety we always watch the development of things in northern Europe and thus the fate of all of you. What is torturous and preposterous about all this is that the little states cling to their "neutrality" until one of them really gets it in the neck! As though neutrality made any sense and these nations could not be expected to know on which side all of them should stand together in their own interests!

I hope you have spent a happy northern 'jul' festival with your charming children! (Is it really still called 'jul' up there?) We all started the New Year with suspense and expectations mingled of hope and fear. What will it bring? Surely not yet the end of the radical process that is in progress. But 1940 is probably bound to advance this process considerably and amidst horrors. In the meantime we must try to fill our days with as many worthy activities as possible that will contribute to a better future. Cordial regards to all of you! Your Thomas Mann.

In my reply to him, dated April 2, 1940, censorship led me to speak only very cautiously of the difficult and terrifying events that preceded our flights to the U.S.:

Dear Doctor Mann, for a long time I have wanted to thank you for your kind letter of January in which you told me that I was able to give you pleasure with the little parchment. You in turn gave me great and enduring pleasure with your letter.

In the meantime the year 1940 has developed in many respects, not all of them favorable, and I suppose it will harbor many more terrors for us. The second Munich Peace was and is a misfortune, and it is particularly oppressive for this country physically and psychically. We have quite exciting weeks behind us in which we were ready to leave; our bags have been packed and, in keeping with the quickly changing circumstances, will remain so.

We spent a very nice 'jul' (which is here still celebrated in altogether heathen fashion with a 'jul' billygoat) and also a still very winterly 'pask' (Easter) with the children. This gang finds life so wonderful and full of adventure and makes the best of all situations, and so we cannot help but do the same. And thus I am heeding your fine statement at the end of your letter that one ought to try to fill one's days with as many worthy activities as possible that will contribute to a better future, and I am trying to do my share in a small way. Heartfelt wishes for you and Frau Katia, Tutti.

We found it alarming to realize that the terror in Germany and Hitler's aggressions basically did not change the Germanophile attitude of the Swedish citizenry. The very same phrases that members of the German middle class had used by way of excusing and exonerating themselves in the face of the excesses of Nazism were now employed by the Swedes in an effort to avoid giving up their accustomed and comfortable relations with Germany. That is how the misfortune started everywhere: indolence, business, neutrality. Thus the typical pattern until the outbreak of the war was that every Nazi excess— the pogroms of November 1938, the occupation of Czechoslovakia, etc.— first aroused palpable indignation, but that this abated after a few days and was forgotten after a few weeks. It was as though the middle class, which had grown up on the soil of democracy and derived its strength and its privileges from it, had taken leave of its senses and was on the point of surrendering to dictatorship. Fortunately it was different with the Swedish workers. They were proud, class-conscious, educated, and clearly anti-Nazi, for they knew what danger to their rights Nazism represented.

German propaganda flourished in the country. The German travel bureau on a Stockholm main street disseminated an abundance of political lies and shameless misinformation. Its subversive activities increased enormously when it became quite obvious that the Swedish government was no longer doing anything about them. But the Swedish police took all the more vigorous action against "British spies." In point of fact, it was the government and the royal house that determined the pro-Nazi attitude of the country in those bad times. To us this attitude became increasingly unbearable and menacing. We wanted to leave the country, leave Europe! There no longer was any other way out for us. To get to America in those days, however, it was no longer possible to use the usual westward route, because all sea routes and air traffic over the Atlantic were closed. Thus we had no other choice but to prepare to go half-way around the world, via Russia and Japan. Securing the necessary visas for the countries through which we had to pass was not an easy matter.

What would life in the "New World" be like for us? What was this "New World"? We were full of curiosity, but it was lying ahead of us in darkness. We received only a first inkling of it through a new friend we had made in Sweden and who had visited us in Stockholm. This new friend was an American named Hendrik Willem van Loon, a unique personality, a friend and schoolmate of Franklin D. Roosevelt, a writer and fighter for human rights and freedom which he preached from the pulpits of churches, proclaimed over the radio networks of America, and defended with his pen. He was a man with a big heart for those in need, and he became a rescue station for uprooted people.

"We shall break with Germany; it would be the best thing that possibly can happen," he wrote us (in English) in 1938 to Stockholm, and in the midst of cries for help from emigrants all over the world he moaned: "Why does not somebody shoot them— him— them? I have given up all my literary work to devote myself entirely to the anti-Hitler agitation . . . There is only one thing to do: get us into war with Germany. Chamberlain betrayed civilization in Munich. We will have to save it . . . but it will be a difficult job . . . "

On April 22, 1939 we received the following (English) letter:

Old Greenwich, Conn., April 10, 1939

Monday morning April tenth and we are getting ready for war . . . unless Chamberlain and Daladier sell us out deliberately we will have war this week and this is that. It had better come or all of us shall go completely and hopelessly crazy . . . which is undoubtedly part of the Hitler scheme. I have sent long and complicated cables . . . let me know if you have received the permission to come . . . if not I shall go over the heads of all officials and go directly to the Prime Minister. Please let me know, for your silence frightens me that something may have gone wrong . . . I do very little writing being too busy trying to make our people wake up and get ready for the war which we will have to fight . . . So here is merely that we love you as always and when everything goes wrong, we have room to take you all in . . . we have enough places for beds and an icebox full of food and a cat and a dog for the kids . . . all our love H.

He became our "good angel" in the gloomy last winter that we still had to spend in Europe. In Sweden we felt isolated and forsaken as though on an island surrounded by Hitler's brown hordes. Hendrik was most solicitous about us and did everything to obtain American visas for us. On November 27, 1939 he wrote (in English):

Old Greenwich, Conn., November 27, 1939

. . . It will have to come to open warfare and we are doing everything we can do to reach that point as soon as possible. I never realized that one could be as tired as I am just now, but I will have to get my rest afterwards. The situation is too ghastly . . . God help us all . . . All our love to you and our deepest understanding. Hendrik Willem.

16
In Police Custody. New Dangers. Hendrik Willem van Loon, the Saving Angel

Through our own efforts and with Hendrik's aid we finally received American visitors' visas. We could hardly wait to leave the continent of Europe, surrounded as it was by Hitler's storm troops. But Hendrik's worries about us were to prove justified, for a bad blow caught us unawares. Gottfried had always had multifarious relations with England, and British publishers and authors had been among our friends. It was known that all his sympathies in this war were on the side of the allies. As a publisher he was a thorn in the flesh of pro-Nazi circles, and an opportunity to get him out of the way easily presented itself. Together with Swedish friends and British ones living in Stockholm he helped forward anti-Nazi propaganda material to Germany by making available his large file of German addresses. But someone had revealed his anti-Nazi activities, and one evening the Swedish criminal police entered our home, searched the entire apartment, and ordered Gottfried to come with them. First they took him to the office, which they also searched, and then to the Stockholm police prison. Those were terrible days of uncertainty for us. For weeks and months Gottfried endured the torments of isolation and worry about our well-being. Any day it could have occurred to Hitler to occupy Sweden as well— Norway was already in his hands— and that would certainly have been the end of all of us. Our well-prepared journey to the United States was now completely up in the air. There began an ordeal of waiting under this constant threat. I ran from offices to ministries, to newspaper offices, and to prominent people of all kinds in order to publicize the scandal of Gottfried's arrest. But the people seemed as though paralyzed; under the constantly mounting influence of the victory-intoxicated Nazis, who increasingly threw their weight around in Sweden, no one dared to champion Gottfried's freedom publicly. Everywhere the famous "neutrality" prevailed! Hans Busch, the son of Fritz Busch, was one of the few people who stood by me in the difficult months in which Gottfried was in custody.

Finally, after five terrible days of uncertainty about his fate, I received Gottfried's first sign of life from detention:

Rannsankningsfängelse, Stokholm, April 24, 1940. Dearest, finally good news. Please visit me tomorrow morning, Thursday, at 10. See Constable Falander, Room 413 (Telephone Police 179). I believe everything is all right now, and I am longing to see you. Greetings to the children and mother and Hilla and Hans. G."

Having been permitted to see each other for only a few minutes, I wrote him on May 1:

"Dearest, we have not been able to see each other or speak with each other for such a long time that I will try to be close to you in this way. I am sure you know that our thoughts are always with you, and you must sense that I wonder every hour and every minute how you are and how you are enduring your isolation. I have courage and am certain that everything will go well, and I want to share some of this certainty and this courage with you! The children are very sweet and always inquire about you. Gaby dreamed today that you were with us again, and surely that is a good omen. They help me get through the long days, which seem so endless without you . . ."

Then I heard nothing from him for two weeks. It later turned out that the letters he wrote during that period were not forwarded. His next letter from jail was dated May 8:

Dearest, to get a letter from you at the end of a long day is a great joy and happiness. Even though I have got accustomed to this situa-

tion and have become completely absorbed in reading and thinking, moments of disquiet keep recurring, and the cause is always the same: Shall I manage to get all of you to the United States in time? After all, I am so cut off from my surroundings that I am absolutely ignorant of the political situation. For that matter, I have little reason to trust the judgment of others. Thus a letter from you is always a great reassurance at such moments . . .

I am just reading The Brothers Karamazov. I had almost forgotten the book, but it is shaking me up completely. It strikes me as especially strange that the Russian Revolution did not occur until almost forty years after Dostoievski and Tolstoi. It is already there in Karamazov and Anna Karenina— with uncanny exactitude. Dearest, I keep hoping that I shall soon be able to get out. Be embraced by your G.

On May 10 I sent him this report: "This evening the war entered a frightful phase. The Germans have invaded Holland and Belgium. I wanted you to learn this from me first . . . Perhaps this new blow will bring a decision . . . I believe in us perhaps more ardently now than I have in a long time, and this is due mainly to your wonderful inner strength. I shall have to work very hard to be your match, but you should know that I shall try very hard! . . ." Eight days later he wrote me:

Dearest, since noon today I have been detained "in custody," which means that I am not under arrest. As I understand it, I must await a decision here as to whether I shall be deported. Thus there will be no court trial. I am well; above all, there is more air here. Till soon, your G.

On the same day I wrote him: " . . . We are all well, but the situation at the front must be described as at least serious. Brussels has fallen, and the troops are advancing at a powerful pace. Nevertheless, we continue to believe confidently in our luck; you ought to do the same, shouldn't you? I feel we shall make it, you and I; I am so full of confidence and would like to embrace you to show you that I am! . . . "

On May 20, 1940 Gottfried wrote:

. . . Everything is bearable— the waiting, the feeling that I am being done an injustice, the worry about the dangerous political situation— all that. But what gnaws deep inside me and torments me and pounds at me and cannot be silenced is my longing for you . . . your eyes, your words, your laugh, and the touch of your hand. It is

only this and always this . . . And here is another sentence from War and Peace that touched me because I wrote something quite similar to the children a few days before I read it: "We always think that we are lost if something throws us off our accustomed track. But it is only the beginning of something new and good. As long as we have life, we are fortunate. There is still much, very much ahead of us." How true that is! Only a person who has experienced and suffered a great deal can say this. And do you know that I would not want to be the man I was from 1926 to 1935, not even the one I was between 1936 and 1938? We probably could have coped with things more comfortably without these circuitous routes and efforts. But then we would not have become the human beings we are today. And I find— without being presumptuous or believing that we have reached perfection— I simply find that we have become somewhat better persons, somewhat more knowing and believing ones. And that is why I also believe in the future, our future.

On May 22, 1940 he wrote:

. . . Oh, these doors, steps, voices, half-understood conversations— all this is now becoming meaningful and revealing, but also frightening and menacing. Footsteps are approaching— no, passing . . . another hearing? Suddenly there is a key in the door, it opens— "Your wife!"— oh, what happiness . . . sure, they are doing their duty, and most of them are even humane, friendly, helpful, and courteous. But what do they know about me, our thoughts, experiences, our knowledge?

Well, I will make no demands— i.e., I have come to realize that one cannot demand anything. I face people with the most profound pessimism. They have lost the only moral basic law that religion gave them, for they no longer believe. Only a few remnants of what is legally permitted and prohibited have remained— a few vestiges whose observance and consideration protect a citizen from criminal persecution and permit him to feel that he is highly respectable. Even this remnant disappears when, as happened in Germany, a party manages to attain to a power that abolishes the basic moral laws of good and evil. In no European country would this meet with serious resistance today, least of all in the so-called neutral countries.

Only the endangering of his property is able to rouse a citizen from his slumber of moral indifference. Then, to be sure, he awakens not to morality but merely— or on the contrary— to the realization that he must now quickly seek to attach himself to forces that will protect his property, and he musters an astonishing hatred and brutality toward anything that might hinder him in this pursuit and call upon him to defend the law, morality, or faith. This circumstance has at all times been the sign of the definitive decline of a prevailing social order. Today we are witnessing the end of the bourgeoisie as a ruling class. There is no telling what may come . . .

It must be noted that owing to a peculiar but logical development the defense of the bourgeois countries against subjugation by fascism can be accomplished only by depriving the capitalist bourgeoisie of power, and this stripping of power is being done by this bourgeoisie itself. It escapes into authoritarian state socialism. Thus it has given itself up and seeks protection in the arms of its enemy.

On May 26, 1940 Gottfried wrote me:

. . . Thus I am leading a monastic life. In my cell there are a bed that can be folded into the wall, a small table and a chair, two diagonal wall shelves next to the door full of books, toiletries, and sweets. A small mirror hangs on the wall, and from 3:30 to 6 the sun shines through the latticed window. Opposite me I can see a hospital situated in a big garden; I believe it is the children's hospital at which Dr. Hindmarsh practices. And if I stand on tiptoes, I can see the "Fanggarden". It looks like this:

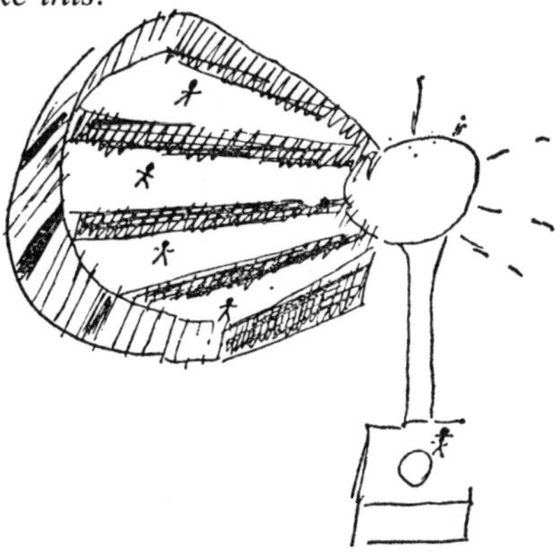

In these acute-angled cages one can run four kilometers in an hour. If one is lucky, the sun will be shining. A guard is enthroned above one to see to it that no one speaks with his neighbor, whom he cannot see. From my window I can see the detainees running around in the morning. I shall never visit a zoo again!

At half past six, a bell rings to wake me. Usually I am up earlier than that and read. Shortly thereafter the door is opened, and with a friendly (really friendly) Gott morgon, the chair with my suit and shoes that was placed outside the previous evening is brought in. There follows a big cleaning in the little basin. By now I am so good at this that I think I get at least as clean as a bath or shower would make me. After my ablutions I make my bed, fold it up, and do some sweeping. At 8 o'clock the trash is picked up. Then comes breakfast. Since I get special rations at my own expense, it consists of coffee and pastry. At 9 o'clock there usually is an hour in the Fanggarden. At 11 o'clock a visitor, or none. At 12 o'clock lunch, usually cold cuts, 5 different items, meat, milk, dessert. Afterwards reading, some sleeping, sometimes sun at 3:30, then again reading and writing, if possible. At 6 o'clock dinner, much too much. In between, by the way, there is again coffee and pastry at 3 o'clock. At 7:30 the bell rings again for undressing, and at 7:45 the chair with my clothes is put outside the door. Then the day is ended. One can still read until 9 o'clock, but after that it is no longer possible. It gets bad only when I start worrying about all of you. Then I run around as if I were in a cage, five steps back and forth, and this makes me feel better. But sometimes that is not so simple. Oh, Tutti, when we can be together, everything will be fine. That is all I am waiting for. From day to day I hope that it may come about. G.

And on June 1, 1940 he wrote:

. . . *If only there weren't this worry about emigrating! . . . What will be the outcome of this war? Is there really to be Hitler tyranny over all of Europe and possibly America as well? For that is what will probably happen if the allies are vanquished and capitulate. I cannot get used to such ideas. If it were a great new idea that was about to conquer the world— certainly that would be plausible. But this barbarism, these wholly destructive forces are supposed to dominate a world? We cannot foresee in what direction things will develop. Teleological thought has no more meaning and justification in history than it does in the natural sciences. Only later observers will be able to see to what final results a development that appeared illogical and impossible to the contemporaries has led, and then they will be able to read some meaning into it. But in the case of the great upheavals in Europe history that would be comparable to a victory of Nazism— the Reformation with all its corollaries, the French Revolution with its consequences up to Napoleon— the contemporaries, at least the perceptive ones, were able to see the background and the new idea (just think of the powerful intellectual forerunners of these movements: Luther, Rousseau, Voltaire, Kant, Schiller, etc. etc.)*

Here, however— where is the idea, the world to be newly conquered, the new class, the new freedom? Nothing— just force, just a fight for pure, brutal power. Utter materialism! Try as I may to be objective, I cannot find anything else. This, then, cannot be victorious— or possess power for a prolonged period of time. Historical analogies probably are no good, but I cannot rid myself of the thought of Napoleon's fate. One must not carry the analogy too far, of course; conditions were different. But Napoleon's betrayal of the French Revolution probably had to be paid for, just as in this case the betrayal of the European development toward humanitarianism will have to be atoned for. This is my last optimism, and I want to preserve it for myself . . .

June 4, 1940.

Dearest, I am not capable at present of making any definite decision for the future— apart from the fact that I want to go to America with all of you as soon as possible. We must be glad that we can live and be together, and we should pray every day that we may be granted this in the future as well. We must live as modestly as possible . . . There remains the hope that this war will not last forever and that conditions will change again. Above all, after a certain period of time I shall probably be in a position to undertake something again and to earn some money. When that will be I cannot predict now. But in the present situation it would be dangerous to plunge into anything adventurous. Let us first observe the situation, bide our time, and then make a well-considered decision. Perhaps we shall move to the country after all and continue our publishing activities in some form. In the near future it may be some literary work that will fascinate me, or it may be medicine. I believe it is too late for the latter. I have hardly any contacts anymore, nor do I have the desire that I once had.

So let us be patient and first lead our own lives, just ours. We now know more than ever what that means. But for the sake of continuity we must first go to the United States. To the extent that anything can be known, I know this, or imagine that I do. After all, what do we know? Or let us say I have a feeling that it would be well and proper to speak with all those people there, particularly Thomas Mann and my business friends. Then, too, I am the only one of the three publishers [Walter Landauer/Allert de Lange and Dr. Fritz Landshoff/Querido, both of Amsterdam, being the other] who would then have a free hand in the U.S. . . . Whether the children should attend college we shall also decide there. We shall then make such decisions in peace. For the time being there is nothing definitive for any European, no matter where, and perhaps this applies to Americans as well, though they are not yet as aware of this as we are.

A great deal will, of course, depend on how long we shall be able to stay in the United States. This, too, we cannot judge until we are there. For now and until our arrival in New York the watchword is this: Get over there as quickly and as safely as possible. There is no thinking of anything else now, and everything else will work out, as it always has up to now.

In those days Gottfried wrote to a friend:

That this time of trial could, in the final analysis, prove invigorating and enriching was due particularly to the constant, unflagging help of my wife, who left no stone unturned to liberate me.

He had to wait until June 24, when the Swedish government finally released him from confinement and passed sentence on him— namely, deportation. since I had in the meantime made all the preparations for our departure, we were able to board the plane for Moscow the very same morning. As Gottfried described it later, "When the soft seat of the Douglas machine received me, in the midst of my family everything that lay behind me already seemed like a dream to me."

17
Involuntary Trip Around the World: Moscow, Japan, Santa Monica. Reunion with Thomas Mann. Old Greenwich, Our New Home

Our first stop after leaving Stockholm was Moscow. There we had to stay overnight in the Hotel Metropol, which was just as run-down as the city itself. Everything was in pitiful condition; there was nothing to buy, and the only displays in the shopwindows were dummies. The wires of the streetcars hung over the roadway in a tangle, and people walked by without looking at one another. It was an oppressive atmosphere, and we were relieved when we were able to board the Trans-Siberian Express. We spent twelve sweltering days crowded together in a compartment, hardly able to escape the roaring loudspeakers on both sides of the carriage or the black soot from the locomotive. On our trip to Vladivostok we did get a glimpse of that immense country, seeing glorious landscapes and for days traversing blooming meadows and wild mountains. Occasionally magnificent peasant types reminiscent of Tolstoyan figures boarded our train. In the small settlements by the railroad tracks we saw the great poverty of the people who, clad in rags, gawked at the train and begged for cigarettes.

We did find accommodations in Vladivostok, but the beds were so filthy that I had to bed our children down on the floor, wrapped in our own sheets. Since not a piece of bread was to be found in the whole city, we went hungry. On the next day, when we were able to cross over to Japan on a spic-and-span Japanese boat, we felt as though reborn and restored to civilization. After three days on the Sea of Japan and a day's train journey through Japan— which at that time was one of the most picturesque and most well-kept countries in the world— we arrived in Yokohama. There a kindly fate once again permitted us to catch the Kamakuru Maru, one of the finest Japanese ocean liners, and cross the Pacific. It was a fabulously beautiful crossing and included one day in Honolulu, the first American "soil" we touched.

The calls of our friend van Loon from the great and free world America reached us and attracted our attention. What openheartedness, what hitherto unknown brotherliness greeted us from there! When we awoke early one radiant morning under the Golden Gate Bridge near San Francisco harbor, our hearts pounded with happiness. We had arrived and reached the shores of this long-yearned-for continent! And already Willem van Loon's first message (in English) was brought on board to us:

Old Greenwich, Conn., June 1940

Dear Friends, for the moment . . . all is well that ends well and you are here and you are safe and we shall see you soon and then we can talk about all the endless adventures of these incredible days . . . The Swedes have lost everything they had ever gained by way of Good Will . . . they have been about as materialistically selfish as any race ever could be and to hell with them says America . . . all their fine trade relations with America and their goodwill in the matter of "Fremdenindustry" is gone . . . but for this we can talk when we meet you here . . . I am working day and night . . . we have got to get America into the war and then all is won . . . otherwise I fear we all will be lost . . . I am glad our friends functioned . . . there is so little one can do these days . . . I can send cables to officials but primo do they arrive and secundo what can the officials do? Not a damn thing . . . so it is mostly good luck and "der grosse

Jehovah", who brought you here and the rest vivavissima voce when we meet you here . . . affectionate regards H.W.

While we were staying for two months in Santa Monica, California, where Thomas Mann had settled, in a spotless little apartment that Frau Katia had found for us, our good fatherly friend Hendrik Willem was thinking of our future abode in the eastern United States. On August 21 he wrote me concerning this (in English):

Old Greenwich, Conn., August 21, 1940

I will tell you what Lady . . . you had better come to New York before the rest of the tribe, for you know what you want and can afford and how far you want to live away from New York . . . of course there are endless little suburbs but personally I would advise you to go as far as Stamford and rather far away from the main road . . . but when you will come we will take you for a day's ride and then you can see for yourself what is what . . . which is never possible in a letter . . .

Of course you are living now in the loveliest and most useless part of America . . . not an idea in a carload . . . nothing but climate and movies . . . but my own guess is that another three weeks will see us in the war . . . that we have made absolutely no preparations . . . yes that too is true but we are a bit further removed from the scene of activities and we will have a chance to set the engines going . . . and once they go they go very fast . . . let us know when you want to come East and then we will find a house for you MIT you . . . love to the family and as ever yours, Hendrik Willen.

And he was as good as his word! When we arrived in New York after crossing part of the wonderful and still so wild giant country with the children in a ten days' automobile trip, Hendrik Willem immediately helped us find a house in Old Greenwich, Connecticut, on Long Island Sound. We have remained loyal to this home to this day.

What kind of New World was this America, then? How often we had heard about America in Europe, and how much we had read about the Americans! A German friend had reported to me about his first impressions:

. . . These Americans . . . There is a great community of spiritual attitude. This uniform friendliness, good humor, and guilelessness, these efforts in behalf of their fellow men are really permanent features . . . The problem of individualism is very peculiar. In their lives and their way of thinking the Americans are the most uniform

people, but as a matter of principle they are so only by free choice. They reserve the right to act just as they please . . . Their lack of tradition extends to the landscape. Sometimes the scenery is beautiful, but it lacks the houses and the villages that might have grown with it. The life of people and the life of nature are not connected in the way we know. The people arrived too late— at a time when ways to live outside nature had already been found. People no longer have any connection with nature.

These were intelligent observations by a European, but one had to have lived in the country, far from the American cities, to find out how strongly Americans are still attached to nature in their own way. Frequently the immense country is still an untamed wilderness, some of which— for example, the Indian Trail that traverses the country from north to south—can only be passed with a machete. Americans are still exposed to the weather and the wilderness in a way very different from Europeans.

The world that awaited us was a very "new" world. There is something lovely, quiet, and dreamy about the small town Old Greenwich in Connecticut, one hour by car from the cosmopolis New York. To this day the New England states on the American east coast display an architectural tradition that is more than two hundred years old. The low, white, wooden houses with their green shutters and the well-tended gardens that adjoin one another without fences and have magnificent old trees are adaptations of old English country houses, and so are the white, wooden churches that go with them.

Such a house had been found for us by our friend Hendrik Willem, and we spent our first winter in it. Immediately after our arrival our neighbors called on us in order to find out how they could be of help. In all matters we received amicable advice. I was taken to see the principal of the elementary school; he welcomed the children in the friendliest manner and did not treat them like strangers at all. He asked them what grade they would like to start with, and all three were placed in a higher grade than was warranted by their age.

Little Annette was now nine, but she had been only four at the beginning of our emigration from Nazi Germany and had been obliged to wander with us from school to school, from country to country, and then half-way around the world. When we had settled in Connecticut, she asked in astonishment: "Where are we going *now?"* That someone could stay and be "at home" somewhere was not yet part of her experience. In her new school she was greeted by a big map in her classroom, and on it she was supposed to show the children her trip around the world with a long stick. Her description of this adventure with the few English words that she knew at the time was later printed in the school paper. No child could have wished for a better introduction to his or her new environment.

After a few days I was personally acquainted with the most important personalities of our community: Johnny from the gas station, George from the post office, Jimmy from the supermarket, Mrs. Watts from the hardware store, Mr. Kerr from the drugstore. All of these could be found on Main Street, and so we immediately became part of the family, as it were. As soon as a newcomer settled there— and all of them had been newcomers once— he belonged like everyone else. This comradeship and neighborly helpfulness constituted an altogether new experience for us Europeans. Something of the old pioneer spirit was still alive here, the spirit of the pioneers who had discovered the New World and had to withstand the dangers there together. Alongside our friend Hendrik Willem, who had filled our ice box before our arrival and lovingly tried to ease our cares, we had a typically American experience on the first day. "The doorbell rang," so Gottfried described it in his autobiography*. "A gentleman with a friendly smile entered, looked at us cheerfully through his goldrimmed glasses, and said: 'How are you, folks? My name is Alfred Harcourt. Hendrik Willem told me about you. You don't know me, but I know *you,* for I have modeled my publishing house after yours. Let me see whether you have anything to eat.' Whereupon he went into the kitchen, looked in the pots and the ice-box, and after inviting us to his nearby house, he left."

The firm of Harcourt, Brace is one of the leading American publishers. Alfred Harcourt invited Gottfried to visit him at his office on Madison Avenue in New York and assigned him a desk with a telephone and a typewriter— "to give him a chance at a new beginning." He also sent for the German-language books that we had produced in Sweden and undertook to distribute them in America. It was an encouraging start and showed Gottfried the way to the establishment of his own publishing house.

My mother had followed us from Sweden to the United States together with my sister and her little baby. One year after us, she took the same route via Russia, Japan, and the Pacific, and because of the exacerbated war situation their trip was particularly adventurous and torturous. Both of them settled in New York, where my sister is still living. She devoted her entire life to the musical world and became the secretary of her close friend Fritz Busch, for whom she worked till his death. Since then she has been active as a representative of many singers of the Metropolitan Opera.

*Gottfried B. Fischer, *Bedroht—Bewahrt,* S. Fischer Verlag, 1967.

18
America, the New World. Franz and Alma Werfel

How could we have imagined that we would meet our dear and admired friend and author Franz Werfel again after so many years in this way? In the fall of 1940 we picked him up in New York harbor where he and Alma had landed with a Greek ship that had brought them to the United States after a long and dangerous crossing of an Atlantic controlled by Nazi submarines. Having escaped from mortal danger by the skin of their teeth, they were exhausted and miserable when they embraced us. We had not seen one another since Hitler's invasion of Austria in 1938. Thank goodness, Werfel had by then already left the country, and the utterly intrepid Alma went across the border with her money hidden in her undergarments. She knew no fear. In France both of them almost fell into the clutches of the Nazis, but at the last moment they were saved by the Emergency Rescue Committee appointed by America. It had them walk over the Pyrenees to Spain under the cover of darkness, and in Portugal they and other refugees, among them Heinrich and Golo Mann, were put on board a ship sailing for the United States.

Now they were standing on the soil of the "New World," with nothing to hope for. But Werfel had brought along a manuscript. It was *Das Lied von Bernadette,* a book he had been inspired to write on his escape as thanksgiving for his salvation. This song of little "Saint" Bernadette touched people's hearts. In very short order its sensational success not only saved the Werfels but also freed them of all material worries. The novel was published by Bermann-Fischer in Stockholm and soon thereafter in English translation in New York. The Book of the Month Club selected it for its hundreds of thousands of members, and the book was printed in huge editions. The film version of *The Song of Bernadette* later became a world success.

Alma and Franz enjoyed their new fame and life in the cosmopolis New York. We spent enjoyable evenings with them in the Hotel St. Moritz, where they were staying. There invariably were Alma's obligatory bottle of champagne and lobster. In those days the two of them were not very fluent in English, and I can still hear Werfel's euphonious tenor voice ringing through the restaurant: "Waiter, smashed potatoes, please!"

The Werfels settled in California and moved into a house in Beverly Hills, where Franz began to write a new book. His health, however, had been undermined by the terrible excitement of the last years of flight. Soon he was hardly able to leave his house any more. To give him some pleasure, I wrote some of his poems that were especially dear to me on parchment for him. He thanked me with a loving telegram (in English) from Beverly Hills dated February 19, 1943, two years before his death: "I am enthusiastic and very touched about your masterful writing of poems like medieval page of illumination, it looks down to me and calms my nerves, I embrace you grateful and with love forever yours Franz Werfel."

He worked tirelessly and with all the strength still at his disposal on the completion of his last, prophetic novel *Der Stern der Ungeborenen* (The Star of the Unborn), a prefigurement of the exploration of space and a vision of the downfall of the "Old World" and possibly of all of mankind. While putting the finishing touches to this work he suffered a heart attack. He was only fifty-five when he died, the same age as Hugo von Hofmannsthal. Shortly before his death I received this poem from him:

Morgensturm

Des Morgensturms aufbrüllende Gefahr
macht diese Erde wieder planetar.

Mit hunderttausend Schultern rennt das Meer
im Urwelt-Irrsinn an das Felsenwehr.

Das Zwielicht der Äonen steigt wie Dampf.
Die Bäume röcheln noch im Todeskrampf.

Der Ortschaft Häuser stehen ausgehöhlt
wie Mumien, von Verschollenheit umgröhlt.

Der Vogel weiß nicht, der darüber saust,
was so ein Haus ist und wer darin gehaust.

Der Sturm hat längst mit seiner Hand aus Gischt
die Menschheit von dem Erdentisch gewischt.

Sie ist in Gottes Schlaf, im Mund des Alls
ein leiser Nachgeschmack noch bestenfalls.

(Morning Storm. The roaring danger of the morning storm makes this earth planetary again. With a hundred thousand shoulders the sea races in primeval madness to the rocky dam. The twilight of the aeons rises like steam. The trees are still rattling in their death struggle. The houses of the town stand hollowed out like mummies, with oblivion bawling all around them. The bird whizzing by overhead does not know what such a house is and who lived in it. The storm has long since wiped mankind from the earth-table with its hand of spray. In the sleep of God and the mouth of the universe it is at best a slight aftertaste).

Alma survived Franz Werfel by almost twenty years. She moved to New York and bought herself a house, where she lived in the midst of her library, her letters and pictures, Werfel's manuscripts and Mahler's scores. She could often be found at her grand piano, playing and improvising. Not infrequently one of her conductor friends, such as Bruno Walter or Dimitri Mitropoulos, would visit her before one of their concerts to have a conversation with her. Alma had completely acclimated herself to the United States and loved the lively artistic and musical scene of New York. She died there without having seen Europe again.

In the meantime Thomas Mann's manuscript of the fourth volume of his Joseph tetralogy, *Joseph der Ernährer* (Joseph the Provider), had reached me, and I wrote him:

Old Greenwich, May 11, 1943.

Dear Mr. Mann: . . . I am quite undeservedly privileged to dig in this treasure of beauty and wisdom before it is opened to other mortals, and I have the feeling that I should immediately tell everyone what awaits him. I suppose it is the inner serenity, the smile that is above knowledge and removes the tragic heaviness from all insight that gives this work such an element of transfigurement. Grace and dignity, humor and wisdom— it is a very special mixture, and one must love it! Gottfried and I read this book to each other, and one really ought to recommend that every reader read it aloud, for then the beauty and the musicality of the language become so evident . . . This seemed to be the right day for me to thank you, dear Mr. Mann. This morning we received the good news that the manuscript has flown over the burning battlefields of Europe and landed safely on the Swedish island to go to the printshop with maximum speed. Apart from the miraculously quick conquest of space there probably is a special significance in the fact that this work, produced and written at a time of deepest darkness, is to come into the world at a moment when the conquest of evil has begun. What is being done with arms there has here been done in the intellectual realm, and it will have an enduring effect. It really seems to me as though your work has always existed, since time immemorial, and at bottom that is the way it is with all great things: They have always existed and will always exist. Accept all my gratitude for this. Tutti.

For me a new life began in America. I was open to all fresh impressions and became more and more fond of this new world every day. What a liberation this was, and not just from the dangers and the oppression of the last years! In America a woman is worth as much as a man and is his equal to a far greater extent than in Europe. Also, male dominance in the family, such as is customary in Europe to this day, does not exist to the same extent in the United States. A woman shares in the responsibility for administering her "community," and her voice is at least as important as a man's. She is the one who fights for innovations in the educational system, for protection, safety, and hygiene. By banding together in the League of Women Voters women have an official representation in Washington. But today's American women are not content with that. They fight with great energy for equal rights in the filling of leading positions in industry, the economy, and politics.

My activities were divided among those of a mother and housewife (which are greatly eased in America by ingenious, practical inventions), work for the community, and helping Gottfried with his professional work.

My studies and my production experience enabled me to do considerable work for the L. B. Fischer Publishing Corporation in New York, which had been founded by Gottfried together with our friend Fritz Landshoff. I was the graphic artist responsible for a number of books, designing jackets and helping with announcements and graphic advertisements.

All of us soon felt very much at home in our new abode. The children became adjusted to their school and age group. In the afternoon the big lawn in front of our house was a meeting place for their friends from the neighborhood. Often they would go rowing or sailing on the sea. A fine sandy beach, reserved for residents of the community, was nearby, and that is where we spent our leisure hours in summer. Our old wooden house, built by an oyster fisherman and at least seventy years old, had three floors and enough rooms for each of the five members of our family. On the ground floor there was a hall from which a wide wooden staircase led to the upper stories. Downstairs we had a dining room that connected with the livingroom, which had an open fireplace and book-lined walls. My good old Bechstein grand piano that had followed us from Stockholm also stood here. From the livingroom one could go out to a covered porch that encircled half the house; this is where we took our meals in summer. We had a magnificent view of the bay over to Long Island and could hear the sirens of the great ocean liners on their outward voyages. In fall and winter there were also the staccato warning signals of the fog horns, and so we often had the feeling that we were out on the open sea. We loved our new home and felt sheltered there. I received much assistance from Queen, an intelligent, kind-hearted, and beloved black woman who came a few times each week to keep the house in order in her efficient and quick manner.

My neighbors and I always took turns hosting the meetings of our chapter of the League of Women Voters. It became my task in the League to give lectures on the fate of the S. Fischer Verlag, its authors, and its emigration as well as to enlighten my audience about the effects of National Socialism in Germany and the crimes that were committed in Hitler's name not only against the Jews but against all of mankind. To my greatest astonishment I noticed that most of our neighbors knew next to nothing about what was transpiring on the other side in Europe, and they could hardly believe my reports about the destruction of millions of people in the concentration camps.

In those days Europe was in the eyes of many Americans still something like a distant, beautiful, and hardly accessible fairy land where everything was "better," "smarter," and "more exemplary." Because I had come from over there, I was gaped at like some outlandish creature. I lectured at some girls' colleges about the S. Fischer Verlag and its fate in exile, and I enjoyed telling the girls how a publishing house operates and what different employment opportunities there are in such a firm.

Occasionally I accompanied our dear friend and neighbor Hendrik Willem van Loon to New York where he spoke about urgent world problems from the pulpit of the Unitarian church near Central Park to a large crowd in his uniquely dynamic and intelligent fashion. Every week he also made a broadcast from Boston to Nazi-occupied Holland, his old home, in order to instill courage in his former fellow countrymen, who called him Oom Henk.

One day Hendrik Willem asked me to write on parchment a text which the Women's Trade Union League had asked him to produce in honor of Eleanor Roosevelt. I regarded it as a great honor to be permitted to write these beautiful words for a great lady who had been active for so many years in behalf of her fellow citizens in the shadow of her outstanding husband, the president of the United States.

19

Hermann Hesse, the Poet, the Painter, the Musician

In 1914, when I was still a little girl of nine, Hermann Hesse gave me some good advice for my life. He wrote in my poetry album:*

Es führen über die Erde
Straßen und Wege viel,
Aber alle haben
Dasselbe Ziel.

Du kannst reiten und fahren
Zu zwei'n und zu drei'n –
Den letzten Weg mußt du
Gehen allein.

Drum ist kein Wissen
Noch Können so gut
Als daß man alles Schwere
Alleine tut.

Von Deinem H. Hesse

(Many streets and roads lead over the earth, but they all have the same goal. You can ride and drive as a twosome and threesome, but the last road you must walk alone. That is why no knowledge or ability is as good as this: that one does everything difficult alone. —From your H, Hesse).

My parents usually met with their friend and author when they stopped in Switzerland on their trips south. One radiant spring he spent with us in Gardone on Lake Garda, at that time still a lovely rural place. Hesse was then still a young man of medium height, lanky, sinewy, and a bit rustic-looking, with tanned skin, windswept hair, and very blue eyes that looked at people penetratingly, with a roguish smile behind them. His gait and his simple clothes indicated a man from the country.

We usually climbed up our favorite path to Gardone *di sopra* (upper Gardone) to a little old chapel that lay before us embedded in meadows. He was full of good cheer and merry tales— just the thing for the little girl I was at the time.

In 1903 Hesse became an author of our publishing house with his first novel, *Peter Camenzind.* My mother wrote in her memoirs:

His main works did not come until his second period, after Demian. He had sent us the manuscript of that book in 1917 as the work of a friend under the pseudonym Emil Sinclair. After reading it I immediately thought that Hesse had written it himself— it was that unmistakable. When we questioned him, he admitted that the book was by him. He asked for strictest discretion, however, writing that his whole enjoyment of the book would be spoiled if the public learned of his authorship; he had used a new tone and wanted to be read in unprejudiced fashion.

The book caused a great stir, and Thomas Mann wrote to my father:

Please tell me: Who is Emil Sinclair? How old is he? Where does he live? His Demian made a greater impression on me than any new book has in a long time. This is a beautiful, intelligent, serious, important work . . . Demian is a work of literature that hit the nerve of the time with uncanny accuracy and filled an entire youth . . . with grateful delight . . .

The "new tone" of *Demian* that shaped Hesse's future work was to gain him readers among the young people of the future as well. After the Indian work *Siddharta,* which enabled youths seeking a new faith to have a first encounter with eastern philosophy, the novel *Der Steppenwolf,* which appeared in 1927, became the book most discussed by young German intellectuals. Forty years later, however, it gripped young people all over the world since it presented the very problems with which youths devoid of intellectual ties were concerning themselves. The young people of today have "adopted" Hesse and literally devour everything he has written. I wish he could have lived to witness this "resurrection."

Hesse repeatedly dedicated handwritten or typed collections of poetry to my mother and me. Every sheet was hand-colored by him. For my parents he wrote, with a hand-painted inscription, his fairy-tale *Piktors Verwandlungen* (Pictor's Transformations), with delightful little water colors scattered throughout the text, and for my engagement he sent me the same fairy-tale with a handwritten dedication and a painted title page of the "Pictor Tree," which has since become famous.

Many of his letterheads carried such watercolors of his beloved landscape around Montagnola and Lake Lugano, where he lived in a beautiful house placed at his disposal by his friend Hans C. Bodmer. There he led a withdrawn life; even his closest friends often found it difficult to visit him there and gain admittance through the always closed garden gate. At the entrance gate there was a sign saying *Besuche nicht erwünscht* (Visitors Not Welcome). Even his friend Thomas Mann once turned back when he saw that sign. Nevertheless, Hesse was sometimes pleased when someone came to see him. He could usually be found in the garden with a large straw hat on his head and a watering can in his hand, tending his plants. My mother fulfilled one of his wishes and gave him a garden hose for his birthday.

Hesse lived very simply, and although the great success of his books relieved him of all financial worries, he gradually became something like a miser. For reasons of economy he wrote his letters on the empty back pages of other people's letterheads and sent them without postage in a large envelope to the publishing house, to be forwarded from there. When we visited him, we were greeted by several weeks' accumulated mail which we had to stamp and mail in Berlin. A postcard addressed to us which he had given to a Viennese friend to forward reached us after our escape, postmarked the day of the Nazi occupation of Vienna: "March 3, 1938. The Führer in Vienna." When he wrote that postcard, Hesse did not know that we had at the very last moment escaped from the Nazis invading Austria and from the Gestapo, which immediately occupied our house, and had found refuge in Italy:

Dear Frau Tutti: Thanks for your dear greeting with the welcome little photo, the sweet photo of the children! I shall soon be watching world history with the malicious joy of an old man who keeps thinking, "Oh well, tomorrow I won't be around anymore." But until then there will be a lot to swallow. May it include beautiful things as well for all of us! Most cordial regards to both of you from your H. Hesse.

His poem *Föhn-Nacht* also dates from the spring of 1938. I received it with a greeting from him before our escape from Vienna, and it conveyed to me much of the magic of his youthful years and the melancholia of his aging:

Föhn-Nacht

Schaukelt im wehenden Föhnwind der Feigenbaum
Wieder wie Schlangen wirr die gewundenen Äste,
Steigt übers kahle Gebirg zu einsamem Feste
Vollmond empor und beseelt mit Schatten den Raum.
Spricht zwischen gleitenden Wolkenschiffen der Lichte
Träumerisch mit sich selber und zaubert die Nacht
Über dem Seetal still zum Seelenbild und Gedichte,
Daß mir im Herzen zu innerst Musik erwacht,
Dann erhebt sich in drängender Sehnsucht die Seele,
Fühlt sich jung und begehrt ins flutende Leben zurück,
Kämpft mit dem Schicksal und ahnt, woran es ihr fehle,
Summt sich Lieder und spielt mit dem Traume vom Glück,
Möchte noch einmal beginnen, noch einmal der fernen
Jugend heiße Gewalten beschwören ins kältere Heut,
Möchte wandern und werben und bis zu den Sternen
Dehnen der schweifenden Wünsche dunkles Geläut.
Zögernd schließ' ich das Fenster, entzünde das Licht,
Seh' die weißglänzenden Kissen des Bettes warten,
Weiß den Mond und die Welt und das wehende Wolkengesicht
Draußen lebendig im Föhn überm silbrigen Garten,

Finde zurück mich langsam zu meinen gewohnten Dingen,
Höre bis in den Schlaf das Lied meiner Jugend klingen.

Februar 38 *Gruß für Tutti von Hermann Hesse*

(When the foehn blows and the winding branches of the fig tree are tangled like snakes, the full moon rises over the bare mountains for a lonely feast and animates the space with shadows. As it dreamily talks to itself between the gliding cloud-ships of the lights and quietly turns the night over the lake valley into an enchanted soul-picture and poem, awakening music deep in my heart, the soul rises in urgent longing, feeling young and desirous of returning to the mainstream of life, struggles with its fate and suspects what it lacks, hums songs to itself and plays with the dream of happiness, would like to start all over again, once more to evoke the passionate forces of youth and bring them to the colder present, would like to wander and woo and extend to the stars the dark ringing of roaming wishes. Hesitantly I close the window and turn on the light, see the shiny white pillows waiting on the bed, know that the moon and the world and the shifting aspects of the clouds are alive out there in the foehn over the silvery garden, slowly find my way back to my accustomed things, and hear the song of my youth resounding till I drop off to sleep.

—February 1938. Greetings for Tutti from Hermann Hesse.)

At a later date, when I was already in America, he sent me the following poem, which is prophetic if viewed from the present situation of the world, with the dedication "For Frau Tutti from Hermann Hesse" and "Greetings for Easter 1940:"

Müßige Gedanken

Einmal wird dies alles nicht mehr sein,
Nicht mehr diese töricht genialen Kriege,
Diese teuflisch in den Feind gewehten
Gase, diese Beton-Wüstenei'n,
Diese Wälder, statt mit Dorn mit Drähten
Dicht bestachelt, diese Todeswiegen,
Drin so viele Tausend schaudernd liegen,
Minen-Netze über Land, Luft, Meer.

Berge werden in die Bläue ragen,
Sterne werden durch die Nächte leuchten,
Zwillinge, Kassiopeia, Wagen,
Ewig in gelassener Wiederkehr.
Laub und Gras mit seinen Morgenfeuchten
Silber wird dem Tag entgegen grünen,
Und im ewigen Wind wird Meerflut schlagen
An den Fels und an die bleichen Dünen.
Doch die Weltgeschichte ist vorüber:
Mit dem Schwall von Blut, von Leid, von Lüge
Ist die Prahlerische als ein trüber
Kehrichtstrom zerronnen, ihre Züge
Sind erloschen, ihre unermessen
Schlingende Gier gestillt, der Mensch vergessen.

Mit vergessen sind die Kinderspiele,
Deren wir so holde und berückende,
Deren wir so unersättlich viele
Ausgedacht, so fremde und entzückende.
Die Gedichte, die wir uns ersonnen,
Jene Zeichen all, die unser Lieben
Rings der willigen Erde eingeschrieben,
Unsre Götter, Heiligtümer, Weihen,
Alphabeth und Einmaleins sind nicht mehr.
Unsrer Orgelfugen Himmelswonnen,
Unsre Dome mit den trotzig schlanken
Türmen, unsre Bücher, Malereien,
Sprachen, Märchen, Träume und Gedanken,
Sie sind ausgelöscht. Die Erde hat kein Licht mehr.

Und der Schöpfer, der dem Untergange
All des Scheußlichen und all des Schönen
Stille zugeschaut, betrachtet lange
Die befreite Erde. Heiter tönen
Um ihn der Gestirne Reigen, dunkel
Schwebt die kleine Kugel im Gefunkel.
Sinnend greift er etwas Lehm und knetet.
Wieder wird er einen Menschen machen,
Einen kleinen Sohn, der zu ihm betet,
Einen kleinen Sohn, von dessen Lachen,
Dessen Kinderei'n und Siebensachen
Er sich Spaß verspricht.

Sein Finger waltet
Tief im Lehm. Er freut sich. Er gestaltet.

geschrieben Ende Januar 1940.

(Idle Thoughts. Some day all this will no longer exist— these foolishly brilliant wars, these gases devilishly blown at the enemy, these deserts of concrete, these forests thickly covered with prickly wires instead of thorns, these death-cradles in which so many thousands lie shuddering, mine-nets over the land, the air, the sea. Mountains will tower into the blue, stars will shine through the nights, Gemini, Cassiopeia, the Dipper, eternally in placid recurrence. The foliage and the grass with their morning moistness will meet the day with silvery verdure, and in the eternal wind the floods of the sea will beat against the rocks and the pallid dunes. But world history is over: With the surge of blood, sorrow, and lies the boastful one has melted away as a muddy stream of refuse. Its features have been extinguished; its immeasurably devouring greed has been sated; man has been forgotten. Forgotten, too, are the children's games, the lovely, entrancing, strange, and charming ones that we have devised in such insatiable profusion. The poems that we have thought up, all the signs that our love has inscribed on the willing earth all around, our gods, shrines, and consecrations, the alphabet and the multiplication table— these are no more. The heavenly delights of our organ fugues, our cathedrals with their defiantly slender towers, our books and paintings, our languages, fairy-tales, dreams and thoughts— they are extinguished. The earth has no more light. And the Creator, who has quietly watched the end of all those horrors and beauties, beholds the liberated earth for a long time. All around him the roundelay of the constellations makes a cheerful sound; the small sphere floats darkly amidst the sparkle. Pensively he picks up some clay and kneads it. Once again he will make a human being, a little son who will pray to him, a little son whose laughter, childish tricks, and all the rest promise to be fun. His finger digs deep in the clay. He rejoices. He shapes.

—Written at the end of January 1940.)

His Easter letter contained another poem, and thereby hangs a tale:

Flötenspiel

Vor einem Hause blieb ich stehn
In wolkiger Vorfrühlingsnacht,
Kaum wissend, was mich hergebracht:
Es war der Flötentöne Wehn.

Das fremde Haus durch Strauch und Baum
Ein Fenster leise schimmern ließ
Und dort im unsichtbaren Raum
Ein Flötenspieler stand und blies.

Es war ein Lied so altbekannt,
Es floß so gütig in die Nacht,
Als wäre Heimat jedes Land,
Als wäre jeder Weg vollbracht.

Es war der Welt geheimer Sinn
In seinem Atem offenbart,
Bezaubert gab das Herz sich hin
Und alle Zeit war Gegenwart.

Geschr. im März 1940

(Flute Playing. I stopped in front of a house on a cloudy night in early spring, hardly knowing what had taken me there: It was the sound of flute music. Through shrubs and trees a soft gleam came from a window of the unknown house, and in the invisible room stood a flute player and blew. It was a well-known song that streamed so kindly into the night, as though every country were home and every mission accomplished. In its breath the secret meaning of the world was revealed. Entranced, my heart surrendered to it, and all time was the present.

—Written in March 1940.)

This poem really enchanted me, and for his birthday in July I wrote it for him on parchment, whereupon he replied:

Dear Frau Tutti . . . This morning I received your dear parchment sheet with my poem. Many thanks for it; it is beautiful and gave me such a good and amicable feeling, as though everything that was ours years ago still existed. And it really does exist, is imperishable, and has more substance than the so-called world history that makes so much noise.

By the way, that poem still is not quite finished; the first stanza has bothered me from the beginning. For the time being it has the following form; look at it again in this simpler form, and accept cordial thanks and greetings from your H. Hesse.

Flötenspiel

Ein fremdes Haus durch Strauch und Baum
Ein Fenster leise schimmern ließ,
Und dort im unsichtbaren Raum
Ein Flötenspieler stand und blies.

Es war ein Lied so altbekannnt,
Es floß so gütig in die Nacht,
Als wäre Heimat jedes Land,
Als wäre jeder Weg vollbracht!

Es war der Welt geheimer Sinn
In seinem Atem offenbart,
Und willig gab das Herz sich hin
Und alle Zeit ward Gegenwart.

The last two lines now read:

(And willingly my heart surrendered, and all time became the present.)

In the definitive printed version Hesse made another small change:

(Through shrubs and trees a house by night . . .)

His great love was Mozart, and *The Magic Flute* was especially dear to his heart. To Tamino he had a kind of brotherly relationship. When I reread his poem *Mit der Eintrittskarte zur Zauberflöte* (With a Ticket to *The Magic Flute),* I seem to hear his voice:

So werd' ich dich noch einmal wiederhören,
Geliebteste Musik, und bei den Weih'n
Des lichten Tempels, bei den Priesterchören,
Beim holden Flötenlied zu Gaste sein.

So viele Male in so vielen Jahren
Hab' ich auf dieses Spiel mich tief gefreut,
Und jedesmal das Wunder neu erfahren
Und das Gelübde still in mir erneut,
Das mich als Glied in eure Kette bindet,
Morgenlandfahrer im uralten Bund,

Der nirgend Heimat hat im Erdenrund,
Doch immer neu geheime Diener findet.

Diesmal, Tamino, macht das Wiedersehen
Mir heimlich bang. Wird das ermüdete Ohr,
Das alte Herz euch noch wie einst verstehen,
Ihr Knabenstimmen und du Priesterchor –
Werd' ich vor eurer Prüfung noch bestehen?

In ewiger Jugend lebt ihr, selige Geister,
Und unberührt vom Leben unsrer Welt,
Bleibt Brüder uns, bleibt Führer uns und Meister,
Bis uns die Fackel aus den Händen fällt.

Und wenn einst eurer heitern Auserwählung
Die Stunde schlägt und niemand mehr euch kennt,
So folgen neue Zeichen euch am Firmament,
Denn alles Leben dürstet nach Beseelung.

(So I shall hear you once again, most beloved music, and be a guest at the rites of the bright temple, the priestly choruses, and the lovely flute song. So many times in so many years I have greatly looked forward to this opera, and every time I experienced the miracle anew and quietly renewed my vow that makes me a link in your chain, a journeyer to the East in the age-old League who is at home nowhere on the globe but always finds secret servants. This time, Tamino, seeing you again secretly worries me. Will my tired ears and my old heart still understand you as of yore? Your boys' voices and priests' chorus—will I still stand your test? You, blessed spirits, live in eternal youth and untouched by the life of our world; you remain our brothers, our mentors and masters until the torch falls from our hands. And when some day the bell tolls for your serene closeness and no one knows you any more, new signs will follow you on the firmament, for all life thirsts for spiritualization.)

Hesse sent me that poem with a letter dated June 10, 1941:

Dear Frau Tutti . . . Today I sent you a new poem; it still belongs with Joseph Knecht's poems [in Das Glasperlenspiel] and is the only one I have written in six months. For over two months I was unable to use my right hand and could not even hold a pencil, and when a new medication permitted me to bend my fingers a bit again, I immediately wrote the poem down so as not to lose it . . . At least summer has finally come, a capricious and wild summer with long, severe thunderstorms (twice our house was struck by lightning, with all sorts of damage) and cloudbursts; but it is not cold anymore, and often it is very beautiful.

A thousand greetings to your family and J. Maass from me and Ninon. Cordially yours, H. Hesse.

From time to time I wrote one of his poems on parchment calligraphically, and he almost always thanked me promptly:

Montagnola, May 1, 1941.

Dear Frau Tutti, your letter and gift reached me two days ago in good order, and I enjoy your beautiful writing very much. The mail does not bring such pleasant things often these days. Many thanks! I wish I could give you my thanks in a real letter, but ever since the bad winter was succeeded by an even worse spring and my articular rheumatism affected almost all my joints . . . I have been very limited even on such matters that have hitherto not been rationed for me. I must be content that I am still able to take a few hobbling steps outside the door every day . . . That there are always young people and sweet unreason on earth was recently shown me by a letter from a 17 year-old youth in Sweden. He informs me that he wishes to become a poet, regards himself as my pupil, and wants to pack his bag, set out, and visit me as soon as the stupid war is over.

The poet A. Mombert has died in a terrible camp in France at the age of seventy. Wolfenstein wrote me a few times from Nice. If possible, I would like to request from Sweden Annette Kolb's book on Schubert and any other new publications. Many cordial regards to both of you from us. Your H. Hesse.

His last and greatest work, *Das Glasperlenspiel* (The Glass Bead Game), the completion of which he mentioned in the following letter, was his legacy to posterity:

Montagnola, September 23, 1942.

Dear Frau Tutti, Your letter gave me pleasure, and I was doubly grateful for it because these are the days when the long, beautiful summer is dead and the fall with its wetness and coolness begins. This time has always been a torment for me, even when I was young and healthy (I wrote about it in [Hermann] Lauscher's Tagebuch [1900] . . . In the spring I wrote the last few sentences of the big book that I started eleven years ago; though I often doubted it, it has now been finished after all. I am doing nothing else, i.e., nothing productive. I am collecting my poems for a complete edition . . . Often one lives as in a nightmare and wishes it were all over. For the rest, I pay very little attention to the details of the war etc. . . . Your H. Hesse.

At a later date Thomas Mann called Hesse's *Das Glasperlenspiel* (The Glass Bead Game, or Magister Ludi), "revolutionary . . . in a spiritual, poetic sense . . . with a vision of the future . . . sensitive to the future." Since then there have been important studies about the significance of "play" and the "play instinct" for present-day society, and the work that Hesse conceived fifty years ago is cited in amazement. Hesse himself begins his novel with "A General Introduction . . . for the Layman." "The Glass Bead Game," he writes, "is a mode of playing with the entire contents and values of our culture; it plays with them as, say, a painter in the golden age of the arts might have played with the colors on his palette. The insights, noble thoughts, and works of art that mankind has produced in its creative eras, what subsequent periods of scholarly study have reduced to concepts and converted into intellectual property— on all this enormous body of intellectual values a Glass Bead Game player plays the way an organist plays on an organ . . . Theoretically, in this game the entire intellectual content of the universe could be reproduced with this instrument . . . "

A handwritten, undated letter from Hesse, probably from 1946, reads as follows:

Dear Frau Tutti, for months I have not been able to write any letters; I am that overburdened with current work. But I found this painted sheet from earlier times, and I am using it to thank you for your kind letter.

The enclosed sheet is a reply to a pile of abusive letters that once again came from Germany, and it appeared in the Zürcher Zeitung.

I hope you are faring well! Cordial regards from your H. Hesse.

The enclosure:

Since Germany in 1914 started an unjust war and an increasingly unbridled war propaganda I have occasionally addressed an appeal or an admonition to the level-headed and fair-minded people there—first in the fall of 1914 and most recently in the spring of 1946. From 1914 to date I have always been laughed at or defamed and vilified for this. Thus your letter, which is far from the worst, is one of several thousand abusive letters that I have received from Germany in thirty-two years.

It is not my fault that my "Letter to Germany" was printed by the Neue Zeitung [Munich] without previous inquiry or authorization and perhaps distorted by cuts.

In that letter, which outraged you so much, I express my greatest respect and affection for those Germans who resisted Hitler and suffered because of him; I even call them the salt of the earth. For this, too, I am now being grossly abused in a flood of angry letters. I cannot understand this at all. Many of my friends have been tortured, robbed, and killed by Hitler's Germany; many have languished in prisons and concentration camps, among them my faithful friend and Berlin publisher P[eter] S[uhrkamp].

My Collected "political" comments will appear in a volume to be published in Zurich in 1946. They have netted me not only those countless hate letters but also the friendship of Romain Rolland and other great representatives of humaneness and reason as well as the affection and allegiance of a small elite among the German people. This small elite is fighting to teach the highly gifted but politically utterly untutored German people reason in political life as well and to show it how to take its proper place among the nations.

Many believe that a sorely afflicted people should not be expected to learn anything. I, however, believe that at no time are insight and soul-searching more necessary than at a time of the direst need and humiliation. Hermann Hesse.

One day he sent me a little prose piece entitled "A Sentence About Cadenzas," and the remark that accompanied it shows what fun he had all his life "playing" with musical forms:

As will be seen, the rather long little sentence is not so much an attempt to explain the phenomenon of the cadenza as an attempt to imitate it, as it were, with the resources of prose and just for the fun of it.

If, as repeatedly happens for some measures in that musical dialogue, contest, or love relationship between the orchestra and a solo instrument which for the past two and a half centuries the technical terminology of musicians has become accustomed to calling a "concerto," said solo instrument, relieved for a breathing spell of dealing with the powerful interlocutor and also of the role of a mere assistant in the development, transformation, and continuation of a musical theme, finds itself released, as it were, from an entanglement in an almost too complex world of functions, claims, tasks, responsibilities, and seductions, from an existence that is exceedingly differentiated, multifariously dependent, and obligated to many other players, and returns to its own, homey, individual world, this short-term return to a realm belonging only to it, to the innocence, freedom, and autonomy of its own nature seems to lend to it an entirely new impulse and rhythm, a buoyance previously fettered and constrained by regard for the partner, a virtually intoxicated delight in itself and its possibilities, seems to invite it to enjoy its regained freedom and luxuriate in the atmosphere peculiar to it alone, to encourage it to become aware of its strength gradually and jubilantly in a long series of trills, like a bird escaped from captivity, so as to experience the seemingly ultimate and even impossible in virtuosic ecstasy in passages, flourishes, and flights that alternately sway, triumphantly soar, and plunge bassward in bacchanalian fashion.

The last letter I received from Hesse is undated:

Dear Frau Tutti,

Thank you for your kind letter of February. To be sure, I am still not able to write you a letter, and perhaps I shall never be, since the bad condition of my eyes and nerves is confronted with increasingly oppressive overburdening. But I do have a little present for you: the enclosed tear sheet that I found last winter in an old book I had taken along to Marin. May it reach you safely and give you some pleasure.

Give my regards to Gottfried Bermann and J. Maass. In a few days I plan to return to Montagnola after an absence of five months, though with very mixed feelings. To derive some enjoyment from life and the world as it has become, one would have to be strong enough to make a completely new beginning instead of returning to an outmoded and antiquated way of life. With cordial regards, your H. Hesse.

The poem that was enclosed with the letter sounds like a farewell to the world:

Herbstgeruch

Wieder hat ein Sommer uns verlassen,
Starb dahin in einem Spätgewitter.
Regen rinnt geduldig und im nassen
Walde duftet es so bang und bitter.

Herbstzeitlose starrt im Grase bläßlich
Und der Pilze wucherndes Gedränge.
Unser Tal, noch gestern unermeßlich
Weit und licht, verhüllt sich und wird enge.

Enge wird und duftet bang und bitter
diese Welt, dem Lichte abgewendet.
Rüsten wir uns auf das Spätgewitter,
Das des Lebens Sommertraum beendet!

September 1947 *Gruß für Frau Tutti*
von H. Hesse

(Smell of Autumn. Again a summer has left us; it died in a late thunderstorm. The rain drips patiently, and in the wet forest there is such an anxious and bitter smell. The autumn crocus pallidly juts out of the grass, and so does the crowd of proliferating mushrooms. Our valley, yesterday still immensely wide and bright, becomes shrouded and narrow. This world, turned away from the light, is becoming narrow and has an anxious and bitter smell. Let us prepare for the late storm that ends life's summer dream!

September 1947 Greeting for Frau Tutti from H. Hesse.)

*The poems Hesse sent me in holograph or typewritten form appeared in different versions in his books of poetry.

20

The War Ends. Reencounter with Europe. The Destroyed Cities. A New Beginning in Vienna. Ilse Aichinger. Doctor Faustus

On May 9, 1945 the war against Germany came to an end. Soon thereafter we received a first sign of life from Peter Suhrkamp, who had taken over the part of the S. Fischer Verlag that had remained in Germany in 1935, when we left the country. As soon as this was possible after the war's end, I regularly sent him CARE packages. On February 25, 1946 he wrote me a report from Berlin that extended over a whole week:

Let me embrace you, Tutti! Usually this is put at the end of a letter, and then it is a handy complimentary close. During the last months you brought me close to tears more than once. And it was not pallid emotionalism of the kind that easily comes over us these days— our nerves are that raw!—but a thanks-offering from a deeply stirred heart. How you have cared for us! I must write it openly for once: Without your constant help since September 1945 I would surely not be walking the earth today. Since I got on my feet again, I too have had the feeling that I have some strength to spare again. You cannot imagine what it means if I write you this now, at a time when people's utterances are chilly with the foreboding of death. This is true of almost all the letters I have received in recent months, even those from younger people. They are still brave, but this winter has— well, not finished them off, but laid them bare, making visible what they have been for a long time. They are sadness— completely and passionately, wordlessly but in their entire appearance and expression; not shamelessly and not desperately. It is like facing judgment naked. This is not an exaggeration on my part. It may be that others do not see it, but the camps have taught me to do so: when the new arrivals undressed, turned in their clothes, then walked naked through a big hall to a man who shaved them everywhere and then had to cover another long distance through the wide, long hall to a little pile of filthy, stinking rags which they could put over their nakedness but which never fully covered them. After that no one dared to look anyone else in the face. This is the scene I have to think of now when I see people. That is all for today. It is late and my little room is getting cold. Tomorrow I shall write more, but I wanted to write down at least this thanks today. As you can see, I am doing so with your pen which was brought me yesterday. More tomorrow!

February 26. It is already late, Tutti. In the afternoon I had to go to Frohnau. Under present conditions this is a long trip. Four hours' travel time for an hour's talk with the French cultural attaché. In the middle of the conversation I had to think of Pierre Bertaux. I wonder why. Do you know how he made it through? And then, of course, Loerke. I would like to visit his grave, but I would not have enough strength for it . . . I am sure you have heard about his death. When the war came, there could have been no other way. He literally died of a broken heart . . . Among his remains I found a letter addressed to me: "Let no one assert that I died of an illness; I died solely of the brown plague . . . "

March 3. Three days have passed before I was able to go on writing . . . Zuckmayer was sitting in the next room; he had come from Vienna in the evening, for just a few days. He has been recalled, and we are as alarmed and sad about this as he is. His open, generous cordiality is captivating and almost overpowering here— like a spring storm. He makes everyone laugh and cry at the same time. People say that if more people like him would come, something could be done here. What a great thing it is, simply a natural and cordial human being! When someone like that comes, we notice that this is what we have missed most for a decade! On Friday two packages from you arrived for the publishing house. You made the folks there quite happy with them . . . Since the middle of January production has stopped altogether, because printing presses and binderies are completely shut down. No gas, no electricity, no coal . . . You can hardly imagine these difficulties. There is hardly anyone willing to work . . .

My regards to Gottfried, Gabi, Gisi, Annette, your mother, Hilla, and Monika, whom I don't know. If I could really embrace all of them! Cordially as ever, your old Peter.

In February 1946 Gottfried flew to Europe for the first time, like the dove of peace after the end of the world, in order to look after the Bermann-Fischer Verlag. It had continued to work by remote control, though it had been cut off from us for six years.

Thomas Mann regarded this first contact of his publisher with his European readers as a promising new beginning:

1550 San Remo Drive, Pacific Palisades, California, February 17, 1946.

Dear Tutti . . . The strike prevented us from wiring a farewell greeting to Gottfried. We do not even know whether he actually flew or went by boat. If the former, he must have arrived in Sweden days ago. Please keep us informed, at least in broad outline, about the course of his journey. You can imagine with what interest we are following it. With cordial regards from both of us, your Thomas Mann.

Here is my reply:

Old Greenwich, Connecticut, February 20, 1946.

My dear Doctor Mann . . . Gottfried left here by plane on February 9 and arrived in Stockholm on February 12. His flight departed 48 hours late because of an atmospheric disturbance caused by sun spots. En route a violent storm over the Atlantic caused a twelve-hour stop-over in Newfoundland. In Ireland he was set down in what evidently was a peculiar and desolate small town, and again it was a matter of being patient, for this time there was trouble with the plane, causing another eight-hour delay. But then there apparently was a very smooth flight to Copenhagen, and two hours later he was in Stockholm.

According to his first reports from there, he faces a huge pile of work, for it is a matter of converting the entire publishing house from wartime to peacetime conditions, or at least peace-like ones. The first interesting offer has come from a counselor at the British Embassy in Stockholm. He is interested in our books and wants to buy them for the British occupation zone of Germany. And the most important thing is that he wants to pay in Swedish currency in Stockholm. It sounds so fantastic that we had better take it with a grain of salt for the time being, but it might be a first step toward Germany. Also, Gottfried met with the Russian ambassador in Stockholm. He gave a dinner for him and the Bonniers, and after Gottfried had been obliged to drink enormous quantities of alcohol, the Russian showed him his great interest in the German schoolbooks that were prepared there.

Gottfried is now trying to get to Germany with the aid of the British and American army . . . The voices from Germany clamoring for books are becoming louder and louder, and under the general pressure the military authorities will have to do something toward clarifying the situation. In any case, I shall immediately notify you of anything that might transpire in this area.

How do you like the January issue of the Neue Rundschau? a critique from you would be instructive and important to those working on the magazine. From now on the Stuttgart radio station will regularly comment on the Rundschau and quote from it . . . With all cordial wishes for you both, your Tutti.

After his adventurous first flight to Europe, Gottfried sent me daily reports of his experiences and impressions. He was again sitting at his old desk on the Stureplan in Stockholm, having set foot in the office for the first time since his arrest in 1940. Together with his associates, who had taken care of the publishing house throughout the difficult war years, he was working to breathe new life into it. But Sweden now seemed to be too remote and in its neutral apathy too far removed from the new, living impulses of liberated Europe. After Gottfried had managed to establish contact with his friend Fritz Landshoff, who had already returned to Holland, he immediately decided to heed Landshoff's urgent request that he come to Amsterdam, where people were starved for free German literature. In those days the Dutch publishers were not able to resume their own production. Gottfried's first letter after his arrival on the war-ravaged European continent was dated Amsterdam, March 4, 1946:

. . . The Schiphol airport, which used to be so beautiful, is in sad shape; all one can see is steel skeletons . . . The same is true of the city . . . Only few stores have lights . . . Taxis are non-existent . . . The people look terribly starved . . . The contrast to Sweden is enormous; the entire history of the last seven years lies between these two cities . . . But Europe really lives here. How friendly the people are, how full of the bliss of freedom!

Everyone is working on reconstruction, full of optimism and enterprise. However, everybody is terribly cold . . . There is no heat in the rooms. The stories about what happened in the last months before the liberation, the shootings in the open street . . . the impossibility of burying those who starved to death— all this is horrible . . . When I walk through the old streets, on which we used to stroll so happily, I have to keep thinking of the horrors that took place there. The Jewish quarter is an empty cave city . . . The prices on the black market are utterly fabulous: a pound of butter is 70 guilders (around $35), a suit 750 guilders. American cigarettes are the most valuable form of payment— between 5 and 8 dollars a pack. Thus one can get a suit for a hundred packs of Chesterfields! . . . The old horse-drawn carriages, pulled by ancient nags or ponies, are very funny. The carriages must be straight out of the museum . . .

Gottfried's visit to Amsterdam was very successful. He was able to sell books of the Stockholm firm for the equivalent of 100,000 guilders and received official permission to transfer what was then a considerable sum to Stockholm. The hunger for German books that was displayed there was a first confirmation of our future hopes after the long drought of the war years.

Since Gottfried was not able to receive permission from the Allied Military Government to travel to Germany that year, he returned to Old Greenwich, hoping to be able to make some decisive progress the following year toward a new consolidation of the publishing house and the importation of the books that German readers had done without for so long. A year later, in April 1947, he flew to Stockholm again and tried very hard to obtain the visas necessary for entering Germany. He wrote me on May 3, 1947:

My darling, today I received the British and American permits for Germany— three weeks for the U.S. Zone and two for the British. I shall obtain the French permission in Berlin . . . I now have every-

thing I need for this trip to uncertain territory— and I only wish you were with me . . .

In the meantime Fritz Landshoff had come to Stockholm in order to prepare a merger between the publishing houses of Querido and Bermann-Fischer in Amsterdam, from where the reactivation of the combined houses could be accomplished much faster and better.

On May 7, 1947, just before his long-desired departure for Germany, Gottfried wrote me: " . . . So I am setting out tomorrow morning . . . I feel very strange. The impending re-encounter is affecting my nerves more than I had thought."

I followed Gottfried's first step in Berlin with all my senses and every fiber of my being, and on May 5 I wrote him: " . . . When you receive this letter, you will already have seen Berlin, and who knows how you will be feeling and how sad and discouraged you may be. In spirit I walk with you through the desolation and wilderness of the city that used to be our home and stand with you before the gate of our beloved Erdenerstrasse."

On May 11 I received his first sign of life from Germany:

When the airport bus brought me to the Frankfurt railroad station, I found myself in the midst of the infinite hopelessness that emanated from the desolate wire-studded piles of rubble and the emaciated human figures that slunk among them, stooped and weary . . . It is hard to describe what it is that has changed these people so. It is not just the frayed suits that droop from them, nor is it their emaciation; it is more the grayness of their complexion and the timidity, the dismay, and the defeat in their eyes . . .

I traveled to Berlin with papers from the Military Government as a V.I.P. These papers have made me a superman able to bring a bit of happiness to the poor figures crawling in the dirt like a god doing magic . . . I had to grit my teeth to be able to stand that . . . Oh Tutti, sometimes I think it is good that you are not here. It is so terrible, so depressing, and so hopeless that the tears welled up in my eyes. From the moment one enters Germany one is in an oddly artificial, strange world. Everything is regulated by a 'higher' power; for everything under the sun there is a special office, and when you get to the American headquarters, OMGUS, you don't believe your eyes, for you are driving through a well-kept, flourishing paradise . . . Through enormous lattice gates guarded by M.P.'s you enter an expansive area with numerous buildings standing in the midst of magnificent gardens. These buildings house the offices of the military government, and that is the location of Truman Hall, where visitors like me as well as many of the American officials take their meals. A sign at the entrance says "No German visitors" . . . To help a starving German girl I went in and bought four doughnuts; I hid them in my hat with great difficulty and then smuggled them to her outside, bit by bit . . . Tutti, even though it is nice to see old friends again, life here makes me sick and miserable, the awareness of the hopeless isolation of this German world from the western world and from the sinister and threatening world of the nearby Russian Zone, which some day may swallow up this isolated island. People here live in constant fear that the American occupation forces might leave them one day . . . Dear one, you wrote me how much you wished you could stand in front of 8 Erdenerstrasse with me. I was happy that you were not with me. You must resign yourself to the fact that there is no 8 Erdenerstrasse any more and there never will be one except in our hearts, in us, and in our children . . . Yesterday I could not stand it any longer, took a taxi, and went out to the Grunewald. There is not a house in that district that is not more or less damaged and looks desolate and empty. The taxi stopped in front of 8 Erdenerstrasse. There it was. It is still standing. Undamaged, surrounded by the old white wooden fence . . . The door is open and I walk in. The tennis court is a vegetable garden. I walk around the house; there are the old plane trees with their speckled trunks . . . I stand on the stone staircase to the terrace where we spent so many happy hours . . . Everything is paltry and dilapidated . . . Some of the glass in the doors has been replaced by cardboard. There are big holes in the plaster in the walls . . . Terribly sad-looking . . . Dearest, that no longer is Erdenerstrasse. Do you understand why I am glad that you have not been here? I would have been even sadder than I was if I had seen you mourn next to me. Let it live within you the way it was when you left it . . .

May 15, 1947 . . . Yesterday afternoon I went to the Weissensee cemetery. Tutti, it was shattering. This cemetery is the only place in Berlin that reflects something of old Berlin. Except for two bomb craters not far from Papa's grave there has been no destruction. There are the old graves and tablets that still bespeak the wealth of the old Jewish families of Berlin, many familiar names of rank and greatness, also a lot of the bad ostentation that simply was part of it, and all this is surrounded by old trees and the old odor; it is incredi-

ble, but the old lives here through the dead. Outside, things are dead and gone. The grave is intact. The big stone with Papa's and Gerhart's names, the fisherman in relief on Papa's side and the harp on Gerhart's, is there . . . The old center of Berlin, the Wilhelmsplatz with the Kaiserhof, the Ministry of Propaganda, and the Reich Chancellery are bizarre rubble. The Friedrichstrasse, the Leipzigerstrasse, the Potsdamerplatz are completely dead; sometimes there is a bicyclist or a pedestrian whose steps resound loudly through the desolation in bright daylight. A gust of wind blows white clouds of dust toward you. At the Postdamer Bahnhof there is a high wall with the staircase at the entrance and nothing behind it . . . The Kurfürstendamm is a glorified village street. The façades are still standing. The people come crawling out from under the rubble . . . At the Wittenbergplatz, however, the great horror begins. All there is there is a big desert of rubble in which you roam around in streets which seem so strange that after a while you have absolutely no idea where you are . . . The Tiergarten is a kind of dumping ground with garden plots. The perdurable Hohenzollern monuments gleam eerily from the tangle; heaven knows why they have not been cleared away. Diana sits on her horse lonely and forsaken; on the right towers the powerful Russian monument; in back of it is the burned-out Reichstag with a twisted cupola, and behind that is the Siegessäule (Victory Column) with the tricolor and the Union Jack . . .

I went to the Städtische Opera, heard Peter Grimes and met old acquaintances . . . They were all absolutely delighted to see me and happy that somebody has come back from the outside. Only now am I beginning to realize that I am one of the very few civilians who have been able to come to Berlin—practically the first one . . .

I would be happy to have you here beside me, though you know how much I also hate the idea of exposing you to these horrible impressions. I need you here every moment— your counsel, your help— but I see no way. I still have a faint hope, however, that you will manage to get a French visa . . .

In the meantime I had pulled all strings in America to receive permission to travel to Germany. My friend Pierre Bertaux, who had become Préfet du Rhône, managed to get the French military authorities in Paris to give me permission to enter the French Zone of Germany. Gottfried wrote me from Berlin on June 4, 1947: " . . . The idea that I shall soon be able to hold you in my arms in

Baden-Baden makes me very happy . . . It is wonderful that Pierre has done such good work! . . . "

We met that same month in Baden-Baden, and both of us felt that this was a new beginning of our life and our work, but that we could accomplish it only if we combined our efforts. Since we were Americans and for the time being were not allowed to resume our publishing activities in Germany, it was our first and very exciting joint task to set up our office in Vienna, where paper was available and the printing of important books could start immediately. There was something unreal and fabulous about our return to the city from which we had escaped from the S.S. by the skin of our teeth nine years earlier. In contrast to the German cities, Vienna was relatively undamaged, but the people were just as starved, scared, seedy, and sobered after Hitler's delusion of "Greater Germany." They looked at us as if we were creatures from another planet, and all doors were opened to us. Within a short time we found a director for our new publishing house, the necessary offices, the paper, and the printing press that started producing the books for which there was such a great demand. We also found a young new author. Shortly after the reopening of our publishing house we were introduced to two young girls who scurried past us shyly and with slightly embarrassed smiles. One of them was said to have recently finished her first novel. Her name was Ilse Aichinger, and her friend was named Ingeborg Bachmann. Both of us read Ilse's manuscript with admiration and pounding hearts. Here was a happy combination of two things: a genuine literary talent and a great subject, namely the drama of her childhood in the midst of cruel persecution by Nazism. We were profoundly impressed and immediately accepted her book, *Die grössere Hoffnung* (Herod's chidlren), for our publishing house. In our room at the hotel Roter Hahn, she jumped for joy when she learned of our decision. Shortly thereafter she wrote us:

Vienna, July 29, 1947.

Dear Madam, dear Doctor:

Since you were here, the whole city has had a new sparkle, and I would really like to tell this to every sad stranger who passes me and prove to everyone that unimaginably beautiful and wonderful things do exist— such as was proved to me just a short while ago! The experience of being happy is for me a very new and captivating one and a great impulse, this knowledge that so much warmth and understanding exists! However, because it is not possible to tell all sad strangers about you, I had better write. And I want this book to become a great thanks to you. No, you have not left at all— you are here, I know it! Your Ilse Aichinger.

Vienna, August 20, 1947.

Dear Madam:

Today it has been a month since we saw each other for the first time. The fact that you, too, felt that we have known each other forever makes it profoundly real . . . Your letter pulsates with the wide world where it is really wide. To know that you exist is such a help to me! All these separations, after all, only seem to be that . . . Work is always like walking on water. It demands so much confidence, and confidence is exactly what you have given me! I have never before been able to work as regularly as I do now. If all goes well, I shall be finished in October . . . In all difficult and unfathomable things both of you have become a support to me! Words can say so little of what one really means; they always remain only gates to something deeper. But I know you know everything that I wish to say. Ever your Ilse.

Since that time we have become close friends. Ilse worked at our publishing house for a while and became part of our family. In the meantime she has written very original and delicate things in an ethereal language— a web of thought and an expression of a sensitive and agitated soul.

Um diese Zeit

Ich lasse mich
von den Jagdhörnern
aus meinen Schlupfwinkeln jagen,
hin zu der Morgenröte
unterm Schnee,
zum vergilbenden Gras.

Mit meinen Händen
erreiche ich
schon die Gelübde der Kinder,
die mich rasch aufwärts ziehen,
hol mir
den winkligen Mond.

Für Gottfried und Tutti
mit vielen herzlichen Wünschen
von Ilse

(Around This Time. I let the hunting horns chase me from my hiding places, down to the dawn under the snow, to the yellowing grass. With my hands I already reach the vows of the children who quickly pull me upward, fetch myself the angular moon. —For Gottfried and Tutti with many cordial wishes from Ilse).

The director of our Viennese publishing house, Joseph Berger, ran the firm with great skill and understanding and became our good friend. We had set up a little *pied-à-terre* for ourselves that adjoined the offices on the famous Graben, with a view of the old roofs of the city, and even though we were able to live there only sporadically, the weeks in Vienna did bring back to us all the charm of old Europe. After the expiration of our visas we had to return to the U.S.A., however, and we were glad to be home in Old Greenwich again.

In the meantime Thomas Mann had sent us a portion of his recently completed novel *Doctor Faustus.* We had previously been able to read some chapters of this book and had heard him read the devil scene before a small group of friends in New York. In the half-darkened room, where only a little light fell on his manuscript, this gloomy vision seemed to be translated into uncanny closeness. After our first reading I wrote him:

"Old Greenwich, Connecticut, November 2, 1946.

"My dear Dr. Mann,

"For ten full days now I have been running around with a letter to you in my head . . . regarding the 713-page manuscript from *Doctor Faustus.* Finally I read those pages again for the second time, but I foresee that I shall not manage to write it even after that. And how could I? It seems presumptuous and immodest to me to express something like admiration or praise for the work that has plunged me into frightened astonishment, that has shaken foundations of thought and set up new ones.

"I would like to quote you, or, rather, Adrian: 'Tell me, what do you think of greatness? I find there is something uncomfortable about facing it eye to eye; it is a test of courage— can one really stand the sight? One does not stand it, one is stuck to it."

"And that is what is happening to me now: I am stuck to it, it is troubling me and will probably do so for the rest of my life. Everyone who comes under its spell will fare the same way . . . My God, where to begin, where to stop with the inexhaustible profusion of figures, reflections, discussions, and investigations that illuminate the intellectual structure of our century? With profound emotion I stand before your work. May we be granted its completion soon. Your B.B. F."

Doctor Faustus was published in late 1947 by the Bermann-Fischer Verlag, Stockholm, and in 1948 there was a licensed edition in Germany. The appearance of this novel evoked great polemics and caused a great stir there. In my letter to Thomas Mann written in Old Greenwich on August 9, 1948 I returned to *Doctor Faustus:*

"My dear Doctor Mann . . . Your "Phantasie über Goethe" is particularly dear and valuable to me. This essay seems to me to be wonderfully close to Goethe's life and presents a rounding off of his personality such as I have encountered nowhere else. Beyond that one could almost call it a "Fantasy About the Nature of Genius." Young Joseph and young Goethe—how they meet in the 'elevation,' in the naturally grown royal element in them . . . This combination of 'tenderness and toughness that constitutes the special vitality-form of a genius'— it is the very key to all masters. After all, the struggle for the perfection of a work of art that recognizes the lack of purpose of artistic creation as a law and regards artistic talent only as a natural task is also Adrian's credo. In him, however, all the divine inspiration of the Goethean genius turns into something pernicious and evil. What pain we must all suffer in seeing him start this descent to hell, with what torment and shuddering do we witness the forces of the abyss that pull Adrian down! Presumably this is the first time that a literary figure was able to become the consummate symbol of an entire people. This ought to help the Germans attain to self-knowledge today, and I am certain that many of them, especially young people, will emerge from this descent to hell purified.

"*Doctor Faustus* has almost nothing in common with the traditional form of the novel, and thus its multifarious episodes do not constitute a retardation of the action but variations on a theme, cross-references and intensifications. In fact, the ultimate meaning, the revelation of an intellectual attitude and its destruction from within would not be comprehensible without those episodes . . . The last ones—the death of little Nepomuk and Adrian's farewell speech—appear to me as the inexorable end, and we must now accommodate ourselves to this end of our world. All these 'episodes' lead, singly and jointly, to dissolution and no longer permit any possibilities of clinging to bourgeois security. Is an alliance with forces of the abysmal depth the only thing that is left to all of us? You yourself leave us a faint, almost touching hope for a resurrection . . .

"The world of the spirit sends icy blasts from inhuman-superhuman closeness, and the beyond moves fearfully close— eternal and cold. It is the horror of greatness that came over me at the end of your book, similar to the horror that surrounds any greatness, even a seemingly cheerful one like that of Mozart's *Magic Flute.* This was the kind of encounter that changes one's life . . . With cordial regards, your Tutti."

1550 San Remo Drive, Pacific Palisades,
California, August 11, 1948.

Dear Tutti, I hasten to thank you most cordially for your letter, which is quite a nice essay and could definitely appear in the Neue Rundschau. Yes, children become people! To think that I used to dandle you on my knees and always threatened to fall off the chair when you were naughty! And now you know how to speak with tongues and gladden an old author's heart . . .

We are now looking forward to seeing you and Gottfried here soon . . . Cordially yours, Thomas Mann.

21

Joachim Maass— Author, Friend, Brother in Destiny. Manfred Hausmann

In the late 1920s a young writer became known in Germany of whom Hermann Hesse, Thomas Mann, and Stefan Zweig were particularly fond, whom they kept encouraging, and whose work they appreciated. His name was Joachim Maass, and like Thomas Mann he was a native of a Hansa town. Maass came into our fold in 1929; his first novel, *Bohème ohne Mimi,* was brought out by the S. Fischer Verlag in 1930 and caused some stir. Stefan Zweig emphatically reviewed this first work by a young writer in the *Berliner Tageblatt:*

It is the special skill of this young Joachim Maass to be just as good at keeping silent as at telling a story, never to speak of passion and yet to make the reader feel it, thus conveying the most personal and intimate things through vibrations rather than words. His unmistakable and natural charm as well as his special literary personality will attract the attention of those who are attentive.

In an essay on Thomas Mann the young writer painted a picture of his generation:

My memories are those of a child of my time, a member of the generation born around 1900, those who still experienced World War I at home and later, when they were mature enough to live the life of the intellect, saw all values hopelessly shaken: money; the material future; professional prospects; the social order that had been regarded as inviolable in our childhood and the fatherland that had been considered sacred; the ideals, all of which seemed to have become questionable, even in art, where the "soul" was now supposed to triumph . . . All in all, it was a dismal period with an aphotic gloss like an early fall evening gone with the wind, and the faces of art tottered about in it like a procession of ghosts . . . The proletarization had begun. In students' rooms, discussions went on till the wee hours . . . People got excited and shouted! . . . In truth it was not the form that left us dissatisfied with The Magic Mountain, but rather the intellectual acuity, accuracy, and clarity of thought in the warmish, drizzly fog of our mystical sense of life. That is not how we had imagined the "new substance"! . . . The direction that mysticism subsequently took in the social and political spheres under the leadership of howling dervishes— the mysticism that evidently was fatefully slumbering not only among intellectuals but among all the young people of Germany— we have experienced it, and the world is still aflame from it . . . It was the same "man" that in speech and writing was always . . . opposed to dangerous mysticism who plunged Germany and the entire world into such horrible misfortune . . . It seems to me that the publication of The Magic Mountain was a milestone in the development and the resolve of the young intellectuals in postwar Germany. This work was a programmatic expression of the greatest and most responsible representative of the bourgeoisie . . . I have never seen a famous man wear his fame more lightly and becomingly. As worn by him, fame produced in those not famous what fame certainly does not always produce: sympathy and even a gentle, heartfelt enthusiasm . . .

In the hard times of Nazi persecution Joachim was faithfully at our side. He had a cordial and humor-filled relationship with my father, and time and again he visited my mother, particularly during the difficult period after our emigration in 1935, when she remained in her house in the Grunewald as its sole inhabitant until 1939. Joachim did not shrink from the personal danger that he incurred through his visits to S. Fischer's widow. He warned her against remaining in Nazi Germany and repeatedly tried to induce her to emigrate, which she finally decided to do in early 1939, when it was already almost too late. Joachim also visited us in Stockholm several times— a daring undertaking that did not remain unknown to the Gestapo. In the summer of 1939 he decided to leave Germany and emigrate to the U.S. Before doing so he revised his novel *Ein Testament* for serialization in the *Berliner Illustrierte* and used the substantial payment he received to enable Hamburg friends to emigrate.

Joachim and I felt like brother and sister; as members of the same generation we were plunged from the seemingly stable "good old" bourgeoisie into a world in which all values and concepts had been upset. Both of us were at home in the field of literature— he from a creative point of view, I as the child of a publisher. We understood each other in many realms. The following poem that he wrote in my album is from this year of our first "inner encounter."

Morgens

Früh die kindlichen Lieder
taten gut;
aber sie kommen nicht wieder,
vertropft ist das Kinderherz-Blut.

Und ein Vorhang zerriß
seither;
Nacht war als Nacht gewiß,
und zu schlafen war schwer.

Doch nun, siehe: der Tag ist nah,
Stimmen schon grüßen dich;
Wünsche sind wieder da,
und das Herz bevölkert sich.

Für Tutti, Stockholm, April 39

(In the Morning. The early childlike songs did us good, but they will not return; the children's lifeblood no longer drips. And since then a curtain has torn. Night was certain as night, and sleeping was difficult. But now, look: the day is near and voices are already greeting you; wishes are here again, and the earth is getting populated.

—For Tutti, Stockholm, April 39.)

Our friendship increasingly solidified during the first years in the "New World," which were hard for all of us. His letters to me testify to his inner ups and downs, to his suffering because of Germany and the world; above all, they show how ardently and devotedly he practiced his profession.

In America Joachim wrote his novel *Das magische Jahr,* which we published in two languages: the German original was issued by the Bermann-Fischer Verlag in Stockholm and the English translation, *The Magic Year,* by the newly founded L. B. Fischer Publishing Corporation, New York. I designed the jackets of both editions. On October 21, 1944 Thomas Mann wrote to Gottfried about this book:

*Dear Dr. Bermann, I have already finished Joachim Maass' manuscript and enjoyed it very much. German exile literature has been enriched by a beautiful, important, highly personal, and highly poetic prose work with which Maass meets all the expectations that he aroused with his first book, Das Testament.**

The introduction to the section "Zwischen den Zeiten," set in a lonely farm house in winter and featuring quite genuine dialogues (which are, of course, in English), is extraordinarily original and grips the reader not only because of the strangeness of the present situation but also through the disturbingly vivid memories of experiences in a homeland "awakened" to fearful nonsense. And surely the recherche du temps perdu, this descent into the depths of childhood, has rarely been practiced with richer poetic results than on the many vibrant pages that follow. There is a profusion of colorful, uncanny, grotesque, tragic, lovely memory portraits whose frame is the great seaport of Hamburg. One outdoes the other in the intensiveness and vividness of the dream; in the entire book I found no empty spot or weak place. Here one learns again that literature is "the life of life", the heightening of life by the spirit, the special situation here being that the heightening role of the spirit is assumed by the fantastically transfiguring and quivering soul of the child.

The finest thing about the book is the "sensitivity to evil" that is at work in it without claiming big words like morality, religion, and humanity, but in a purely painful way, as a profound, delicate, and invincible no. It is this delicate, seemingly helpless and yet powerful touch of vulnerability that even today lets the most secret things at the bottom of an epoch groaning with cruelty resonate and that a none too distant future will appreciate even more consciously. Your Thomas Mann.

Joachim's friendship ultimately encompassed a third generation of Fischers as well— our children, particularly our oldest daughter Gaby, who studied for two years under Joachim at Mount Holyoke College, where he had become a professor of German literature. She was initiated into the mysteries and backgrounds of German literature through his brilliant lectures. He wrote:

I would hardly have dreamed that some day I would be a teacher at an American women's college and talking about literature, modern German literature, in awkward English. But I was comforted by the fact that the things of the spirit that I had learned to love ever more deeply had accompanied me. I have talked to my young ladies especially about Thomas Mann, and whenever I talk about him I feel at home in the alien surroundings. I feel that I am speaking about what is best about the German spirit— its ever-recurring shift from personal fascination with death to great, comforting friendliness toward life, from nationalistic wilfulness and reclusiveness to cosmopolitanism.

With great good humor Maass attempted to reconcile his two professions— that of a teacher who had to teach something to his "snow geese," as he called his students, and that of a writer. He prepared his lectures on German literature intensively. When I visited Gaby at the college, I utilized every opportunity to listen to Joachim, and I always left enriched by the wealth of ideas in his exposition. He wrote:

Yesterday I gave my final lecture for this academic year about Grillparzer, Grabbe, and Büchner. The story of Büchner's life and the circumstances under which Danton's Death *was written are as though from time to time history favored ingenious repetitions. What this brilliant young man, who died in exile in Zurich before his twenty-fourth birthday, experienced has also been experienced by most of us who for one reason or another could no longer endure the preponderance and idolization of shameful monsters like Hitler. What always shakes me most, however, when I read such a story is not the spirited congruence between then and now, but the fact that we did not understand these stories before we had experienced them ourselves. This makes me sad, for if the experiences of those long-forgotten people did not teach us anything, why should our experiences instruct those coming after us? Oh, Tutti, it is a world without much hope, destined to fall prey to the scoundrels; the apathy of people is stronger than all the grief and suffering that are being experienced here. This feeling often threatens to paralyze me, but I am helped by Dostoievsky's words which you wrote for me so beautifully, like a medieval monk, and on which my eyes often rest when I sit at my desk: "Work, work tirelessly."*

In 1941, when I quite unexpectedly lost my dearly beloved and adored uncle, my mother's brother Ludwig Landshoff, a Bach scholar, musicologist, and conductor, and was disconsolate about his death, Joachim wrote me:

. . . When something like this happens, I always ask myself whether we do the right thing if we mourn too much. Is it not highly desirable to take leave quickly of a world which with its filth and bestial depravity cannot possibly have anything to offer an experienced and satiated heart? That we are gripped by melancholy is proper, but by pain? When I hear about a consequential death, I always think of Grabbe's magnificent words that one man says to another when it is a matter of dying: "Oh, we shall not fall out of the world; we are simply in it." This is what I believe, too, and it mystically eliminates pain and transforms it into a great perspective of the fate and destiny of us all . . . If one has strong feelings, one must demand a lot of them and particularly that they rise to greatness and permanent validity and solidity and ennoble themselves on a purer plane. Sometimes I wonder compulsively whether life is perhaps not a dream of every human being and whether he dreams exactly what he needs to experience and to know . . . Think about this idea at a quiet, dark, solitary hour and see whether it changes some things for you and suddenly shows them to you in a different light. That has been my experience . . . In any case, it is so profoundly and closely connected with death that I am not quite certain whether it is an idea about life or about death . . .

At a later date, when Maass was working on his new novel *Der Fall Gouffé* (The Gouffé Case), he described the inner situation of writers of his generation on the basis of his own creative process:

If I compare my work with the works of earlier writers (at the moment I am reading Fontane by way of preparing my lectures for the coming semester), I get a strangely uncertain feeling: I don't know whether I should envy those sons of better times or whether I ought to regard myself as superior to them. Their great assurance, their almost astonishing unpretentiousness which, however, yields such a lot; the integrity of their psychology and the childlikeness of their technique— my God, what an easy time of it they had! In those days everything was clear and unambiguous; God was still in his heaven; the state was not an institution of bandits; there were classes, and people were content with that . . . We, however, are sitting on ruins under a deserted heaven. But it seems to me that our visions are igniting new stars, and the torches of our anxieties shine into the deepest abysses; the ghosts, enemies of every epoch that is sure of itself, come staggering along again; the nights, the hearts, our horror, and our piety— all this appears to me infinitely more mysterious, even though it may not yet let itself be formed into a great harmonious structure. And I wonder whether I would have preferred to live then and shape things in peace or whether it is not a greater privilege to have been cursed to live at this time and to serve it creatively— without much hope of the great completion, but with one's eyes not diverted from the everlasting secrets of human destiny and human dignity. Surely it is honorable, intellectually honorable, to have to wade around in this brew and not have one's beloved eyes soiled by this filth! Tutti, I must confide in you: No matter how horrible life almost always appears to me, I am a happy person. I look back on my sorrowful years with joy and find that I have not once been beset by serious confusion. I have been deceived by neither friend nor foe, and in hours of grace I have been guided by a divination of what I feel to be my mission as by another star of Bethlehem. And I am confident that I shall not give this up until I die.

The way that this man, who was delicate by nature, time and again attained to faith in himself and his work was admirable, though he often regarded getting through the hours and the days as an unreasonable burden.

To have Joachim's friendship was a precious and rare gift; he fulfilled the ideal of the friend *per se* as it was actually expressed only in the age of Romanticism. He was always there when he was needed, always ready to forget his own problems and concern himself with those of another person and to solve them in accordance with his absolute conviction of what was "right." In so doing he always tried to proceed in a loving but quite vigorous manner, and in the end one had the feeling that one had been guided by kindly thoughtfulness. At the present time, when this feeling of responsibility for one's fellow man threatens to be lost entirely, it seems very important to me to sing the praises of this kind of friendship, which by now has become a thing of the past. It should be revived among people. "Let us stick to our friendship; there is nothing better in the world and nothing more needed in these apocalyptic times, when we should all help one another to survive, to hate clearly, to love clearly, and never to become bitter. For all this is equally necessary." That is what he wrote me.

When I wrote for him a verse by Schiller of which he was particularly fond on parchment in beautiful lettering, he thanked me as follows:

. . . I am gradually becoming saturated with pretty Tutti things, and I like that an awful lot. For people can be close to each other in things, too, if these things bear their personality; whatever comes from you has your personality . . . You are a good thought in my life— in the sense of Schlegel, who always regarded as an artistically good idea one that was also a feeling!

Before the war ended in 1945 he was beset by great fears about the future:

. . . Where shall the great compromise on the problems of the postwar period, which are so fraught with catastrophe, come from? Despite all the brilliance of his temperament, Churchill is a fanatical conservative, and what Stalin's political ethics was all about became clear when he concluded a treaty with the Nazis on the eve of their attack on Poland . . . We shall perhaps never experience good times any more, Tutti; inwardly, too, our time seems evil to me, and one cannot escape from it anywhere except to the "Mount Ararat of the heart," but who has the strength to get there? And I feel that this is what I am working on; actually, it is not so much my "novel" that I am writing. As I write, I try to climb upward to the ridges of the stony cliffs of the heart. Up there it will be pure, cold, and clear, and down here our earthly fate is brewing in thick clouds. Forgive me . . . I am really incapable of writing a letter today. If only you would come soon! Ever your Joachim.

On August 15, 1945 he wrote me:

. . . I am feeble and weak, presumably because I drank all sorts of things yesterday to celebrate the end of the war. But I felt anything but festive as I did so, because the enormous problems of the near future seem to be casting their gloomy shadows over the entire world.

God only knows what will become of the invention of atomic fission in the hands of this immature, stupid, and vicious mankind.

And on September 30, 1945 he continued as follows:

. . . *With burning interest and an uncertain impression I have studied the news from Germany. Oh, it is all so sad, Tutti, heartrending and wretched. But then again, what else could have come from the dominion of the filthy demons but complete disintegration, the most strangling poverty, and shameful humiliation? What else have these evil spirits ever blessed mankind with but the gifts of degradation and death? But the feeling one gets from the news that the Germans are accepting all this comparatively calmly, as though it were simply the result of a lost war— that is more horrible than anything else. What? They are not outraged, they are not trying to get hold of any Nazi beasts that may still be found in order to stone them? That is terrible, it is criminal nihilism, and it seems that they have not gained the slightest moral insight from the dreadful devastation— the only thing they could and should have derived from it . . . A last hope is fading for me . . .*

On November 17, 1948, during the second year that Gottfried and I spent in Europe together in order to prepare the rebuilding of our publishing house in Germany, Joachim wrote:

. . . *I am, incidentally, pleased to hear that you appear to have concrete plans for your publishing house. Are they connected with the printing project that Washington once suggested? To be sure, I doubt whether you will manage to influence Suhrkamp in your or in any spirit, for he is as stubborn as a mule. Do you think he ever answered my letter, even though I enclosed international reply coupons? No, evidently he doesn't answer letters as a matter of principle, and though this is a considerable savings of time, it is a bit embarrassing. I would be happy if I had nothing further to do with him. The distrust that I have felt toward him from the beginning (though this never concerned his political character) has been confirmed all too fully . . .*

In 1949 Joachim went to the west coast of America to spend a few months with friends, and despite a profound depression about "wrecked Europe" he tried to work on the completion of his novel *Der Fall Gouffé*. The following poem dates from that period:

Die Nacht des Einsamen (Juni 1949)

Allein gelebt in deinem Heiligtume,
mußt du allein dich auch zum Schluß versöhnen;
Zu spät zur Liebe und zu spät zum Ruhme:
du mußt dich an den Tod gewöhnen.

Es wird dich keiner preisen, wenn du gehst;
die Zeit sei, wie sie mag: in Flor und Rechte
verwuchert sie die Stelle, wo du stehst,
dem jetzigen, dem kommenden Geschlechte.

Vielleicht, daß sich die Nacht erbarme
in der ein Maienglanz von Mondlicht liegt,
und dieses sich wie weiche Arme
um deinen stolzen Kummer schmiegt.

Für Tutti,
Joachim, Hollywood, Juli 1949

(The Night of the Lonely Man. June 1949. Having lived alone in your shrine, you also have to make your peace alone in the end. Too late for love and too late for fame; you must get accustomed to death. No one will praise you when you go. No matter what the time may be like, in blossoms and rights it overgrows the place where you stand for the present and the coming generations. Perhaps the night in which there is a May gleam of moonlight will take pity and this glow will wrap itself around your proud grief like soft arms.

—For Tutti, Joachim. Hollywood, July 1949).

In the fall of 1926 Gottfried and I read in a periodical a short novella that impressed us with the great narrative talent of its author, Manfred Hausmann, then still unknown. We set out to visit him at Worpswede, where he lived in a small country house at the edge of a big moor. We found a tall, thin young man with blue eyes and a melancholy smile who went well with the seclusion of this austere, isolated region. He already had a contract with another publisher for his first book, *Lampioon küsst Mädchen und kleine Birken,* but with his big novel *Salut gen Himmel* he became our author and friend. This work, which Hausmann dedicated to me, showed a different literary talent of both delicate melancholia and dramatic dynamism. Later he made me a present of the manuscript of the first chapter, "Die Achterbahn," a mysterious, spooky occurrence described with vehemence. *Salut gen Himmel* found a large readership that henceforth remained loyal to the author, and the literary critics also hailed him as a promising talent.

Hausmann also attached himself to my parents, who took an amicable interest in him. He often came to see us and shared our enjoyment of our baby daughters Gaby and Gisi. He wrote a craddle song in my album for the three of us:

Ein kleines Wiegenlied aus Worpswede

Da hinten auf Wendelkens Weide
Da scheint die Sonne so warm,
Da sitzt Maria im Grase
Und hat ihr Kindchen im Arm.

Sie legt es in die Wiege
Mit ihrer mageren Hand.
Der Hütejunge hält ihr
Das goldene Wiegenband.

Die Wiege geht auf und nieder,
Die Schafe weiden heran.
Da fängt der Hütejunge
Ganz leise zu pfeifen an.

Seine Augen sind so ernsthaft,
Er weiß es selber nicht.
Er pfeift nur und sieht dem Kinde
Ins schlafende Angesicht.

Für Tutti, Gabi und Gisi
Worpswede 17-IV-30
Manfred Hausmann

(A Little Lullaby from Worpswede. Back there on Wenedelken's pasture the sun shines so warm. Maria sits on the grass and has a little child in her arms. She puts it in the cradle with her thin hand. The shepherd boy holds the golden cradle strap for her. The cradle rocks up and down. The grazing sheep come closer and the shepherd begins to whistle quite softly. His eyes are so serious, but he is not aware of it. He just whistles and looks at the face of the sleeping child.

—For Tutti, Gabi, and Gisi. Worpswede, April 17, 1930. Manfred Hausmann).

Manfred Hausmann was courageous enough— and it did take courage in 1934— to speak at the grave of my father, whom he so deeply respected, in his name as well as in that of the young generation:

. . . *For us younger people who did not witness the growth and evolution of the S. Fischer Verlag from the beginning but joined it only a few years ago, when everything was already big and firmly established, it was a rather singular experience when we came into personal contact with the man who was to become our guide, friend, and fatherly counselor . . . There came the day when one bowed to a short man with very intelligent light blue eyes and had to admit that S. Fischer was not only an institution but, strange as that might seem, a human being as well . . . Certainly, a human being, but, Good Lord, what a human being! Such a human being that anyone who was privileged to be with him, be it socially or alone in blessed hours, did not primarily think of the publishing house, the literary program, and the superior authority. Here, after all, was something entirely different, here was much more! We grew up at a time marked by a lack of reverence; we neither would nor could have any real, heartfelt reverence. People and things seemed too dubious for us to want to genuflect before them. S. Fischer, however, was among those who, simply through their humanity, through their existence and unique being, brought us to the point of feeling reverence again, whether we wanted to or not—reverence especially for so much modesty and reserve coupled with so much true wisdom; reverence, to use Hölderlin's mystical words, for the sacred sobriety of his personality; reverence for the gentle and reserved manner in which he presented his thoughts; reverence for his steadfastness, a reverence that one could also call loyalty to oneself; reverence for the enchanting intellectual charm of this old man; reverence for his deep-seated smile that reflected so much awareness of the sadness and darkness of existence; reverence for his helplessness in the face of all meanness; reverence for his nobility, which was the most natural thing in the world to him; reverence for his dreams and longings which made him love Romanticism; reverence for his compassionate kindness toward all weakness; reverence for the breath and the openness of his soul. And reverence for his so-called faults which, after all, made him even more lovable than he was . . . Only now, with a knowledge or at least an idea of the human being, did we also perceive the greatness, the significance, and the hovering unity of his creation, the S. Fischer Verlag. Nothing impersonal was there any more . . . He brought out only literary works that he himself loved. And what is love of literature but surmising in it a part of one's self? . . .*

In 1937, after we had opened the Bermann-Fischer Verlag in Vienna, Hausmann wrote:

. . . The packages of books that I receive from you astound me over and over again. What a publisher, what a publisher! Who can compare with this? . . . I hear more about you than you may think . . . I am always pleased that everyone has only pleasant things to report . . . Your astonishing publishing program tells me that you were right to leave Germany, and with all my heart I wish you peace, work, and success. To be sure, I hardly dare look into the future . . . I mean the future of Austria.

At Christmastime 1938 he sent us this little poem:

Unser Schifflein mag nun schweben
Recht ins unbekannte Leben,
In die Ferne und Gefahr,
Also daß wir uns erheben
Über das geringe Leben,
Das noch gestern unser war!

(Let our little boat float now right into the unknown life, to distant and dangerous places, so that we may rise above the modest life that was still ours only yesterday!)

Hausmann's first sign of life after the end of the war, brought us from Germany by an American friend, was dated September 1945:

You know that we have bitter times behind us and such times still ahead of us . . . What has tormented us most is not the events of the war that roared over us in their whole frightfulness; the moral misfortune was much worse. You know that I foresaw what the Nazis would bring upon us from the first day. It made me despair, and I am desperate even now—not about the destroyed cities, though the dimensions of the destruction are horrendous, but about the destroyed soul of my people . . . What revealed itself here during the Nazi rule defies description. You are probably familiar with the horrors of the concentration camps, but you do not know everyday life in Germany during the past ten years. You are not acquainted with the criminally stupid, megalomaniacal average German. I got to know him, and at times this took my breath away.

During the difficult starvation period following the war, in February 1948, he wrote us:

. . . *Things here are lousy, but I never forget why things are lousy for us, nor do I ever forget that I share the blame for it. Please believe me! And please remember that everything I write you has as its premise and is based on a feeling of guilt. Of course, I am not sitting around wringing my hands and despairing. Rather, I am rolling up my sleeves and trying to clean up the mess . . . When, oh when will the longed-for Bermann-Fischer books appear? You simply cannot imagine, you really can't, how famished people here are for them! I greet you in old friendship as your grateful and faithful Manfred Hausmann.*

*Actually, Joachim Maass had published three novels before *Das Testament* (Hamburg, 1938): *Bohème ohne Mimi* 1930; *Widersacher* 1932; and *Die unwiederbringliche Zeit* 1935.

22
Carl Zuckmayer, an "Original Talent"

"Zuck is an original talent," wrote my mother about him in her diary. After his first great success, *Der fröhliche Weinberg* (The Merry Vineyard), and before my father's death Zuckmayer frequently was our guest on Erdenerstrasse. When my parents invited him for the first time, he arranged with his friend Erich Maria Remarque, whose book *Im Westen nichts Neues* (All Quiet on the Western Front) had been a sensational success, "to disturb the good old bourgeois atmosphere of this house a bit. *Épater le bourgeois!*" When, however, the two men, so cocky with success, faced the venerable and yet so humorous S. Fischer, their youthful conspiratorial fervor ran out of steam and they were captivated by his charm. From that moment on they were among the admirers and friends of the house. After my father's death Zuckmayer wrote affectionate letters to my mother during the first terrible Nazi years, such as this one from 1935: " . . . The difficult period that all of us are now going through is creating a closer bond between us, and this connection will endure no matter where the paths of individuals may lead." Soon thereafter he wrote, on the occasion of the New Year: " . . . Remember how many good wishes of those who love you and your house accompany you into the new year!"

Later, when my mother had emigrated to the United States, he sent her this poem for her seventy-fifth birthday:

Das Alter

Ach das Feuer das in Dir einst brannte –
Nur zum Scheine sank es aschenwärts.
Was uns in der Jugend übermannte,
Unvermindert schürt's das alte Herz.

Wie's die Amsel frühlingsfrüh gesungen
Tropft's am Abend, – nachtigallenhold.
Fischer – tief in Deinem Netz verschlungen
Glänzt das reine, meerenthobne Gold.

Ach das Feuer, ach das heiße Lieben –
Oh wie leidet, wer die Freude kennt!
Heb den Blick! Die Sterne sind geblieben!
Horch! Die Stimme spricht. Der Dornbusch brennt.

(Old Age. Oh, the fire that once burned inside you only seems to have turned to ashes. What overwhelmed us in our youth provides undiminished fuel for the old heart. What the blackbird sang with the freshness of spring drips at eventide with the nightingale's loveliness. Fischer, deeply entwined in your net there gleams the pure gold lifted from the sea. Oh for the fire, oh for ardent love—oh, how anyone who knows joy suffers! Lift up your eyes! The stars have remained! Hark! The voice is speaking. The bramble is burning).

In 1934 we took over Zuckmayer's story *Eine Liebesgeschichte* (A Love Story), which had already been set in type by the house of Ullstein, as well as his works that Ullstein, now directed by Nazis, had previously published.

In the first years of our Austrian emigration our friendship deepened. We met in Vienna at the home of mutual friends, in our house in Hietzing, and at theatrical premieres. We saw the Zuckmayers in their beloved Wiesmühl at Henndorf near Salzburg, and from there we attended the Salzburg Festival together for the last time in 1937. A magnificent performance of Mozart's *The Magic Flute,* conducted by Toscanini, seemed like a farewell to our world! After the glamorous performance the iron curtain got stuck and one could see the stage hands striking the set. It was like a sinister omen. At that time Zuckmayer wrote the following poem into my album:

Kleine Strophen von der Unsterblichkeit

Dauer, Zeit und Raum
Sind wie Brandungsschaum,
Der verweht, indes die Flut sich wendet –
Doch das kleinste Sein
Schließt ein Wesen ein,
Das von Anfang ist und niemals endet.

Der Du Dich besinnst,
Ob Du einst verrinnst
Gleich dem Sand und gleich dem Regentropfen –
Denk, daß Meer und Land,
Wasser, Fels und Sand
Steter sind als Deines Herzens Klopfen.

Nur was in Dir brennt –
Was kein Wort benennt –
Dauert über der Vernichtung Flammen.
Wärst Du nicht geweiht
Zur Unsterblichkeit –
Bräch die Schöpfung in sich selbst zusammen.

Carl Zuckmayer
für Tutti 18. 9. 1937

(Little Stanzas About Immortality. Permanence, time, and space are like foamy surf that disappears when the tide turns—but even the smallest being contains a substance that is there from the beginning and never ends. You who reflect— even though some day you may vanish like the sand and raindrops— consider that the sea and the land, the water, rocks, and sand are more enduring than your heartbeat. Only what burns inside you, what no word can name lasts beyond the flames of destruction. If you were not consecrated to immortality, Creation would collapse.

—Carl Zuckmayer, for Tutti, September 18, 1937).

When on March 13, 1938 a friend in the Austrian government informed us about the imminent occupation of Austria by the Nazis, we called up Zuck, who was alone in Vienna at the time (Jobs, his wife, was staying for the time being in the Grunewald with my mother) and implored him to leave Austria with us immediately. He, however, insisted on "taking a look at things." His last words were "I shall join you tomorrow." Joining us tomorrow very nearly cost him his life. If he had not been so good at appealing to the authority mania of the S.A. officer who had pulled him off the train at the border— Zuck put on a veritable Köpenick comedy for him (the reference is to Zuckmayer's play *Der Hauptmann von Köpenick* —The Captain of Köpenick— based on a real-life incident and illustrative of the German's overwrought reverence for authority— in this case a faker in a captain's uniform)— he would not have been permitted to pass.

After our flight from Austria we met the Zuckmayers again in Zurich. It was an oppressive atmosphere, for none of us had any prospects. Zuckmayer decided to seek asylum in French-speaking Switzerland and went to Chardonne, while we traveled to Stockholm and rebuilt our publishing house there. Two years later, however, we met again in the United States. We had settled in Connecticut, while the Zuckmayers found their rural *ritiro* farther north, in Vermont. There we visited them on a radiant day when they were able to rent the farm that they had long had their eye on. The "green hill" afforded a magnificent panorama of the whole countryside. Zuck wrote me on August 6, 1941:

Dear Tutti . . . The refurbishing of the house is proceeding apace; every time we go there we get enthusiastic all over again. Our two children were here over the weekend and almost cried when they saw it; it must have matched their dream image of a new home. The upstairs rooms are already finished and look enchanting; the new brick fireplace in the barn has been built, and next week the electricity and plumbing for the bathroom will be installed . . . You haven't even seen the big skiing slope that is part of the property; it also offers the most marvelous view. All this we didn't discover till later. The only thing that worries me now is the wood, because it is practically impossible to get anyone to fell trees here . . . Incidentally, last Sunday, in an isolated clump of raspberry bushes on a nearby mountain, I had my first encounter with a fully grown black bear, who looked at me suspiciously and then cleared out. I saw him quite clearly and smelled him, too . . . Most cordially yours, Zuck.

Barnard, Vt., August 30, 1941

Dear Fischers, first a zoological note: In the meantime I have secured exact information about the existence and living habits of the North American Stachelschwein and also observed one near here. There are two sorts in the woods of Vermont. The big kind, the one you have seen, is called porcupine, and I have encountered one. Michi saw two little ones, called bush hogs. In all areas in which there are porcupines there is also the Canadian lynx, the biggest local wildcat, which eats primarily porcupines: I saw two of its cubs the day before yesterday. C'est ça. Gaby is a young lady. The question about her behavior is simply grotesque. It is the other way round; there is something about her that causes us to be on our best behavior— insofar as possible . . .*

Good-bye and all good wishes. Your Zuck.

Next week we shall move into our house. It will be wonderful.

Despite all the hard work Zuckmayer was very enthusiastic about his new life in the country. The work demanded all his energy, but for the time being he did not mind this because he felt so well on his farm up in the "Green Mountains" of Vermont. We frequently visited him and Jobs, spending with them radiant summer days as well as ice-cold winter days with snow and ice. There was always a splendid meal; Jobs cooked her favorite dishes, and Zuck was a gourmet.

On April 20, 1944 he wrote:

If you see a chance of coming, hang on to it and don't let it go . . . Our gasoline situation is good enough for us to pick you up, and by that time the road to our house may be such that we shall be able to drive up . . . I shall kill two ducks and perhaps also a rooster. I shall take pork from our last sow out of the freezer; we could also start a ham we smoked ourselves, and for breakfast you will get at least six eggs (but no more than sixteen in accordance with Bismarck's principle). Should you wish to bring something, alcohol is always welcome and in any form (except rubbing alcohol).

To be sure, you must be prepared for me to read something to you. After all, during the past few years I did not just lay eggs and give milk. But seriously, I recently made a very quick and final decision— namely, to plant next to nothing this spring, not to make a new milk-selling contract, and to make a substantial reduction in our animals and the entire farm, keeping only what is easily movable . . . You see, experience has now taught me that this work can definitely not be combined with writing, unless one has real helpers. And I must write again and complete what I have started. For the time being this decision poses certain financial problems, but this, too, is an incentive for me to complete plays and books again instead of sketching them or devising them. For it is true that we were able to squeeze by the last few years with the farm; but if one does not do it on a very large scale with a big financial investment, one can never achieve more with a farm than eking out a living and maintaining the existing stock— and even this is not always possible without financial loss and only with so much hard and time-consuming physical labor and so much constant "planning" that one is completely absorbed by it. Not for one moment do I regret having lived like this for the past few years. Today I am quite certain that I needed this break, that it saved my life in every respect. And I have learned an enormous amount from it—something that no other life-style could have given me. But the break is over; things are starting up again, they are sprouting and budding, and I must now concentrate all my energies on not letting any growth get stunted. I was recently asked in a written interview what I could say about my "literary" development, and my answer was that I hoped it would begin in 1944-45.

At Christmastime 1944 Zuckmayer wrote us:

Dear Tutti, dear Gottfried . . . I hope and am sure that you are having a good and happy holiday with your three daughters— as happy as it can be this year, when no bells of peace are ringing as yet but, rather, the earth seems to be gently trembling and swaying always and everywhere— as from a distant and heavy impact whose tremor one feels without hearing it. In this all but impenetrable and oppressive fog that surrounds us and afflicts us from all sides the best thing we can do is to stick firmly together, so as not to lose our way. Friendship means more than anything else. I am joyfully certain of yours, and on mine you can put down full glasses without a drop getting spilled. In this spirit, Merry Christmas from your old Zuck.

At a later date he sent me a vision of the future titled "Elegie von Abschied und Wiederkehr," written seven years earlier, with the following letter:

January 11, 1946. Dearest Tutti, today I am finally sending you a poem I wrote years ago and that no one but Jobs has known . . . It was written in 1939, during the first months of our American period, when no bomb had as yet fallen on Germany but its real destruction had already taken place. Today it seems to me like a lyrical version of the letter in which Thomas Mann explains the fate of an emigrant and his attitude toward "returning." In any case, after almost seven years I had no alterations to make— it has come true in horrendous fashion— and its last line already contains an invitation of our future.

Elegie von Abschied und Wiederkehr
geschrieben in Amerika, 1939

Ich weiß, ich werde alles wiedersehn.
Und es wird alles ganz verwandelt sein,
Ich werde durch erloschne Städte gehn,
Darin kein Stein mehr auf dem andern Stein –
Und selbst wo noch die alten Steine stehen,
Sind es nicht mehr die altvertrauten Gassen –
Ich weiß, ich werde alles wiedersehen
Und nichts mehr finden, was ich einst verlassen.

Der breite Strom wird noch zum Abend gleiten.
Auch wird der Wind noch durch die Weiden gehn,
Die unberührt in sinkenden Gezeiten
Die stumme Totenwacht am Ufer stehn.
Ein Schatten wird an unsrer Seite schreiten
Und tiefste Nacht um unsre Schläfen wehn –
Dann mag erschauernd in den Morgen reiten,
Wer lebend schon sein eignes Grab gesehn.

Ich weiß, ich werde zögernd wiederkehren,
Wenn kein Verlangen mehr die Schritte treibt.
Entseelt ist unsres Herzens Heim-Begehren,
Und was wir brennend suchten, liegt entleibt.
Leid wird zu Flammen, die sich selbst verzehren,

Und nur ein kühler Flug von Asche bleibt –
Bis die Erinnrung über dunklen Meeren
Ihr ewig Zeichen in den Himmel schreibt.
C. Z. für Tutti

(Elegy About Farewell and Return, written in America, 1939. I know I shall see everything again, and everything will be completely changed. I shall walk through extinguished cities in which no stone will be left standing; and even where the old stones will be left, it will not be the familiar streets any more. I know I shall see everything and no longer find anything that I once left. The broad stream will still flow westward and the wind will still blow through the willows which, untouched in declining times, will keep the mute death watch on the shore. A shade will walk by our side and deepest night will blow on our temples. Then may he who has already seen his own grave in his lifetime ride shuddering toward morning. I know I shall hesitantly return when no desire propels me forward any more. Our heart's desire to return home is soulless, and what we ardently sought lies lifeless. Sorrow turns into flames that consume themselves, and only a bold flight of ashes remains—until memory writes across dark seas its eternal sign into the sky.
—C.Z. for Tutti).

Our future is memory (not retrospect)— and from the soil and the wellspring of memory a new and multifarious growth will arise for us. Only he who remembers with every fiber of his being can let the past be the past and strike out for new shores. Only he who loves more intensely than he hates has life.

*This poem, you see, was in Job's little fireproof steel box on the farm in which she keeps my manuscripts; I tend to be rather careless with them, and in recent days the farm has been hard to reach.*** *Before that I went there on skis twice and each time forgot the house key. Skiing over the hills was so wonderful that I did not feel like taking my skis off . . . And now I had to undertake a sort of glacier expedition with cleats on my boots, since Joachim had reminded me of the poems and I definitely wanted to have the thing. We have glare ice everywhere and people play Sonja Henie on the streets, which is especially charming when one goes shopping for milk and eggs. But I am sure it will snow again soon— that is, as soon as the storm that is blowing today has abated; I know about that. By the time you are* *able to come we shall have the finest snow for skiing. You must go skiing with the girls and me on the farm this winter, for it is the nicest place in the area. Then we shall light a fire in the fireplace and grill steaks.*

Cordially, Zuck.

As the war went on, food became scarcer in America as well, and we started converting our lawn into a vegetable garden. On his free weekends Gottfried toiled very hard to dig up part of our land for planting corn, and our magnificent corn crop made us famous among our neighbors. Zuckmayer helped by sending fresh butter and eggs, and on June 19, 1945 he sent us this report: "Dear Tutti, it got to be four dozen— the eggs, that is; that turned out to be more practical and can be repeated every two weeks." And he added to this brief report: "Received the terrible news that my friend Theo Haubach, the Castor to the late Mierendorff's Pollux, was hanged by the 'People's Court' in Berlin on January 23, 1945. Unfortunately this is authentic information. Other friends of mine are also dead."

More and more news of this kind reached all of us, and the truth about the concentration camps increasingly leaked out. In those days people were scarcely able to comprehend the dimensions of these horrendous murders. This was the beginning of the terror that today is threatening to destroy our civilization.

Not only had Zuckmayer's "literary development" begun again, but he had already completed a new play that was destined to become one of his greatest successes, *The Devil's General.* In several letters he announced that he would visit us in order to read it to us.

Barnard, Vt., July 10, 1945.

Dear Gottfried, dear Tutti: Last night Joachim and I finally established contact. The public conveyances in America seem to be worn out and journalism seems about to become extinct. We have decided that we want to go to New York together or at the same time— for me it is of the greatest importance to have him present at the reading, and then you will be able to determine much better, together with him, whether the third act is suitable for the [Neue] Rundschau . . . The whole thing is a tremendous undertaking, but I venture to say that it seems to be successful— that is, for me it is a satisfying result of all those years . . . We shall probably be at your place around July 20. Meanwhile, be embraced by your old Zuck.

On July 24, 1945 he wrote:

Dear Tutti: so it will be Saturday; I shall let you know the train . . . You will pick us up in Stamford, won't you? . . . Regarding the reading, which is particularly long and exciting (a premiere for me—even Jobs has only read and not heard the second and third acts): Would you mind perhaps inviting the old Osborns? They are such dear, brave people, and it would please them so much . . . So that it won't be such a late evening and anyone from out of town might still catch a train, and so we could discuss it afterwards, I would suggest that I start around five in the afternoon. The first act is the longest, and if I take my time, it will require two hours and a half. I suggest that we take a short break for eating. But please, in the interest of the reading, if possible no long sitting around for a regular dinner, but perhaps only a few sandwiches! Afterwards we can fry ourselves some eggs; I shall bring along at least two dozen. I suppose you will have a drop of alcohol on hand. For the listeners it would be better to have as much coffee as possible ready, especially for Gottfried, who would otherwise drop off on me. But I myself don't doze off, even if I have beer or something else.

I am very excited (seriously; it is my most important work to date of my entire life) and I am so much looking forward to you. The girls have to be present! (I fear that Annette is in camp, but the other two must be there— dead or alive).

The reading of his play took place in our house— before a small group of friends, as proposed by him. Zuck was right: It was an exciting and unforgettable experience for all of us. How on earth had he managed to conjure up in America, so far from Nazi Germany, that country's atmosphere, its tone, its abysmally mendacious mentality so dramatically that one felt as though one were in the midst of those creatures, hearing them and feeling their menacing presence as well as the presence of their victims?

Incidentally, there had been an earlier reading by Zuck, and I shall always vividly remember that winter evening in the deep snow of Vermont. He read to us his novella *Der Seelenbräu* (The Soul Brew), a popular music-filled story from the Salzburg area, and as he read it, he acted it out and also sang. Soon it appeared in the Stockholm Bermann-Fischer Verlag with great success. With great joy I designed the jacket and drew little vignettes for certain sections suggested by Zuck. This work brought me the author's praise; he wrote me from Barnard on November 10, 1945: "Dearest Tutti:

Say what you will, I like it! Jobs and I find the little volume quite captivating and your design beautiful. It turned out charming . . . Everyone will like it, and I only hope that the contents will not be considered inferior."

His next letter dealt with his financial cares. He was, of course, not the only one who did not know where the next day's sustenance would come from. On February 19, 1946 he wrote from Barnard:

Dearest and Best One . . . I have written to Gottfried about our Seelenbräu and given him the names of Swiss editors who are acquaintances and friends. Perhaps he will be able to do something for both of us from there. I hope he has transferred some money; if he has, please remember my $200. We are under great pressure— in fact, in a rather tight situation. Last night Jobs went to Washington with our last dough. I am literally vis-à-vis de rien until my new English work is sold. By the way, I have an idea which I think is quite commercial and could put us on easy street: I am planning to rewrite my play [Carl Michael] Bellman . . . quite airily and cheekily, bringing out the playful and fantastic elements. With all the music, the songs, etc. this would surely be a hit as a musical . . . something like that could give us financial security for years . . . Just wait: In a year or two we shall be laughing about today's financial worries! (But today they are still here). Give my regards to the beautiful girls and be embraced by your Old Zuck.

His prophecy that we would be "laughing about . . . financial worries" was to prove correct, for as soon as the German borders were opened also to "intellectual" imports after the end of the war, Zuckmayer had an enormous success with his play *Des Teufels General* in particular. After its premiere in Zurich the new play was performed on all German stages and greatly stirred people with its true-to-life quality. The controversies about the "ennoblement" of the figure of the general only made the play even more popular.

In 1946 the American military government, which occupied Western Germany together with the French and British, began to invite certain personalities among the German emigrants to Germany. Zuckmayer was among the first to receive such an invitation. On March 5, 1946 he wrote me from Barnard:

Dear Tutti . . . In the meantime all sorts of things have happened and come about. Via the State Department I have received the army's definitive assurance that they want to have me over there— under the condition, however, that I accept a commission as "theater officer" *and stay there for a year . . . But I am by no means certain that I shall accept. If it can be clearly established from the outset that I shall be able to perform a consulting, mediating function between the German theater people and the appropriate military authorities— a position that can only be understood as a good-will mission in Germany as well— then I will do it . . . I must also have a guarantee that I shall be able to speak freely, give my lectures, express my opinions, and establish full contact wherever that seems proper to me . . . Without such assurances there would be no point in sending a German author. I have to make this clear to the people . . . I shall not leave before the beginning of next week, have to complete all sorts of work here, and also am in the most embarrassing financial bind right now— which means that even if Washington pays for my trip, I cannot get away until I can raise some money. How are you doing in this respect? Has Gottfried been able to transfer anything for the publishing house? I know it has been a bad year, but after all, we share the consequences, and so I ask you kindly to help me out a bit. Next year will be better for all of us . . . I hear that L. B. Fischer has been sold.*** Under the present circumstances this was probably the only right thing to do. Let us all concentrate on the Bermann-Fischer Verlag, our old racing stable in which I am pawing the ground. Please let me hear from you, including the news you have from Gottfried and when you expect him back. Cordially yours, Zuck.*

And on March 25, 1946 he wrote:

Dear Tutti, in recent nights we have had such fantastic Northern lights here that I thought this must surely be connected with Gottfried's return trip. When is he actually coming? My project is making progress. I just received the definitive official inquiry as to whether I would accept the assignment, and I have answered in the affirmative . . . The army has sent the State Department another telegram from Germany in which it says: "We are convinced that Zuckmayer as Theater Officer in Berlin or Munich would make great contribution and at the same time have opportunity for bringing his unique qualifications to bear upon reorganization of theatrical life in Germany— Plan would be to use his advice on zonal matters and his special personal supervision for exchange of theatrical possibilities between all four zones involving official travels through Germany and Austria." This sounds good, doesn't it? Well . . . I gave my definitive consent . . . Please let me know when Gottfried is expected and how everything is going. Most cordially, Zuck.

He wanted to know how everything was going! In order to find out, Gottfried had ventured to fly to Germany for the first time in February 1946— an event that I had told Thomas Mann about earlier.

As an officer of the U. S. Army, Zuckmayer wrote us from Zurich in December 1946:

Beloved friends, the long letter to you that I started weeks ago refuses to get finished; there is such an awful lot to report, too much, an indescribable amount, and when would I ever have the time? In Germany I didn't have a free moment day or night, and here, where I arrived two days before the premiere [of Des Teufels General] and where hundreds of people were waiting for me, including at least a dozen of our best and dearest friends— who had come here for the occasion—I had to schedule every hour in order to be a match for the onslaught . . . It was worse than on the most glittering occasions of my heyday in the past, and of course, from a personal and human point of view it was much more intensive than ever before. In Germany: arduous trips, horrible weather, rides in open jeeps, overheated quarters of the Americans, freezing habitations of the Germans, constant rushing through the occupied areas plus the inner shocks and excitement— in short, I arrived here the way one comes from the front. Then this exertion here, mitigated by fine living and success! . . . The success of the General is hardly to be believed— it is tremendous. A magnificent, masterful, simply unsurpassable production by Hilpert, a grandiose actor playing Harras, a simply riproaring, thunderous success— so that on all the streets strangers talk in Schwyzerdüsch about the "Düfels Cheneral." The play has now been cleared for Germany . . . There is not a German stage that does not want to do it, but first it will be produced by Hilpert in Vienna . . . Engel in Munich will probably be the first in Germany . . . Your Zuck, who is very much in demand, which is quite all right with him.

The negotiations about a prompt reopening of our publishing house in Germany and the merger of the exile branch with the one that had remained in Germany and was now functioning again under Suhrkamp's direction dragged on and on, and the path to this goal was to be long and thorny. All of us realized that we would have to be extremely patient. Concerning this need to wait, Zuckmayer sent me the following epigram from New York on March 30, 1947:

Spruch auf diesen Tag:

Die Langsamkeit
Ist die schönste Keit
Mit der Schnellig-keit
Kommt man auch sehr weit,
Doch weiter kommt man
Mit der Langsam-keit! *Merks!*

(Maxim for This Day. Slowness is the finest-ness. With quickness one also gets quite far, but one gets farther with slowness! Remember that!)

In the spring of 1948, barely three years after the end of the war, something like war fever broke out in the United States. The Russians attempted to extend their boundaries within Germany as far west as possible. How far would they be able to get without America stopping them? It was a time of terrible tension for the western world. Zuckmayer wrote me about this as follows:

Currently Belsito, Cademario-Lugano, March 26, 1948.

My dear Tutti . . . Please do not let yourself get worked up to a war psychosis. I know there has been such an outbreak in America . . . but I don't believe there is a real reason for it—though unfortunately, unfortunately by now I can hardly imagine how we can escape experiencing the third catastrophe of this century. From the viewpoint of foreign policy, I believe the Russians now want to push as far ahead as they can without active warfare— that is, in Europe they want to impose their system on the area up to the Elbe river, preferably including Berlin. Even if the western occupation forces are determined to keep Berlin for reasons of prestige, which is probable, the Russians want to exert such pressure on Berlin that in practical terms it will not be an impediment to their Eastern zone policy, which is in line with their policy on Czechoslovakia etc.— not even a real island, but a sort of mixed first-class to fourth-class waiting room in a railroad station. They will continue to use the Allied Control Council as if it were the United Nations, which can be rendered powerless by a veto, in order to implement outwardly what they call the "Potsdam Agreement." Presumably the Allies will have to continue to engage in psychological warfare with them without there being an appeasement like the one in Munich. But there won't be a rift either, for the Russians themselves are justifiably in a blue funk about that. I know what seasoned communist ideologues are thinking here: They are counting on a catastrophic economic crisis in America . . . and believe that if they continue until then with their policy of constant sabotage of all European proposals for reconstruction and of fomenting panic and a crisis atmosphere, their ship will come in . . . I feel that at the very least we shall have a prolonged respite and that during this period we must live and work as though there were peace . . . This respite is our only chance, and we must not let it pass unutilized . . . Your Zuck.

At Christmastime 1966 we received the following little prose piece from Zuckmayer:

When I think of the brightest and the darkest hours in my life and in the lives of those who have been close to me, friendship is intertwined among them like a strong, visible, unbreakable chain. In good times it strengthened mutual giving and receiving. In times of need it became an anchor, the last to cling to, a pilot, sometimes a life preserver, and always, even in times of breakdown and defeat, it has remained an earthly beacon, a lightship, a signal in the fog. Even when death snatched friends away— something I had to experience all too early in life, and it goes on happening— every time I have felt as if I have lost a part of myself.

Our good friend left us in January 1977, when he died high up in the mountains and was buried in Saas-Fee, a place he loved so much.

**Our Oldest daughter.*

***In early 1946, when there was a prospect of reopening the German S. Fischer Verlag, the L.B. Fischer Publishing Corporation, New York, was sold to an American publisher.*

****In the winter of 1944-45 the Zuckermayers spent a few months in a house near Woodstock, Vt, where he was able to complete his drama (The Devil's General), something that work on the farm would not have permitted him to do.*

23

Reopening of the S. Fischer Verlag in Germany. Inge Scholl's Courageous Act. Encounter with Albrecht Goes. His "Unquiet Night"

For me the new beginning in Germany dates from 1948. The cities were destroyed; the winter months were grey and icy cold, with scant possibilities of heating habitations. I shall never forget the dismal days we spent in a newly opened tract of the once imposing but now dilapidated Hotel Frankfurter Hof in Frankfurt am Main. The hotel could be entered only through the rear gate, the walls of which threatened to collapse at any moment. The people were as gloomy as their environment, and it was hard to find one's way through the maze of destruction and to keep from feeling completely crushed by that atmosphere. But we had a goal before us, the rebuilding of our publishing house, and with a great deal of patience we managed bit by bit to clear away the obstacles in our path.

One of the first German women I met at that time was Inge Scholl. She had survived her heroic younger siblings who had rallied the students of the University of Munich against Hitler and who had had to pay for this heroic deed with their lives. In Inge I got to know the integrity and strength of character of a young German woman who had defied the Nazis. Immediately after the end of the war she had made it her task to shake up her environment, the distraught people of her hometown Ulm, and to convene them for evening meetings and discussions. Thus there came into being the first adult-education program that became a center for the exchange of ideas as well as a forum for important lectures, discussions, poetry readings, concerts, and performances of all kinds. Writers, musicians, artists, and scholars from Germany and other countries addressed young people who had been completely cut off from the world during the Hitler years. There could not have been a more grateful and receptive audience. I was attracted to this enterprise, which was so full of courage and faith in the future. Here one could learn to understand how the German people actually felt and it was possible here to tell them about that great "other" world, America. What I had in mind was a dialogue between the continents of Europe and America, and in Albrecht Goes, a Swabian country pastor and writer, I found an ideal partner. Our first encounter marked the beginning of a friendship. Goes was ready to prepare such a dialogue, and he asked me to visit him in his small country parish to discuss all the details— for he "hated vagueness."

The Swabian village with the little old church and the parsonage adjoining it in which he lived was embedded in a lovely countryside. The simple farm house in which he had his office and his study was surrounded by a sleepy little garden. I felt as though I had been transported back to the days of Eduard Mörike, and Goes himself seemed to belong to that period. One sensed in him a tough character capable of fighting for his ideals— and he *had* fought. As a chaplain in hospitals and prisons during World War II he had comforted and encouraged men who were dying or under a death sentence, and in the midst of a Nazi world possessed by the devil he had lost neither his courage nor his faith. After barely escaping from this hell with his life, he transmuted these experiences into literary works, like fanfares of the Last Judgment. As we strolled through his little parish garden and across the adjoining fields, there was no end to our talks. Was it the spatial closeness of Friedrich Hölderlin's birthplace that made his verses float through the air to us? One Sunday I listened to his morning sermon and was touched by his voice, which called upon his small congregation, using a short, obscure Bible text, to form a great brotherly and spiritual community and which lifted them above their everyday concerns. He had been vouchsafed a dual calling, caring for the people of his parish and addressing his poetic words far beyond that circle, to all people.

We carried on our dialogue "from continent to continent" and "from person to person" in the Ulm Center for Adult Education. There was lively participation from the audience, which consisted almost entirely of young people who picked up the word "freedom" and wanted to know how one could live in accordance with it. They were thirsting for contact with the "outside" and received my reports about daily life in the United States so joyfully that immediately after my return to the States I started a book collection for German youth. "Food for Thought" became a big success, and thousands of books were sent across the ocean to those hungry to read and thirsting to experience the world.

This initial encounter with Inge Scholl and Albrecht Goes made me realize how oppressive the isolation and the exclusion from the world during the Hitler years must have been for these people. A poem that Goes sent me at that time testifies to this:

Aber im Winde das Wort

Gut ist die Hausung, der Hort,
Und der Menschen zu zwein und zu drein,
Aber im Winde das Wort
Heißt: immer ist einer allein.

Glückliche Stunden am Meer,
Und der Einklang des Lebens so groß
Vogel Flug – und wie leicht ist das Schwer!
Weiße Flut – und wie lösest Du los!

Und der fremde Schritt wie vertraut,
Wie verwandelt das Fern und das Nah.
Wir wagen den leisesten Laut,
Und die Botschaft des Trostes ist da.

Und wir wenden den Fuß, und es schließt
Sich der Tag und es schließt sich der Kreis.
Schicksal selbst, das zornige, fleßt
Gelind und gelinder. Ich weiß.

Aber da stürzt es herein,
Dunkel ins selige Licht:
Immer ist einer allein
Und ich helfe ihm nicht.

entstanden im Oktober 1948 in Kampen/Sylt
Gruß an B. B. F.
Albrecht Goes.

(But the Word in the Wind. A habitation, a shelter, and human twosomes and threesomes are good, but the word in the wind is this: Someone is always alone. Happy hours by the sea, and such a great harmony of life. A bird's flight— and how light heaviness is! White flood— and how you let loose! And how familiar a stranger's steps are, how transformed distance and nearness. We venture the softest sound, and the message of comfort is here. And we turn around, and the day and the circle are completed. Even an angry fate flows ever more gently. I know. But then darkness irrupts into the blessed light: Someone is always alone, and I am not helping him. —Written in October 1948 in Kampen/Sylt. Greetings for B.B.F. Albrecht Goes.)

And he wrote me:

. . . *Now there is again a night as quiet as the one when you were here and we walked through the night; we could do so again now. The trees in the little front garden are budding and the scent of spring rain is coming in; it arouses great yearning in one . . . It is good to add: because you came . . .*

Early in 1950, when we had returned to Germany from the U.S.A., I received a very perturbed letter from Albrecht Goes, who had just received a rejection slip from the editors of the publishing house, then still under Suhrkamp's direction, along with the manuscript of his story *Unruhige Nacht* (Unquiet Night).

Gebersheim, February 9, 1950

Dear Tutti,

A hearty welcome to the old continent. I was pleased to get the news of your daughter's wedding . . . and now I hope good things will flow from your presence at the publishing house. I am glad also for the sake of my own work that you are someone who knows what makes my little watch tick and who has confidence in me— which unfortunately cannot be said about the editorial office in general. Forgive me for speaking right out, but yesterday I got such a bitter taste in my mouth that I am still quite sick from it. Enclosed with my manuscript Unruhige Nacht there was (intentionally or inadvertently) an evaluation from H.K. dated September 26, 1948 (H.K. probably stands for Hermann Kasack) . . . This evaluation reflects such an unfathomable and arrogant low opinion of my work ("conventional narrative . . . quite thin . . . reworking it would require a talent greater than that of Goes") that I really thought I was in the company of murderers. I am a bit consoled by the fact that Mr. Kasack is in disagreement with Hermann Hesse (who wrote me "I shall often think of your serious and magnificent story"), with Thomas Mann, with Reinhold Schneider, with Nelly Sachs (incidentally, a Swedish translation is being prepared), with the 3500 people who bought the book in seven weeks and the hundred correspondents from all walks of life and all parts of Germany and Switzerland . . . but you will understand: I have had such hostile vibrations from there that I am utterly upset. Seven years ago Mr. Kasack disposed of my poems as inconsequential imitations of Mörike; I believe since then some people have realized that this was an absolute misjudgment. Some people simply fail to notice that eschewing window-dressing, intellectual sleight of hand, exalted incomprehensibility, and intellectualistic pseudo-mysticism need not be a matter of simple-mindedness but might derive from a lengthy process of purification . . . How good it is that you are there, Tutti . . . In the days to come I shall be rather busy, because I have to devote what little free time I have entirely to the work that Kasack thinks so little of. I am now preparing a collection of my poems and plan to submit it to the publishing house at the end of the month. Perhaps you will then save it from Dr. Kasack's misjudgment.

Forgive me for not writing a beautiful letter of welcome; it is impossible today. But I shall write again soon, and then you shall also hear the cheerful voice of your friend, just as today you are hearing the dark and agitated one. Your Albrecht.

I, too, was full of consternation at this arrogant rejection of *Unruhige Nacht,* that moving testimony, by the publishing house that would soon bear our name again. The book was published by Friedrich Wittig and could not be taken over by the S. Fischer Verlag, again under our direction, until a much later date. In France it caused a stir in Pierre Bertaux' translation, and the same was true in many other countries where people took notice and were deeply impressed.

That same year he wrote in my album:

Nehmen, Geben. Wer zu rechnen liebt,
Der wird nie auf seine Rechnung kommen,
Leben lehrt: wer einen Finger gibt,
Dem wird gleich die ganze Hand genommen.

Gabst Du? Wohl, Du gabst. Nun warte nicht,
Daß die Jahre Dir die Schuld begleichen.
Wags, ob auch die Klugheit widerspricht,
Soll und Haben kühnlich auszustreichen.

Dieses nur. Dann leg den Stift beiseit,
Armut wird Dich unversehns versöhnen.
Ja, sie selbst, die karge Endlichkeit,
Will Dich ans Unendliche gewöhnen.

Für Tutti, zu Gesprächen zwischen Gebersheim
und dem Homburger Park,
herzlichen Gedenkens, Dein Albrecht Goes.

Frankfurt am Main, 10. Mai 1950

(Receiving, giving. He who likes to calculate will never get his money's worth. Life teaches: He who gives a finger will have his whole hand taken. Did you give: All right, you gave. Now do not wait for the years to pay the debt. Even if prudence decrees otherwise, dare to draw a bold line through debit and credit. Just this. Then put your pen aside and poverty will unexpectedly placate you. Yes, poverty, that meager finiteness, tries to habituate you to infinity.

—For Tutti, in cordial memory of conversations between Gebersheim and Homburg Park, your Albrecht Goes. Frankfurt am Main, May 10, 1950).

24

My Work at the Publishing House. Mother's Death. My First Grandchild. Thomas Mann's "In Praise of Transience"

In the meantime we had regained possession of the S. Fischer Verlag. We had to spend the major part of the year in Frankfurt, and at first we inhabited a building in the old West End which also housed the publishing firm. The two of us did not find it easy to have to live in Germany again and to be separated from our children and our home in Connecticut for many months. But the rebuilding required all our energies.

For the first time I was able to devote myself completely to my work in the publishing house. I did so with great enthusiasm, and henceforth there was not a moment that was not devoted to this work. Our private life had stopped; a department of the firm was installed in every room of the house, and our colleagues were everywhere. Only for the meals and at night did we retire to our private rooms on the top floor. Morning, noon, and night authors, friends, and co-workers would drop in. Occasionally we invited people to readings of our authors, and at such times our living room was overcrowded.

Soon, however, this place became much too small for the ever-expanding publishing house, and it moved to one of the Frankfurt skyscrapers, called Bienenkorb (beehive). Our large, modern rooms there overlooked the city, and through the huge glass windows we were able to see as far as the Taunus mountains.

I now had an office of my own. There I sat day by day at an old rustic table that I had chosen as my desk because it was so warm and cozy, and I felt like a cog within the ever-expanding machinery of the publishing house. It was fascinating to work within such an organism. The nice thing about this work was the opportunity to develop initiatives of my own. These were, of course, coordinated with and adapted to the whole.

At first I concentrated on giving the publications a special appearance in order to establish the character of the S. Fischer Verlag. This also applied to advertising, which had to be channeled in new directions and for which new outlets were found. When we began to issue a series of paperbacks and established the Fischer-Bücherei, I was put in permanent charge of the graphic design of these paperbacks. New books appeared every month, and I worked on them with young graphic artists. I was now able to apply my extensive study of typefaces and composition in practical terms.

In my visits to numerous bookstores I found that they were hesitant in getting accustomed to inexpensive paperbacks. I brought them revolving bookstands that they were able to place outside their stores, thus inducing many passers-by to make purchases, and I suggested special window displays, some of which I was able to help arrange.

The variety of my work in the publishing house gave me a great deal of pleasure. In addition to all my other activities I organized a foreign department by establishing personal contact with publishers abroad and literary agents all over the world. Every year I went to see European and American publishers in order to sell them translation rights to our books and to acquire the rights to their important new books. Given the increasing competition from other German publishing firms, anyone who did not keep his or her eyes and ears open and knew exactly who was being published where did not have much of a chance to acquire the rights to the relatively few important works published abroad. Only a handful of German publishers participated in the first Frankfurt Book Fair, which has now assumed tremendous dimensions. The personal shape we gave our booth precipitated a hard fight with the administration of the Fair, but we were finally able to convince it of the advertising appeal of original ideas.

After his "legacy," *Doctor Faustus,* which he had regarded as his last work, Thomas Mann had written an exquisite and highly imaginative story that delighted all of us. After reading it I wrote him:

At present Amsterdam, December 11, 1950.

My dear Dr. Mann,

I would like to give you my heartfelt thanks for the wonderful gift of your new book. We have spent long evenings lasting till the wee hours reading *Der Erwählte* (The Holy Sinner) aloud to each other, evenings on which I entrusted myself to your "spirit of the narrative" with profound joy. This joy kept increasing as the story progressed. I feel that this dual love story is among the purest and most transfigured stories ever written. The humor inherent in all the seriousness of the story changes languages like a game, enlivening the narrative, and this world of ideas which hovers between the spheres makes it easy for the amazed reader to regard the wondrous and the supernatural as the natural . . . To encounter this masterpiece of the purest art is a great experience. May it give similar happiness to innumerable human beings.

Your Tutti B. Fischer.

1550 San Remo Drive
Pacific Palisades, Cal.
December 17, 1950.

Dear Dr. Bermann, your words and Tutti's equally fine ones written after you had read my Gregorius book gave me pleasure. They are a friendly and encouraging reaction for the beginning, and after delivering of such a years and days work, one always needs some comfort. I hope the judgment of the public will not be far different from yours. In this curious case all my hopes lie more than ever with the German edition, for how can these jests be translated? . . .

With Christmas greetings and all good wishes for the New Year,
Your Thomas Mann.

The year 1952 brought two far-reaching events in my life, the death of my mother and the birth of our first grandchild. How strangely close death and life came to each other here! A scant three days after Mama's death the great-grandchild for whom she had waited so long came into the world.

My mother died at Königstein in the Taunus mountains. Some time before that, and at her request, we had brought her back to Germany, for she had never been able to become acclimated to America. Although she spoke English well and found old and new friends in New York, the "New World" did not become a new home for her, and she missed Europe at every turn. She breathed more freely when she visited us in Connecticut, but otherwise she led a rather isolated life in that enormous city. Unfortunately we were never able to induce her to live in the country with us permanently.

She spent good years in Germany, where she lived in a beautiful countryside and was cared for by a nurse touchingly solicitous of her. She took pleasure in the new beginning of the publishing house and in her granddaughters, but she increasingly lived in the past. During her last year her beloved husband became almost alive to her again. It mysteriously turned into a reunion with him in her old world and was like a blessing that would make dying easier for her. In the last months of her life I could overhear her speaking with him, convinced of his physical closeness. It was impossible to talk her out of it; for her the present did not exist any more. For me her passing meant the end of an epoch, and I felt uprooted and homeless without her.

At Mama's grave our friend Joachim Maass spoke the following words:

Hedwig Fischer's life had a richness that is vouchsafed to few women; it was vouchsafed her by the circumstances and the gifts with which nature had blessed her. For spiritual richness is a gift that only a blessed person can receive, a gift that thrives only in knowing, loving hands. The products and representatives of the intellect were close to her heart—in such a natural way that both were secure in her custody.

Almost all the names that have meant literary fame in our country from the end of the last century are chapters in the story of Hedwig Fischer's life . . . That most of them were associates and authors of the S. Fischer Verlag will surprise no one, for Samuel Fischer was one of the truly able, brilliant German publishers. But they were also friends, friends of the house of Fischer and of Hedwig Fischer.

A correspondence of immeasurable proportions— unfortunately largely lost, like so much else— attests to these venerable friendships, to the closeness and spiritual affinity which the great creative spirits felt to her. It also bears witness to the almost vehement, indefatigable, and always gloriously youthful sympathy which bound Hewig Fischer to these significant and often careworn personalities.

Is there a greater richness, one that would be more worthy of a eulogy? To us it seems as though the life to which we bid farewell today was as fulfilled as a woman's life can possibly be . . .

She experienced the joys of an intellectually glorious epoch and contributed to those joys. She knew that only a person who gives joy receives genuine joy.

It was a loving heart that has ceased to beat, a lovable heart . . .

Thomas Mann dedicated to Mama's memory a little essay, "Lob der Vergänglichkeit" (In Praise of Transience), which he wrote for "This I Believe," a series of the Columbia Broadcasting System of New York, and which we printed as a Christmas and New Year's greeting for the friends of our publishing house. "Transience is the soul of existence," he wrote; "it is what gives worth, dignity, and interest to all life, for it creates time— and time is, at least potentially, the greatest, most useful gift, in its nature related to, and even identical with, all creativity and activity, all alertness, all volition and striving, all perfection, all progression to a higher and better life. Where there is no transience, no beginning and end, birth and death, there is no time— and timelessness is stationary nothingness . . . Among the primary qualities that distinguish man from the rest of nature is knowledge of transience . . . This knowledge is privileged to consecrate time . . . and with its aid to wrest the everlasting from the transient . . . At the bottom of my soul I harbor the presumption that with that "Let there be . . . " which produced the universe from nothingness and with the creation of life from inorganic existence God had man in mind and that man represents a great experiment whose failure through human fault would be tantamount to the failure of Creation itself and to its refutation. Whether or not this is so, it would be well if man behaved as if it were.

I was deeply touched that Thomas Mann had dedicated this particular essay to Mama's memory, and I wrote him:

Old Greenwich, Conn.

December 31, 1952

My dear Dr. Mann:

I would like to give you my heartfelt thanks for your telegram on the occasion of Mama's death and above all for the worthy and beautiful memorial that you have created by dedicating your "Lob der Vergänglichkeit" to her memory. I have become especially fond of this little work of yours, which appears to me like a kind of essence of your wise and mature knowledge of life, and I hope that its substance has been heard by people like a clarion call . . . And it has many a connection with the life of my mother, which was fulfilled in so many ways. How pleased she would be with your dedication if she were still alive! It was astonishing how tenacious Mama clung to life even in her last years and how many things she perceived with astounding alertness. Nevertheless, death must have come as a release. As far as we are concerned, she took much with her, and with her passing the living thread, the connection with her time of great intellectual wealth has been severed. But her memory continues to live in many people, and this is a great comfort.

Your family has suffered a great loss, too [the death of Mann's son-in-law Antonio Borgese]. We share your grief and in particular mourn with Medi. I hope very much that she will find her way back to life and that her children will help her do so.

Let me send you and yours my heartfelt good wishes for the coming year. Your Tutti B. Fischer.

Erlenbach-Zurich, March 8, 1953

Dear Tutti, your letter arrived long ago, but I was ill, laid up with an ugly influenza or viral infection which made me so tired that any exertion makes me perspire and shake. As a result I make only painfully slow progress with my urgent work. I have not known such a nervous nadir for a long time, or ever. Well, things will look up again. But when is the S. Fischer Almanac supposed to appear, and when is the deadline for contributions? I fear I shall have to limit mine severely, provided that my poor head does not break down completely. In that deplorable event I would have to console myself with the fact that I have dedicated "Lob der Vergänglichkeit," that little New Year's gift, to your dear mother's memory. But I will not give up completely, and if there is still time, I shall try to produce a few simple sentences of remembrance and devotion. With amicable greetings to you and Gottfried, your ancient Thomas Mann.

In 1954, when I was heading the Frankfurt firm during a period when Gottfried had to stay in the United States, I had my last correspondence with Thomas Mann before his death.

Frankfurt/Main, June 16, 1954.

My dear Professor Mann,

Gottfried must have recently told you about our plan to mark the appearance of *Die Bekenntnisse des Hochstaplers Felix Krull* (The Confessions of Felix Krull, Confidence Man) with a record that would enable readers to hear a chapter in your reading style. The Northwest Radio Network in Hamburg has placed the tapes of your Hamburg readings at my disposal, and I have now excerpted from them, stopwatch in hand, the Professor Kuckuck chapter, which will fit on two sides of a long-playing record. I hope that you will agree to this choice. I regard this chapter as a little gem, and it really contains all aspects and profundities of the book. And how wonderfully you read!

We thought we would print your introduction, in which you give readers the history of the book, on the sleeve of the record. Would you be good enough to send me the manuscript directly so that we can pass it on to the artist who is designing the sleeve?

I am taking Annette to Italy this weekend and hope to see Medi and the children in Florence. At the end of July Gottfried and I will come to Zurich to visit you. I am greatly looking forward to a speedy reunion. With cordial regards to you and Frau Katia, your Tutti.

Alte Landstrasse 39

Kilchberg am Zürichsee, June 20, 1954

Dear Tutti,

Many thanks for your letter. Your plan to accompany Krull's memoirs with a record gives me particular pleasure, and so I am enclosing the text of the little introduction with which I preceded my reading of the Kuckuck chapter in Hamburg.

It is also a fine idea to give the Thamar story to the readers of the paperback editions as a gift, and I gladly give you my approval.

How nice that Annette has now recovered sufficiently for you to be able to take her to Italy, and let us hope that her health will improve further there.

Your coming to Zurich at the end of July is a pleasant prospect for us. On the 27th, to be sure, we are planning to go to St. Moritz, where we are expected at the Suvretta house. Perhaps you can so schedule your trip that you will still find us here; otherwise your visit will be welcome in the Engadine as well.

Auf Wiedersehen, and cordial regards,

Your Thomas Mann.

Falkensteinerstr. 24 Frankfurt/Main

October 25, 1954

My dear Mr. Mann, I would not want to leave Europe without sending you a farewell greeting and conveying many good wishes to you and Frau Katia.

You will surely be glad to hear of the strong reaction to the appearance of Krull everywhere. Even though we at the publishing house feel that no reaction, no matter how strong, is sufficient for the reception of a masterpiece like this one, we nevertheless feel daily the mounting wave of delight that this work is producing. This is borne out by many communications from readers that already add up to a chorus of enthusiasm. I know from my own experience how greatly the delight factor is involved in the reading of the book, for the realm that one enters lifts the reader into a world and a spiritual climate in which he can move freely and with almost playful delight. Without being aware of it, he moves into a spiritual zone of ultimate clarity of insight where he is able to forget the burdens of the mundane completely. When he receives such a pure gift, is he not bound to be full of happiness and gratitude?

Have you already received the Krull record, and are you pleased with it? Here, too, the success is great; the first shipment of the first edition is almost sold out, and we are already producing a second edition of 1000 records . . .

Gottfried and I expect to be in Europe again at the end of January, and we hope to be able to visit you then. Cordial regards from your Tutti.

25
Thornton Wilder, a New Friend and Author. Visit with Albert Schweitzer

We spent a summer during the war with our children on Fire Island, a narrow spit of land off Long Island. Our bathing at the beach, at that time still sparsely populated, was interrupted by a pleasant event. We attended the performance of a visiting theatrical troupe in the summer theater of the small town of Southampton. The play performed was Thornton Wilder's *Our Town.* To our great surprise we saw the author at the entrance to the theater, wearing a beret and watching the audience stream in.

We admired and loved Wilder and had recently acquired the German rights to his works, but we had not yet met him personally. But now we greeted him, and he mentioned that he would himself play the part of the Stage Manager that evening—"but the trouble is, I keep forgetting my lines," he added with a roguish smile. How his eyes sparkled when he spoke his own words, just as if it had all occurred to him at that moment! He took great pleasure in acting at America's summer theaters, which often consist only of improvised stages in barns. At a later date I saw Thornton on the boards again— this time in his play *The Skin of Our Teeth,* in which he played Mr. Antrobus.

When we reopened the S. Fischer Verlag in Germany, we began to print Wilder's works immediately, and our theater department supplied his plays to German stages, where they have become a permanent feature. At that time he wrote us: "I am glad to be a fisherboy." He became a new member of the "Fischer family," and the following letter (like the succeeding ones in English) refers to this:

Princeton, N.J., March 24, 1948

Dear Mrs. Fischer:

It was a great pleasure receiving your generous and thoughtful words. So few readers seem to have felt that the book was also an earnest book.

It will be a proud day for me when I see your father's name on a book of mine and feel that I am taking a small part in that procession which he assembled and directed— and from which I derived so many rewarding hours.

Kindly convey my regard to your husband, and again accept my thanks for your letter.

Sincerely yours

Thornton Wilder

In my letter I had thanked him for his first great novel, *The Ides of March,* that "reconstruction of historical material." How shrewdly he utilized history to express contemporary truths!

For his sixtieth birthday we gave him a lithograph of Picasso's celebrated dove. He was pleased with it, and later he wrote us that on his next crossing to the U.S.A. on the Giulio Cesare he would take the "Picasso Täubchen" with him.

Paris, Hotel Continental, April 29, 57

Dear Mrs. Bermann Fischer:

Many thanks for your letter. I have been seeing many of Picasso's pigeons here and, like you, I rejoice in them for their own sake rather than as symbols of the Kremlin's peaceful intentions . . .

Sincerely yours

Thornton Wilder

Bonn, May 31, 1957

Dear friends:

Long ago I should have thanked you for your most friendly letter on my birthday. I hear that one of you is also about to cross that decade-line. I send all my cordial best wishes. And I like to point out that one's age is a "statistical fiction" and that I know many joyless thirty-years olds who are far older than we are . . . Again a world of thanks— of felicitations— and regards

Sincerely ever Thornton Wilder

On June 27, 1957 we joined Wilder for the German-language premiere of his *Alkestiade* in Zurich. It was a brilliant performance with Maria Becker in the title role, and even then it already was a great success. Soon thereafter, shortly before leaving Europe, Wilder wrote to Gottfried:

Hotel Colombia Excelsior, Genova, July 4, 1957

Dear Gottfried—

In a few hours I get on the Giulio Cesare for an eleven-days crossing.

I've just finished sending Herbert Herlitschka the last of several hundred addenda and corrigenda (and delenda) toward the revised acting edition of "Die Alkestiade" (Much ignored by certain suggestions of Gustav Gründgens). As to the " Sisters", I don't know what to do about that: Lindtberg thinks that Herlitschka translated "Alkestiade" admirably and the "Sisters" very badly. Of course I am not competent to judge in such verbal matter . . .

All in all I am very pleased with the work in Zurich. I still believe that the Satyr-play will go well, if it is simply and attractively and rapidly presented.

I take on the boat with me my precious Picasso Täubchen—please thank all who had any part in making this beautiful present to me. And very many regards also to your gnädige Frau,

Cordially your Thornton

In the fall of the same year Thornton returned to Europe, for, two important events awaited him in Frankfurt. On October 6 the Peace Prize of the German Book Trade was bestowed upon him there, and on the preceding evening the German premiere of his *Alkestiade* took place in his honor.

The address he gave on the occasion of the festive presentation of the prize at St. Paul's Church was taken amiss by certain groups of people. We, however, were captivated by his openness and his demand for human rights and the dignity of the individual. He concluded his speech as follows:

. . . Democracy is not just a striving for social equality among men, but also an effort to give them the assurance that they are equal before God's grace— they are not sons or subjects or lowly born. This effort will require some time . . . Culture under a democracy has its risks— but also hope and promise, for there opens up to it a new and vast subject that needs to be described, intellectually penetrated, expressed, and investigated:"Man with His Head Raised High . . . " Democracy has a great task— namely, to create new myths, new metaphors, and new images, and to indicate the state of the new dignity that man has assumed.

When we established the paperback series Fischer-Bücherei, we chose a translation of Wilder's *The Bridge of San Luis Rey* as the first volume. Since then many hundreds of thousands of copies have been printed, and this story has given pleasure to generations.

In 1959 Thornton Wilder was in Europe again and wrote me:

Neues Posthotel, St. Moritz,

Sunday, November 8, 1959

here until Nov. 20— then weiss nicht wo [don't know where] best c/o American Expr. Zurich

Dear Brigitte:

First: thanks for the salon in your home on Wednesday night. And suddenly I remembered that I had forgotten to thank you for the beautiful flowers you and Gottfried sent me to the Hotel in Hamburg. They were still d'une beauté when I had to leave Hamburg and I gave them to Margot Schrepfer of the "F.d.K. Freiheit der Kultur". As I have a bad character I did not tell her that I had first received them from valued friends in Frankfurt; so I received a thousand thanks from her which I now re-direct to you.

I am still covered with confusion about missing the appointment at Bienenkorbhaus— I cannot even remember making the engagement and I never miss engagements. I suppose I must have thought that when I heard that I would meet Der Gute Hirsch** at your house— having already seen Frau Hunzinger—that it was the same as a Zeile-visit. Anyway, I deeply apologize.*

St. Moritz is absolutely dead. The first class Hotels are closed. All the several class Hotels are closed except this. All the bars are closed except one, so modest that it thinks a Martini is a glass of Italian Vermouth.

But I am as happy as I can be. The sun poured into my room all day— hot hot hot. The mountains and lake are glorious. In the absence of tourists the Gemse [chamois] comes right down to the water to drink.

*Give my best to Gottfried, den lieben Töchtern, dem gekrönten Schwiegersohn, to Steffi Hunzinger, dem Dr. Hirsch der erlaubt sich kein Urlaub*** and to the charming poet who was with us.*

And to yourself

devoted regards Thornton

The Claridge Hotel

Atlantic City, N.J.

Election Day Nov. 8, 1960

Dear Brigitta:

In Europe you produce Dichter and hommes de lettres; and they can produce many kinds of literature. Von Hofmannsthal could do Der Schwierige and beautiful critical articles like the letter to the Duke of Chandos and many essays; and Gide could do Faux-Monnayeurs and a book on Dostoievski.

But we in America don't have that practice.

O'Neill was a great dramatist, but it never occurred to him to write an essay about Strindberg who influenced him powerfully. I worship Faulkner but I would not expect (nor highly anticipate) a work by him on his Dostoievski.

Similarly I am not a critic nor an essayist. The few attempts I've made cost me endless work and they aren't good. It's hard to explain this to Europeans. They don't believe me. The editor of Corriere della Sera, supported by Prof. Cecchi of Rome, have recently asked me to do something for their feuilleton page. I'd love to! I think that page is of a very high order— almost as good as those in the golden days of Vienna— but I can't. I sat up almost all night trying to do a charming light essay . . . but the sun rose and I saw that it was all forced and voulu.

I am sorry to send you this disappointing answer, but I am pretty sure you know what I mean.

But this gives me an opportunity to send you all my deep regards and my pride in being a member of the HAUS.

devotedly Thornton

For the seventy-fifth anniversary of our publishing house he wrote:

50 Deepwood Drive, Hamden 17, Conn.

October 15, 1961

All cordial greetings to the great house of Fischers on its seventy-fifth birthday, and to all connected with it— and particularly to my friends Brigitte and Gottfried

ever cordially

Thornton Wilder

Just crossed from Genova

to Curaçao by S.S. Rossini

last day in Miami, Florida, June 3, 1964

Dear Gottfried:

Many thanks for your letter and greetings. Yes, I went to Italy for a retired corner . . . but spring was so late this year— snow and rain in Milan at the end of March that I became discouraged. I'm returning to Hamden for the quiet summer months, but I'll be going back to the desert soon after.

I heard that there were many conflicting stories about reorganization in your firm, but I've never understood anything about business and I leave that to others or I'd never get anything done.

Tell Brigitte that I've been working well on a novel— it's showing a tendency to grow into a rather long novel, which I don't like! I'm going to try to keep it down.

Please give my best to your delightful young people. And to Frau Stefi.

I hope I thanked you for your kind invitation to visit Forte di Marmi (I'm afraid I've spelled that incorrectly), next trip I shall plan the season better for visiting Italy.

With all cordial regards to you both

Euer Thornton

For his seventieth birthday we sent him an early printing of a Mozart piano sonata for four hands with this English covering letter:

Camaiore, April 12, 1967

Dear Thornton,

congratulations and all our best wishes to your 70th birthday, a fate which I, Gottfried, will have in common with you within a few months.

Our wishes are accompanied by the same mail of a first or very early print of Mozart's second Sonata for four hands, a "ricordo" of our four hand playing in your house in Hamden.

This special copy of this rare edition, published by Pleyel in Paris, has its own history. It's an old family property which was stolen by the Nazis together with our other books and music in Vienna in 1938, then handed over by the Nazis to the National Library in Vienna and returned to us after the war, as you can see from the rather gruesome blue marks.

We hope very much that you will enjoy it.

A short time ago we learned form the Fischer Verlag in Frankfurt that the sheets of your new novel have arrived. We have received so far the first 40 pages only, which we enjoyed reading tremendously. Already after these first pages we can feel the hand of the master with his humor and wisdom and the tension of a detective novel. Congratulations!

We are very anxious to hear from you after three years of silence! We are living now most of the time in our house here in Camaiore (Tuscany) and we are still hoping that one day you might visit us here.

Love yours G.T.

50 Deepwood Drive, Hamden, Conn. 06517
April 16, 1967
Dear Brigitte and Gottfried:
Many thanks for your kind greeting—

and for the rare and delightful ricordo that you tell me is to arrive. That is wonderfully kind of you— I shall leave it in my will to the library of the Yale School of Music— which has many early editions of the great composers, but almost nothing of Mozart.

But while I live I shall treasure it as a precious icon—then it will enrich the minds of the students.

During the last year of writing the novel, I withdrew (even more than usual) from all the world about me; since then I was aware of a deep fatigue— from which I am only now emerging.

Spring is late arriving here. I hope you are in the full beauty of a Tuscan spring.

With deep regards and many many thanks
your old friend Thornton

50 Deepwood Drive, Hamden, Conn. Again in hermit-retirement on the Island of Martha's Vineyard, Mass., May 14, 1967
Cari Amici:

Many thanks for your generous and thoughtful letter. Yes, the work was planned consciously on musical forms. I have recently read Professor Adorno's remarkable essay on Gustav Mahler: he finds that those symphonies have often the form of a novel— he instances Jens Peter Jacobson's way of introducing characters late in his story who bring the themes of the preceding narration together. (But I've only learned to know Mahler's major works since writing the novel— and was deeply impressed.)

I hope my little sketch of the Hamburg milieu sounded fairly all right. I know nothing about such lives; I merely "invent"— as I did Chile— solche Freschheit! (sic)

All cordial best to you and the children— and again many thanks

your old friend Thornton

yes, indeed, the Mozart arrived— to my great joy—

Herzlichen Dank TNW

In the meantime his delightful novel, *The Eighth Day* has appeared.

The last sign of life we had from him, a postcard, probably dates from the year 1967:

Dec. 27: Semmering

then January 3, American Express, Vienna,

then I don't know where

Dear friends:

Many thanks for beautiful card and kind words. Have been working so well that I may go home earlier than thought . . . but have no idea where I shall go for late January and February . . . maybe Baden-Baden, maybe Engadin . . . I've been working fine—but you know me: I'm never working at the thing I ought to be working at. (So I never dare to write to Cas Canfield of Harpers or to you!)

I came to Europe to settle down to work at Bad Gastein— and within two days I hated Bad Gastein— so where to go I do not know. Maybe I shall be seeing you both soon.

Your old friend Thornton

In 1955 we acquired from Harper's New York, the European rights to the book *The World of Albert Schweitzer*. Erica Anderson, a photographer and friend of the great man, had contributed numerous photos that illustrated Albert Schweitzer's life and self-sacrificing work in his African hospital at Lambarene. A brief text by Eugen Exman, a friend of Schweitzer, provided a commentary on these photos:

Eighty kilometers below the equator, not far from the west coast of Africa in the French colony Equatorial Africa, lies the village of Lambarene. In 1913 Albert Schweitzer chose this remote place on the banks of the Ogowe River for the founding of a hospital. Since then the road to Lambarene has been walked by untold numbers of people who wished to encounter, in the depths of the forest, a man of unique greatness, the man who in 1952 was awarded the Nobel Peace Prize.

If Albert Schweitzer had done nothing but found a hospital in the tropical forest, his name would by now probably have sunk into oblivion. Even the variety of his extraordinary gifts, which brought him doctorates in theology, music, philosophy, and medicine, can hardly explain why his personality and his work have all over the world become the object of astonished reverence and why he alone is above the strife among the nations in our time out of joint. The reason for the loving veneration that he is accorded everywhere is that through his works, which have been translated into many languages, he has given the world joy, comfort, and courage, demonstrating that he is prepared to translate his teachings into action. He is not only the greatest literary interpreter of Johann Sebastian Bach, but also his great interpreter on the organ. He has not merely preached "reverence for life" as a theologian, but he has practiced it in tropical Africa in arduous, tireless labor. As a thinker and physician he has become for all the world a symbol of human faith in mankind and a model of human compassion in the days of mass hatred.

Concerning S. Fischer's edition, Schweitzer wrote us:

Lambarene, March 20, 1955

French Equatorial Africa

Dear Sir,

My Paris publisher, Albin Michel, informs me that you have acquired from Harper Brothers in New York the European rights to Erica Anderson's The World of Albert Schweitzer. Since the book is about Lambarene and myself, I take the liberty of submitting to you a few requests for the European editions.

The value of the book lies in the beautiful photos. The text of my friend Exman is beautiful as well. I believe, however, that the book is too voluminous and too replete with pictures; thus it would be well to omit some of them, and this would also reduce publishing costs. Unfortunately I was too busy in 1954 to concern myself with the preparation of this picture book; otherwise I would have suggested even then that the American edition contain fewer pictures. Here are my proposals:

The book contains too many pictures of me, and the uninteresting pictures detract from the interesting ones. After all, it is supposed to depict the world of Albert Schweitzer rather than always letting him appear. [At this point there are specific proposals for omissions].

If you remove these photos from the book, it will be a beautiful picture book from Lambarene. You must consider that European readers care far more about the uniformity of an illustrated book than American ones. And if there are fewer pictures, they are more effective.

I shall also send you corrections in the text as soon as you inform me that you are willing to accept them . . . Frau Erica Anderson's pictorial material is wonderful. After all, she visited Lambarene on several occasions.

With kindest thoughts, Yours sincerely, Albert Schweitzer. Forgive me for presuming upon you to read my handwriting, but on account of the noise I do not use a typewriter.

In the meantime I had tried to get Harper's to agree to his changes, but since the American copyright holder did not give its consent, I was not successful. I wrote Albert Schweitzer about my attempts to accede to his wishes and drew his attention to the sketch of a Bach trill that was greatly enlarged in the American edition and thus was not comprehensible. Concerning these matters he replied as follows:

Lambarene, March 3, 1955

French Equatorial Africa

Dear Mrs. Brigitte B. Fischer,

Many thanks for your letters of March 19 and March 20. Too bad that Harper's did not agree to the version you put together. It is not good to issue an illustrated work designed for America in Europe without changes. I was interested to note that your proposal and mine were along the same lines. So now you are issuing a book that does not give you full satisfaction any more than it does me. As regards the sketch of the Bach trills, unfortunately I cannot help. I do not know how those people came to publish, without my permission, a sketch about the execution of Bach's trills which I gave to someone as an autograph. The second part of this sketch is quite incomplete and incomprehensible, and I do not want to have it published in

Europe, where people will wonder whether I have taken leave of my senses. All the pictorial publications that I have to endure cause me terrible suffering. But the publication of musical sketches that I gave away as an autograph is too much for me. Thus I cannot offer you any revised sketch and ask your forgiveness for this. I am sure you will think of a way to handle the technical aspects. Of necessity you should also omit the photo that goes with it; it represents no loss. There are too many pictures of me in the book, and as I wrote you in my first letter, this has been a cause for regret to me.

All right, and now let us drop this illustration book and talk about the unillustrated one that your publishing house is issuing in its own spirit. That is a source of joy. Stefan Zweig, Feschotte, Grabs— you let these three understanding friends express themselves. This is typical of the Fischer-Bücherei! My sincere thanks for this. I am writing this late at night, for my work in the hospital does not leave me any other time. Forgive my tired hand for the bad writing. With kindest thoughts of you and your husband, Yours sincerely, Albert Schweitzer. I have not forgotten the beautiful hour with you in Günsbach.

We have never forgotten the "beautiful hour" at his home in Günsbach either. Decades earlier Albert Schweitzer had built a home for himself on the outskirts of his hometown; it was peacefully embedded in a pleasant valley and afforded a view of the nearby Vosges Mountains. This house became the goal of pilgrims from all over the world, and most of the time it was surrounded by people who wanted at least to catch a glimpse of the great, venerable man. On the day of our visit a big bus stopped in front of the house; it was full of school children who were to be shown the home of Albert Schweitzer. When he was told about the bus, he immediately went outside to greet the children personally. He never tired of radiating his kindness to people. Over and over again he manifested his sense of responsibility and his reverence for all living things in word and deed. He said: "Through reverence for life we become pious in an elemental, profound, and vibrant way." And his advice to young people was this: "Our world will not get back on its feet until it learns that its salvation lies not in measures taken but in new ways of thinking."

On May 5, 1955 there arrived an envelope from Lambarene in which Schweitzer's associate Emma Haussknecht informed us about the return of the corrected galleys of *Die Welt Albert*

Schweiters and which also contained a letter from Schweitzer himself:

Dear Frau Bermann Fischer,

I am so sorry that it was not technically possible for you to effect more of my proposed changes. The text drawn from my book on Bach cannot be published together with the sketches of my work on Bach's ornaments (this publication is a delicate matter!) which appeared in a volume of Bach's organ works issued by Schirmer in New York. What you quote from my book on Bach is no longer correct, for it has turned out that in the manner of Bach's ornaments, Bach's son parted company with his father. The father does not leave the execution of the ornament to the player, but gives explicit instructions for it.

I am enclosing a text that might get you out of an embarrassing situation. I am writing the enclosure late at night. But now I ask you not to oblige the publishers of the French and other editions to take over the text of the German edition, for it has many flaws taken over from the American edition that seriously jeopardize the success of a book with such fine pictorial material . . . The fundamental fault of the American text is that it was written by people who do not know Lambarene and hence were unable to provide a proper text for the picture; this is also why they include a biography of me in this picture book. With my kindest thoughts, Yours sincerely, Albert Schweitzer.

Frau Anderson knows Lambarene well, having stayed here on several occasions. Too bad that they did the text without her.

The enclosure:

Text for the Page with the Trills.

In his work on Bach, Albert Schweitzer, along with others, still took the view that Bach, like French masters of that period, gave the player a certain freedom in the execution of the ornamentation signs. But his continued occupation with the problem of Bach's ornaments has convinced him that the marks used by Bach, if properly interpreted, exactly prescribe for the player when he has to execute a trill ending on the note or continuing for its entire value, or whether or not the trill is to have a Nachschlag [springer or termination].

This text was included in the book *Die Welt Albert Schweitzers* together with a sample of Bach's music and Schweitzer's commentary on it.

At the same time we published in the Fischer-Bücherei the paperback *Albert Schweitzer, Genie der Menschlichkeit* (Genius of Humanitarianism) which he mentioned so positively in one of his letters. Its three essays (Stefan Zweig, "Unvergessliches Erlebnis" (Unforgettable Experience); Jacques Feschotte, "Das Leben Albert Schweitzers"; Rudolf Grabs, "Sinngebung des Lebens" (Giving Meaning to Life) as well as an important address by Schweitzer himself give a comprehensive picture of this great personality. The paperback soon sold 150,000 copies.

The S. Fischer Verlag was located at the Haus Bienenkorb on a Frankfurt street called Zeil.

****Dr. Rudolf Hirsch.**

*** . . . *who does not permit himself a vacation.*

26

Kurt Heuser, the Friend Who Saw Everything With His Own Eyes

"Tutti, after dragging this book [my poetry book] around with me for two years without finding a verse that would be beautiful enough for you, I am returning it. And now, to keep the page from staying empty, I shall recite for you the three wedding rhymes with which the husband, Kuve, and the wife, Kokun, are handed three presents in the film about the genie in the bottle: a lamb, a loaf of bread, and a jug of wine:

Dieses Lämmchen, grad geboren
nimm es an an Kindesstatt
denn ein Wesen ist verloren
das nicht Deine Liebe hat.

Dieses Schwarzbrot, frisch gebacken
mache Dir den Hunger satt

denn ein Wesen beugt den Nacken
wenn es nichts zu essen hat.

Dieser Becher, voll von Wein –
trink ihn aus auf einen Zug!
Er macht glücklich. Glücklich sein
kann ein Wesen nie genug.

Im fünften Jahr unserer Freundschaft, Kurt
8. Dezember 34, zwei Jahre zu spät!»

(Accept this new-born lamb in place of a child, for a creature that does not have your love is lost. May this freshly baked dark bread satisfy your hunger. for a creature that does not have anything to eat bows its head. Empty this goblet full of wine at one draught! It will make you happy. A creature can never be happy enough.

In the fifth year of our friendship, Kurt. December 8, 1934, two years too late!).

With this unusual entry in my album— which, however, was typical of him— Kurt Heuser wrote a kind of self-portrait. Seven years earlier his entry into the S. Fischer Verlag had been just as unusual. "Since there are no books around here, I have started writing them for myself"— this is what a letter from Africa said that arrived at the office of the *Neue Rundschau* one day in 1927. It contained the manuscript of a story, "Elfenbein für Felicitas" (Ivory for Felicitas), which delighted the editors and immediately captured our hearts as well. The rather slightly built, shy young man with the big smiling eyes who followed his letter a bit later had lived in the African bush for years, running a cotton farm, and so he was quite estranged from European civilization. The publication of his story made Kurt Heuser's name known overnight and meant a turning point in his adventurous existence. He stayed in Germany and immediately plunged into the maelstrom of Berlin.

For us this encounter marked the beginning of a lifelong friendship. The young new author, whom Oskar Loerke, at that time the editor of our publishing house, called "a poetic talent into which all the passions of a new time flow," was also given an amicable reception by my parents on Erdenerstrasse. Although the unaccustomed approval at first embarrassed him a bit, Heuser very soon felt at home among them and was attracted by the human warmth that was extended to him. He became a regular Sunday guest of the house, invited by my mother to the famous "turkey," and my father liked the adventurous young man and asked him to tell him about his life among the African blacks.

A year later there appeared his first great novel, *Die Reise ins Innere* (The Journey into the Interior), a book written from first-hand experience of the African world.

Yet Kurt, a man who loved life and people, wholeheartedly plunged into the maelstrom of Berlin, and we, his friends and publishers, noticed with consternation that he was no longer able to concentrate on his work. We sought a way to tie him down to work and took him along on a summer trip to Kampen on the island of Sylt. There we installed him in a bungalow in which we locked him up for several hours each day. Under lock and key he actually managed to complete his second novel, *Abenteuer in Vineta* (Adventure in Vineta), which appeared in 1932. Unfortunately he soon fell silent, like so many of his generation, under the pressure of a barbarism that left him no choice but silence.

Since Adolf Hitler's accession to power both the future of our publishing house and our private life were in extreme danger. Kurt did everything to help us. Thus one night, when we were beset by fear of the Nazis' nightly raids, he sheltered us and our three little daughters in his little wooden house on the outskirts of Berlin. When we precipitately left Berlin with our children in an effort to escape the "Night of the Long Knives" scheduled for April 1, 1933, he traveled to Switzerland with us in order to get at least the children to safety if we were removed from the train at the border. All his life he remained this kind of faithful, fearless, and loving friend.

At present Henndorf near Salzburg, Spring 1938.

Dear Tutti,

You know the old inn up there on the village street. That is where I took a room, fulfilling an old wish. You see, I have to be here to work with Hilpert on a film that has wishing as its subject— based on Balzac's Peau de Chagrin. But the thing about wishes is that they are no longer a joy when they are fulfilled, or they are fulfilled only when it is too late. The friends are no longer here, the brook rustles as it always has, but the house, and more than the house, is dead. The* *deer is here in its enclosure, and it came up to me without any fear . . .*

*I admire your courage; I don't know whether I would have it. And I wish you, Gottfried, and the children much luck with your new undertaking.** . . . Even if you don't hear from me, don't think that I have forgotten you and Gottfried. But there are so many things about which one should keep silent— and some day you will get good news from me. The millstream rustles and says, "I shall be heard when all of you are long gone from the earth." Let us, however, send each other greetings because we are souls that are on earth at the same time. Farewell, and take care of yourselves. As ever, Kurt.*

This was the "farewell letter" to us from the friend who had stayed in Nazi Germany, who were in Sweden working on the reestablishment of our publishing house— the farewell of those "inside," who now had to live as though behind barbed wire, to those who had emigrated to the free world. Years passed before we heard from him again. His next letter came a few months after the armistice:

Altaussee/Puchen 79, Austria

September 5, 1945

Dear Tutti, dear Gottfried. A Turkish acquaintance of mine is going to Switzerland today and he is taking this greeting along— in the skeptical hope that it will reach you as a sign of life. I don't know whether you are so through with everything that is called German that you won't have anything to do with us . . . It occurs to me that one autumn day I walked through Gneiststrasse past the burned-out ruin of your house and suddenly had a vision of all of us sitting, drinking, and talking on the balcony terrace. It was a vision of perfect happiness. In the background and in reality another villa was quietly smouldering, but the old Fischer house stood unscathed, and perhaps it has survived. Yes, Tutti, Gottfried— I, too, have survived, though at my age, and in general, this is a miracle. I did not even have to wear a uniform. The film that cost me so many productive years, or, more accurately, Goebbels' film craze, saved my life. And upon closer examination you will note that most of the writers who stayed in Germany behaved well. Only in few cases was that integrity betrayed. "They" simply weren't able to get what they wanted from us. They remained what they were: a foreign occupation force.

Any American is less of a foreigner than they were. Intellectual life assumed vegetative forms; it went into exile, withdrawing to the conventicles or the rooms of village schoolmasters. It was a subterra-

nean mycelium, tough and indestructible. People met and recognized each other, and at some later date you will learn that the power that ruled over us was also undermined from within . . . It may sound strange, but often we sat in the midst of hell laughing, and we also loved. And the poorer we became, the more external things dropped off from us, the more free we became inwardly, and if the word did not sound vain, I would say that we became more mature, too. And even when the sky roared with bombs, next to the organ sound of death there always remained the sweet music of life, indestructible, the deepest ultimate substance. And the impotence of power went to extremes. Some day I would like to tell you about all this . . . The notes that I collected over the years— fragments that were to compose my works some day— have gone up in flames. But all this does not matter. I am now forty and have felt grown up for only a short time. Now one could begin— if the world returns to its bounds. All that the politicians need to do is not to impede this process.

I don't know whether you will be able to reply to me. The nets are still destroyed. Perhaps there will be an opportunity. With all my heart, your Kurt.

Altaussee, late March 1946.

Dear Tutti, upon my return from my first major excursion to the "world"— Vienna— I found a lot of mail, good as well as sad.

The good kind is headed by your letter. You may not be able to gauge what it means to us to hear the voices of old friends talking to us; and this handwriting of yours that once was so familiar to me! We are living half a life as in a realm of the dead, surrounded by the souls of people we loved and who are no longer on earth. Thus it almost seems as if our existence is a very dogmatic course about the vanity of precisely this earthly life— and about the vanity of all our efforts . . . No, Tutti, nothing has happened to me physically, though this often was a miracle. One time, when I was sitting in a hollow fruit tree overlooking a vineyard, a blanket of bombs came roaring down a scant hundred meters from me, intended for a bridge over the Main river that I had left moments before. At that instant it was as if I were watching the destruction of a city from a box in a theater. And it was nothing other than a natural catastrophe, an earthquake or the eruption of a volcano. I was seeing it, while at other times and in the cities people usually were blind as moles as they felt the unleashed demons of technology roaring overhead. Later I looked for the partisans in the mountains, but I did not find them, for there were none. There were only deserters, and later a great deal of bragging and lying. And after the catastrophe there began a satyr play of justification and falsification that is still going on, and it is best not to participate in it even if one can adduce reasons . . . But we have been able to do some peeking behind the curtain; a few insights did gleam at the bottom of the well; and an infinite number of stories and a history are to be told. For the past six months I have been working on sketches and drafts for this big novel. If I ever manage to write it, you shall be pleased about our friendship again— a little. In general, your thinking about reconstruction is like the rays of a lighthouse before the dawn. And that the Neue Rundschau is alive— that is even more for shipwrecked people, that is a plank! The flood is still running high, and I don't want to let my goddamned optimism deceive me once more— and yet! There is a spirit that is like a piece of home— and for me this home is the Neue Rundschau, my last contribution to which was an obituary of your father . . .

A person is almost always bound to something, and even if one is free of what you call the earthly goods— all of us became free of them— there still remained the silken, invisible threads that bind our hearts to other people. And one of these threads— delicate as cobwebs but, I hope, untearable—, a thread that long floated in nonexistence, is now aimed at Old Greenwich, Connecticut, America . . . Tell me sometime about you and your three daughters. Do you remember that I am permitted to take Annette out on her seventeenth birthday— or was it the eighteenth? That was our agreement upon her reception into the world. In the meantime, to be sure, I have started to turn grey— at least my hair has. Otherwise, I believe, I haven't changed much. A person does not change in his nature— and that is what I sense from your letter. Don't forget your old Kurt.

Altaussee, June 1, 1946.

Dearest Tutti . . . the letter you wrote me was a good one. I keep noticing with joyous astonishment how little people change if they have been "centrally structured." and thus I perceive the familiar warmth of your nature as a climate that makes the drift ice of the years melt. You must not forget either that we here are at the very beginning of our second reencounter with the world— ploughed up and curious about everything that has developed in the meantime.

There still isn't much; we are still as though quarantined, and an invisible flag warning of an epidemic hangs from the mast of our wreck, which a demented pilot has steered into the cliffs. But as though from spice islands the smell of freedom is already reaching our senses. No wonder if we get impatient.

I have just returned from Vienna, a city that has regenerated itself to an astounding extent in the eight weeks since my last visit. Sure, a lot of people are still starving, but there must be some subterranean springs that feed the city, or is it just hope that has made the women more beautiful and the grey faces happier again? It is hard to comprehend what these masses are living on; presumably everyone solves his existential problems in his own way, as I do. It is a miracle— but is it not a miracle how every European has survived this destruction of the world? And it is strange to see how the old habits are already beginning to nest in the rubble like colorless birds— in fact, how the rubble itself is beginning to become a habit. Well, in Lisbon the rubble piles from the earthquake of 1790 are still lying around, and no one who sees them thinks any longer of the collapse, the screams, and the fires. This is how it will be with the ruins of many of our cities as well.

While your spaces kept shrinking— as you write and as I know—, while the streamline ought to be the magical symbol of our age, it still takes twenty-four long hours out of one's short life to get to Vienna, not to mention dozens of documents. I recently got hold of Stefan Zweig's book Die Welt von gestern (The World of Yesterday), which you published, and he complains about the same symptoms and suffers because of them. Added to this are controls, delousing, problems with food ration cards, certificates from the labor bureau, residence permits, trips of hundreds of kilometers for a single stamp from an office that is not yet or no longer in existence— and all this in a small country. And the people—patient, patient as cattle— endure everything without grumbling, for they hardly know anything different.

The terrible thing is that one always, and once again, has to be in opposition to all divisions along party lines. For after this shake-up of all standpoints and principles, what is red and what is black and what is left and what is right? . . .

And if you debate with Communists, as I did several times on recent evenings, then you really have the "decent Nazi" with reversed premises, you get the very dangerous doctrinaire idealism which, as

Thomas Mann so aptly remarked, bears a major part of the blame for this whole incalculable filthy mess. For it obscures the only and grandiose reality with veils of ideas; it is basically unworldly; and it forgets that the whole game is for man himself, his happiness and his sorrow, and nothing else.

. . . What you report about your mother is sad enough, but unfortunately I can understand her only too well. She simply belonged in the house on Erdenerstrasse and the patriarchal world of security . . .

I was an occasional Sunday guest in your mother's house until that, too, was dissolved . . . One day I came back from a trip and the house was an empty shell . . . And yet today one must praise the fate of those who were able to leave the country in time . . .

Please tell me a little about your house and its surroundings so I may picture it. Give my regards to your flock of daughters— engaged, married, or not— Gottfried . . . and then Joachim Maass . . . and farewell from your old Kurt.

Altaussee, Puchen 79
September 30, 1946

Dear Tutti . . . Funny that now, after so many years, I am still thinking of you and writing you as though you were my publisher— which means, the great friend of the poets.

Yes, much has been dissolved that had been regarded as indissoluble, and other things have joined together about which no one had suspected a secret bond. Much of what we loved belongs in a museum; suddenly we find ourselves in the middle of a new, grey, cruel millenium dominated by technology. We must see to it that it does not become the millenium of the atom bomb or the millenium of Asia; that is what we are here for. The outlines of the future are still indistinct in the smoke of past fires, but soon they will be recognizable. But they will have to be given new names in place of the antiquated, dusty nomenclature ending in -ism. In conclusion, therefore, I will tell you about a little schoolteacher who attended a spirited debate among intellectuals arguing about socialism and Marx and Leninism and capitalism and the more subtle concepts and distinctions. He said to me in a soft voice:"I can't really participate in the discussion. For me all this is much simpler. Call me stupid, but I find that the reason why people are unhappy is that they become so godless." It seems to me that he has a point.

Take care of yourself, Tutti, and give my regards to Gottfried and the children. Until next time, your Kurt.

Altaussee, Puchen 79, New Year's 1946.

Dear Tutti . . . All of you who have been living out there since that time seem to have been transported to an inaccessible beyond and thus have become a species of demigods. We used to speak about you as one speaks of those who have been spirited away to another world, and by this we recognized ourselves and our utter forlornness. And, Tutti, that is why your and Gottfried's letters are gifts so precious that you may not be able to estimate their full value yourselves . . . It was our special situation that made us strain our ears to hear the vox humana in the thunderous sound of all organs. That was a stop which Thomas Mann did not pull out, for he is already surrounded by the glacial air of the absolute . . . You have aroused in me a burning desire to read his new work, and I recognize you again by the enthusiasm with which you speak of it. For this, oh Fischer's daughter, was among your most lovable qualities: your love of your authors when you were truly spoiled by your association with great personalities, when it would have been natural for you to break away and become snobs. But no! You never let it become a habit; you loved the books you printed and you printed what you loved. And this, you see, is the way publishers have to be. Your Kurt.

The year 1947 was finally to bring us together again. When we met again in Salzburg, it was as if we had never been separated. Although so many experiences and so much suffering had intervened, this reunion, as Heuser himself says in one of his letters, was "like an encounter with oneself," with one's own life. We were happy to find one another unchanged and enriched by a large slice of lived life.

November 4, 1954.

Dear Tutti, all right, now I have closed the book, taken a deep breath, and thought: I hope he lives much longer— Thomas Mann, that is— for the book was "Felix Krull", Confidence Man. I hope he lives much longer— that's what I thought— so he may give us many more of these colorful, opaque toys that he quietly manufactures, the old magician. Every time something different, new, surprising . . .

And Albrecht Goes! It brought back memories of the May afternoon on which we visited him in the town with the red roofs, in his parsonage with the tiny church in which you played the organ and we worked the bellows, and with the little cemetery that virtually enticed us to lie down in the grass and among the wild flowers and slumber thus till Judgment Day! And this story of his [Das Brandopfer (The Burnt Offering)] which I would have preferred to call "Die Feuerprobe" (The Ordeal of Fire) and which is told with the classical composure of a Storm novella and which yet leads the reader into the most frightful things— calmly, by the hand, as it were. I wish it could be brought into the homes and read aloud to all those who like to forget or have already forgotten. But for anyone who believes in the quiet, incessant workings of the spirit, this story is one of those elemental ones that open up in reading like a mustard seed, over long periods of time, until they fill the spirit and those living by it with roots, sap, stems, and blossoms. Such is also the silent work of Albert Schweitzer—his life as an example in itself. And many other unknown spirits are at work as well, and I also believe that they are being heard, more than before. They are a measure of the future, or there will be no future . . . We shall live for a long time and have a lot to do. A love can fade, but a friendship never. Kurt.

Here ends our correspondence, for we were now in the same country, Germany, again, at least for a time. In 1972, after the sudden death of my daughter Gaby, in whose memory I had written an essay, there came a letter from Kurt Heuser in which he closed a circle, remembering shared experiences and confident of a reunion after death.

Kampen/Sylt, Ginsterhof.

Dearest Tutti, your dirge and lamentation for Gaby reached me on this island which, as it is, is full of memories for me down to the dunes. Thus I can see you standing on a little hill with flowing hair. They are the preliminary gusts of a powerful thunderstorm that is still over the sea . . . And since I am now here alone, I walk along the beach and by the mud flats with many deceased people and hold conversations with them. Your essay came at just the right time for this. I find it marvelous that you should have expressed your grief in this way. It is the best remedy for despair and transience; perhaps this is the unconscious reason why we all write. But do not despair, Tutti! We shall all meet again when we have crossed the threshold of the temporal, sooner or later. For that is the solution of the secret that death is to us (and I mean this not speculatively but scientifically): it lies in the nature of the unknown dimension which we have agreed to call "time." By this I mean not only the measure that is granted us down here; the way we exist, we are only the projection and the reflection of what we are intended to be. The appearance can fade, but not the origin, which is called spirit. What was, is; what is, will be— be forever, for otherwise everything would be meaningless, and there is no such thing. There is always a beginning, there is always an end. This is the only possibility of thinking about beginning and end, and thus about time. Proof? Look at nature, right now, when everything is renewing itself— there this doctrine is opened up as in a book! That has nothing to do with religion— at any rate, not the kind that we practice— but with observation, insight into the nature of the things around us. And in truth "religion" means connection with something higher, doesn't it? And now Gaby! I have thought a great deal about her and why she may have been destined to be called away so suddenly. I do not know that, of course. But it just might be that she was complete in herself, that she had completed her circle early on, that nothing would have come for her but aging, grief, disappointment. But, as I have said, I do not know. But you found such beautiful words about her dreamy nature, about her eyes, about her belonging to that other world— the world that had always been there when she came into it and that will be there when we shall leave the earth, when we return home. Do not despair, Tutti . . . You rightly keep referring to music. One doesn't think music; one sings it or plays it. And I have always perceived you, too, as a definite melody. And melos is imperishable, too. Greetings to you and Gottfried from your friend Kurt.

Our friendship with him was imperishable, too, whether we met or not, but we always knew about one another. Suddenly his end was fated for him. We saw him a few weeks before his death, and he was full of plans, thirst for knowledge, and loving interest in everything, as he had always been. We, however, knew that it was a leavetaking.

Gottfried wrote in his obituary: "He belonged to our life. When he came, it was as if a beloved brother came. When he went, he left a gap. Now it will never be closed."

**The reference is to the Wiesmühl, Carl Zuckmayer's house that he was forced to leave after the occupation of Austria.*

***Bermann-Fischer Verlag, Stockholm.*

27
Pierre Bertaux— Fighter, Scholar, Interpreter

In 1927 a twenty-year old Frenchman lived in Berlin whom I had met a few years earlier in Austria. A brilliant pupil at the Ecole Normale in Paris, Pierre Bertaux was the first student who came to Berlin after World War I to study German language and literature and write a dissertation on "The Spirit and Nature of the Poet Hölderlin". Since that time his life was devoted to Hölderlin, but his career as a specialist in German literature was soon to be disrupted and he was to be involved in the political confusion and struggles of World War II.

At the time of our meeting it seemed as though we had in times past been brother and sister and had known each other forever. A lifelong friendship developed.

Pierre took a student's room in the Grunewald, quite near us, and became a frequent visitor to our house. In the meantime his friendship had extended to Gottfried as well. He brought to our house his friend Pierre Viénot, the head of the Franco-German study committee in Berlin, as well as other friends and fellow students, including his friend Roland de Margérie, the son of the then French ambassador, who was helpful to us later at the time of the first Nazi threats. Two extraordinary American personalities also were part of that group: Dorothy Thompson, the correspondent of the *Herald Tribune,* and Edgar Mowrer of the *Chicago Daily News.* Both of them early on recognized the dangerous political development in Germany and incessantly, though for a long time futilely, warned their government in Washington about the true nature of incipient Nazism.

In his memoirs Bertaux recalled a Sunday in February 1928 at our house, a day on which he met many of our friends there: Jakob Wassermann, Alfred Döblin, Ernst Toller, Alfred Kerr, George Grosz, and Joseph Roth. The last-named said: "In ten years a) Germany will be at war with France, b) we shall be living in Switzerland, if we are lucky, c) Jews will be beaten up on Kurfürstendamm." No one believed Roth, who smiled in despair, but soon enough these prophetic words were to come true.

We experienced the onset of disaster together with Pierre and became joint witnesses to the macabre spectacle of the burning of the books. On the huge square in front of Berlin's venerable university a pyre had been erected, and from a tribune the devilish clubfoot Goebbels consigned the books of twenty-four "undesirable and corrosive" authors to the flames. For each of the burned authors, among them Freud, Marx, Heinrich Mann, Stefan Zweig, Alfred Kerr, and Alfred Döblin, Goebbels had prepared an indictment which he spoke into a loudspeaker for broadcasting over all German radio stations: "You do well . . . to entrust the evil spirit of the past to the flames . . . From now on the state will decide what is wholesome and what is pernicious literature. Now the pen must serve the people in the same way as the sword and the plough." It was a ghostly scene: up on the platform the shrieking dwarf, eerily illuminated by the flames, and down below a silent crowd that circled the burning mountain of books and tried to get hold of any that were still intact. A witches' sabbath.

In 1933 Bertaux became the director of the "Spoken Word" at the French radio in Paris, PTT, and the following year he was appointed department head in the Foreign Office there. He directed French German-language broadcasts as a counteraction to Nazi broadcasts in the French language over the Stuttgart radio.

In 1936 Pierre qualified for a university appointment and became a professor of German language and literature at the University of Toulouse. In addition he served the state in various missions, and upon the outbreak of the war he became an interpreter attached to the General Staff. After the German invasion in 1940 he organized one of the first underground actions of southern France, which caused the Pétain government to sentence him to three years' confinement in fortress. After his release in August 1944 he entered liberated Toulouse as a commissioner of the Republic.

French emigrants in New York told me that Pierre had survived the war, and when I set foot on European soil again in 1948 I visited him in Lyon, where he was residing in the enormous old palais of the prefecture as Préfet du Rhône. The abyss before which we had stood together years ago had now been filled in, but many things had been destroyed, and rebuilding was the order of the day. The atmosphere in France at that time was a weird one. The communist workers's movement was trying to control the streets and the administration even though it was not able to seize power. With prudence and determination Pierre managed to lead the unions and the organized workers' groups back to a democratic form of cooperation. In that dangerous situation he performed a great service for France, and he was called to Paris as director-general of the Sureté Nationale, minister of police. Confronted with the great political problems of the time and exposed to constant threats, he worked day and night, prudently and calmly and with the greatest energy, in the Ministry of the Interior opposite the Elysée Palace.

"In his life is refracted all the story of France," wrote the American writer Theodore H. White about Pierre Bertaux in his book *Fire in the Ashes,* published after the war.

When we took over our publishing house in Frankfurt again in 1950, Bertaux became one of our closest associates and consultants, particularly in the establishment of the Fischer-Bücherei, a paperback series that was then still a novelty for the public and the book trade. He was tireless in sending us suggestions for political, philosophical, and literary subjects. The volume of selections from Hölderlin that he compiled for the Fischer-Bücherei was particularly close to the heart of this Hölderlin scholar.

A new event interrupted this work, however. Pierre had been elected a senator for the French Sudan, today called Mali. In 1953 he wrote me:

. . . Tutti, everything is happening at once . . . High season in Paris . . . Voters from the Sudan . . . No time to think . . . Much African activity; I organized the contact with sixty Sudanese students in Paris to whom no parliamentarian has ever paid any attention

before and who are growing like wild grass . . . At the end of September I shall fly to the Sudan where my constituents are getting impatient. How smart, prudent, and politically mature my Sudanese are! Come to Timbuktu; you will also enjoy them. And they are so pleasant and have so much humor. They will probably outlast the Occident. My idea of entrusting our "higher" values, our most sacred things to them is not so bad. Perhaps they will succeed more easily than we. Ségou on the Niger river is not a metropolis, but it has long been called the Athens on the Niger, and I have met wise people there.

On October 20, 1956 he wrote:

. . . Light again at last; perhaps some things will become brighter and lighter. It was so nice, so true, so real with you . . . I am continuing to work on our preface to the Hölderlin volume and have discovered Heraclitus and Parmenides. Hölderlin is really a pre-Socratic, and he knew it— with Empedokles as an "apocryphal book."

In November 1957 the Hölderlin paperback appeared, and he wrote about it as follows:

"Tutti, this morning the most beautiful surprise: our Hölderlin; yes, it will stay with me wherever I may be." He had prefaced the book with the following lines:

Today Hölderlin is in the forefront of the poets. Why? The perfect, glorious beauty of his writings is not the only reason. Rather, through his work and his person the nature of poetry reveals itself, and far from being a game and an ornament it is a deep penetration into the structure of the world. Hölderlin teaches us also that a work of art is not the monologue of a lonely man but an appeal, a demand of the "coming generation," of us, of our turn to a new era of which he is part.

I heard a lecture about the concept of "turnabout" in Hölderlin, and this set me off in a new direction. Has a "psychoanalysis" of Hölderlin ever been attempted? An exceedingly rich subject. His relationship with his mother. The "turnabout" is the longing for the state before birth. "There is a yearning for the unrestrained . . . " "Birth is capable of doing the most . . . the cradle."

Hölderlin, according to Bertaux, can be a guidepost to us in a world that grows ever more menacing and is destroying itself. He wrote:

It is not yet fully realized that a limit has been placed on a society based on technological and industrial development by the fact that the pollution of the air and the water, the destruction of the natural balance, places the survival of mankind in doubt. Man's relationship to his environment is being menacingly destroyed. What remedy can there be if not Hölderlin's "new" religion— the religion of nature, the cult of the elements— light, air, earth, water?

Viewed in this light, Hölderlin's definition of "fatherland" sounds astonishingly modern. It certainly does not involve any geopolitical or historical concept. It has nothing to do with "homeland" and "patriotism." To him, "fatherland" is an ecological-sociological concept, as we would put it today: "Nature and man, insofar as there is a special interaction between them." If the "fatherland," that is, the existing order of society and the world, is antiquated, it should "rejuvenate" itself. The old and the outmoded should dissolve itself, and from its passing a "new" world will arise, creating a new, mutual relationship of man to his environment, a new covenant with nature. "Oh give yourselves to nature before it takes you . . . But you will judge, holy nature! . . . Is that which you mock and call soulless not divine? Is the air you drink in not better than your babbling? The sun's rays, are they not nobler than all you clever ones? The springs of the earth and the morning dew refresh your grove; can you do that, too? Alas! You can kill but not restore to life, unless love does so . . . You worry and scheme how to escape fate and do not comprehend it."

Pierre managed to keep returning to his main profession, German language and literature, and in 1958 he was appointed to a professorship in that field at Lille. He turned it into a comprehensive study of "Germanness," being concerned with plumbing the nature and the psychology of the German character in order to acquaint his French students with the thinking and striving of the Germans. In 1960 he wrote me:

. . . I am just jotting down a few lines; perhaps they will include something for your work and for the direction of Germany's future development as we try to observe it . . . You know my opinion that the attitude and mentality of the Germans has been shaped by theology. Everywhere one encounters the theological orientation. Perhaps this is connected with the fact that between the eleventh and the fifteenth centuries German culture developed in the cities founded at that time. In the universities theology was the only subject that could

be studied; it was the form knowledge took in general, and it served as a model for the other forms. The Reformation was a dissemination, popularization, and generalization of theology—precisely at a time when language and "culture" were fixed in connection with the guild system of the German cities.

In Germany philosophy is a theology of ideas (more recently a theology of being), art a theology of the beautiful, politics a theology of the state and power. Theologians know only one truth, and everything else results from that: the claim to a monopoly on faith; all those who think differently must be wrong, etc. Anyone who does not submit to that is cast out, and hence all who are dear and precious to us in Germany are outcasts.

"The near-arbitrariness of feasibility"— that is the original sin and inherited affliction of the German people.

Anyone among the Germans who does not agree with this delusion is proscribed as an enemy of the people, as anti-social, alien . . .

I am now making excerpts from the works of Georg Büchner, a fantastic figure— also misunderstood in this way. One only has to read him; he says everything there is to say. Dead at age twenty-three . . . Do you know the story of his résistance? . . . Broadsides, flight from the police, arrest, examining magistrate, secret societies . . . we know all that. Someone ought to write a history of this résistance in Germany, the members of the secret societies: Hölderlin, Kleist, Nietzsche— on the whole, from the viewpoint of success, a sad story that always ends with misery, deprivation, illness, isolation, proscription— or worse (as with Nietzsche), with misjudgment and misinterpretation, misrepresentation and distortion. And it is precisely these people who speak the most beautiful German, and there probably is good reason for it . . . And who else should be admitted to this secret society— Lenz, Lichtenberg, Hebbel? There are many more among the outlawed.

In July 1961 Pierre wrote me from Berlin, where he was staying with some of his French students:

Oh, Berlin, it was very nice with the students— and we arranged a small reception on Erdenerstrasse on Sunday afternoon. Such a pity that you were not present. All the time I had to think of the time we spent together there . . . The days in Berlin were full of experiences, as always in Berlin . . . Almost every day I went to the Eastern sector, also to the Academy and the Heinrich Mann Archives. This gave me an opportunity to tell these young people that Heinrich

Mann's greatness is tolerance . . . that one doesn't say: "We are right, and so the others are wrong" . . . They were somewhat surprised when they heard this, especially when I said that this made Heinrich Mann quite timely, even prophetic, and that this was the meaning of his work (Henry IV, the religious wars, Protestants and Catholics). There is something stimulating about the Berlin air; I am enjoying work and life again!

In 1970 Bertaux, who had already met Heinrich Mann as an adolescent, gave a memorial address on this admired writer upon the invitation of the Academy in the Eastern sector, saying, among other things:

Forty-two years ago a French student of German language and literature was the guest of the Prussian Academy in Berlin. The invitation was issued by Heinrich Mann . . . That period is as alive and Heinrich Mann is as present to me as they ever were: the dignity of his figure and demeanor, the gleam in his eyes— fire and tenderness at once— his smile, his understanding, his kindness and courage . . . What is to become of the delicate, sensitive, intuitive poetic types? Should one not declare these receptive, porous, and therefore jeopardized types endangered species and create reservations for them where the species will be preserved? . . . For these people see what others do not see . . . The gift of vision and astonishment is one reserved for such poetic types . . .

The subject of "mutation" occupied Bertaux for years. He wrote:

There are so many new things; life goes on so magnificently. I now have much more time for writing and thinking, and now I have proof that I am working in a good direction. From all sides come signs that what I have imagined for some years is becoming reality. But it is not so easy to be the first to enter this "eternal wilderness" through all but impassable brushwood, to glimpse the hitherto unseen and to express the unexpressed . . . It is so exciting— I am carried away with enthusiasm. We are facing an entirely new development; whether or not it is gratifying is of no interest. It will be "different" and we shall participate in it . . . It will even go beyond the human; what is taking shape will be dehumanized . . . After all, the machine, the mechanical is the new creature . . . It has the capability to think, to reproduce itself . . . We have to make a fresh analysis of the concept "man" and distinguish what about him is the "apex" of development (this will continue) and what is "animalis-

tic." Up to now the two have been combined; perhaps now the two elements will separate, like the stages of a rocket . . .

In April 1963 his book *Mutation der Menschheit. Diagnosen und Prognosen* (Mutation of Mankind. Diagnoses and Prognoses) appeared in the Fischer-Bücherei as an exhortation to his environment. In his introduction he writes:

To regard and evaluate the human history of our time as a biological event is not only permissible but virtually unavoidable. Anyone who shrinks back from this does not understand the full import of what has happened and thus the dimensions of responsibility . . . The species man has far more ahead of it than lies behind it. It is questionable, to be sure, whether the descendants of today's mankind will not belong to a different species from the one that we designate as homo sapiens. It is actually my view that a mutation is taking place at this very time . . . When I voiced this view for the first time a few years ago, it was not even deemed worth discussing; in a short time it will be banal. Be that as it may, our generation has been given the chance to observe this unique and magnificent biological process from the inside and consciously participate in it. Added to this is the fact that precisely the awareness which we have of this process plays a decisive role in the process of mutation . . . Here we shall try to interpret the signs of the times from this perspective and to throw out a new and very timely subject for discussion.

How timely these ideas of a biological mutation were to become could only be surmised at that time, but Bertaux' book did arouse some attention. Kurt Heuser wrote me in March 1964:

. . . I have just reread Pierre Bertaux' Mutation. I regard it as one of the most important books of recent years . . . because in it prognoses are made, quite scientifically and yet boldly, which make the future of all of us seem transparent. And some of his ideas, such as those about war and peace, are so unconventional that one steps into them as into an ice-cold bath, shuddering with the chill of truth.

Similar reflections about the perspectives of the future gave rise to the series *Welt im Werden* (A World in the Making), which included books on cybernetics, linguistic theory, games theory, social psychology, and many other problems of today's world. Regarding this series, which Bertaux co-edited with our scientific associate Ilse Grubrich-Simitis, he wrote:

The diagonal sciences open up a new perspective. What appears at the vanishing point of this perspective is nothing else than the future of mankind.

Never before have so many and such radical changes occurred in a scant fifteen years:

1) Mankind today has the technical capability of destroying itself as a species and also of changing itself genetically. We are gradually ceasing to regard man as a stable species. We know that he is subject both to destruction and a spontaneous or induced mutation.

2) Up to now men believed they were alone in the world and, having been created in God's image, were the only intelligent beings in the universe . . . Man is on the point of abandoning his illusion of an absolute central position and a monopoly on intelligence.

3) The departure from the planet earth has begun. Even though we may hardly expect practical results from this in the foreseeable future, the very possibility of flight is already bringing about a shift in our entire system of coordinates. To promote an understanding of this shift is the meaning and purpose of the series Welt im Werden.

At that time Bertaux also compiled an anthology of French storytellers for the Fischer-Bücherei and became a contributor to our latest enterprise, a history of the world which has since appeared in thirty-four volumes. He took charge of the volume on Africa and wrote it on the basis of personal experience as a senator of the Sudan and first-hand knowledge of the African continent.

The student unrest of 1968 also affected Pierre Bertaux, who had been a professor of German at the Sorbonne since 1964. The old style of the University was now outmoded. He wrote me soon thereafter:

. . . After the events of May and June at the French universities the Sorbonne was out of commission . . . In October a colleague asked me why I did not open my own institute outside the Sorbonne. This seemed to me a chance that one gets once in a century. I submitted my plan for an "Institut d'Allemand" to Edgar Faure, the Minister of Culture; in three minutes he had comprehended everything, and a few hours later he said at a conference of ministers: "Et nous savons décidé de créer a Asnieères un Institut d'Allemand" . . . It is to become a European institution, integrating German and French students and teachers . . . If I succeed, it will be the great achievement of my life and the concrete result of the efforts of three generations of Germanists and Europeans . . . The Institut

d'Asnières is also yours— that is, the consequence of our first conversations forty-five years ago, when you told me about Coudenhove and Pan-Europe . . .

His institute at Asnieres became the center of free, European exchanges. During my visit I had an opportunity to become acquainted with the joyful and harmonious atmosphere between students and teachers at a time of great tension at other institutes. Two years after the founding of Asnières Bertaux wrote:

. . . It is probably an opportunity to create something for the world that is truly significant— a beginning of a "new university," a new concept not only of instruction but of education in general . . . It is a great success and continues to develop— like a miracle, with cheerful, happy students and enthusiastic teachers . . .

Years before that, Bertaux had come to Camaiore for our house-warming; he had visited us there on several subsequent occasions, and planted one of his favorite trees, the conifer *Libocedrus decurrens,* which has by now grown to enormous size. After another visit in 1971 he wrote:

. . . Those were such beautiful days . . . as always when we are together. The scenery is even more beautiful than the memories I had of it, and the house is a paradise; time stands still when one is in it, and it is not so easy to find one's way back to normal life afterwards. But all this— the scenery, the house, the life— that is you . . .

In parting I gave Pierre a piano score of Mozart's *Don Giovanni* that had been in the possession of my grandmother. This work had played an important role in his life for a long time, and he wrote me about it as follows:

. . . The Don Giovanni has a place of honor in my library, and I keep hearing his "Non l'avrei giammai creduto, ma farò quel che potrò." Its echo in Hölderlin: "As for me, I have done what I could." And here is the same thought in the peasant language of my ancestors as handed down by my mother: "J'avou fait ce que j'avou poullu" (j'ai fait ce que j'ai pu), which means that one has been a "man." This has also remained my ideal . . . The authorship of the libretto of Don Giovanni has always been a mystery to me . . . How much did Mozart himself contribute? What is the origin of this magnificent, manly tone toward fate? Well, I discovered that Lorenzo da Ponte was a friend of Casanova and that Casanova was in Prague during the months when Lorenzo da Ponte had no fewer than three assignments to write libretti there . . . What is more

natural than to think that Casanova at least helped him? But now the most exciting thing: In Casanova's (unpublished) literary remains at Dux there are supposed to be sketches and variants of Don Giovanni!

In 1975 Pierre Bertaux was awarded the Heinrich Heine Prize of the City of Düsseldorf. The mayor wrote him about that: "With this prize the committee recognizes your exemplary work not only through your scholarly activities but above all through your militant championship of freedom and human rights at a time of the harshest oppression as well as through your efforts toward Franco-German reconciliation."

After years of work Bertaux completed his "Poetics," "an entirely new theory that no longer has anything to do with literature, a scientific investigation of a matter that far transcends 'literature.'" Some day he will publish the story of his eventful life on which he has been working since his youth.

Pierre never contents himself with the results of his research, and to the end of his life he will surely not be an idle onlooker but will always attempt to save "freedom."

28
Boris Pasternak, the First Voice from Russia

In 1957 we acquired at the Frankfurt Book Fair the German translation rights to *Doctor Zhivago,* a novel by the Russian writer Boris Pasternak. It was the first time that a voice from Russia had penetrated the Iron Curtain and reached the West through that hermetically sealed wall. This author and his book were shrouded in mystery. An Italian correspondent had brought the manuscript he had received from Pasternak to Berlin and handed it to the Milano publisher Feltrinelli there. After making a contract governing the world rights, Feltrinelli published an Italian translation of the book, thus securing for it the protection of copyright. Shortly thereafter the German edition appeared in our S. Fischer Verlag, but the book has been barred from publication in Russia to this day.

After reading the German translation it immediately became apparent that this work was one of the great human documents of our time. The brisk demand for the book when it appeared in the fall of 1958 was like an explosion. For years the western world had been waiting to get a first-hand report about life in Russia, and the mysterious rumors that circulated about the way the book had reached the West made the curiosity about it even greater. When

Pasternak was awarded the Nobel Prize and the Russian government prohibited him from accepting it, the international success of his novel was assured. Millions of people were shaken; the darkness that had hitherto lain over this unknown world grew lighter, and a bridge had been built. Pasternak received a flood of letters from his readers in the western world; requests of all kinds reached him and threatened to swamp him. All he heard from his own country, however, was the voice of the court that sentenced him to complete retirement to his small country home near Moscow. There he lived under the constant surveillance of the G.P.U. and was not allowed to move about freely. No wonder that this meant the ruin of a delicate soul like his.

We were not vouchsafed a personal meeting with Boris Pasternak. He died suddenly in 1960, before we had had a chance to visit him and before he could complete any of the three great works on which he had started to work passionately. In the fifteen months of our relationship our correspondence developed into something like friendship between people who have known each other for a long time. What a great heart and what profound sorrow were reflected in each of his words to us!

I was moved to tears when I read his first handwritten postcard, written in his expressive German:

September 26, 1958

My dear Mr. Fischer, I hasten to confirm receipt of your soulful, noble-minded letter. I thank you particularly for the cordial, personally tinged tone of your letter . . . This friendly tone happily fills me with a feeling of spiritual closeness to you and your sphere of activity. Should you ever have another opportunity or desire to gladden me with a letter, please address it to my country home at Peredelkino near Moscow.

It would greatly please me to receive a copy of the German edition of my book . . .

Please do not be surprised or offended that I answer your expansive, generous letter with a meager, unsigned postcard. This is being done for the sake of a safe delivery. I hope that in future I shall be able to send you long letters in envelopes, but today I do not wish to postpone indefinitely this expression of my delight at the newly won friendship, and this way it is most likely to reach you. It is a great satisfaction to me that my book appeals to you and yours. It is my conviction that we are living in days of the consequences and final results and not of the continuation of what we have long seen and suffered, that the few and only important things that wars and revolutions ought to do have long since been attained, proved, and drilled into people. One no longer needs to shout oneself hoarse about this. I am surprised at artists and thinkers who are still loyal to the many useless and antiquated political, aesthetic, and other forms and counter-forms, for the only thing that matters is the new, uncomprehended, and barely germinated substance, like the fields and sprouts after the Thirty Years' War or the fall of the Tartar yoke. A new age is dawning . . . I close my letter with the expression of my deepest devotion to you and the highly respected Mrs. Fischer.

All subsequent letters were also written in his peculiar German, which deviated from the standard language and sometimes was almost creative.

December 14, 1958

My dear lady, how easy it was for me to hasten gratefully toward Mr. Fischer's first letters. In the face of your two letters and also one from your husband, I remain like a permanently insolvent debtor.

These letters from you are a whole world of thought and feeling. The honor you do me with them is no less than the honor the publishing house shows me so enormously by devoting its New Year's issue [the reference is to the Neue Rundschau]so skillfully and tastefully entirely to me.

Forgive me, then, not only for leaving your generosity unthanked and unanswered for so long, but also for not making a response comparable to your letters. Your superiority is my excuse. And I did not keep silent because of some impediments. I simply spent the past month with craftsmanlike translation work done in debilitating concentration in an effort not to hear the dangerous unpleasantness that has roared all around me . . . Regarding the impossibility of speedy postal service and giving advice: To an actor who was putting on poetry readings and wanted to consult me regarding mine (when I was still young and legal) I replied that every work of art that is genuine and perfect is posthumous even if its author is still alive. Thus no one should be asked for elucidations and explanations (which cannot add or impart anything to the real work). If it is untrue and imperfect, then the matter is not worth wasting any words on. You need not consult me regarding the prose anthology. Go ahead without my advice.

Among the countless letters that I receive from the four corners of the earth— from madmen (complaints about courts, governments, reigning royal houses, etc.); from givers of practical advice (who propose that I do not decline the prize but assign it to them, whereupon they will concede me one-half or one-tenth etc.); from enthusiastic young readers, male and female, who tell me many fine and cordial things and ask me for photos and autographs— among these and other categories of letters there are requests for material help from at home and abroad. For the time being I am obliged to put off satisfying the one kind, since my financial and legal affairs will evidently be in abeyance for a long time— until they are decided by an aphoristic statement from someone in power, though such a statement may not be forthcoming. As for the requests of the other kind, I shall shortly ask that they be fulfilled through your good offices or those of Kurt Wolff or Feltrinelli.

Now I finally give you a reason to breathe freely. Please accept my best heartfelt wishes as well as my expressions of profound respect.

Since there is some doubt that this letter will arrive, please confirm its receipt as quickly as possible. Kindly write me about the decision of the Swedish Academy. It is said that they have preserved not only the honorary title for me, but everything else as well. I do not believe this, because from what I have heard I believe that this runs counter to the statutes of the institution . . .

February 5, 1959

Dear Mrs. and Mr. Fischer, I am bent and breaking down and foundering under the weight and number of the letters of which I am able, permitted, and willing to answer only the smallest part (and even that with terrible delays). Thus I shall be quite brief.

The selection of the little volume in the Fischer-Bücherei is very good. I thank you, the translator, and everyone, and I have no criticism to make. In general, my refusal, my evasive way of speaking about almost everything from my "early period" should not be taken too much to heart. The publishers, translators, and others concerned should not take offense at this estrangement. It is not meant for them but for this past of mine. I am not dissatisfied with them but with myself.

But shall I be able to make up, in the few years I have left, with new original work for the loss of fifteen years spent in the pure translation trade? Very doubtful. Do I then have the right and the opportunity to abandon everything (and I do mean everything) I wrote prior to Zhivago and renounce it completely? That is probably impossible. Some exceptions have to be permitted, but which ones? If I only knew that!

. . . Now, however, that people want to publish all my failures not only in Germany but everywhere and seem to have partly succeeded in doing so, it is too late to lament this. What remains for me now is to swim across this sea of the unwanted and not to drown in it . . .

A great many letters are getting lost . . . Several letters addressed to me have disappeared in recent months. Four months of my correspondence to and from France have simply been wiped out. That need not discourage us, however. (I did receive your congratulations from Italy some time ago). Let us continue to use the mail to write each other.

For the time being I will not and must not engage in financial negotiations with any of you. What good would it do me if I knew something definite about that?

. . . As regards the projected comprehensive poetry volume, I have looked over the pertinent manuscript (Wenn es aufklart [When It Clears Up]. I could not have done all this in greater detail and with more care than someone was good enough to do. The title Wenn es aufklart remains for this series of poems.

I certainly do not want to influence the selection; that must be done by the editor of the collection. May he be guided only by a feeling of immediate, irresistible, free, and sincere liking, not by secondary considerations of fashion, political seasoning, etc. etc. For example, if the poem "Der Nobelpreis" (in the supplement) is not a poetic piece in itself, he should not be swayed by the secondary value of the poem. The same goes for the poems "Die Seele" and "Änderung," which leave me cold.

As I looked over the selection, "Bacchanal" seemed to me to be the best, perhaps the only dynamic one that moved me.

I am interrupting this letter without reading it again. Gratefully and sincerely yours, Boris Pasternak.

April 6, 1959

Mrs. and Mr. Fischer, dear, highly respected friends, oh, for the annoyance! If only I could tell you everything!

Do not think me forgetful and ungrateful. I should have thanked you immediately for the beautiful dictionary which I found at home after a brief sojourn in the Caucasus. (Thanks to your kindly obligingness, additional impertinent requests for books will appear).

But the fine present was not the only thing that awaited me upon my return. I shall spare myself and you the description of all that. Well-meaning patrons advise me to refrain from writing letters altogether. Should one also refrain from breathing in and out? Thus you will hear from me less frequently, and I shall be briefer. But letters to me can and should be sent as before. I do not know if I have already had an opportunity to address the following request to you. In Marburg an der Lahn lives a Frau Käte Becker who has an obvious and lively literary talent. She is the owner of the Marburg gasoline station on Bundesstrasse (Marburg Krummbogen 57). She sent me birthday wishes and a present— for the single reason that she saw from a Hessian newspaper report that I studied in Marburg in 1912 and wrote a nice description of the city afterwards. She is the only person who writes me from Marburg, but she is a special case— dynamic and touching. With your kind help I would like to give this lady a valuable, palpable surprise. She must definitely receive a gift copy of Doctor Zhivago by mail and then nothing else by me, except, perhaps, the new poems (Wenn es aufklart) . . . but none of my expressionistic sins! A few other books, however. The woman likes to travel, thus perhaps some books about cities (monographs with many pictures, Swiss scenery, Italian cities, Venice, Florence, Rome). That is not all yet (I ask you— what are the limits of unscrupulousness?) If some member of your publishing house came driving along and stopped at that Marburg gas station, would it not be possible to bring her a big cake or perhaps something better that might occur to you or your wife? (Marburg has many gardens, and a bouquet of flowers would not be a surprise for the woman in summer).

Then I have a whole lot of other encumbrances for you. I am planning to write three different works in prose and verse: a play based on Russian history toward the time of the liberation of the serfs; then a poetic work about the thirst for freedom as a natural goal to the point of madness, based on some Slavic-Illyrian, Dalmatian-Adriatic materials— half original, half derived from books in which I might find something if I obtained them. For the third work, which deals with Georgia, pre-Christian antiquities, early Christiani-

ty, archaeology, excavations, and finds, I shall now ask you for four books. During my life I have on several occasions given away and sold all the books from my years in secondary school and at the university, and so I have no classical dictionaries. Therefore, be so kind as to send me 1) the Greek and 2) the Latin dictionaries from the bilingual Langenscheidt series. Then (and I derive the information from two reviews in the Vienna bibliographic journal Biblos) two books about the finds at Qumran: 3) Davies, A. Powell, Der Fund von Qumran (German translation of this work). Die Schriftrollen vom Toten Meer . . . Wiesbaden, Brockhaus, 1957, and 4) (but 3) is sufficient, for 4) may be too costly and too heavy for mailing as printed matter), 4) Burrows, Millar, Die Schrifttrollen vom Toten Meer (German), Munich, Beck, 1957.

Unlike many to whom almost all my letters get lost, I hope this registered letter will reach you. I have good luck with you . . . But if you, Collins, or Gallimard (please write them about it) should think of sending me some of my newly published books (I know almost nothing but the novel), it would give me pleasure.

July 31, 1959

My dear Mrs. Fischer, I have resolved to refrain from pleasant letter-writing and do only real, undissimulated work. The most difficult thing during these abstemious weeks was to leave your angelic message uncheered and unthanked. Now I can no longer resist the temptation, but this will probably not turn out to be a real letter. Look for nothing here but grateful glances and exclamation points. . . . It was easy for me to evaluate and admire Keil's accomplishments. Apart from the fact that these are really excellent achievements of the art of poetry and translation, the originals, too, are normal human products, which is something that transfigures and facilitates the matter . . .

Oh, how much time I have for failing; oh, how little I have left for improving and catching up!

At this point I was going to write an introduction to all future aesthetics for you, but today's mail was brought in in large quantities, and so that the signs of my admiration may not remain outside your knowledge and perish, I hasten to sign as your devoted servant B. Pasternak.

September 9, 1959

My dear Mrs. Fischer, again it is not the time to write you a long letter. I only want to inform you gratefully of the arrival of yours of August 8 from your Tuscan casa.

I have been in a peculiar mood in recent days. My work is making very slow progress. I am not working more than two hours daily. It is not that the intention is an unfounded self-deception, that this thing, writing, does not constitute a natural need for me. But even assuming that after immensely long work this play turned out to be a powerful masterpiece, in my life and my career it will not have the importance or play the role that was the case earlier. This form of fate has become so unalterably disastrous that it cannot be managed and guided with productions of art, with will-power and zeal.. And since all this is always bound up with reliable, fulfillable vital instincts, this hopelessness probably curbs my diligence.

I was never an expert on Nietzsche or an admirer of him. Now that I cannot harbor any hope of ever getting away from here into the bright world, I would like to pay homage to his memorial place via my photograph if not in person. I now feel like one of the realizations of his feverishly bitter, insanely effective and utter solitude . . .

This is not a letter. What do I intend with this nonsense? But something intelligent remains to be said: I like Thornton Wilder exceptionally well; he delights me! Please give my heartfelt greetings to your husband. Your B. Pasternak.

November 14, 1959

Dear Mrs. Fischer, my heartfelt thanks for your inestimable letter and the invitation card . . . For some time I shall not be able to write many and long letters . . . From the words on your card I conclude that you have magnanimously forgiven me for my silence . . .

The piles of letters which at another time it would give me the purest pleasure to answer (and I hope that time will come, perhaps in the Spring) are divided into two parts: the theater and the field of literature. It is a real heartache for me not to be able to write reviews immediately of collections sent me as a present, as for example those of T. S. Eliot or Stephen Spender, and to postpone letters to them indefinitely. But is it not my duty to subject the new piece of writing (with all the inner elements that gave rise to it) to the almost unattainably difficult goal, a complete external embodiment? And how much time and effort are demanded by this goal! Best regards and wishes from all my heart, your B.P.

December 17, 1959

Happy New Year, my dear Frau Brigitte, please convey my best and warmest Christmas and New Year's wishes to Dr. G. Fischer. One after another the presents are coming from the publishing house (most recently the record and the Neue Rundschau,) faster than I am able to thank you for them and start reading them. I am aware of the excellent accomplishments of Celan . . . and of the fact that there are young poets. It weighs heavily on my mind that there still are unacknowledged poetry collections of T.S. Eliot and Stephen Spender lying around here. That I never wrote you anything about Kafka or other books sent me does not mean that I have nothing to say about them or that all these names were completely new to me. (But I repeat in every letter that I am delighted with the splendid Thornton Wilder). But my lack of time is indescribable. To write the drama "Blind Beauty" is a matter of honor, a bounden duty for me. After one has produced so precious little of one's own (owing to the long period of numerous translations) it is impossible to revel parasitically in the success of a single work for such a very long time. That is tactless and vile. But of course it is not this secondary consideration that makes me want to be diligent. I have an inner impulse and a most ardent desire to work on and polish this piece of writing.

Life keeps going on, however, gets ahead of me, and brings events, disturbances, distractions, and entanglements. But these complications of my life bear only a small part of the blame for the slow progress of my work (and it was the same with Dr. Zh.). I am one of those who have always turned their favorite work into the drudgery of a galley slave. What one puts on paper is far less than what one revises and changes and— oh God, oh God— strikes and scratches and crosses out to the point of madness . . . The Hamburger Schauspielhaus gave guest performances here for a week. This time I shall not expand on the lively, sparkling freshness and great splendor of the performance, because this letter is dangerously long as it is. But owing to my request there is a small secondary matter that I must touch upon here. If I am not blinded by my vain stupidity, the people were extraordinarily nice and kind to me.

Now I would like you to keep something in mind. If you and your husband are satisfied with the production of my poetry volume (in America, for example, they put a monster on the cover with the presumption or assertion that it was I), if the early reception strikes you as favorable, if, in a word, this present will be a worthy one and will not appear offensively valueless to the recipient, then I would ask you to induce the publishing house to send the book in my name to a number of the leading personalities of the Hamburg theater— to Ella Büchi, Elisabeth Göbel, Ehmi Bessel, and Werner Hinz (I hear these are husband and wife). To Gustaf Gründgens. When do you hope to have the poetry printed and published? I am ending this letter abruptly. Gratefully and sincerely, B. Pasternak.

December 18, 1959

My dear lady, this is a supplement to my letter of two days ago, or rather, a continuation of my constant importunate begging. Forgive me for bothering you so often. But I wrote you the letter of the 16th after a performance of Faust and one day before seeing Der zerbrochene Krug and one act of Wallensteins Tod.

The scenic art, the art of playwriting and dramatic performance, is a field of its own. Two days ago I would have denied this, but today I must admit it.

It was startling to witness the rich, colorful, life-saturated (logically clear, like the zigzag course of lightning) effects that are produced by Kleist's one-act comedy and a separate fragmentary act of Schiller by comparison with the meagerness and weakness of Faust, with only one part, the first part! When I was translating it, the whirl of work made me forget that the second part is incomprehensible, and this forgetting unexpectedly made me understand it. If, modesty aside, I constitute a link in the development of Russian literature and Russian literary forms, the same thing must be acknowledged about my Faust translation. This work on Faust is an enormous intermediate stretch covered on this road. The same laws of originality (that originality which is superpersonal and whose origins and possibilities are inherent in the nature of every great, rich mother tongue), the same laws that may have guided my own unpretentious attempts also guided me in this work, since Goethe's text was for me not literature but a raw and deep elemental document, equivalent in reality to nature. There is no need, then, to sell me on Goethe.

But what is the first part alone, as an independent, self-contained whole, without reference to the second part, without the admixture of its presentiment? A simple, lower-class girl is ruined by an educated man and finally executed. This would make us swim uncontrollably in our hottest tears. But to make things easier for us and harder for the girl, a millstone of brilliant lyrical-philosophical dialogues and monologues of the perpetrator is hung around her neck. And it is surprising that it takes such an effort, such aids and stimulants, devil's work and many magic tricks, to have a man fall in love with a girl and lead her into temptation. I was not able to understand how the director suffers this incompleteness, which makes the work of the two actors performing the major roles infinitely more difficult. Only today did I learn that in Hamburg both parts are performed and that they brought the first part here as the great half, a huge, one-evening fragment of the complete performance . . .

What is the meaning of the notation "Suhrkamp Verlag vorm. [formerly] S. Fischer" which I found in a book? Are you planning to turn your enterprise over to someone else? Oh, how sorry I would be about that! Since these two letters seem destined to get lost, please wire me immediately if the opposite is the case.

Please do not be angry with me for tiring you so. Your B. Pasternak.

February 14, 1960

Dear Friends, Mrs. Brigitte and Mr. Gottfried, Goethe's holograph letter has arrived. I am speechless and cannot find words of thanks. You should not do this. I shall of course put this original in a glass frame and hang it on the wall of my study, but I am not the person in whose life it belongs as something important, nor am I (by nature) worthy of such a rarity. You have far too high and noble an opinion of me. And then I am bothered by the fact that you have expended so much effort on me in finding this and so much money in acquiring it!

After a long interruption and postponement I have returned to my own work. Your B. Pasternak.

February 16, 1960

My dear Mr. and Mrs. Fischer, today I received Wenn es aufklart. *I am overjoyed. Thank you, thank you. Permit me to embrace both of you. And as always it comes at a time of terrible haste and hurry. Tomorrow morning I have to go to town to do many errands and get things for the neighboring house of the Ivanovs (he wrote* Der Panzerzug *(*The Tank Platoon*) and very colorful stories in our expressionistic period at the beginning of the Revolution).*

Well, then, to choose gifts for the house of the Ivanovs, who are very nice people and are having a family celebration tomorrow, is anything but an easy matter here. And so I shall get up at six in the morning.

I have already taken care of my shopping in town, but the celebration will not be until this evening. I have returned from town and will continue this letter. Do you not think that Keil is brilliant? I swim in tears when I read it. That is me, taken over by a masterly, truthworthy hand. Keil sent me the first chapter of Eugene Onegin [the play by Alexander Pushkin]. I read two or three stanzas to people who do not know German well and asked them what it was. They immediately recognized the work by the flow of the rhetoric, the zigzag of the syntax, the sound of the sentence structure. Every judgment about Wenn es aufklart will be a judgment on me; in the original it is not any better or different; the main thing, the essence, has been captured and royally reproduced. Everything he does is in accordance with the laws of his talents and thus brilliant and right. This is how one must translate. I can guess what his first draft must have been like and what he cut; even the genesis of his work, the way it took shape, is so dynamic and natural. This guarantees him a higher insight into the meaning and purpose of the original text in my work, the Shakespeare sonnets, and Pushkin than mere metrical ability and knowledge of language can afford. He is destined to grasp, master, and continue the movement and life of the original. For to bring a work of literature (a flowing, rolling document) to a standstill is to kill it.

That a judgment on Keil will also be a judgment on me has a negative sense as well. It is so convincing in substance and so faithful that if I am on the wrong track, he exposes things more fully than I would myself.

To draw a sharp distinction between life and art is the soul of creativity, a paragon of taste, an aesthetic commandment. The symbolists drew this line very high and atmospherically; the post-expressionistic currents widened the gulf quite differently after their own fashion. The first half of my activity was very much subordinated to this feeling that art was "different." All this was very nice before us, among the beginners where this boundary line was still based on discoveries and revelations and was serious and dramatic. But afterwards it became all too mannered. The unique and revolutionary supplied its own succession and tradition. Surely it is paltry and petty when, e.g., Dadaistic mischief becomes tradition.

Shortly before the war and especially in the postwar period I developed an irresistible urge to overthrow all that, these habitual tastes and usages of the time. I did so in my novel. In prose this attack is not so perceptible; in poetry it is clearer and more transparent. Do you think that I have carried this too far? Does this worldly brave simplicity not become empty, prosaic, banal? In order to be lively, a translation should not remain at the geometrical point where the original stops. Sometimes the tone of sociable familiarity is heightened in translations when it is modest or nonexistent in the original. But that is not Keil's fault. It should and could not have been different. Please write Keil about my great delight; I do not know when I shall find the time to do so myself. Kindly write me as well what your honest opinion of this kind of poetry is.

With infinitely augmented thanks, your B. Pasternak.

These were his last words to us; never again was his voice to speak to us. Three months later this great heart stopped beating and this poetic voice fell silent. The new works that he had barely begun and that were intended to express the fate of his people were buried in the Russian earth with him. The news of his death spread from mouth to mouth in Russia, and many hundreds made pilgrimages to his dasha on foot and accompanied him to his last journey despite the official prohibition. But he will live on, and not only in *our* hearts.

Epilogue

In 1954, during a summer sojourn on the Tuscan coast of Italy, we took little exploratory trips to the interior of the country toward the enticing, picturesque mountains that jutted out into the blue sky. Thus we found ourselves one day at the top of a hill in an uncultivated vineyard with a wide panorama of the valley below us, as far as the Mediterranean. The sight of this harmonious beauty caused us to fall silent. Behind us were olive groves right up to the rocky, Alpine heights; before us there were lovely, terrace-shaped, vine-covered hills and the steeple of the old village church; and all around us were old farmhouses built with rocks. Such was the countryside that surrounded us, and we knew: This is where we want to and must stay!

We managed to acquire that piece of land, and a few years later we had built a house there. It had become a small estate with walls and yards and a patio at the center of the house in which we planted a tree, surrounded by a vineyard and a big lawn.

Henceforth we spent all the free time that our work in the publishing house left us in this new home. Here we planned new publishing projects with our editors in the free, fruitful, and stimulating atmosphere of our *collina.*

In 1965 I bade farewell to my place of work in the firm, the old farmhouse table which I had chosen as my desk, and this also meant good-bye to my fellow workers and authors. The friends among them remained my friends, and "they wrote me." [An allusion to the original title of this book, *Sie schrieben mir, oder was aus meinem Poesiealbum wurde* (They Wrote Me, or What Became of My Poetry Album)— Translator's note.]

A new life in a new world began for us. This life on the slope of the Tuscan mountains, where humans had settled since prehistoric times, was full of wonders. I discovered what it meant to possess a piece of land, fruitful land like this one which needed tending to derive the utmost from it. Little by little I became familiar with the special quality and nature of this soil. There was hardly anything that could not grow in it. We planted trees of all kinds, particularly cypresses, in Tuscany the sign of a human settlement. But we also planted cedars, pines, olives, gingkgoes, and oleanders, and soon the entire house was covered with a fragrant jasmine. The mimosas began to bloom and smell as early as January, and April brought the bloom of the wisteria, whose long, quite gnarled vines twined and crept from yard to yard. We planted lemons along the southern wall that reinforces our hill, and with astonishment I experienced the miracle of this constantly self-renewing fruit. We also planted oranges, apples, pears, and peaches. As we harvest almost all kinds of berries and most of the vegetables of both northern and southern regions, we enjoy everything that surrounds our house and our yard with fragrance, blossoms, and fruit. Our vineyard supplies us with good red and white wine which we have learned to press ourselves.

I have got to know and love the people of this region. The farmer who takes care of our vineyard and vegetable garden and his wife, who bakes bread for us in an oldfashioned way, still live in patriarchal fashion in close contact with their children, who are grown but are still attached to their parental home with all fibers of their being. Here life still has something lasting in the midst of a world that is destroying itself.

On our Tuscan hill the circle of my life is closing. From here I look back on my parental home in the Grunewald, the place of my happy childhood and youth where the circle of parents' friends began to write to me. And I look back on the later years by the side of my husband in the midst of my own family— as a publisher and publisher's wife, persecuted with him; cast out into foreign countries where it was a matter of holding our own and preserving the publishing house, our heritage; finding a home in the "New World," where we were surrounded by new friends and new authors and where Germany became a foreign country to us; and finally I look back on our return to Europe, our reunion with old friends, and the successful rebuilding of the publishing house.

I feel that the "hourglass" is emptying. The threat to our life from a very rapidly changing environment is becoming ever more evident; time is racing on, and water, air, and quiet, those priceless values which mankind regarded as its unquestionable, inalienable possession, are becoming more and more scarce. Survival is becoming harder and harder.

What is there left for young people to do? What advice can one give to one's grandchildren? Do they still have a task before them? How can they help to forestall a catastrophe? How can they guard against a "progress" that is fast outpacing all reason and prudence?

They are the generation that will decide whether mankind can survive. By renouncing the mania for "more," may they find a new freedom that will perhaps enable them to save their future.

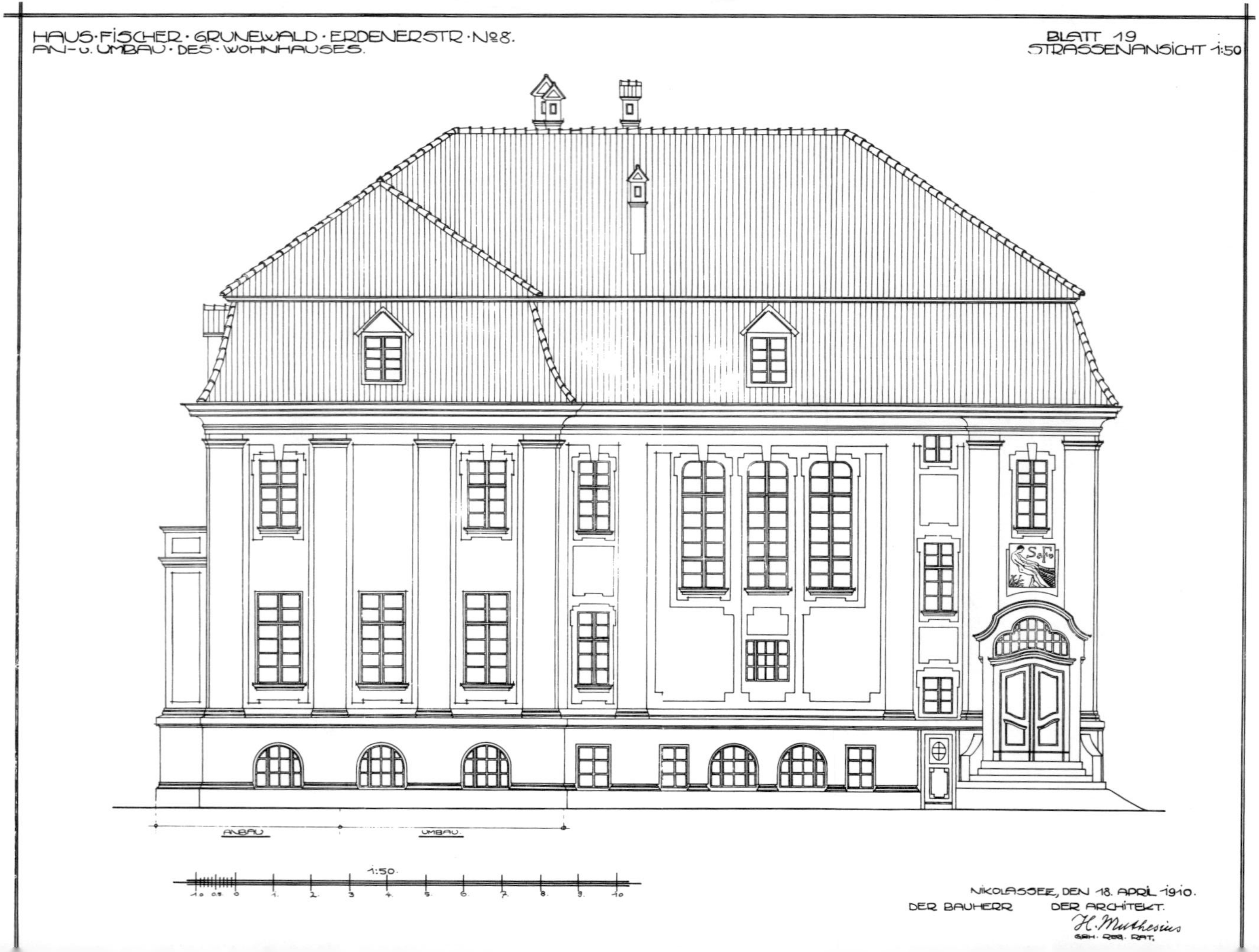
HAUS·FISCHER·GRUNEWALD·ERDENERSTR·No8.
AN-U.UMBAU·DES·WOHNHAUSES.
BLATT 19
STRASSENANSICHT 1:50
S&F
ANBAU
UMBAU
1:50
1.0 0.5 0 1 2 3 4 5 6 7 8 9 10
NIKOLASSEE, DEN 18. APRIL 1910.
DER BAUHERR
DER ARCHITEKT.
H. Muthesius
GEH. REG. RAT.

Index of Names

Our home in Berlin-Grunewald, number 8 Erdenerstrasse.

Our Sunday dinner in 1910.

Mother receiving our guests in the vestibule.

1908: in front of our house, on board the Benz.

With dad, mother and my brother Gerhart on the stairs of our terrace in 1908.

Berghof, 1911: with mother and Gerhart.

Santa Margherita, 1912: with my brother, Gerhart Hauptmann, Margarete Hauptmann, Benvenuto Hauptmann and dad.

Mother (1920)

Dad in 1909.

With dad (1911).

On my twelfth birthday (1917).

Moritz Heimann at the spa of Altheide (1923).

With Otto Flake at Obersdorf in 1915.

With dad, Thomas Mann, Hans Reisiger and Annette Kolb in Partenkirchen, in 1914.

Felix Salten in 1911.

Arthur Schnitzler in Engadin (1930).

Samuel Fischer and Jakob Wassermann in 1926.

Holiday in Unterach am Attersee, summer of 1911. With Franz Blei (top) and with my friends Paul and Annerle Salten (below). In the background, mother and Bertha Seele ("Lau").

Franz Blei and Annette Kolb in 1911.

With Rainer Maria Rilke, mother, dad and (behind him) Jakob Wassermann in Rome in 1910.

Hugo von Hofmannsthal and his daughter Christiane in Rodaun in 1917.

Thomas Mann in "Weisser Hirsch", Dresden, in 1905.

Thomas Mann in Glücksburg in the summer of 1919. It was here that he received the news of the honorary doctorate granted him by the Department of Humanities Bonn University.

Gottfried in 1925.

With Gottfried (1927).

After the wedding (1927).

Dad in 1933.

Our daughters Gaby, Annette (below left) and Gisi.

Our home on the Dalarö hill (summer 1938).

Skärgarden panorama from Dalarö (drawing of Hendrik Willem van Loon).

June 3, 1940: view of cell 127 (drawing of Gottfried B. Fischer).

In front of our new home in Old Greenwich, Connecticut, in 1940.

With my daughters in Old Greenwich, in our garden on Long Island Sound (1944).

Franz Werfel in his Beverly Hills home, in 1945.

At Rockefeller Center in New York in 1951.

Old Greenwich, Connecticut, 1943: with Hendrik Willem van Loon and two friends.

With Hermann Hesse in Montagnola in 1933.

Grunewald, May 1932: with my sister Hilde, Gottfried, and Manfred Hausmann.

Joachim Maass (1929).

Ilse Aichinger in Vienna in 1947.

Entrance of the Frankfurter Hof Hotel in 1947.

Carl Zuckmayer, Grunewald, at Pentecost of 1937 (above) and (below) at his desk in Saas-Fee in 1964.

Albrecht Goes in 1954.

Gottfried B. Fischer in 1960.

Thornton Wilder in 1961.

With James Jones in 1953.

Kurt Heuser
(May 1930).

Samuel Fischer, Kurt Heuser, Gottfried B. Fischer and Manfred Hausmann in 1930.

Pierre Bertaux with Samuel Fischer in Berlin in 1933 (above), as a young Hölderlin scholar in 1925 (below left) and commissioner of the republic in Toulouse with General De Gaulle in September 1944, after the retreat of the German troops (below, right).